O9-AID-365

"Heru has captured the voice of a generation and a movement. . . . [A]n absolutely great read."

—Ben Vereen, Broadway legend

"Heru Ptah does an unprecedented job in transplanting the reality of the world we call 'hip-hop' onto the pages of his very first novel. . . . [A]mazing! For those of you who like to mentally tread the thin line between art and life, this one's for you!"

—Paul "P Moor" Moreland, *Four Korners*

"Heru has crafted a masterpiece with his first novel. Each page draws you into the very beat and soul of hip-hop."

—Tehut-Nine, author of *Mental Eye-roglyphics*

"The definitive novel to be written on hip-hop is here and it is a masterpriece! This book is not only entertaining but educational on the rap game as well. . . . It's definitely a classic!"

—Tahir, producer/rapper

"Heru Ptah . . . is a consummate and effective storyteller who weaves a narrative that strikes a chord."

—Karu F. Daniels, journalist and author of *Brandy: An Intimate Look*

"A hip-hop masterpiece! Every hip-hop head needs to read this! *A Hip-Hip Story* goes beyond what any other movie or story about hip-hop ever has. It mixes a beautiful fusion of *West Side Story, Belly,* and *The Ausarian Drama.* I look forward to seeing it on the silver screen."

—Jehvon Bruckner, *DaGhettoTymz*

A HiP-HOP STORY

HERU PTAH

ORANGE COUNTY LIBRARY
146 A MADISON RD.
ORANGE, VA 22960
(540)-672-3811

POCKET BOOKS
New York   London   Toronto   Sydney

POCKET BOOKS, a division of Simon & Schuster, Inc.
1230 Avenue of the Americas, New York, NY 10020

This book is a work of fiction. Names, characters, places
and incidents are products of the author's imagination or are
used fictitiously. Any resemblance to actual events or locales
or persons, living or dead, is entirely coincidental.

Copyright © 2002 by Henry "Heru Ptah" Richards

Published by arrangement with SunRaSon Press

MTV Music Television and all related titles, logos, and
characters are trademarks of MTV Networks, a division
of Viacom International Inc.

All rights reserved, including the right to reproduce
this book or portions thereof in any form whatsoever.
For information address Pocket Books, 1230 Avenue
of the Americas, New York, NY 10020

ISBN: 0-7434-8323-5

First MTV Books/Pocket Books trade paperback printing September 2003

10   9   8   7   6   5

POCKET and colophon are registered trademarks of
Simon & Schuster, Inc.

Cover Art Direction: Stacy Drummond and Deklah Polansky
Cover Design: Stacy Drummond
Cover Photographs: (Top) GettyImages (Bottom) Warren Darius Aftahi

Manufactured in the United States of America

For information regarding special discounts for bulk purchases,
please contact Simon & Schuster Special Sales at 1-800-456-6798
or business@simonandschuster.com

All lyrics written by Heru Ptah

To any and everyone, from street corner
to street corner in all of the boroughs
of the world, who has ever picked up
the pen and dared to rebel; dared to dream,
to see the big picture to take over the world.
This is for you, stay true, keep on spittin'.

It is Ptah the Most Great who has given
existence to all divine powers and to their
essences through his heart, mind and tongue.
And he thinks as heart and mind and commands
as tongue whatever he wishes. Indeed, every
word of God came into being through that
which the heart and mind thought and the
tongue commanded.

the *Husia*

Micah and Erika entered the middle car in the midst of the melee and surprisingly they were able to find a seat together. It was evening time, late rush hour; at this stop the train should be brimming. It was not empty by any account; nevertheless, sardines would have begged for this comfort. Today was a colder day than it had been in the recent weeks and they had dressed warmer out of protection. They were fashionable in their wool overcoats, but heavier and more cumbersome for it. Once in the heated car they took the chance to undo their bindings. Once his coat had been opened she sat her head upon his chest and he placed his arm around her shoulder. There they sat as young lovers, layered by cloth and comfortable in their skins.

With her ear to his heart she listened attentively for its beat. Through the thick fabric she was not able to hear one.

"I can't hear your heartbeat," she looked up and said to him.

"Don't worry, it's there," he replied.

"I don't know, I can't hear it, I think you're dead," she remarked playfully.

"If I were, how would I be able to talk to you now?"

"Well, maybe you're dead and you just don't know it yet."

"So then, you're saying that we only die if we acknowledge death."

"Maybe. And maybe we only live if we acknowledge life, but I'm not quite sure."

"Well, then, I will never acknowledge death and I will live forever."

"And what would you do if you could live forever?" she asked him.

"I would stay here, with you, in this moment, in love."

"But I won't live forever. What will you do when I die?"

"Girl, you will never die. I'm not sure about a lot of things, but of that I am."

"So then, we will both live and love forever," she stated and asked him at the same time.

"Why not, why not."

In like vein the two lovers found each other's lips there in the crowd of the not-so-packed train. They kissed, eyes closed, hearts entwined and minds miles away, in a haze of purple.

When they came up for air the train had come to a stop at Fifty-ninth Street subway station. Many of the passengers got off and were readily replaced. A young man came on and sat directly across from them. In his hands he carried a periodical; he held it spread-eagle before him. It covered him from stomach to brow and brought the full picture on the cover of the publication within eyeshot. There they were shown profiled head to head, Flawless and Hannibal, and above them were the words Crown Warfare. The airbrushed tableau stood before them like a hanging harbinger, as if they had needed any reminder of war.

BOOK ONE

ONE

I ain't gotta spit
'Cause ma farts
Flow better than you
Smell better than you
Ma shit is just better than you
I'm a skinny dude
But dude don't be fooled
I'll knock a fat fuck
Back to Bellevue
'Cause you must be crazy
Comin' wit' that weak shit
Cough one line
An' yo fat ass is outta breath

The words are sharp, pungent and cut through shells with a razor's edge. It takes a thick shell to bear it, to hear it, to stand still, all the while crafting an evermore denigrating comeback. As such this pudgy prodigy waited his turn, engulfed in the melee of his peers, pretending not to be fazed by his skinny opponent's stinging aspersions. Waiting for his retort, he meditated on his course of action and how to turn the affections of the ever-growing goading crowd to his favor. It was coming, he could feel it now, Skinny Man had come to the climax of his tirade; the beat was turning to his favor.

No time to be tired, think fast, the beat is on me now, here

I go . . . *and then nothing.* What the hell! Oh shit . . . I just went blank. Shit, niggas is looking at me. What the hell was I gonna say again? It was something about what he said. But what the fuck did he say? I don't remember. Shit, how the hell I don't remember what to say? If I don't say something, this kid's gon' eat me. I won't be able to open my mouth on the street again. C'mon, God, you can't let that shit happen. Think, think. What the hell was I gon' say? All right, I'll just keep sayin' "yeah yeah" until something comes to me. All right, that did it. Cats stop staring for a second. But I gotta have something by the next time the beat turns over. God, don't do this to me. Here comes the beat. I gotta say something, but what to say? "Yeah, yeah." Think, think . . . aahhhh-hhhhh . . . there it goes.

> *Nigga you fart*
> *'Cause you all gas*
> *You just garbage*
> *So you talk trash*
> *But I'm the trash collector, garbage disposer*
> *An' I ain't overweight*
> *I'm heavyweight, motherfucker*
> *Dirty wit' mine*
> *Hit below the belt line*
> *Give you a uppercut to the cup*
> *Have you cough yo' balls up*
> *You should know better*
> *Than to battle the Brooklyn brawler*
> *When I'm done*
> *I'ma have yo' ass bawlin' fo' yo' momma.*

He felt his stride and rode the rhythm. The obligatory *Oh Shits* began to turn his way. He held nothing back, doing the dozens with precision. It all ate into Skinny Man. He was not as good at concealing his feelings as his robust counterpart.

Seeing this, Fat Man edged in for the kill, close enough to kiss. He held the death blow upon his tongue . . . and unleashed it: along with an inadvertent wad of spit. The *Oh shit*s of the crowd came through clenched teeth. Skinny Man did not wait for an apology. He threw up a fist and connected quickly. Fat Man replied and the entire crowd exploded.

The fight ensued outside of the club, Rampage. It was one of the more popular hip-hop nightclubs in lower Manhattan. At seeing the progressing affray two very big, well-dressed bouncers parted their way through and quickly put an end to it. They pulled the two young men apart; who in truth did not want to be fighting, but were merely caught up in the adrenaline of the movement.

There were SUVs and all manner of expensive cars parked outside, from the Lexus to the Benz. The bouncers dressed in black suits stood at the door. There was a railing that kept the people lined against the wall. The dense procession extended the stretch of the block and around the corner. The line was a dichotomy of gender and style. The women were dressed from head to toe in the most revealing, tight-fitting things they could have squeezed their frames into, while the men wore loose-fitting denim, complemented by work boots or sneakers, with a T-shirt or some form of sports jersey. The pounding music from inside was well heard. The beat beckoned the people in with baited anticipation.

A young man at the front made his way past the bouncers and was handed a flyer as he proceeded. Upon the flyer it read: *Hip-hop speak out for justice, Speak out for truth, Free all political prisoners, Fight against the war on terrorism.* And on the cover it showed a man with profound eyes, dreadlocks and handcuffs. There was more to be read, but the young man paid it no mind and quickly folded it into his pocket. His mind was already well engaged by the beautiful young girl walking in front of him, keen to the manufactured faded area about her rear. They arrived at the security check where they were frisked. While the muscled guard grabbed at all parts of his body he was far more concerned with the aggressive gropes that the stout female security guard addressed to the girl. When they were finished the girl walked away and the young man approached the female guard.

"Yo, Ma, tell me how can I get yo' job?"

She curled the corner of her lips in sarcasm and prodded him along. He tried to catch up to the girl. He, however, entered the main floor to complete confusion. The club was packed, the crowd thick and the music loud. He looked about without discretion but it was all for naught. He had lost her in the shuffle of flesh and the psychedelic pattern of lights. But within a minute he didn't seem to mind as another beautiful girl squeezed her way across his brow and his thoughts followed the sway of hips.

The crowd was dense, being anywhere from fifteen hundred to two thousand people. While bopping their heads to the beat and dancing as much as the space would allow they focused their attentions toward the stage at the DJ. He was well known and, by the smoothness in his scratches, well deserving of his accolades. He was RA, the hottest DJ in the city. Above him, an all-encompassing banner for Bin Laden hung. Bin Laden was the most popular hip-hop act at the time. He was the premier artist in the Crown Records roster; as such, the name of the ubiquitous music juggernaut was imprinted alongside his. And just below Bin Laden's banner was another for BET Freestyle Championship; again the symbol for Crown Records was imprinted, as Crown was the sponsor of both events.

The music began to fade as a man and a woman entered the stage. She was cute, medium-tanned, stockily built; well-fitted in her mix of bohemian and hip-hop. He was lean, tall, dark, handsome; attired in a mix of thug and preppy. They were Free and AJ, the hosts of BET's 106 and Park. He was the first to address the crowd, "Hey what's up, New York, how are y'all doing tonight!" And Free followed, "Yo, how's everybody doing out there? Alla y'all lookin' so beautiful. Ain't I right, AJ? Isn't everybody just looking so good tonight?"

"You are definitely right about that, Free. Especially the sistas; damn, sistas you look good! Y'all making a brother have thoughts to . . ." He then looked over to Free, who playfully slapped him on his shoulder.

"Boy, you better stop, before you get yourself beat down looking at some other man's woman."

"What you talking about, Free? I can handle my own now. But you're right, you're right, you're right. But I'm just sayin', though, that the sistas look good. And y'all need to give yourselves a round of applause for that."

"All right now, everybody, do we all know why we are here?"

Reacting to Free's question the crowd shouted out, "Bin Laden!"

"Yes, we are definitely here in support of our terror boy, Bin Laden," Free responded. "Doing his thing, dropping the bomb shit as always. But what else are we here for?"

The crowd again shouted out, "Freestyle Championship!"

"That's right, y'all, this is it," AJ remarked. "This is the grand championship of our Freestyle Battles, where two local unsigned talents are going to come up on this stage and do their thing. And when it is all over, one of them won't be unsigned anymore, 'cause he's gonna walk away with a fat-ass record deal from Crown Records, home of Bin Laden, Stalin and Lil' Hitler. Not to mention also being the sponsors of our event tonight."

The crowd cheered again as if playing a round of call and response. "Now, AJ, let's tell the people how these two guys got here."

"To get to this point both of them had to win an almost impossible nine weeks in a row on our televised Freestyle Battles. It was hard work but they both did it. And they are both here tonight to determine who is the best of the best."

"Now, do y'all know who we are talking about?" Free asked.

The crowd began to shout out, "FLAWLESS" and "BULL!" The mob was all but evenly split between supporters of Flawless and those of Hannibal. "Damn, AJ, it looks like it's gon' be a war tonight."

"That's right, Free; so let's not keep the crowd waiting anymore. Let's get this war started. Let's bring out my main man, Flawless the word shifter; and the undeniable, I tell you I'm scared of this guy, Hannibal the Cannibal."

Flawless entered the stage from the left, and Hannibal did so from the right. They were both attractive black men in their early twenties, of average heights and slim builds. Flawless however was the pretty boy. He was more neatly dressed; with his white shell-top sneakers, his light blue jeans, his black loose-fitting T-shirt and his hair: a well-cut blowout. In his Timber-land boots Hannibal appeared more rugged. His clothes were darker and baggier, his demeanor sterner and his head was bald. The crowd reacted to the difference in their styles. The women screamed and swooned for Flawless, while the men barked and howled for Hannibal. Through the noise they remained silent; Free broke through the barking. "Now, gentlemen, let's get the rules straight. Basically there are no rules. This isn't like our televised show, so there are no censors. Only rule is: you keep it verbal."

"Yeah, brothers, there is no need for any physicalities here. And that goes for the audience as well. I know we all like to keep it gangsta. But let's keep it peaceful as well. Keep it on the mic."

"Without further ado, let's get started. Flawless lost the toss backstage, so he will be going first. There will be three rounds, one minute each. The audience will judge the winner of each round and the best two out of three wins." She then looked over at both men. "Brothers, are you ready? This is it. DJ, turn up the beat."

TWO

Flawless lived in a decent home, on a fairly peaceful block, in a rather modest part of Queens, New York. On the steps leading to the house, his sister Erika and her date stood talking. She was nineteen then, beyond beautiful and had a hypnotizing smile; as such, the young man stood mesmerized in her presence. He was dark-tanned, thug in appearance but a kitten at heart. He attempted to be suave and respectful while trying to conceal a growing nature, seeing her through X-ray vision, imagining the firm of every curvature. He spoke with enamored timidity:

"So we're here," he said.

And she responded, as was her custom, in a very quiet, subtle, almost seductive but never forced tone, "Yeah we're here." Simple words seemed so much more palatable coming off of her tongue.

"I had a really good time tonight."

"Yeah, I had a really good time as well."

"Yeah, yeah, that's really good. 'Cause y'know, I mean . . . I really would like to . . . y'know, maybe we can go out again."

"Yeah, why not. I think I would like that."

"Good shit, good shit."

Feeling a bit more confident about himself he stepped in, closing the gap between them. This was the closest that he had been to her all night. He could smell the shampoo in her hair, the engaging scent of her perfume, and look into the brown depths of her eyes. He lost himself there in her presence. He lathered his lips and dreamed of a kiss, hoping that his translucent attempt at seduction was enough of a clue; and that Erika too was of like mind.

As he mulled over his approach a car pulled up to the house, music playing loud; but not enough to wake the neighbors. Flawless was in the passenger seat while his best friend Tommy drove. Tommy was Flawless's peer in both age and taste, of the same build and just a shade lighter than Flawless's brown complexion. They had been friends from freshman year in high school unto manhood. They had been through it all together: Flawless and faithful Tommy, always by his side. Tommy drove but Flawless led. This was never an outright rule. It was a relationship implicitly arranged, subconscious and as natural as an instinct.

"Yo, you did your thing tonight, man. I'm mad proud of you," Tommy congratulated his friend.

"Thanks, I really appreciate that."

"So you on your way, man. You won the deal, nothing but the big time for you now," Tommy said with pride and the slight apprehension that he may be losing his friend to the gravity of success.

Flawless quickly dissuaded his fears: "It's big time for us. Wherever I go, you coming with me. Like it always been, like it always will be. I mean that, we gon' take over this whole world, change the game."

With his fears eased, Tommy's pride showed through more clearly. "Blessings, god, blessings." His light heart then strayed to the doorstep, where he saw Erika and her date. "Yo, I see that Erika got herself a little boyfriend." Flawless, being so engrossed in his glow from earlier, was ignorant to all things outside of the tinted glass.

"What?" he asked. Tommy then gestured with his head about that which he spoke. Flawless turned his eyes in that direction and became . . . silent.

"So, when are you supposed to meet wit' dem cats and make the deal official?" Tommy spoke but Flawless did not hear him. "Yo, you hearing me, man?"

"What was that?" Flawless reacted, sharing his focus between Tommy and the doorstep.

"I was asking you when you was gonna meet wit' dem cats from Crown and sign the deal?"

"Oh yeah . . . I'm supposed to meet with them tomorrow," Flawless said, for a moment letting go of his preoccupation.

"You need a ride over there?"

"Yeah, that would be cool. We'll roll over there together."

The two friends then exchanged their good-byes and their love the way that men do; through the use of a pound, more fervent than a handshake, but not as intimate as a straight hug.

Flawless waved good-bye as Tommy drove off. Upon seeing her brother, Erika and her date pulled away slightly; and slightly Erika smiled at him, already intuiting what he was thinking.

"Michael, you're back," she greeted.

Her date, at seeing Flawless, showed him the respect due to the older brother of a prospective mate; also, being aware of Flawless's gifts on the mic, there was a mix of awe in his tenor. "Yo, what's up, Flawless?" he greeted with outstretched palm. Flawless shook it without any real sincerity. "I seen you do yo' thing over on One-oh-six. You nice, god, you nice."

"Thanks," Flawless replied as lifelessly as his handshake.

"So you was in the finals tonight. How did that go?"

"It went all right." Flawless spoke with his attention squarely focused on Erika, seeing her date only as a peripheral annoyance. "Hello, Erika. I see that you're getting in late tonight."

"So are you, Michael," she responded in downplayed sarcasm.

"Well, I had a reason."

"And so did I."

Noticing that she was neglecting her date, Erika returned

her attention. "Yeah, so I had a really nice time tonight. So just give me a call and maybe we can hook up again."

"Yeah. I'll definitely do that."

It was time to go and he knew this, though his affections urged him to stay. He thought to give her a customary kiss good night or at least get a hug. However, he looked over at Flawless, who looked back at him as if to say, Why are you still here, and he decided not to. He headed down the steps and toward the gate. Erika opened the door to the house and went inside. Flawless watched her enter and made a motion to do so himself. But then he turned and called to her date. Her date at hearing the call veered back.

"Yo, what's up, Flawless?" he said.

"Yo, listen. You a man, and I'm a man, so I'm gon' keep it as real with you as possible."

"All right."

"I know what you're trying to do."

"What do you mean?"

"Nigga, don't play dumb with me. You trying to fuck my sister!"

"Wait, hold up, man. I'm not trying to do nothin'," he reacted.

"Oh, so you telling me that you don't wanna fuck my sister?"

"Yo, I'm not saying none of that. I'm just saying that I like her."

"So then you do wanna fuck her?"

"Yo . . . you, you puttin' words in ma mouth."

"Naw. You see I'm not really concerned with the words coming out of your mouth; it's the ones in your thoughts that I'm interested in. See, I know that my sister is a very beautiful girl. And every nigga around here is trying to get a piece of her. But you see my sister is different, she ain't like all them other tricks and hos around here."

"I know that. That's why I like her."

"Why, because you wanna be the first one to turn her out?"

"Naw, man, that ain't it at all."

"Yeah, that's exactly it. And that shit ain't gon' happen. So you know what? Do yourself a favor and don't call her or come by this house again. Ever!"

"Yo, man, you ain't serious."

"Fuck yeah I am. Now I'm done talking. Good night!"

Before her date could get another word in, Flawless turned away and walked inside. Her date was left alone standing at the gate stupefied. He stood there for a moment in disbelief and then walked away.

Inside, it was a nice home; a handsome floral-patterned sofa set encircled a wooden unit. Flawless entered the house into the living room to find his mother sleeping on the larger of the two sofas. To the immediate left was the red-carpeted stairway leading to the second level. To the left of the living room was the dining area and straight ahead a door led into the kitchen. As soon as Flawless entered and locked the door behind him, Erika came at him from upstairs.

"What did you do, Michael? What did you do?" Erika attacked.

"What are you talking about?" he replied with a smirk.

"You know what. You were out there talking to him, about what?"

"I was just wishing the brother a good night."

"Yeah, right. Mom! Michael scared off another boy again!"

Their mother rose groggily, fixing her nightgown beneath her. This was one of her few nights off. Working two jobs at a time at times made sleep a luxury. Her forty-something face looked more drawn and fatigued for it. Being so accustomed to constantly being up, she found it hard to surrender herself to somnolence. Annoyed at her insomnia and half-asleep she said, "Michael, I told you about you and them boys. Leave your sister alone. Let her live her life."

Flawless, still playing the game, answered, "Mom, I didn't do anything, I swear it."

"Yeah, well, we'll see," Erika added, then forcefully walked upstairs while looking back at Flawless.

Flawless now directed his attention to his mother. He was proud of himself and his night's accomplishment and he wanted his mother to share in his joy. He was twenty-three years old and one year out of college. He hadn't graduated. He left during his junior year due to a lack of passion. He had sat in class after class for over two years crunching numbers, all for the purpose of becoming an accountant. He did this while daydreaming of rhyming. With his head down alongside his notes of charts and figures, the words flowed through his pen. This was his passion. He played accountant for his mother. It was a respectable profession and the responsible thing to do. However, responsibility was seldom liberating. In truth, the only liberating thing about campus life were the biquarterly talents shows; which he always won. His gift of gab had made him a star on campus, though campus celebrity was not his aspiration. His vision was grand and so the city called him back from upstate.

He wanted more. He didn't just want to study; he wanted to be studied. When he was in school, he took a far greater interest in literature classes. He learned about all of the greats: from Shakespeare and Wordsworth to Hughes, Angelou and Sanchez. He admired their works while believing that he could do better. It was the ultracompetitive nature of hip-hop to be the best that always ate at him.

Far beyond the naked word, the beat was much a part of his consciousness. He was married to the two in a polygamy of rhyme. He loved what he did and saw school as a waste of time. So he left, to his mother's chagrin. In the year since she had made nagging him her daily harangue. He asked for patience and faith. She told him to go back to school. And many times, after he had won battle after battle but still had nothing concrete, he questioned if his decision had been folly. Now that he had the deal he saw that it had not been, and he wanted so much to share his news with his mother, so that she would look at him once again with pride anew.

"So Mom, I got some news for you."

"Yeah, well, Michael, if it's not about you going back to school, I'm not interested. I don't know, boy. You're just sitting here wasting your life and your education."

"I'm not wasting my life, Mommy. I'm just trying to live my dream."

"I tell you this, son. If you always do only what you want, you will always be unhappy. Believe you me, go back to school, grow up and take care of your responsibilities. All this rapping nonsense is not going to get you anywhere."

Flawless smiled to himself. The words still stung even though he had already won the deal. His mother's disregard curbed his enthusiasm, so he chose not to share his news, at least not for now.

"Yeah, Mom. I guess it won't."

"Trust me, you're a smart boy, go back to school. Go back to school," she repeated. "Now be a dear and get me a blanket."

Flawless went upstairs, retrieved a blanket from the hall closet and returned and covered his mother. He kissed her forehead, turned off the living room light and headed quietly upstairs.

He began to go into his room when he decided to go to Erika and tell her the good news. She would understand. Unlike his mother, Erika had always been supportive of his vision. She listened to him. He shared his thoughts with her. He expressed to her those thoughts that he would not share with Tommy, for the simple fact that men never liked to appear weak among other men; and still those thoughts that he felt were too intimate to share with the other women who came in and out of his life. He felt close to no woman save his sister. Now he couldn't wait to see the expression on her face as he told her the news.

He was about to knock, only to find her door slightly ajar. In her room some distance away he was able to see a full-length mirror. In the mirror's reflection was Erika, half-dressed, in the process of putting on her sleepwear. This caught him by surprise. He stepped back, waited a few moments and then knocked at the door. He looked only for a second; the image lingered for a few moments longer. She had truly grown into a beautiful woman.

"Who is it?" she called from inside.

"It's Michael," Flawless answered.

"Okay, come in," she said after a moment.

Flawless entered her room. It was much like Erika was, sweetly feminine without being overly girlish, save for the vanity bureau and mirror. As Flawless stepped in he noticed the mirror from before. He turned his head so as to get away from the thought. He saw her now dressed in a matching fuchsia pajama shirt and shorts. He felt weird about what he had seen and almost wanted to leave so as to get away from the image.

"What, you came to see if I had any boys up here so that you could run them off?"

"Yeah, I did. You got any hiding under the bed?" Flawless then jokingly went and looked under the bed. For this, Erika swatted him with a pillow.

"Stop playing. I'm upset with you. Why did you do that?"

"I just thought that you could do better than him."

"Yeah, but you do that with every guy I bring."

"Well, I thought that you could do better than all of them."

"Yeah, whatever. If I listen to you I would probably end up as a nun."

"That wouldn't be so bad."

She hit him again.

"Don't take it out on me because you had a bad night."

"That's funny. Who told you that I had a bad night?"

With a half-excited expression she asked, "What do you mean . . . you won?"

"Well, maybe I did."

"Don't play with me, Michael. Tell me, did you win or not?"

"Yep," Flawless said with contained exuberance.

"You won the contract? You got the deal?"

"Yeah I did."

She ran and hugged him, closer than he would have liked her to at the time.

"Oh, I'm so happy for you! How come you didn't say anything?"

He broke the hug and stepped back. "Well, I'm telling you now."

"I mean before, why didn't you tell Mom?"

"Well, I was going to but then she got on me about school again, and y'know . . ."

"So what, you're not going to tell her?"

"No, I am, I am. I'll tell her tomorrow."

"Oh man, you won. You finally got the deal," she repeated.

"Finally."

"I'm so happy for you." She hugged him again. He wanted to push her off but gave in and indulged in her affections.

"Be happy for us. It's a whole new world for us, a whole new life. We are gonna move out of this house, out of this hood. It's just the good life from now on." Finally he broke the hold.

"Damn, Michael, it must have been so exciting. I wish I had been there."

"No, I'm glad that you weren't. If I had lost I couldn't stand to have seen the expression on your face."

"Yeah, I guess you're right. So was it close?"

As he reflected his expression became focused; Hannibal always had that effect on him. As Erika was the light to his heart, Hannibal was the dark. "Well, it was Bull. Bull is always hard. I'm just glad I was able to pull it off. That's one chapter of my life finished with now. I never have to deal with him again."

THREE

Hannibal's black Lexus shimmered in the moonlight as he pulled into the parking area of the Brooklyn project. It was somewhere between late night and early morning. Hannibal sat silently in his car and looked out into the maze of apartment buildings of the Cypress Hill projects. Through the moonlight, through tired eyes, it all appeared somewhat majestic. Hannibal, however, knew too well the true grimy reality.

He was exhausted both emotionally and physically. He really wanted to win. Going up against Flawless, he knew that it would be hard but he believed that he had had a shot. He wanted it not just for the deal but more so for the escape. Losing knocked him down to square one. He questioned how to pick himself back up again and if he even should. Was it all worth it? He looked at himself in the rearview mirror. He could see into his eyes. He was tired but there would be no relief just staring into oblivion.

He made his way through the maze toward his apartment building, slightly inebriated in his stride but not in his bloodstream. He walked past the slew of local boys; everyone stood almost at attention in his presence, there was an air of reverence in the gesture. It was the usual custom to chat with the boys at the steps before going in. Tonight he was in no mood for conversation. He desired only to sleep this night away.

He entered his apartment building. There was a green hallway leading to the elevator. It was dimly lit and wreaked of urine. The fetid smell was the accustomed aroma to the air, yet it seemed all the more pungent tonight: with the paint-chipped walls that swelled with moisture being an effective breeding ground for mold and all manner of carcinogens. Hannibal called for the elevator. Tired and almost falling over, he awaited its arrival.

When the door opened, an attractive young woman, well-shaped in her tight jeans, walked out, invoking thoughts of sex with her every gesture. "Hey, Bull baby. How are you doin'?" she greeted. He found her voice somewhat shrill and annoying as she spoke in stereotypical *Jerry Springer* low-brow twang.

"I'm fine," Hannibal replied, feeling a bit more excited, but nevertheless, still drained.

"You don't look fine, baby; you look real tired."

"Naw, it's nothing. I'm cool."

"Are you sure? Because I could always come up and take care of you."

Hannibal looked at her and her offer seemed inviting. Then he remembered how tired he was and how he couldn't be bothered with sleeping with her and then kicking her out of his bed an hour later.

"Naw, girl, it's all right. I'll be cool."

"Well all right, but if you change your mind, you know how to reach me." She kissed him on the lips. Hannibal did not kiss back. She then turned off and began her saunter down the hall, swinging her hips a bit more than her natural stride suggested to better emphasize her point.

He went to step into the elevator, but it closed just before he could get in. He pushed the button furiously but it had already left for another floor. Exasperated, Hannibal shouted out his feeling of the entire night, "Fuck!"

All was dark at first. Hannibal pronounced *lights* and the entire room became alive. It was a surprisingly big apartment with a well-spaced living room. It had a very black metallic feel to it. There was a black leather sofa, set against the wall, facing an immense big-screen television. Truly, it was immense: it was sixty inches square and sat on a stand that was a foot and a half. Hannibal walked to the television and at its height it was taller than he was. He rubbed the belly of it with familiar endearment, much the same way that one would do a pet. To his left behind the television was the kitchen. It was neat and not laden with week-old dirty dishes. He looked at his fridge; he was hungry and he was tired, he debated, and fatigue won out. He went straight ahead toward the bedroom. He was so tired that he didn't hear the pants of sex coming through the door.

The room opened lit only by the light from the kitchen. Once inside, Hannibal could see the shadowed contours of a man and a woman in the midst of an act. They were obviously comfortable with the voyeurism of their intimacy, as they paid little attention to him and he in kind paid little attention to them. He merely walked over to the minibar in the corner and proceeded to fix himself a drink.

Who the girl was, he did not know. The man he knew was Mook. If Hannibal were to have a best friend, Mook would be the closest thing to it. They were business partners. They shared liabilities in commerce, and at times they shared a bed in conquest; though it was Hannibal's bed and Hannibal's apartment and Mook had his own of both of these. Many times he had come home to the familiar pants echoing out of his door. For the most part he was generous to the closest thing to a brother he never had—but not tonight, tonight he was tired.

"Yo, Bull, what the fuck you doin', man? I'm in the middle of something here," Mook gasped.

Without turning his attention toward them, with a restrained voice, Hannibal answered, "Yeah, I can see that. Now get that bitch the hell out of here."

"Nigga, you ain't for real."

"Fuck yeah, I'm for real. Now you and the bitch get out," Hannibal answered, never raising his voice. He then left the room with his drink in hand, leaving the door open and the sting of the light behind him.

Hannibal was slouched on the sofa watching the movie *Hannibal.* He watched it, engrossed in every word with a virgin's interest, though he had long since been a prostitute. At the count he was somewhere between seventy or seventy-two. The only other movie he had seen as much was its predecessor, *The Silence of the Lambs,* which over the years he had seen close to a hundred times. At the rate he was going, *Hannibal* was well on its way to beating that record. He never seemed to count. It was his diversion from the real in all of its gory psychological angst. And even more than that, it was his namesake.

The twenty-four-year-old had been calling himself Hannibal for the past ten years; and he kept himself in the company of those who only knew him as such, so much so that he had all but forgotten his given name. Hannibal had become for him not just a name but also his being. And though the character had inspired him, he was not Lecter, and did not aspire to be. He was another type of devourer. Still, beyond all that, he just thought the name was cool.

Hannibal sat focused with an unwavering gaze as the girl exited from his bedroom. Buttoning up her shirt and straightening her bottom, she walked into the view of the immense television. She was attractive but all Hannibal could see was that she was obstructing his vision.

"Hey, Bull," she greeted flirtingly.

"You're standing in front of the TV," he said with an annoyed calm.

"Oh I'm sorry, I'm sorry."

She hurriedly walked out of the view of the immense TV as Mook, a dark-skinned man much like Hannibal, came into the living room. He was shirtless and wore baggy jeans with the waist of his boxers visible. He had a prisoner's physique, with his defined arms and chest, but less defined stomach and legs. He calmly crossed the path of the television and went over to the girl. He whispered something in her ear; kissed her, pulling on her bottom lip; then opened the door for her and smacked her on the rear. To this she reacted playfully and was set to leave, but first said, " 'Bye, Bull," and waved. Hannibal barely raised an eyebrow in response.

Mook closed the door, walked over and sat in the loveseat to Hannibal's right. He leaned over the coffee table and began to roll a blunt from the recesses of marijuana left on top. With his head tilted down, "So what's up, nigga, you lost tonight and you pissed?" he asked.

"Who told you I lost?"

"Come on, nigga, I know you. If you had won, you woulda came in here with two bitches of your own and joined in." Hannibal silently looked toward him. "All right, maybe you wouldn't have joined in but you get what I'm saying. So you lost, right?"

Hannibal took a sip of the drink in his hand. The Alizé tasted bitter tonight. "Well, I guess if you was there you wouldn't have to ask. Thanks for the support."

There was an uncomfortable pause as Mook sat wondering what to say next. "So it was Flawless?" he finally asked.

"Yeah, it's always Flawless. Some nights he wins, some nights I win. Tonight he won. And he got the deal."

"Shit, so Flawless got signed. Shit! Fuck it, it ain't nothin'. We just go back to plan A."

Hannibal took another swallow of the embittered drink and remarked, "What's plan A?"

"What the fuck you think, man? Plan A is what we been doing. It's what got you all this fly shit in your crib and that pussy-catching car you got. We need to, hell, you need to get your attention solely back to pushing this weight."

"Yeah, pushing weight." There was a bit of sarcasm in Bull's voice.

"C'mon, nigga, don't act like you don't know. You one of the biggest dealers in Brooklyn, but you been getting your perspective all fucked up trying to be some rapper. An' I'll admit it, you got some skills an' all, but I never seen why the hell you wanted to do that shit anyway."

"What am I gonna do? Sell drugs for the rest of my life?"

"Why the fuck not? We know mad niggas who have."

"Yeah, and most of dem niggas are either dead or in jail."

"Nigga, I been in jail. That's the business, that's life. Don't act like this is something new."

"Listen, I ain't in this shit to get shot or to go to jail. I'm here to make money. And that's it."

"And we are making money, a lot more than most a dem niggas on BET. Check the shit out. Most a dem renting the cars you see in those videos. We own the shit. That whole industry is just a big front on what we doin'. Faggot-ass niggas talkin' like they killers. There ain't nothin' about it real. I mean, this is the thing that I just don't get; we already got the money, the cars and the hos."

"I'm tired of fucking these project bitches."

"So what? Now you wanna fuck some million-dollar model?"

"I'm not talking about that. I'm talking about something more. I'm tired of living in the projects, seeing these same niggas everyday."

"Well, these niggas around here love you and more than that they respect you. We can walk down any street and park our shit with the doors open and never worry about that shit getting robbed. How many a dem fake thug hip-hop niggas can say that? Yeah, a motherfucker may listen to the music, but have one of them come bling-blinging down the wrong street and that nigga is gon' get jacked. Shit, I would personally like one of them to come my way. He would go back broke and with something up his ass. And plus, there ain't nobody sayin' that

p living here. You wanna move to the suburbs, let's
where most of our customers live anyway. But that
ain't it, is it?"

"You're right, you're absolutely right. That ain't it. I got big
plans for the future and this shit ain't it."

"No, man. You need to get your perspectives straight."

"Nope. I got everything in perspective. I see the big picture.
Yeah, I see the big picture. And right now it's me and that bed."
Hannibal crossed Mook's path and went toward the bedroom.
He stepped in for a moment, held his head down, calmly
walked over to the kitchen counter, picked up a bottle of disin-
fectant and placed it in Mook's chest.

"What's this for?" Mook questioned.

"Go in the room, change the sheets and fumigate the motherfucker," he replied with dead calm.

"What the fuck for?"

"Because the motherfucker smells like a mix of weed, sweat
and stank ass. Now go spray that shit out."

Mook got up and walked angrily over to the room. "I don't
know what the hell you talking about. There ain't nothin'
wrong in here." He then got a foul whiff of something, "Whoo,
oh shit," and began to spray the room fervently.

Hannibal walked into the kitchen and looked out the window into the cluttered, claustrophobia-inducing expanse—at
the back of buildings, at the fire escapes, the lines of clothes
that hung across them—and how they glowed in the blue black
of the coming dawn. It had not arrived quite yet but it was no
longer night. There in the sky it seemed as if the two times of
the day were fighting each other for supremacy and Hannibal
with a vigilant eye to the battle watched on quietly and said,
"Yeah, I see the big picture."

FOUR

It was a beautiful day; one of those clear spring days that made you so happy that winter was over and heralded thoughts of an even more promising summer. Though spring is a fickle season, it is not static and ultimately undependable. It will start off beautiful in the morning, can become wretched in the afternoon, comfortable by the evening, reminiscent of winter by nightfall and beyond all that . . . it can rain. In truth, spring promised to be nothing but itself; ultimately inconstant in nature, much like a lover's affections. Nevertheless, today was a beautiful day.

Flawless, with a worm's eye, admired the day through the New York City skyline. He was the furthest thing from a tourist yet he still walked through Manhattan's streets with awed admiration. In the apex of capitalism he many times felt like a speck in the great expanse, lost in the shuffle of money. So much money, he could literally taste the rich; not the people but rather the intangible. This made it all the more frustrating for a hungry man to be teased with the smell of food and not be able to eat. The entire world looked through the glass window on the outside of this great restaurant with hungry eyes. They watched as the occupants dined on excess with a heart quicker to discard than to give. And now in the midst of all this, here was Flawless, approaching the threshold of capitalism, with an invitation.

Flawless and Tommy entered the great edifice of glass and

steel that housed Crown Records. The two friends walked with a virgin's excitement and a sense of belonging. They headed toward the security desk; as Flawless arrived he took notice of an exceptionally beautiful woman who was signing in at the time. He was so enthralled that he did not notice the older fat female security guard calling him.

"Excuse me, but may I help you?" the security guard called again, now with a bit of an attitude.

"Oh, I'm sorry. I had something on my mind," awakened, Flawless answered.

"I can see that. Now what business do you have here, young man?"

"I have an appointment with Mr. Jennessy."

"And what is your name?"

"Michael, Michael Williams."

The security guard checked her list and then shook her head negatively.

"I am sorry, young man, but there is no Michael Williams here."

Flawless looked at her almost in disbelief, his feeling of belonging waning in the confusion. "There has to be a mistake," he said.

"That's what they always say but the list is never wrong."

The security guard then looked over to the beautiful woman and smiled at her, mocking the young man; the beautiful woman did not share in the mockery. Flawless wanted to curse out the guard for trying to steal his sense of belonging; but he knew that he had to go through her so he played the diplomat.

"You know what, try Flawless, look for Flawless."

"Flawless?"

"Just look for it," he stressed.

She again checked the list, not expecting to see anything, waiting to look up at the disappointed young man and send him off. "Well, what do you know? There is something here for Flawless/Michael Williams," she said disappointingly.

"Great." Flawless then called to Tommy and the security guard likewise turned an eye in his direction. Seeing this, Flawless responded, "Oh, he's with me."

"I'm sorry, but if he is not on the list, he's not going up."

"Maybe you could call upstairs and ask them."

"No, I cannot. That's the rules!" she retorted in vintage stank.

Flawless was angered and already having gotten through was prepared to curse out the tubby nobody.

Tommy, seeing this, broke in, "It's no big thing. I'll wait down here."

"Yeah, all right man. But yo, as soon as I get in there I'll have them call you up."

"Now, you're going to be going to the seventy-second floor. After you go through the security check, you are going to take the elevator around the corner to your left," the security guard instructed him.

Flawless went to the security check to find an airport-style metal detector and a very big male security guard. "Place all of the metal objects you have in your pockets into this container. And take off your jacket and your shoes and put them on the conveyor belt," he commanded in a deep tenor.

Five years ago such security measures to get into a building would have been considered excessive; however, in the new era, the excessive had become the norm. Given that, Flawless followed orders without argument. He was set to walk through when the security guard stopped him. The beautiful woman was still being checked on the other side. Another female guard was scanning her with a hand-held detector. At first her back was to Flawless and he admired her figure from the back. Then she was instructed to turn around and now they faced each other and he admired her even more from the front. They made eye contact for moments and Flawless could feel the heat rising within. She wore a tight-fitting lavender dress that extended to her knees and fixed to her frame almost like a second skin. Flawless took notice of every form and curvature: the shape of her bust and the gold pendant that hung down into the sweet slit of cleavage; she had locks, well groomed and worn up in a bun; she had an immaculate caramel complexion that seemed so smooth to the touch and even more palatable to the taste; she had edible lips and deep brown eyes, set upon a face that rounded at the cheeks and narrowed neatly as it came to the chin; she was truly beautiful, and in many ways, in many moments, she reminded Flawless of Erika.

The security guard finished with her and sent her on her way. Flawless then hurried through the detector, fortunately unobstructed. He put back on his shoes and jacket and went to the elevator, hoping not to lose sight of the beautiful woman. Even if he never spoke to her, even if just to look at her again . . . it would have all been filling. He bent the corner coming to the elevator to find, to his elated surprise, the beautiful woman holding the door open for him. Flawless stepped in.

And then she spoke in a dreamlike contralto, "The seventy-second floor, right?"

"Yes, how did you know?"

"I overheard. Plus that's where I'm going as well."

Wow, he thought to himself, she was listening. He offered his hand in greeting.

"Hi, I'm Flawless."

She took his hand; hers was soft and smooth. "Yes, Michael, I know," she answered like a tacit coquette. It was strange. Flawless was only accustomed to family calling him by his given name. Though he did not know this woman, she called him with innate familiarity. It was engaging; he loved it, and wanted her to call him by nothing else.

"Let me guess, you overheard that as well," he replied. And she smiled, and then he smiled, and he held back words on the tip of his tongue, and before he could utter one, the elevator opened and she stepped out.

The elevator opened to Crown Records. The nameplate of the label hung above like a prow a few feet ahead by a long stretch of windows. It was an office complex, much like any other, with personal cubicles and employees busy working. Throughout the walls were posters of Crown Records artists. There was an especially enormous one of Bin Laden.

"I'll see you around, Michael," the beautiful woman said to him with her back turned walking down the hall. Flawless watched her walk off, admiring her every step and murmured beneath his breath, "Yes, you will."

"Flawless!" an enthusiastic voice called from behind. Flawless turned around to find Jennessy: a white man in his late thirties, of average height and build; dressed in a Bin Laden T-shirt, opulent brand-new wornout denim and a NYPD baseball cap. He was in casual wear but seemed strangely uncomfortable. For some reason Flawless figured him to be better fit in an Armani suit.

Jennessy was the president of Crown Records and from his succession to the throne he had changed the entire dynamic of the company. Crown was at first a haven for country and pop iconography, hosting such talents as Cherry Pop and Sync Street, which were very successful multiplatinum late nineties boy bands. But as the millennium came in, they began to wane in popularity. Country stayed static, showing neither growth nor decrease. However, it was not the mode of the youth. And as it was known it was generally the youth who bought *Billboards*.

Jennessy altered the path and rode the hip-hop tide as rivaling labels had been doing for years before, heralding Crown into a genre they had, to their discredit, previously stayed far away from. Though with Jennessy at the helm, and due to aggressive and somewhat unethical practices, within seven years Crown had become the most lucrative hip-hop label and Jennessy was the mogul to be for the moment.

"Mr. Jennessy, it's good to see you again."

"No, my boy. It's good to see you. You're the man of the hour. Let's head over to my office." Jennessy spoke with affluent confidence and hypnotic subtlety. This beyond all of his attributes was his most profound, his gift of gab. It was his verb, and not his birth, that got him to where he was, a self-made man of sorts, who had articulated his way to the top.

"One second. My boy is downstairs, I just want to call him up."

"We will. We will. But let's have our meeting first."

Flawless saw no reason to press or to refuse. "Okay," he replied and then followed Jennessy as they turned right down a long hall of offices until they had arrived at the office at the end. Jennessy invited Flawless in and then addressed his secretary. "Jane, I'm in an important meeting, so hold all of my calls until I tell you otherwise," he said, loud enough that Flawless, who had just stepped into the office, was able to hear.

"Of course, Mr. Jennessy," Jane responded, wondering why he pressed on a point that was already a given.

The office was immense; larger than the average living room, and fully carpeted in fuchsia fiber, the type that feet sink into. There was a white sofa set, placed with a coffee table, in direct view upon entering. Behind the set was Jennessy's personal bathroom and shower. To the distant left was Jennessy's large mahogany desk. On the walls there were numerous framed gold and platinum records. There were also pictures upon pictures of Jennessy with all sorts of celebrities. From Michael Jackson to Bill Clinton, Jennessy had met them all. Thoroughly impressed, Flawless walked the length of the room, mouth practically agape, all the while looking out of the window that stretched the entire length of the office. He took a seat at one of the two leather chairs; they still had that new leather smell. The entire office had the taste of wealth.

"So have I impressed you enough?" Jennessy asked.

"Yeah, man, I think so."

"Good, that was my objective." Jennessy then noticed that Flawless's eye had strayed from him and was focused on something on the floor behind the desk. It was Jennessy's parachute. "Crazy, I know," Jennessy said to him before Flawless had time to question. "But this is a new era and I am on the seventy-second floor. Better safe than sorry, no? I tell you, man, they should just bomb and lock up all of those fucking people. . . . But let's not worry about that now." Although he was taken aback by Jennessy's statements Flawless gave up his preoccupation.

"So, my man Flawless, tell me about yourself."

"I don't know. What's there to say? It's not too complicated; I rap and I wanna take over the world."

"Take over the world! Slow down, brain, one thing at a time. But that is a good attitude. And you now what? I believe you. I believe that you are going to take over the world. But how about we do it together?"

"I have no problems with that."

"Great. Because I see a great relationship starting up here with you and Crown Records."

"I see it as well."

"Great, great. It is good to see that we are on the same page. So Flawless, tell me about your family. Do you have one?"

Flawless was thrown off by the last question and looked back at Jennessy, who looked back at him, simply waiting for an answer.

"Yeah, yeah I do," Flawless replied. "I live with my mother and sister."

"And how do they feel about you rapping?"

"My sister is cool, but my mother hates it."

"Your mother hates it, even after you told her that you won the deal."

"Well, I haven't really told her yet."

"Well, you trust me, when you do, everything is going to change. I got big plans for you, Flawless. You have just become my number one priority."

"Really," flattered Flawless remarked.

"Yep. What you did last night was pure genius. I listened to your demo ten times. Everything you do is genius. I'm telling you, I have met and produced a lot of rappers, and I got to tell you that nobody has got anything on you. You are the best in the game."

"Thank you."

"You don't have to thank me. I'm only stating a fact. With your talent you can tear the entire competition apart—with the right backing and promotional campaign behind you. And that's what we are going to give you here."

"That's good shit."

"That's really good shit. And even better shit. I already got you a feature on the new Bin Laden track. All we need from you is 16 bars. You think you can do that?"

"Fuck yeah, I can. Whoa . . . Bin Laden; that's the hottest cat in the game right now."

"You're right, but you know what? You're gonna eat him alive. From what I heard on that demo, nobody's got anything on you. Trust me, I got some more features and work on sound tracks coming up. We are going to create such a buzz behind you that by the time your album comes out nine months from now, it's gonna go straight to platinum."

"Whoa. Shit."

"Trust me. It can all happen that fast, but it takes talent and a good team behind it, and together we got it all."

"Well, then I'm ready. C'mon, let's do it."

"Fuck yeah, that's the type of attitude I like."

Jennessy then pulled out a prepared contract, which he handed over to Flawless. "You're name is already on the contract, you just sign right there and we can get started." Flawless took the ten-page document and began to look it over. Jennessy tried better to direct his vision. "The X is right there at the bottom."

Flawless was, however, a bit overwhelmed by the weight of the matter.

"Yeah, I just wanted to read some things over."

"It's a lot. I know what you mean; but there is nothing to read over. All you need to know is that you get a two hundred fifty thousand-dollar advance, fifteen cents off of every record sold, you get a fifty thousand dollar bonus every time you go gold and one hundred thousand dollars for every time you go platinum. That's right man; you sign that line and you're already a rich man on your way to becoming a millionaire. Take a check home for two-fifty large and I'll bet your mother will not say another bad word to you about rapping again."

"Yeah. Yeah, I'm sure she won't. Still, I just wanted a chance to look some things over."

"Okay, sure." There was a break in Jennessy's speech. It lasted exactly seven seconds, and then: "But this is the deal, man, and it won't change. And maybe if you walk out of here today, maybe it won't be here when you come back tomorrow. Or if it is still here, maybe I won't consider you my priority anymore because you wasted my time."

"Hey, what happened here? Slow down a minute. Nobody is trying to waste nobody's time. I just wanted to look some things over."

"But it is a waste of time, son. I got things that are already in motion, only waiting for your signature. This slows up a lot of things and aborts others. And in this business that could all equate to millions of dollars, all to look over a contract that is nonnegotiable."

"I see."

"I'm glad that you see. So what's it gonna be?"

Flawless sat there confused as to what to do exactly. Jennessy's turnabout had come so quickly. Jennessy, sensing the change in the young man's mood, softened his tone. "You know what, come here. I wanna show you something." Jennessy then led him over to the window and handed him a pair of binoculars. "I was saving this as a surprise for after you signed but I think that I'll show it to you now. Now look directly down there. Do you see the red SUV with the bow on it downstairs?" Jennessy asked.

"Yeah," Flawless replied, while looking through the binoculars.

"Well, it's a Benz: it's brand new, all paid for, fully loaded and it's yours."

"Shit!"

"That's only the beginning. I'm going to share something with you, Flawless. There are a lot of talented guys out there, some more so than you. And you know what? Most of them are just bums on the street or working a nine to five. And do you know why? It's because they're scared to live their dream. They're afraid to succeed. I'll tell you this, something I learned a long time ago in this business. And that is: The only thing worse than a 'has been' is a 'could have been.' Don't be a 'could have been,' Flawless. Let me ask you something. Do you know what deism is?"

"Yes," Flawless replied, though he was a bit thrown off by the question. "It is the belief that God only created the world, but ever since has no control or is indifferent to the creation." Flawless had learned that in philosophy class. He failed to see its relevance to the argument at hand.

"Well, I am what you would call a deist," Jennessy continued. "That means that I don't believe in fate, destiny, religion or all that other shit. I don't believe that the future is written. I believe that God created the world but your life is your own to do with as you choose. So make your choices, decide your own fate. Never let anyone define for you who you are. God wrote you into existence, Flawless, but now the pen is in your hand. You write your life the way you want it and then put a beat to it and rhyme. This is your opportunity; don't blow it trying to be conservative. Take the pen and save conservatism to the elderly. Don't wake up thirty years from now in a pissant job that you hate, with a wife that nags the hell out of you, thinking always about how much different your life could have been. Make your life the way you want it. I see what you want, Flawless, you want the same thing that I want: a chance to live, love and prosper. Everything that you want can happen, all of your beliefs, all of your desires, just write it into being. I know what you're thinking: you wanna get a lawyer, you wanna get an agent, get someone to look things over. Why? So that they can take fifteen percent of something that is rightfully yours? Something that you have worked years for. Flawless, listen to me. This is your chance. This is the contract; it's nonnegotiable; it's not going to change and Crown is the label. This is your opportunity, don't blow it, take it, pen your future and have no regrets and know that God no longer has any bounds on you."

After ingesting all that Jennessy had said, Flawless took in a deep breath, smiled and walked over to the desk and signed the contract. Jennessy patted him on the shoulder. "All right, my boy, it is written. Now let's go take over the world." He then pushed a button on his phone. "Jane, a son is born. Bring everybody in and let's introduce them to our boy. I feel like a drink. Would you like a drink?" he asked Flawless.

"Sure."

It had all happened so fast, Flawless found it hard to be happy. Had he made the right decision? Was this the way that it all really went down? He had heard the horror stories of bad deals before, but was that only the talk of the disgruntled? Everything that Jennessy said vibrated well; the Jeep downstairs was even better. But what had he signed really? He didn't know and was in a manner afraid to know.

Jennessy led him to his personal bar set to the left of his desk. He opened up a small refrigerator and pulled out a bottle of champagne.

"What are you doing tonight?" he asked Flawless.

"Nothing that I know of."

"Great. You're going to a party. It's an album release for Stalin at the Goldstein."

"Cool." Anything to take his mind off of what had just occurred.

"Now, how about some Cristal? Have you ever had Cristal?"

"No."

"Well my man, it's all Cristal from now on." Jennessy uncorked the bottle and its contents spilt over. "Whoa there," he reacted.

He handed Flawless a glass and filled it. At that moment Jane led five people into the office. Flawless noticed that the beautiful woman from the elevator was one of them.

"Everybody, come over here and let's celebrate the birth of a new Crown Records artist. Everybody, this is Flawless, and Flawless this is everybody. Flawless, this is the team that's going to make you number one."

Flawless exchanged greetings with everyone, giving a special eye to the beauty from before; upon seeing her, and touching flesh again, all of his prior worries began to fade away. For now, he pitied nothing but the depths of her eyes, and the gravity of their brown.

"This is Trish. Trish is going to be your publicist. She is new to Crown and publicity, but already she's the best in the game. A sure testament of that is what she has done for Bin Laden. Without her no one would know Osama from Saddam. I don't know where she came from, now I don't know what I would do without her."

Trish, that's her name—sweet. But then again, what's in a name? Even phlegm would take on new definitions when coupled with her frame. Flawless's thoughts stayed with Trish while Jennessy continued the introductions: introducing everyone from marketing, to media, to radio, to stylist. They all had names, but Flawless was cognizant of only one: Trish. She stood there like a dreamlike creature of his making, penned to perfection. With her there, Flawless felt at ease with the future he had signed.

FiVE

Hannibal sat with his legs sprawled before the immense television, watching the movie *Hannibal.* This was count seventy-three. He was coming to the close of the film. It was the scene where Hannibal Lecter fed agent Krendler his own brains on a hot plate.

Now this is the shit right here. That's the way you kill a nigga, Hannibal said to himself.

At this time Mook and two older well-dressed Italian men entered the apartment. The door had been locked but Mook had a key. Hannibal looked up at the figures with silent familiarity. He knew Jersey and Jacobin very well. If he were to have a boss, Jersey would be it; a man slim in build but fat in style. He had an air of charisma, an aura of cool that a professional gangster possessed. He was a killer but he was admirable; though to say killer may have been a misnomer. Jersey ordered hits, but in recent years had rarely been the facilitator. That was where Jacobin came in. He was a bit taller, a bit bigger and dumber in thought. And he looked up to Jersey, so he dressed like him; today they were in matching gray suits. Jersey was a businessman, as he liked to call himself. He dabbled in gambling, construction, sanitation and drug trafficking, the Brooklyn arm of which Hannibal ran. In all he oversaw a multimillion-dollar operation in condoned illegalities, though he had such a sense of professionalism that it all but legitimized everything that he did.

"What's going on, Bull?" Jersey greeted.

"Yeah, how's things rolling?" As a custom, Jacobin followed after, and only after Jersey spoke. Jacobin was Jersey's right-hand man, his cousin, and beyond the suit, his carbon copy.

"Things are going great, gentlemen. To what honor do I owe the visit?" Hannibal asked while looking up from the sofa. The two men were standing in front of the television, blocking his view. This annoyed Hannibal. If it were anyone else, he would have already been barking. He however knew better than to tell Jersey to move.

"You know us, Bull. We always like checking up on our investments, make sure everything is moving properly."

"Well, everything is straight."

"Yeah, I don't doubt it, but let's talk business anyway."

"All right then, let's go into the bedroom," Mook interjected.

"Naw . . . the kitchen will do," Hannibal said, shutting down Mook's suggestion.

He then led the others into the kitchen; Jacobin started off the meeting. "So Bull, how is business?"

"Like I said, man, everything is straight, more productive than it has ever been," Hannibal answered him with his eyes on Jersey.

"Yeah, yeah, I know it is," Jersey responded.

"Then why the visit? It's not time for your pickup, and plus I usually deliver that to you."

"You're right, Bull. Business is good but we're concerned nevertheless. You're drawing too much attention to yourself."

"How so?"

"With all this hip-hop shit you been doing," Mook again interjected and Hannibal became quietly irritated at his obtrusive friend. Now he saw what was going on. This meeting was all because of Mook. He looked over to his friend, gave him a cold eye and then turned his attention back to Jersey. "Trust me, it's nothing."

"Bull, you been on TV. Multiple times."

"And we can't do what we do and draw so much attention to ourselves. It makes other people *nervous!*" Jacobin emphasized with tacit intimidation.

"Understood," Hannibal replied without an argument.

"Listen here, Bull. I love you, man. I love you because you make me money," Jersey intimated with sincerity. The proof of this was that he had come to Cypress to address the matter to Hannibal personally. If it had been anyone else he would have merely sent Jacobin and muscle. "I ain't seen nobody run the streets as efficiently as you do. You're wiser than your years and you command respect, which is absolutely necessary in this business. I know guys twice your age who ain't got your calm and control." At the end of Jersey's last remarks, he nodded his head over to Jacobin, inclining Hannibal to do the same; Bull got the point. "But even the wisest of men are known to do stupid things, like all of this rapping shit." Jacobin came in, being unaware of the unspoken conversation.

"Now, I am sure what we are saying to you is not unreasonable. Surely you can see the discrepancies in your behavior. So it's like this, Bull: you give up this hip-hop nonsense and we continue business as usual. But you cannot do both," Jersey stressed.

"Understood," Hannibal answered again without an argument.

"Yeah?" Jersey verified.

"Yes."

"Excellent. I take you at your word. Ma main dawg Bull. Now give us a hug, and we will be on our way."

They all exchanged affectionate hugs, after which Jersey and Jacobin left.

"All right. Now that all that shit is settled, let's get back to work," Mook stated, feeling as if he had done the right thing by calling Hannibal to the principal's office, or as it were, brought the principal to Hannibal's office.

"I need some air," Hannibal said, feeling a bit sickened and sold out.

It was the afternoon of that beautiful spring day and in true spring fashion the weather had turned. The rain had come—not a downpour, just a drizzle—but nevertheless an annoyance. Yet much like postmen, the weather was no deterrent for the boys, forever engaged in their customary game of dice by the side of the building. They were sidetracked only by the occasional passing by of tight-fitted flesh, a prey that they would jump on in true hound fashion. Or perhaps by the starving John, the dignified and homeless, who came searching for a fix. This was their true occupation; dice, however, was their living, or so it seemed.

They were Hannibal's foot soldiers: sixteen in total, though only nine were now present. Among the nine was Terrence. Terrence was Hannibal's third in command and a liaison between the boys and himself. He was a natural to this role due to his charm and personality. He was the classic class clown, and as such he was attractive. The brown-skinned, skinny twenty-one-year-old drew people's attention not so much for any physical prowess but more so for his mental acuity. He was intelligent but not educated. He was street, born and bred in the proverbial gullies of Brooklyn. He was a hustler, he was a survivor, he was hip-hop: dressed in oversized baggy jeans, the latest Jordans, Allen Iverson's jersey, a do-rag over his corn-rows, a hat over his do-rag and a chew stick in his mouth.

Hannibal exited his apartment building into the downstairs courtyard amid a maze of buildings: Cypress all concrete and inorganic. The boys stood at attention and spoke in unison, "Yo, what's up, Bull?"

"Nothin', nothin', just life, man. Who's winning?"

"Who else, god? I'm bussing they ass as usual," Terrence replied to Bull's question, as was ritual. Even if Terrence were losing, which was rarely the case, he would have still been the one to talk. The others many times just gathered around as mindless, backup automatons.

"Good shit. Yo, let me holla at you boys for a minute. I wanna show you something." All of the young men gathered around Hannibal as he pulled out a CD plainly marked *Hannibal: The Silence of the Lambs.* "This right here is my CD."

"Yo, god, this is you?" Terrence asked.

"Yeah, man, it's all Bull. And the shit is hot."

"No doubt, no doubt."

"Now, this is what I want y'all to do. I got about two thousand a these made up in the basement. I gotta move them. So I want y'all to sell the shit."

"When we gon' find time to do it though? We already mad busy as it is."

"Yeah, playing dice. It won't take up any extra time. You'll sell it while you push the regular shit. Sell it to the customers; especially dem white heads."

"What if a nigga don't wanna buy shit though."

"Fuck it, make them. Sell the shit. By any fucking means necessary. Now, you gon' sell them for ten dollars each and you get to keep four." Terrence nodded his head in agreement and the other boys followed suit. "All right, so we all down?"

"Yeah, man."

"Good shit. Now you gon' bring the profits straight to me. This operation is just between me an' y'all. Nobody else is to know; not even Mook." Everyone agreed. "Cool, y'all find the boxes downstairs in the basement. All right, ma niggas, let's get to work."

SiX

The Goldstein Ballroom was alive with splendor, decadence and a pounding, heavy hip-hop beat. The lavishness of the atmosphere was customary to the ballroom. The beat was new. The Goldstein in its hundred-year history had normally catered to the reproductions of Bach and Mendel, though like all capitalistic ventures, it was wholly adaptable to the green. And as the hands of green changed with the make of the music, from jazz to rock to pop, hip-hop now found itself the pet of the Goldstein in the new millennium.

The crowd below was the folk of the industry, all mingling, all smiling, all fronting. The dress code ranged from semiformal to bohemian to thug. In this new hip-hop era, baggy jeans and work boots had been made chic. The room was also a world of techno fantasy, with a wide array of the most expensive Palm Pilots, two-way pagers and cell phones. Everyone beaming information back and forth with more ease seemingly than Scotty did on *Star Trek*.

They were not in the space age, but not that far away either. Reality had become science fiction. Pagers and mobiles had become appendages to the anatomy, seemingly as natural to their being as a hand, or at the least an extension thereof. Wherever they were, they were forever online, hooked, like a new form of addict. And they never argued the addiction or the fact that they existed just fine without it. In truth, how did they exist back then: ten years ago, or just five? Life seemed so grossly different; and now different was anyone who had not evolved with technology. Much like a dinosaur simply waiting for extinction, or eventual absorption into the larger collective of the Borg. And so Flawless embarked on this voyage at first as a curious voyeur and as always at first, voyeurism was sweet.

Flawless and Tommy entered the ballroom through the big white doors, looking up at the majestic grand chandelier, the ceiling-high columns, looking out at a sea of faces and being greeted by an assortment of pretty waitresses offering all manner of entrees. The two indulged themselves in a little eye play and subtle foreplay, as they stood on a plateau that descended by seven steps into the main floor.

Before Flawless could think of Jennessy, he looked down and saw him calling from a tidal wave of people. Flawless acknowledged. "C'mon, Tommy, I see Jennessy down there."

They began to cut their way through the crowd. The melee was a motley crew. There was a mix of races, being mostly black, Latino or white. There was also the flavor of homosexual flamboyance, which at times Flawless thought was at an abundance. Added to this was a mix of thug life, there, he thought, to keep things in perspective. They arrived at Jennessy's position, to find him garbed in opulent denim.

"Flawless, my boy, how you enjoying the festivities?" he greeted.

"Oh, I'm enjoying it."

"I knew you would. I knew you would. I want you to meet some people."

"Cool, but, oh yeah, Jennessy, this is my boy, Tommy."

Jennessy and Tommy greeted and shook hands. "So Tommy, do you rhyme as well?" Jennessy asked purely for the sake of pleasantry.

"Yeah, I do a little sumthin'. But I mostly do production."

"Really?"

"Yeah, Tommy produced my demo," Flawless remarked.

"Whoa, that was pretty decent work," Jennessy flattered.

"Thank you," Tommy accepted.

"I would like to see what you could do in a big studio."

"Yeah, man, me too."

"Great, we'll work on that . . . but if you'll excuse us for a second, Thomas, I have to show our boy around."

"Yeah, all right," Tommy replied feeling a bit disappointed.

"Yo, I'll be right back," Flawless said to his friend before getting lost in the crowd, leaving Tommy alone, surrounded and by himself.

Jennessy led Flawless through the shuffle until they had come to Noah's position. Noah was currently the best producer of the day. It was a new phenomenon in music in which producers were as heralded as the performers. In the current wave of hip-hop, amid all of the redundancy in rhetoric, it was the beat rather than the lyrics that was the sugar. For this reason, the stock of the producer had risen. More times than not the shelf life of a producer far exceeded that of an artist. In truth, performing was a fad; producing was a career. Noah had more than made a career out of the game. He had been in the business for ten years. He only worked with the most popular acts because only they could afford him. Noah was a brand name in the world of beats, and his contribution was all but a guaranteed hit, with the hook included.

Though Noah was a man, he represented far more than that. He was a corporation of production, so to speak. He was a team of producers. In his studios, at any one time, he had up to seven producers working for him; fingers to ASR-10s, crafting the rhythm for the next club banger. And when a client desired a beat with Noah's distinctive sound he would walk the halls of his studios, see what his subordinates were offering, take the track that was best fitting, add to this beat his own characteristic flavoring, take full credit and publishing rights for the production, sell it to the client for up to $100,000 to points on an album and give to the particular producer 50 percent of the monies earned and no credits. The producer who, more often than not, wouldn't be able to sell his beat for any-thing more $5,000, would still be happy to get the cash and to be in the company of Noah's greatness, as Noah was once happy to be in the company of Adam's greatness, being a sub-ordinate, crafting beats for cash and no credits, until he real-ized that the credit was the thing, and that in this game name recognition meant more than anything else. Ever since he had learned that he had been on his own, with his own sound, and with his team he now outshadowed everyone else in the game.

He stood in the crowd now: slim, dark-skinned and locked, draped by two beautiful girls, fiddling with his two-way pager, when Jennessy approached.

"Noah, my man with the beats."

"Yo, what's going on, Jennessy?" Noah replied, looking up from his pager.

"Well, what's going on is Flawless here." At hearing Jennessy call his name, Flawless stepped forward. "Flawless here is my new boy, my number one priority."

"Oh, it's like that," Noah remarked.

"It is most definitely like that." Jennessy turned his attention toward Flawless. "Noah here makes the best beats in the busi-ness."

"Yeah, man, I know Noah. You did a lot of work for Bin Laden."

"Yes, he did. He even wrote his hooks for him. And now soon he will be working with you."

"You getting high praise here. You must be nice."

"My man, you have no idea," Jennessy cut in before Flawless could answer. "But you will be seeing it for yourself soon enough. But until then . . . well, until then."

"Well, then, until then," Noah concurred.

Flawless, standing there feeling much like an embryo amongst giants, just kept the rhythm of the flow. "Until then."

Flawless and Noah exchanged pounds and then Flawless and Jennessy walked off.

"There are a few more people that I want you to meet," Jennessy said, as they began cutting through the crowd, passing by a myriad of faces that Flawless recognized from a video or a magazine or some other medium of media. And those he did not recognize, he recognized that they were important behind-the-scene brokers. He knew this to be so because despite their anonymity they were heavily courted. And eventually he knew he would meet them all, and they would all court and covet him. He would rule this world. It was happening, he could feel it in his bones; he could feel it in his teeth.

As was becoming a custom, as his mind ventured off, he would run into Trish; and so they did. As always, it was a per-spective-altering experience. She was breathtaking, wearing a slinky fitting black dress that was cut to be a mini and expose the thigh. She was with three other girls, who were attractive in their own right, but to Flawless they were only accessories to her adornment.

"Hello, Trish . . . ladies," Jennessy greeted.

"Mr. Jennessy . . . Michael," Trish replied. And there she went again, speaking his given name. It seemed out of place but, nevertheless, sweet: because it came off of her tongue. Her tongue. At that moment he wondered just how she would taste. "So what's the plan for tonight, boys?" she asked.

"Just meet and greet, Trish, meet and greet. You know the biz," Jennessy answered.

"Yes, but you have ample time to do that . . ." There was a break in her beat as she looked at Flawless, and of course he looked back at her. ". . . How about I borrow your boy for the night? We don't want to bore him with all of the plebs of indus-try life already."

"Really . . . well, it's not up to me. What do you think about that, Flawless?"

"I have no problems with that," Flawless quickly answered.

Jennessy had not wished to cut the evening short so soon; he rather liked walking Flawless around on his arm. But one man cannot argue with another man's hormones. It was almost always a losing battle. "Well, then, I guess we'll save the introductions for another night."

"Great," Trish replied.

Jennessy said his good-byes and walked off, quickly losing himself in the crowd. Trish addressed her company and the girls offered no audible rebuttal for being ditched. She then placed her arm through Flawless's and began to lead him through the crowd, stopping occasionally only to exchange brief salutations with the rest of the melee. Flawless, lost in the moment, pondered what to say.

"Would you like to get out of here?" she asked him.

"Ah, sure, where to?"

"I don't know, anywhere. I just need to get away from all of these . . . people."

"Okay, but I came with my boy and I just need to tell him that I'm leaving." Flawless looked around, realizing that he was far away from where he originally left Tommy. "Now I just need to find him." He didn't even know in which direction to begin walking and if Tommy had been roaming himself this would be a task.

"Does he have a cell phone?" Trish asked.

"Yes."

"Well, then, call him. It's going to take you forever to find him in all of . . . this."

She handed him her phone. Flawless stepped aside and covered his ears while he made the call. After a minute he walked back to where she stood.

"You told him?"

"Naw. I couldn't get through. I left a message on his voice mail. I hope he gets it."

"So are you ready?"

"Yes."

"Then let's go."

• • •

Flawless and Trish stepped out into the night air amid the traffic of people coming in and out of the party. That beautiful spring day had now become a chilly winter night. The weather caught Trish off guard. She was dressed to be cute, not seasonable.

"Oh God, it's cold!" she said through clenched teeth and then hugged Flawless tightly for body heat. She did this out of reflex and not any planned attempt at seduction, though there was a sense of comfort in the embrace. She would not have thrown herself so easily into the arms of just any man.

This was the closest that they had been; so close that Flawless was able to feel the suppleness of her breasts pushed up against him, her nipples tickling his torso. It felt good, too good. He separated himself from her just a bit. He didn't know if she would take offense to feeling him so soon.

"I am so sorry. I didn't mean to attack you like that," she said.

"It's all right, it's all right. Believe me, attacks like that I don't mind. Would you like to borrow my jacket?"

Trish smiled at the chivalrous offer. "Thank you so much," she said and then coated herself, and walked down the steps to the valet and handed him a ticket. The valet left and in a minute a silver Camry SUV pulled up.

"Would you like to drive?" she asked him.

"I don't drive," Flawless replied.

"Really." Trish reacted with surprise, but not overtly so.

"Naw, I don't," Flawless remarked, feeling slightly embarrassed.

"That's so cute," she said with a smile; and he didn't know whether to be pitied or flattered, but her smile made him feel more to the latter.

And at that moment there came a thunder, a roaring bass, an earth-shaking rhythm: the Boss was here; a Mack truck, an eighteen-wheeler, pulled up to the Goldstein with all of the pomp and circumstance of a circus, and the ring master was

Stalin. He was an oversized man who did everything over the top. Most artists had promotional vans, he had a promotional eighteen-wheeler, with all eighteen wheels blindingly rimmed out, its exterior plastered with his enormous visage in promotion of the new album and in its interior there was a big-screen TV, a sofa, a stereo system, a bar, a Jacuzzi and an entourage unparalleled in the industry. The man was a party in and of himself.

The truck came to a halt and the Boss and crew stepped out. Stalin was bulbous, light-skinned and bald; and hungry, as he eyed Trish upon the steps like a tender piece of meat. He stepped to her position and probed her company, looking Flawless up and down as if he were somehow . . . less than. Flawless saw the challenge and returned the rapper's gaze with likewise intensity. Seeing this, Stalin broke off his stare and turned his eyes to Trish.

"So what's up, sexy? What's goin' on, Trish?" he greeted.

"Nothing but the biz, Stalin. You know how it is."

"Yeah, yeah. So . . . who dis?" he asked her in reference to Flawless while his eyes never left her cleavage.

"Oh well, Stalin, this is Flawless. Flawless just signed on to Crown today."

"Really . . . Flawless, huh?" Stalin asked.

"Yeah, Flawless." Flawless answered.

"That shit supposed to mean something?"

"Yeah, it means everything," Flawless replied with intensity in his tenor. He didn't like this man; he didn't like him at all.

Stalin thought about the meaning of what Flawless had said for a second and then he gave up. "Whatever, nigga. Whatever." Then he turned his attention back to Trish. "So Trish. When you gon' leave that bum Bin Laden and come work on my project? Y'know I'm taking it to a whole new level with this album. I'm seeing five p's with this shit, at least."

"Well, Stalin. Y'know, Jennessy is *the boss;* and now he has me working on Flawless's project."

"Oh, so it's like that?"

"I'm afraid so."

"Cool. It ain't nothin', ain't nothin'." He then looked Trish up and down again and bit into his bottom lip. "So Trish . . . when you gon' stop frontin' and let me hit that?"

"Good night, Stalin," was Trish's sharp reply to Stalin's grostesque proposition.

"Whatever, bitch; your loss," was his reply to her refusal. He then turned to his crew. "All right people, let's roll through this shit." With that, Stalin and company took their leave and paraded themselves into the party.

Flawless watched them leave, still feeling a bit heated by the encounter. Trish then gently put her hand to his cheek and turned his brow back in her direction.

"Are you all right?" she asked him.

"Yeah, I'm cool," he answered.

"Don't let that bother you, Michael. Don't ever let it. You will be bigger than him. You will be bigger than them. You already are, tenfold." Her words filled his ears and soothed his temper; after a moment he could think of nothing else but being in her company.

They got into her Jeep and for seconds merely stared at each other. It was rare to find someone and be able to get lost in their silence. So they just stared, reveling in the beauty of the moment. They did this until a car honked from behind, prodding them to move.

"So where would you like to go?" Trish asked.

"Anywhere."

"I'm a bit tired. You don't mind if we just go back to my place?"

"No . . . I don't mind at all."

"All right then, we're off."

Flawless and Trish, like seasoned lovers, walked hand in hand up the steps to her apartment, both feeling at peace and comfortable with the person they had met less than twenty-four hours ago. She lived in a brownstone in the Fort Greene section of Brooklyn. Fort Greene was home to the artsy and the up-and-coming of the borough. Given the ambition of the neighborhood the rent did not come cheap. Trish could afford it. She was twenty-five and in a good place in her life and profession. Crown paid her well for her status. She was the new millennium's independent woman, self-sufficient as it came to the material; the heart, however, was a matter of a different making.

The door opened to darkness. She felt for the lightswitch and flipped it on and Flawless found himself in the middle of a stunning living room, well decorated in a mixture of Ikea and a fetish for African art. There was a mood of brown to the entire apartment, the color being present in varying degrees; it led from the parquet floors to the beige sofas to the brick walls to the handcrafted wooden African figurines, which either came straight from the continent or by way of the shop down the street. There was a very organic feel to the apartment, alive with art and style, as original Mshindos hung on opposing walls creating balance in beauty. It was like a dream, a beautiful still life, all mixed in an aura of purple.

"Whoa, this is a great place," Flawless said, as his eyes roamed the room.

"Thank you," Trish replied. "Excuse me for one second."

She walked over to her answering machine. As she leaned her locks fell over her shoulder, covering her face somewhat. She then gently pulled them back over and there was something about how she did this that Flawless found to be such a turn-on. Inspired by his heated desires, he slowly walked up behind her. He placed himself about two inches away from body contact. Trish had not felt his presence as she listened to a message.

A man's voice came over, "Trish, this is the umpteenth time that I'm calling. Baby, I can't stand this. I need to see you. I need to—" His speech was cut short as Trish erased the message. She tilted her body slightly. With that motion her rear rose and gently rubbed against Flawless's being. She finally noticed his presence and paused at the recognition.

He spoke to her in an octave just above a whisper, "Who was that?"

"Nobody," she responded in kind.

"Ex-boyfriend."

"Something like that."

"I understand his pain."

"Really."

"I would feel the same way. And so . . . now, who am I?"

"Michael, you are whoever you want to be."

"And who are you?"

"I'm just Trish, nothing more, nothing less."

"I don't know Trish."

"Would you like to get to know her?"

Flawless placed his lips to her ear. "I think so." He melted his face into her neck and she reacted as he fell into the trenches of her scent.

"Girl, you smell so good."

"You feel so good," she said as her hands massaged his thighs beneath the denim.

Flawless pulled the straps of her dress down past her shoulder, and the garment slowly slipped to her ankles. She wore no bra and only a thong. His hands moved down and gently cupped the shape of her breast, then the curves of her flesh, past her waist and then onto and around her ass, which he drew in closer to his being. He was now completely aroused and likewise, so was she. At the moment there were no thoughts of propriety. Was this the right thing to do, was it not? Today was their first meeting but they didn't feel like strangers. Stranger yet, she felt no weirdness or uncertainties about sharing her body with him. True, it was in her nature to be bold, but still this seemed too much, too fast, but nevertheless just right. Why? She didn't know, she merely felt, and it all felt good. The way he looked at her, the way she looked at him. Never before was the retina such a clear channel to the soul. She took solace in his eyes, a peace that she had not seen in any man before. She saw it clearly from the moment she first eyed him this morning. It was a corny sense of comfort that all made sense in a dream.

"Tell me, Michael, do you think that you could ever love her?" she asked him.

Of all the things he expected her to say . . . that wasn't it. The shock of it woke him from his nebulous. Because of his affections for her there was something extremely endearing about the question. Still, the thought of love, so soon in the midst of lust, was somewhat scary. "What does love have to do with it?" he asked.

"Everything. So . . . do you think that you could?"

"Do you think that you could?" he replied, returning the question.

"Strangely, yes."

"How can you? How do you know that? You don't even know me."

She then turned around and gently kissed him on the lips. "I don't know, but I just feel it. And I see it."

"See what?"

"I don't know exactly. But tell me, what do you see?"

"I don't know, Trish. I see you here before me."

"And how do you feel?"

"With you in my arms, better than I ever have."

He had desired her all day and perhaps even longer than he had known. Holding her now seemed almost unreal. His words to her heart rang sweet. She again placed his hands upon her waist. The intimacy of flesh was a distraction.

"So tell me, Michael, do you think that you could love her?"

He pulled her in closer, and not being exactly sure of what he was saying, save that it all felt right in the rhythm of the moment, he uttered the words, "Yeah, I think so."

SEVEN

It was a cloudy day in the maze of Cypress. The skies above foretold of rain. By the density of the clouds Terrence could tell that it wouldn't be a drizzle. He was among the boys as they were captivated in their customary game of dice. Throughout all of the shouting, through the corner of his eye Terrence was able to see a familiar car pull up to the parking area. With the purpose of his day in sight, he retrieved his winnings from the concrete playing field. "All right boys, that's me right there, so you niggas get to keep the little money that you got left." Terrence pocketed his booty and began to walk away.

One of the dice players shouted him out, "Yo, c'mon, T. You gotta give us a chance to win back some a dat money."

"Win back what? Nigga, you lost, deal wit' it. Shit, you fucking lucky I'm letting you go home wit' yo' drawers on."

Terrence pulled out his Discman and put the headphones to his ears. Within two seconds the music came on: loud enough to drown out all the other noises of the maze. He was deaf to the boys still hollering for a rematch, deaf to a mother's crass admonishments of her child, deaf to a teenage boy's threats to his girlfriend, deaf to a police siren blaring. He was also deaf to the young couple strolling by with a newborn child, deaf to the Rastafarian tutoring the surrounding youth, he was deaf to the brothers' engrossment in their game of chess, deaf to the children's laughter as they diverted themselves in a game of tag. To this world of sparse trees and cheap brick, low-maintenance buildings, Terrence became deaf to many things; but what his ears didn't see his eyes heard very well. As he walked over to the parking area toward the beckoning BMW, he took in all that was his environment and knew well that it was home.

When he arrived the occupants greeted him. A young blond white male drove. A brunette white female was in the passenger seat and another was in the back. They stunk of suburbia.

Terrence approached the passenger side, leaned against the car with his headphones still blaring, saying nothing, merely chilling in his repose. Though he knew them very well. They were some of his best clients. They came every week at almost exactly the same time looking for their fix: Sometimes they wanted ecstasy, other times heroin, rarely they wanted blow, a few times acid; but always they wanted pot, or ganja, as they preferred to call it, as they came wearing Bob Marley T-shirts or that of any other dread that was in vogue.

Amy, the brunette sitting in the passenger side, shouted, "Hey, what's up, T?"

Terrence didn't respond, being so engrossed in the music from his phones. Darrin, the driver, leaned over to the passenger side and stressed the greeting, "T, are you hearing us, man?"

"Yo nigga, you said something?" Terrence answered, pulling down his headphones.

"Yeah, we were just saying hello." Amy replied.

"Oh yeah, sorry. I'm just so *imbued* in this shit right here; I wouldn't hear my name even if my momma was calling it. An' that woman's mouth is big, y'know."

"I hear you, man, I hear you," Darrin remarked.

"So what is it, a new Bin Laden track?" Amy asked.

"Bin Laden! Please, girl, this mofucka right here will smoke Bin Laden and his Taliban ass outta dem fucking caves."

"Wow, it's like that?" Darrin reacted.

"Fuck yeah. Here, give it a listen."

Terrence took the disc out and held it as an offering. Amy took it from him with a smile and proceeded to pass it onto Darrin. Darrin, however, was unwilling to take it.

"Well, T, we don't have that much time," he stated.

"Shit ain't gon' take no time."

"Yeah, Darrin, be cool. I wanna hear it," Amy added to Terrence's point.

"Yeah, Darrin, be cool." Terrence repeated. Terrence and Amy then looked over at each other flirtingly as Darrin reluctantly inserted the CD. A thumping beat came on and then over that came Hannibal's distinctive voice. After a minute everyone was bopping their heads. "Yeah, yeah, shit kills like crack, right?" Terrence remarked.

"Yeah, man, it's hot."

"Who is it?" Darrin asked.

"It's my man Bull."

"Bull. Wow, that's dope," Amy remarked, still flirting.

"Well, he is the dopeman, nigga. And now back to business."

Darrin was glad that Terrence changed the subject back to the original purpose. No matter how many times he had visited the maze, his soul still felt uneasy there. Every time he came he fidgeted in anticipation of leaving. He only came because he was always assured to get quality product from Terrence. A good dealer, much like a good doctor, was hard to give up once you had grown attached to their healing touch.

"Yeah, T, so you got the stuff?"

"Motherfucker, I'm a professional. Fuck yeah, I got the shit."

"All right."

Darrin went into his pocket and pulled out his money while Terrence fixed in on Amy. "So you feeling my man Bull, right?" he asked her.

"Yeah man, the shit's dope."

"Exactly, the shit's dope. So listen. I'm selling these."

"Yeah, how much is it?"

"For you, Ma, only ten dollars."

"Yeah, I'll get one."

"Yeah, Ma, shit that's cool, that's why I gotta love my peoples. That's good shit. But you know what? I got a lot of these to move. So how about you get ten?"

"Ten!" she blurted in disbelief.

"Yeah, ten," Terrence calmly repeated.

"Terrence, you can't be serious, man, you don't expect her to get ten CDs by herself?" Darrin interjected in pure suburbanese.

"No, no, of course not."

"Okay then."

"I wouldn't put all of that love on Ma alone. Naw, naw . . . alla y'all gon' get ten CDs . . . *each!*" Terrence exclaimed, placing extra emphasis on the last word.

"Each! Oh, fuck no. You must be crazy!"

"Nigga, did you just call me crazy?"

Amy tried to temper matters. "No, he didn't mean it, he didn't mean it," she said while reaching out for Terrence's hand.

"Better not had meant it. 'Cause you wanna see crazy? Crazy is your ass trying to get outta here in one piece without ma fuckin' say."

"You're not serious!" Darrin retorted.

"There goes that serious shit again. Motherfucker, do I look like a fucking comedian to you? Fuck yeah I'm serious! Now that's thirty CDs, at ten dollars each, equals three hundred dollars. Now add to that the two hundred dollars for the regular shit, an' we looking at what . . ."

"Five hundred dollars!"

"See, nigga, you got it before me. That's what a college education will get for you."

"I don't have that much with me!"

"That's why you walk with friends, nigga. Now, all you put together and add up that shit. Now get to it, I'm a busy man. I got a dice game to get back to. In the meantime, let me listen to some Michael here."

Terrence pulled out Michael Jackson's CD and placed it into his Discman. He gave a look to the boys in the corner of the building with a sign signaling thirty. Following the cue, they walked over to him with thirty CDs and placed them in the backseat of the car, frightening the silent white girl in the back into shimmying over and then returned to their pose back in the corner of the building.

The music from the Discman played loudly and Terrence began to feel the melody. "Oh, now this is the shit here." He began to sing along, *My life will never be the same, 'cause girl you came and changed, the way I walk, the way I talk, I cannot explain . . .*"

While he did this the occupants of the car bickered. Darrin was reluctant to comply. But the two girls outvoted and out-yelled him. In agreement, they went deep into their pockets and put together the cash, after which Amy handed it over to Terrence.

"Good shit, good shit. I can always depend on ma people to look out. Aw'ight, y'all, you have a very beautiful day and get home safe, okay. I'll see you next week."

"Now, what are we supposed to do with all of these CDs?" Darrin asked in anger.

"Ain't nobody ever teach you how to share, motherfucker? *Disperse* them shits amongst your friends. Now *tarry* on." He smacked the roof of the car, prodding it to move as if he were smacking a donkey. Darrin began to drive off, visibly upset.

" 'Bye, T," Amy said sullenly, but still flirting.

" 'Bye, Ma," Terrence replied.

He began to sing along once again. Walking off from the parking area he felt a trickle of water on his forehead. He held out his palm and felt that the rain was coming, and, given the speed of the drops, it was coming heavy. He threw on his hood and headed back toward the building, deafened to the oblivion, walking through the maze, singing along, *"Hee hee, ooh, you rocked my world, you know you did."*

BOOK TWO

EiGHT

Yo, I'm shameless, man
I'll bang a fan
Even do her mom
If her daughter that ass is fatter than
An' I'm flattered, ma'am
That you wanna get wit' the plan
Tie the back of her hand
Put it to her in a caravan
An' she's such a character
Makes me wanna bite her
No, not eat her, just bite her. . . .

"Yo, New York. Dis is yo' god, RA, live and in effect again, here on the frequency to be, WHRU, the home of the *hottest* Hip-Hop and R'n'B." The DJ's voice came on loudly over the lyrics, gradually fading the beat to a null. "Now, what does that mean? It means if it ain't on fire we don't play it! No mediocrity here, only the premium tracks. The stuff that's more addictive than crack. Will get out that crick in your back. Forever making your fingers snap. Yeah, I know that that rhyme was whack, but it's aw'ight, they don't pay RA to rap. I don't spit, I just spin, I wheel and deal with all the big Willies; 'cause RA is always in, the place to be, WHRU, home of the hottest hip-hop and R'n'B. Holla at yo' God."

DJ RA did his trademark ebullient rant over the airwaves to an audience as large as the bandwidth and with the advent of the Internet his range expanded beyond the bounds of which he was conscious. He had the most influential daily four hours on hip-hop radio in the city and quite possibly the nation. Anyone who was anyone and anyone who wanted to be anyone had to come over his mic. He had power and the ability to make, and at times, break careers. So in many respects, on radio, RA was God.

He sat now: a stocky, light-skinned twenty-eight-year-old, with studio headphones to his ears and his lips to a mic. He was seated on the inside of a crescent-shaped table. On the other side sat Flawless, likewise geared with studio headphones and a mic, awaiting his introduction. Behind Flawless, Malik and Devon from the Crown marketing department were standing silently against a padded wall. Behind DJ RA was a sound-proof booth where his engineer was busy at work.

"Now, who is in the house wit' RA today? None other than the man of the hour, the most hyped man that I have ever seen, ma brother, ma god, y'all were just listening to his song in the intro, give it up y'all for . . . FLAWLESS!" After addressing his audience, RA turned to Flawless and began the interview. "So whud up, god? How you livin'?"

"I'm good, I'm good; glad to be here."

"All right, ladies you have heard his voice, feel free to scream." RA pushed a button and played a recording of women screaming. This evoked a slight chuckle from Flawless. "But now, c'mon, Flaw, you doin' just a little bit better than good, aren't you?"

"Naw, I'm all right."

"I'd say you all right, making it on the cover of just about every hip-hop publication in the same month. And you did all of this without your album even dropping yet."

"Well, that's all blessings to having good people around you and having good promotions, y' know. And speaking of promotions, I would just like to add that my album is dropping today, today; so everybody out there, go cop that."

"Trust me, they know, they know. And everybody in the industry knows that this whole game is about to be shut down. Cats are scared of you."

"Well, what can I say . . .?"

"You ain't got to say nothin'. You been killing it on the wax. You been eating up everybody on every track you been on. You just about ended Bin Laden's career. I think that's the worst mistake he ever made, putting you on as a feature. How did you get on that anyway? Naw, forget all that, how did you get put on to all of this so quick? I mean, the last thing I knew you was up on One-oh-six doin' yo' freestyle thing, then all of a sudden, like a thief in the night, you here taking over the airwaves."

"That was well put, exactly. I came like a thief in the night. But truth be known, nobody makes it on their own. I've had help. I have a supportive label and great management. So you know I have to give it up to the people behind the scenes for helping the movement happen."

"Exactly, exactly. We gotta keep everything in perspective."

"And speaking of giving thanks, I gotta give it up to you, and all the other cats on radio for showing me mad love and playing my music, making me have the number one single in the country right now."

"Much love, but you ain't gotta thank me for that. We always play the most blazing tracks. And your stuff, beyond the hype, is hot. I will go out on a limb and say that you the best lyricist in the game today."

"Respect, RA. That's high praise. I might have to join you on that limb."

"Trust me. There's a whole lot of us out there. The praise is well deserved and well worth it. And right about now we gon' be worthless if we don't take a commercial break. Wish you could stay with us for the hour but you a busy man. So I would just like to thank Flawless for being here today. An', yo, the door is always open."

"No doubt, man, anytime. Thank you again for having me."

"And for all of you living on Planet X, who don't know, ma man's album drops today, so go cop that. And with that we gotta go pay some bills, so y'all, this is RA, this is HRU an' I'll see y'all in a few."

"And we are off in five, four, three, two . . . good show, y'all." The voice of the engineer rang through dry and loud, signaling that it was now safe to talk and move around with liberty. RA and Flawless removed their headphones, reached over the table and gave each other a pound.

RA, being the God of radio, had come across just about every rapper in the industry, from the green to the rotten. In all, he respected about three percent of them. Some he had to simply because of their commercial appeal—you sell one million records or more and even God has to respect you. Others he respected truly for their talent. Though as a DJ, RA lived by the proverbial club banger in order to keep the people sated, in his heart he placed a higher esteem to lyricism. And so he respected Flawless.

Though it was his custom to be skeptical of those who came with an avalanche of hype behind them as Flawless had, Jennessy had kept his word. He made Flawless his number one priority. With the effort he placed behind him, the entire industry had no choice but to react to Flawless in kind. RA knew that there were very few times in which hype lived up to its billing. Flawless, however, was a thing of another matter.

"Good show, good show," RA said to him.

"Yeah, man, thanks for having me."

"No time to rest, we gotta swing over and do One-oh-six," Devon said to him before Flawless could think to protract the conversation. It was Devon and Malik's job to get him prepared, get him from show to show on time and to make sure that everything went smoothly.

"All right, let's roll," Flawless, who was rarely one to argue, agreed.

Exiting the Midtown Manhattan building, Flawless was met

by a group of thirty who had waited outside in the winter cold just to get a look, a touch or an autograph, or perhaps all three. He greeted and smiled with them, signed a few posters and then was hurried into a limousine.

Entering the limo, Malik handed him a cell phone. He had an interview with a reporter from one of the daily periodicals. While Flawless spoke to him, Devon handed him a laptop. He had to do a live feed chat for an online magazine. Surprisingly he handled doing both of these at once as Malik and Devon chatted away as well on their mobiles, setting up other meetings with the media; all this while they drove to Harlem to do yet another interview. It all seemed hectic but this was the life he wanted, and for now he had no complaints.

"Hello everybody. Welcome back to another edition of BET's One-oh-six and Park," Free announced.

"We here at BET are all pleased to bring out someone very special. This is a real success story born right here on the stage of One-oh-six," AJ continued.

"He took over the stage here, then he went on to take over the airwaves, and now he is about to take over the record stores as his debut album drops today, today."

"So now everybody put your hands together and let's give it up for the man of the hour, One-oh-six and Park's own, Flawless!"

Flawless made his way onto the set from behind the stage. The audience was on its feet in an instant explosion. He waved, acknowledging their affections, and came onto the set, counting his steps so as not to trip on his way up. No matter how cool you are, and how much they love you now, you fall on your ass on national live television and your career is over, he kept on thinking. He got to the set without incident. He gave a hug and a kiss to Free and a strong pound to AJ. Flawless then took a seat on the lavender sofa to the right of the stage, Free and AJ sat on the fuchsia couch to the left. He had never been on this side of the set before. This was the side saved for the super-stars. Now he knew that he had arrived.

AJ began the interview amidst the yelling and hollering of the audience. "So my man, Flawless, what's going on, how does it all feel?" The hollering began to fade allowing Flawless to answer.

"It feels good, man. It feels really good to get all of this love."

"It's all love indeed, 'cause the ladies love Flawless, don't they?" Free's question was the impetus for the women in the audience to test the limits of their vocal cords, screaming in a unified soprano.

"Now hold up, Free, it ain't just the ladies, 'cause I know that the fellas are feeling Flawless's flow as well." After AJ's prompting, the men likewise reacted with barks and hollers.

"That's peace, that's peace," Flawless replied to the ovation with modesty.

It was so strange. It had only been nine months, but his life had changed so much. Many times he still had to pinch himself to make sure that everything was real.

"So, my man, much has changed since you last graced our stage. You got the record deal and then in only a few months you've been on two hit movie sound tracks and have had hit collaborations with numerous artists, including Ms. Mariah Carey, I might add. Now you have the number one single in the country and your highly anticipated and critically acclaimed debut album, *Flawless Victory,* drops today."

"Whoa, that's a lot," Free added.

"You're right it is. It has been a blessed year. I have met a lot of good people and a lot of good things have happened to me. And I am just glad that the work is finally being heard."

"I hear it, brother, and I must say that you are an amazing talent. Something more than just a rapper, they're even calling you a poet."

"Better than that, Free, a wordsmith," AJ remarked.

"Yeah, I like wordsmith. But y'know, that's all part of the

plan, because a lot of people don't like to recognize hip-hop as poetry. And you know they do this so that they don't have to respect it. But it is poetry, just like Shakespeare and Hughes. And I wanna take it to that next level and give it that respectability as an art form. Y'know what I'm saying; I wanna write lines that's gon' be studied in school books, studied for lifetimes."

"Wow, that's beautiful."

"I hear you, Free. And, man, I just feel mad proud to have been part of your progression. Y'know many have graced this stage, but none have done what you have done."

"That is so true. I mean, the only other person who came half as close as you was my man Hannibal. Y'all remember Bull, right?" Free asked the audience. The audience members answered her by shouting out, a number of them chanted his name.

"Speaking of which, how is Bull? Have you any idea what he is doin' right now?" AJ asked Flawless.

Hannibal, Hannibal, Hannibal. It had been nine months, nine months in which he neither heard nor thought of the name Hannibal. Then it all came crashing back with the suddenness of a pubescent girl's period. Flawless never liked thinking about Hannibal; he was grateful to have passed that stage in his life and was hell-bent on keeping Bull in the past tense. Nevertheless, he now had to answer the question.

"Well, you know, I've known and battled Bull for a while in the beginning. We had nothing personally against each other but we were never friends. So I really couldn't tell you how he's doing. But I will tell you this. Bull is a hustler, and I mean that literally. So wherever he is, whatever he's doing, I'm sure he's fine."

His answer seemed to satisfy his hosts and the audience. He hoped that they wouldn't pry any further. The thought of Bull had just brought back a series of past anxieties, all of which he couldn't wait to repress into his subconscious, so he could move on and live his life in a Hannibal-less existence.

NiNE

A close-up of Flawless could be seen on the screen. It was a large image, which occupied only a small section of the righthand corner of Hannibal's immense television. On the larger screen was a close-up of Lecter's face. This was somewhere between count 105 and 106. The two images competed with Hannibal for his attention. Strangely he was able to take in both without losing a beat from either. Even stranger, though Flawless's was so minuscule in comparison to Lecter's, yet for Hannibal, it carried as much weight.

"Interesting, very interesting," Hannibal thought out loud in reference to Flawless's last remark. Flawless, Flawless, Flawless. Not a day within these last nine months had gone by when Hannibal did not give some thought to the man and their last encounter. It was a constant annoyance: much like a cut on the tongue, a pebble in the shoe or a boil on the butt. No matter how hard he tried, Hannibal couldn't seem to get past him. He had gone through it in his mind many times. This, however, was not just a psychological struggle. The Crown promotional juggernaut was in full gear and Flawless was everywhere, physically. He was on the cover of magazines, he was on billboards, he was on the radio, he was on television and he was on the 'Net. For Hannibal, the stink of Flawless had become an all-encompassing omnipresence; like a fart that lingered in the air, refusing to fade away.

While Hannibal meditated on the profundity of stank,

Mook entered the apartment with two suitcases; as usual, he used his key. He quickly walked across the floor, only giving a glance to the television. He knew that Hannibal was watching Lecter again, as he always did. In the beginning Mook shared in Hannibal's zeal for cannibalism but over the years he had grown sick of the habit and the sight of Lecter had become repulsive. But then something bit his eye.

"Oh shit, is that Flawless? Fuck yeah, it is Flawless. Damn, that nigga is everywhere nowadays."

"Yeah, everywhere," Hannibal remarked.

"Well, I guess a nigga is doing his thing."

"Hmmm. Well, speaking of doing his thing, you got the shipment?" Hannibal quickly diverted the subject back to business. He knew it was the only true language that Mook understood. And also he had no intention of speaking about the successes of Flawless.

"Nigga, you don't see the shit in my hand."

"Had any problems coming through?"

"Nope. I tell you, man, establishment ain't watching niggas anymore. Now, if I was an *A*-rab coming through, my ass woulda been fucked. I tell you, this terrorism shit has been the best thing for business."

"Nigga, you funny."

"Naw, I'm serious, man; business is good, greed is good and I'm a greedy motherfucker."

There was a characteristic knock at the door. From the pattern of the call, Hannibal knew that it was Terrence. Mook let Terrence in.

"Yo, what's up, Bull . . . Mook?" He delayed saying Mook's name for a reason. He didn't care for Mook much. It was nothing serious; it was just that Mook wasn't the most personable of people.

"What's up, T? How's commerce?" Hannibal asked.

"It's all gravy; profits is up on all fronts." Terrence then looked over at the television. "I see you watching ma nigga Lecter again."

"As always," Mook said in sarcasm, and it raised not even an eyebrow from either Terrence or Hannibal. Terrence then noticed the smaller screen in the corner. He noticed a particularly beautiful girl dancing in skimpy attire in one of the videos.

"Yo, y'all check out the ass on that one! Oh God, she is nice. I see that girl in everybody's video. Damn, she sweet! I tell you, that's the ass of ma dreams right there. Man, I be having the sweetest jerks when I be looking at her shit." Terrence's last remark evoked a mutual look of repugnance from both Hannibal and Mook. Terrence sensing this, responded, "What y'all lookin' at me like that for? Like I'm the only nigga who jacks off." In response, Hannibal merely shook his head, smiling. Mook kept his look of indignation. Terrence returned his attention to the television where he noticed Flawless. "Yo, is that Flawless? Oh, this is his video. Damn, ma man is all over the place. I just caught the bootleg to his shit. The fucker is hot." Flawless's name was again the last thing Hannibal wanted to hear. Noticing this, Terrence reformed his speech. "But you know, shit don't compare to yo' shit though, Bull." The thought of music reminded Terrence of the reason why he came to visit. "Speaking of which, we gotta talk."

"So speak," Hannibal replied.

"In private," Terrence said an octave lower.

"Understood. Mook, give us a minute."

"What the fuck for?" Mook questioned, not liking the idea of conversations going on between Hannibal and Terrence that he wasn't privy to; even worse, he hated the idea of Terrence suggesting that he should leave.

"Because I said so!" Hannibal said, shutting down Mook's argument.

"Oh, so it's like that," Mook remarked. Hannibal had just shown him up in front of a subordinate. Hannibal, realizing this, tempered his tone.

"Don't make it out into anything more than what it is. Just give us a minute."

"Cool. I dig."

Mook left the apartment, giving the evil eye to Terrence as he passed. It was the kind of look where Terrence knew that Mook was silently cursing him with every profane noun, adjective and combination thereof.

After Mook had left, Terrence responded, "Yo, Bull, what's up with your boy?"

"Pay no mind to that. So what's the deal?"

"We need another shipment."

"That's it . . . we just got in a shipment."

"Not that kind of shipment. We need another batch of CDs."

"Really. What about the ten thousand we got last month?"

"Dem shits is gone. Shit is selling better than the blow now."

"Get the fuck out."

"Yeah, I know. It's surprising to me too. In the beginning I had to thug them shits off, almost by gunpoint. Now muthafuckas are requesting the shit. And it ain't just customers either. Be some new cats that I ain't even seen before. Word a mouth is spreading."

"Fuck, that is crazy. That's about fifty thousand CDs sold in about nine months."

This was surprising to Hannibal. Though he was the one who initiated the business, for the most part he had paid little attention. He accepted the payments that Terrence was bringing in but had been so downtrodden that he had given it little mind. Terrence, on the other hand, had taken full charge of the operation. It was his idea to order more CDs when the first batch was finished and for each one in succession. Yet now it was obvious that the operation was getting bigger; Terrence felt that it was time to up the ante.

"Yep, and niggas want more. White cat was telling me that he's playing the shit on his college radio station. He say the crackers up there lovin' the shit. They want you to come and perform at their school."

"Get the fuck outta here!"

"Naw, man, I'm serious. So bottom line is we need more CDs."

"Gotta give the customers what they want, right?" Hannibal replied through a grin. This had been the best news that he had heard in a year. All at once the world held some measure of promise. He felt alive again.

"Yep, but this time I think you should print up an insert with it. Y'know, just something listing the tracks an' shit that got your info on it; you know, for bookings an' shit. We'll get another phone, set up a website, the whole deal."

"Website? You know how to set that up?" Hannibal asked.

"C'mon, god, I'm a multigenius. Terrence can do anything."

Terrence at the time did not know how to set up a website but he knew that he could learn. He always had a special aptitude for doing just about anything.

"Cool then, let's make it happen. But you know what, let's not stop there. Let's do flyers, posters, stickers and plaster the entire fucking city with it. Brooklyn, Queens, Bronx, everywhere. And shit, let's not even stop there. I'm ready to travel and do the same thing. Push this shit hard. Dem cats want me at they school, fuck it, I'll do it." Now it became clear to Hannibal again, the grand scheme, the big picture. He had stopped dreaming within the last few months. He now felt like breathing again.

"Yo, Bull, I'm down one hundred percent for whatever you do. But I thought you wanted to keep this on the low. All this commotion is gon' make some noise."

"You're right, but fuck it. I can't sell drugs all ma life. How about you?"

"Shit, Bull, I'm with you, any which way you go. If you slinging crack or tracks, it's all dope to me."

"Good shit, good shit. So you see the big picture?"

"I see it, god, I see it."

"So let's make it happen."

As they planned for the future, the immense television loomed in the background with Lecter's burning eyes; in the right hand corner was Flawless: sitting, smiling, laughing, chatting, glowing in the present.

TEN

Open your eyes. Open your eyes, Flawless, he said to himself, as his lashes slowly became untangled and his lids, like blinds to the world, folded up into a crinkle. He could see clearly before him—there was a microphone, being an emcee a microphone was like a tenth organ—however, seeing it so close to him he took extra notice of it now, of its globelike shape and the multiple tiny perforations that were imbedded in its metallic frame, housed upon a square box measuring an inch and a half in every dimension, and on the side was printed the letters *MTV* in characteristic fashion. It was a powerful tool. So powerful that just the lathering of his lips produced a sound that went throughout the audience. An audience of a little over one hundred, only two feet away, cropped on the floor, looking up at him with baited anticipation. It was an intimate audience. That's what he told himself but he knew better. He knew, though he saw only one hundred, there were millions watching him. The thought of it was as nerve-wracking as it was exhilarating, as he stood surrounded by cameras and that audience of one hundred here in MTV studios.

He was here on the top of the world, like a fish in a bowl, and all of a sudden he felt alone, before millions. Then he looked to his right and he saw Tommy. Tommy was there to play back up, to be his hype man. He saw Tommy and he felt calm. Flawless gave DJ Shu the go-ahead and then pulled the mic free.

He heard the beat. It was the rhythm to his second release,

"Pretty Brown Thing": a sexually laden, but ultimately sad, violent narrative. It was one of his favorites and he enjoyed performing it. The ladies loved it even more. They were the ones who made it a number one single, his second thereof.

It was marketing genius. Crown had perfected the game into a science. A hip-hop artist was to enter the market hard at first. Flawless did this with the title track of his album, "Flawless Victory." It was a wordplay piece; it was work written for men.

Though a number of women had made strides in the industry, hip-hop at the time was a very heavily testosterone-driven market, built upon the testicles of the streets. An artist had to win the respect of the streets first and foremost. Then after they had the men, they went after the women. It was simple: women bought more, they supported more and they were far more loyal. Men, for the most part, rarely jumped on bandwagons but were the first ones to jump off. Women would jump on and crash and burn with you. Though an artist had to be careful not to ride the female bandwagon for too long, for once the men and the streets stopped respecting you, it was over.

As Tommy hyped the crowd into a frenzy, Flawless scanned the room for a girl to serenade. He always did this whenever performing this particular song. It made everything more intimate. His eyes searched for the prettiest girl he could find. He found one. She was beautiful, she was fitting; she was his sister. Naw, that won't work, can't use Erika. He had forgotten that he had invited her. She smiled at him with pride and he was happy that she could see him in that way. Yes, she was pretty but she would not do at all. However, the girl who sat next to her was just as good. He looked at her, and his muse looked back at him amorously. He began the performance.

I seen this pretty brown thing
Diminutive Dominican
Tanned Tanzanian
Tantamount to a tangerine

Ma was sweet
Sista was complete
From the kinks in her locks
To the tips of her feet
An' I was a, fiend for the flesh
Had a fetish for the breast
Took my breath away
In everyway, she swayed them hips
Thick, like that accent
To accentuate dem assets
An' the way that ass set
Would off set my interests
Shit was intense
Burn sweet like incense
Touching my intestines
I was in suspense
I was dying to meet her
Fiending to feel her
'Cause sister
Had me doggone
Like a Doberman pincher
Makes me wanna howllllla
Make me wanna grab her
Undress her
An' put two in her
An' I'm too into it
I say I'm losin' it
Ain't even met this girl
An' I already wanna wife this chick.

He flowed the first verse, the story of praise. The second and third would tell of death and sadness. At the end, a sweetly sullen audience erupted in kinetic applause. Ananda Lewis, the special guest host of the program, made her way through the crowd, mouth agape. She was a beautiful caramel sister in her midtwenties with a look and a voice made for media.

"Wow, my man Flawless. That was beautiful." After speaking to Flawless she turned her attention to the audience. "Everybody, wasn't that beautiful?" This was an open invitation for the masses to go berserk. It took almost a minute for them to calm down.

"Flawless, y'know there are a lot of people who want to see you. Why don't you go to the window and say hello?"

Flawless cut his way through the endearing crowd, over to the window, looking out at Times Square. He had walked the streets of Times Square many times before. He had never seen it from this perspective. It was mind altering. Here he stood in the epicenter of capitalist opulence, seemingly on top of it all. There were no walls before him now. Then he looked down and was in for more than he could have fathomed.

Four stories down stood a swarm. Much like a mass of bees, five thousand people gathered in the early April cold; it was the type of cold that seared through fabric and touched the bones, caressing with a lover's intimacy (the weather was not aware that spring had begun), yet, there they stood, thousands screaming his name. That's crazy, he thought. That's insane. They stood there warmed by their mass and his presence. The NYPD tried their best to contain them, as fans waved signs, banners, posters and other manner of Flawless paraphernalia, whether they were homemade or Crown issue.

Flawless had no idea that his influence had reached this level of fanaticism. This was the stuff of Michael Jackson videos. The stuff he dreamed of. Now it was real and it was really happening to him. Shit, this is cool.

"Hey, Flawless, come back over here before you cause a riot," Ananda called to him; yet Flawless, being so imbued in the moment, did not hear her. Ananda then playfully shouted, "Flawless! Come back over here." He finally reacted to her call and returned to her beckoning arm. "Wow, there is a lot of love out there for you, brother, and you're feeling it, aren't you?"

"Oh, most definitely."

"Well, you should be. Your album is already certified five times platinum with only three months in release."

"Like I have said, the words are being heard and it just all around has been a blessed year."

"Well, you deserve all the blessings, man, because your work is awesome. They are saying that you are the best lyricist in the game today."

"Well, I'm not exactly going to get into all of that but I ain't gon' lie. My work is good; takin' it to another echelon, y'know. Comin' to take over the world."

"Well, brother, I believe you will. And thanks so much for coming through today."

"My pleasure, my pleasure. But before I go, because she is going to kill me if I don't, I wanna give a shout to my sister, Erika, who is sitting right there in the audience."

All of the MTV cameras focused on Erika seated in the front row.

"That's so cute. Hey, why don't you come up here?" Ananda asked.

Erika joined them in the center to cheers and a few hollers from the male members of the audience. She and Ananda hugged. "Wow, Flawless, she is so pretty. I see that good genes run in the family."

"Well, of course."

"Well, thanks again to both of you for coming through. Audience, let's give a big hand to Flawless and his sister, and we will be right back to more of your top ten most requested videos in just a minute."

"And we are off in five, four, three, two . . . clear." The invisible voice came over the intercom.

"Great show, Flawless." Ananda spoke now in a more sedate, nonetheless sincere tenor. They hugged and exchanged kisses on the cheek.

"Thanks for having me," Flawless replied.

Ananda's personal assistant approached her. "Nandie, Chuck needs to run something by you before we come back from commercial."

"Okay, cool." Ananda turned her focus back to Flawless. "Sorry guys, but I gotta go. So Flawless, I'll see you later."

"Mos' def."

"And it was a pleasure meeting you, and I'm sure we'll meet again," she said to Erika.

"Sure, I'd like that," Erika replied.

"Yeah, Flawless, make it happen. You should take her out with you more often." Ananda then hurried off the set.

"You heard that Michael? You should take me out more often," Erika restated.

"Listen, I'm not trying to get into any brawls, all right."

"Brawls for what?"

"Brawls because I ain't tryin' to see no degenerate big-head nigga try to turn you into some video whore or his latest one-night stand."

"That's all in your head. That's not going to happen."

"Well, you keep being naïve and I'ma keep leaving you at home." They tilted their brows, giving each other a look; it was a silent language implicit between siblings.

At this point Flawless became surrounded by audience members. As he greeted and smiled he kept an eye on Erika, who had stepped back out of the way of the crowd. His eye became fixed when a young man approached and began to speak to her. We can't have that, he thought. He sent a signal to Tommy. Tommy understood and walked over and gently broke up the conversation. Tommy was accustomed to this. He had acted as chaperone for Erika at Flawless's request many times before. Erika tried to argue but found Tommy's look of indifference immutable. So she sighed, playfully stuck out her tongue at Flawless and then cut her eye. To all this, Flawless laughed.

Malik cut through the crowd and handed Flawless a cell phone.

"Hello! What . . . who is it?" he said, straining to hear.

"It's me, my boy. I just saw the show. I loved it." Jennessy's voice registered loudly over the phone.

"Yeah, it went well!" Flawless replied.

"Yes, it did. I was just calling to tell you that you got the night off. So enjoy it, rest up; tomorrow is going to be another media blitz."

"That's good to hear." It was great to hear. Flawless loved all of the attention but he was tired. This had been a hectic three months.

"All right, my son, until tomorrow."

Flawless, Erika, Tommy, Malik, Shu and his bodyguard began to exit MTV studios. While walking down the hall Flawless felt a buzz in his pocket. Knowing the distinctive vibe of his two-way pager, he pulled it out.

I know you got the night off.
I'm at the hotel, can't wait to see you.
Love Trish.

The thought of Trish put a smile on his face. He continued to smile as he walked forward, seeing Erika as she walked in front of him.

They exited the building from the back. They all hurried and got into a black limousine awaiting their arrival. Flawless was about to get in when he looked down at the ground and noticed a flyer lying on the gum-laden concrete. Something about it caught his eye. He began to read: *Hip-hop take a stand, Fight for justice, Fight against the war on terrorism, Fight for reparations, Fight the death penalty, Free all political prisoners.* Flawless found it interesting and picked it up to read further, when he also noticed another flyer at his feet, and it read:

Cannibal Records proudly presents, Hannibal: The Silence of the Lambs. *The rawest, most controversial hip-hop album ever made. It cannot be found in stores, and will*

*not be heard on the radio. You can only receive by order-
ing at www.cannibalrec.com. Order now, and be prepared;
the rap game is about to be devoured.*

"Michael, are you getting in or what?" Erika shouted from
inside the limo.

"Yeah, yeah," Flawless answered. Somewhat in a daze, he
retrieved the second flyer and stuffed the former deep into his
pocket. He got into the limo and they drove off. Inside,
Flawless handed the flyer over to Tommy. "Check this out."

Tommy read it casually and then remarked, "You think that
this is the same Hannibal?"

"Who else?"

"Looks like he got signed to a label."

"Naw, he started his own. That whole cannibal shit, that's
all Bull."

"Well, then, I guess Bull is doing his thing as well."

"Yeah, I guess so," Flawless said while looking at the passing traffic. Hannibal: the name was like a bane to his existence.
Seeing that second flyer had irritated him to the core.

The limo pulled up to the Millennium Hotel. Flawless was the
only one who got out. He was the only one with a reservation. He
had an early morning interview in the city; it would have been too
much to return from the new house in Jersey tomorrow.

"All right, Malik, I'll see you tomorrow. And Tommy, do me
a favor and see that Erika gets to the new house."

"Hey, I am not a child!" Erika shouted.

"Yeah, whatever. I love you too and I'll see you all tomorrow. Peace."

He closed the door and the limo drove off. As the doorman
was escorting him into the hotel he noticed another flyer laying
on the ground. Closer inspection revealed again that it was one
of Hannibal's. Then he looked down the block and noticed that
the entire sidewalk had been littered with Hannibal flyers. A
troubled look came across his brow. What the hell is going on?

ELEVEN

Be prepared; the rap game is about to be devoured. Devoured, huh? Yeah, we'll see. Flawless stared at Hannibal's flyer, intently reading the words over and over again. For some reason there was something about this flyer that troubled him. What was it? Was it the dimensions of the flyer? No. Was it the blood-red lettering or the scripted font? No. Was it the eyes, Hannibal's eyes, reimagined and fashioned onto the paper? No, not exactly. It wasn't any of that. It was Hannibal himself. This piece of paper was of Hannibal's making and that alone was reason for a contempt with the same degree of loathing that he held for the man himself.

Damn it, what was he doing on a flyer and what are they doing all over the streets? This whole cannibal thing; he formed a label, and with his crew of dumb-fuck thugs he was pushing it hard. Damn, I thought I got past this guy. Shit, what the hell was he doing forming a label? Calm down. Cool it, it's nothing, Flawless. He's probably just working out of his shihole apartment in the projects. What are you concerned about? This is far from competition.

While Flawless pondered all of this, soapsuds began to fall from above onto the flyer, slowly dissolving it into a soggy mess. Flawless tilted his head upward to find Trish, as beautiful as ever, smiling guilty; her majestic locks hanging down, a soapy sponge in her hand.

"Why did you do that?" he asked. To that she only smiled at him. "Anytime now."

"Why, because you're here with me on one of the few nights you have off and you're staring at some piece of paper."

"I'm not staring at it. I'm just checking it out."

"I'm sorry, baby, but when you look at something nonstop for over an hour, that's staring."

Over an hour . . . wow . . . had it been that long? Flawless thought as he gazed at the clock on the wall. Yes, it has. Man, where did the time go? "All right, all right. I'm getting rid of it," he said to her. He rolled up the soapy flyer and threw it away. It fell on the reflective marble floor of the bathroom. It was a large bathroom; every feature was meticulously carved out of exotic stone, creating a striped, reflective surface fixtured in gold.

Flawless sat in the middle of the white floor, inside of a golden tub, in between Trish's legs, with soapsuds all around them. "Are you happy now?" Flawless asked her.

"No," Trish answered while placing her lips into a pout.

"And why not?"

Trish was quiet for a moment and then she said jokingly, "So tell me, Flawless, when are you going to marry me?"

Flawless heard the humor in her tone; nevertheless, he was silenced by her question. "Okay. You know what, let me face you, because this seems like it is going to be a serious conversation." Flawless got up from in between her thighs and moved over to the opposite end of the tub so that he was able see her face-to-face.

"You didn't have to move. It's not that serious."

"Actually, I think it is. It's not the first time you've brought up the issue."

"It was just a joke, and that being the case, it shouldn't be so surprising."

"Actually, it is. I mean, don't you think that this is a bit soon? We've been going out for only a year."

"What relevance does time have in perspective to love? I mean, Romeo and Juliet met, fell in love and married all within three days."

"Yes they did, and they also died within three days."

"Yes, but it doesn't make the love any less sweet." ,

"Yeah, but it is less real."

"What is truly real in this world?"

"Oh, c'mon, let's not philosophize."

Trish was annoyed that the conversation had taken this path and even more exasperated that Flawless felt the need to debate the issue. She decided to play her trump card. "Fine. I'll make it simple. Do you love me, Michael?"

What is it about this question that women love to ask it so? Flawless thought before saying, "Yes I do, I've told you this . . . many times. But I'm also only twenty-four years old and in the last year my life has changed completely. I'm just trying to give myself some time to take this all in."

"I can't argue with that. I understand," she said.

"Do you?"

"Yes . . . now, I gotta get out of this tub before my skin shrivels up."

Flawless watched her as she rose and the foam gently fell from her form, revealing her naked body. Beautiful. Over the year he had seen her body many times, in many different positions and every time he did, it never failed to arouse him, as it did now. He began to grow beneath the foam and water.

She slowly got out of the tub, her right leg first and then her left. Flawless studied her entire movement; especially giving an eye to the wet spot between her thighs, gently shaved into a triangle. Out of the tub, slightly tiptoeing, she walked naked across the tan marble floor. Flawless continued to watch as the water trickled down her wet body, going from her back, down the curve of her hips, around and then falling from the firm smoothness of her ass and onto the floor. She left the bathroom, picked up a white robe and walked into the main room of the suite. He wanted her. She was so beautiful, but even more arousing, she was confident.

Flawless rose from the tub. He stood, allowing the water to drip from his slim, muscular form. He stepped out, still wet, and walked naked across the bathroom floor heading into the main room, being led by his erection. He neglected to grab a towel or a robe. His wet body dripped water from the marble floor of the bathroom and unto the plush carpet of the main room. He walked, following the lavender imprints her wet feet had made on the fuchsia carpet.

The room was big and ornately furnished in brown. There was an immense window that encapsulated the entire suite, revealing the beautiful New York City skyline at night. This was the presidential suite. This was the opus of the opulent, gorgeous in its splendor. It carried with it a $5,000 bill per night.

Trish was robed and leaned against the window, looking out at the night sky. The window provided a view to the world and also a translucent reflection of the surrounding room, enabling her to see Flawless enter and walk directly toward her. She closed her eyes and within a second she felt his hardened nature pressed up between her thighs. It felt good. Her nipples stiffened beneath the silken fabric.

Flawless caressed her thigh beneath the silky smooth. She reacted to his touch by leaning her head back, her locks falling onto his shoulder. This was what she wanted. Over the year she had grown to love his touch. In truth she had grown to love him. She had loved him from the beginning. Why did she, why so fast? She still didn't know. It was as if she were written to do so. "I do love you, you know that, right?" he said to her.

"Really," she replied. Did he really love her? She didn't know and, in truth, nor did he. He did know that he cared; he cared a lot. But there was something that he didn't trust. He didn't trust her completely. It all seemed too good, unreal in a way; like a dream come true, with all of the trimmings. In her words, she loved him from the beginning. Could this beautiful, professional woman who was able to have any man she wanted truly love him and so profoundly? This was not a battle of his esteem. He knew that he was an attractive man; still, this all seemed too good. Did she really love him or was it that he was a successful rapper and she was an opportunist who saw a pay-day coming from that very first day in the elevator. Which was it? He didn't know but he would give her the benefit of the doubt. But he would doubt. He would always doubt.

"Just give me a year. Just time to get everything settled."

"Okay," she replied; there was no rush in love.

Flawless slowly raised the bottom of her robe past the curve of her ass. She separated her thighs slightly and he was able to slip between her inner depths. It was warm, soft and wet. It was so inviting how her body called to his. He could tease his desires no longer. He pulled back and enjoyed the sensation and the rhythm as he entered her, her flesh sucked onto his and pulled him in; then all at once he lost his mind. Trish likewise lost herself and the rest of the robe in the embrace as they both stood, naked bodies exposed to the world, her breast imprinted, hard nipples pressed in gently upon the window, making love.

"I love you, Michael," she said, as naturally as a heartbeat.

"I love you, too," he replied, without forethought; after saying it, he thought, I think I meant that.

TWELVE

The number 4 train was in sight. They heard the beep of the bell and the sterile automated female voice of the conductor: "Please stand clear of the closing doors."

"Oh shit, it's about to leave," Flawless said to Trish. They made a mad dash down the stairs. Flawless ran ahead, cut his way through the departing passengers and wedged himself in between the doors of the train. Once Trish was safely in, Flawless released the door. Inside they both breathed heavily.

"You're out of shape," he said to her.

"So are you," she replied.

"Well, I'm a rapper, not an athlete."

"Yeah, yeah, whatever."

"C'mon, let's sit down," he said. They sat in the car, his arms around her shoulder and her head to his chest. There was a beautiful comfort about them as they looked about their surroundings. This was a nice car. It was a nice train. It was brand-new, clean and automated; a big improvement from the gum-laden, graffiti-stained and smelly old cars of yesteryear.

The car wasn't full but it wasn't empty either. The passengers spaced themselves out, sitting in comfort. Some had eyed the young couple when they entered and then after a second looked away. Others continued to look at them in their embrace. A few teenage girls sitting across the way began to giggle over recognition of Flawless's identity. Flawless was a millionaire who was now taking the train merely for the fun of it. In his past life he never would have thought that a tryst on the train could be enjoyable.

"You see that? You're a superstar," Trish said to him.

"Naw, I think they either looking at how fine you are or they're jealous of how fine you are." The two lovers began to smile and look into each other's eyes.

"Tell me, Trish," Flawless said, "do you believe in soulmates?"

"Yes," she replied quickly, as if the answer were already on the tip of her tongue.

"But it is such a corny and played-out thing. You really believe that there is somebody out there who you were written to be with?"

"Yes."

He smiled, thought for a moment, smiled again and then said to her, "Yeah, me too."

They began to kiss, completely oblivious to the eyes of others. This was the thing that Flawless loved most about Trish. She was a free being; free to express herself wherever, whenever. Liberation was such a turn-on. It spoke to his soul; so for there and then they were mates.

In the middle of their embrace Flawless opened his eyes slightly. From his periphery he noticed an ad above and across the car.

"What is that?" he thought aloud, and broke the embrace to get a better look.

"Baby, what is it?" Trish said, as if awakened from a sweet dream. Flawless went across the car to see the ad more clearly. It was an ad for Hannibal, much like the flyer from before.

"What is this, he's in subways now? I don't even have ads in subways. He doesn't have a major deal. How's he doing all of this?" Flawless blurted, irrespective of where he was or who could hear. His reaction seemed odd to Trish.

"I don't understand, why do you even care? Hannibal is doing his thing. So? We're not the only ones in the game."

"Yeah, but you don't know Bull."

"What's there to know? It doesn't matter. Your album was number one for four weeks in a row. In one more, you will have sold six million records domestically. Not to mention when we add in the international market, you will do over ten million by the end of the year. Hannibal has flyers on the streets and ads in the subways; baby, I don't see how it compares. Why does this concern you?"

His actions didn't make sense. Then again, Hannibal having ads in the subways didn't make sense either. That was a major promotional achievement that only people like Michael Jackson could afford. It didn't make sense. And all Flawless could say in response was, "I don't know. I don't know. But you don't know Bull."

THIRTEEN

Hannibal's eyes burned. There was so much intensity behind them that they appeared to glow crimson like ember. He looked out into the dark beyond and could feel the energy as they pushed and hollered in anticipation. Then it began, "BULL, BULL!" they chanted; sparsely at first but soon in orchestrated unison. Hannibal could not see them but he felt them in his blood as it pumped through his veins. Hard. His heart felt as if it was going to rip out of his chest. This was not nerves but rather pure, raw, concentrated exhilaration. He felt higher than he ever had. Then the lights came on.

Hannibal could see them, all two thousand of them, all packed into the Speed. It was the hottest hip-hop nightclub in the city and Hannibal was performing. He stood on the stage with his DJ, Amra, behind him. At the sight of the devourer the chanting became louder. Then Amra began to scratch, putting fingers to vinyl, mixing sounds, working the one and twos with precision. It was a loud milieu of chaos and order. This was the sound of the youth. This was their music. This was hip-hop. It was an art form young in definition but as old as time. The spoken word put to a beat. Everlasting; ever since the Creator uttered the word that brought creation and itself into being. They were the reflections of the more, uttering words to percussion, forever amorous of the beat, craving to hear the loud.

The makeup of the crowd was hard-core. There was a mix

of races: black, Spanish, white, Asian; all thugged in their
robes; even the women, to a lesser degree. They were thugged
in attire but not so much in character though many had the
character; Hannibal attracted that kind of flock. Others were
geared as such, more for style and a degree of necessity. There
was a dress code to such an affair: baggy jeans, work boots, do-
rag or scarf. These were Hannibal's people, all cannibals, all
here to see the king devour. Within the past months the lore of
the man had captivated the entire underground.

Amra played a rhythm familiar to the crowd. Having never
seen Hannibal perform live before, hearing this distinctive
beat, they all broke into a frenzy. Bull felt it and unleashed.

The silence
The silence
The silence
The silence
The silence
The silence
The silence
The silence
There's malice in the lambs
Sheep are envious motherfuckers
Talkin' violence in the camps
Tryin' to fuck the big picture
Want beef with Bull
Dem fools so gullible
Thinkin' they untouchable
But I'ma devour them like a cannibal
Hannibal the general of Brooklyn
Pushing mad weight in Crooklyn
With ma crew full of sixteen
Packing Tec-nines and Mac-tens
Know ten ways to kill niggas
Ten ways to eat niggas

Cook up the remains
So moms can't identify the features
While I'm the feature in these streets
I own these streets
Bull been packing heat
Killing niggas
Before the beat.

He gave a low-pitched, high-energy performance. They loved it, not so much for the lyrical content but for the energy of the delivery. This was Hannibal's talent; he made them feel the words in a way that few others could.

At the end of the performance Hannibal left the stage, shirtless and drenched in sweat, as if he had bathed himself in the endocrine. As he descended the metal steps, club bouncers created a path for him, blocking the ensuing mob. Then a man, well dressed in denim, emerged from the dark shadows. It was Jennessy.

"Mr. Hannibal . . . a brilliant performance. I think that we should talk," Jennessy said to him without thinking of giving an introduction.

"About what?" he asked the man, already knowing well who he was.

"Why, what else? Making money."

FOURTEEN

Jennessy sat before his desk attired in vintage casual with an FDNY baseball cap and his hands clasped before his lips. Hannibal sat in one of the two chairs placed before his desk, Mook in the other and Terrence stood to the side of Hannibal's chair. Jennessy stared at them and they stared at Jennessy. It seemed as if they were in a Mexican standoff. They could almost hear the whistle refrain of *The Good, the Bad and the Ugly*. Jennessy drew first.

"I see you have brought your boys with you," Jennessy said to Hannibal.

"Never leave home without them."

"Fraternity is an admirable trait but perhaps we should narrow this meeting to only relevant parties."

"These are all relevant parties. I am the founder and CEO of Cannibal Records. Mook seated to my left here is the president of said label. And Terrence is the senior vice president."

"Yeah, VP, baby," Terrence cut in with his distinctive exuberance.

"Cute . . . All right, I'll play. Let's get to business. My man Bull, the entrepreneur, you are an impressive young man; I've had my eye on you."

"Really."

"Yes, we have been tracking your movements for some time now."

"Tracking me. And why is that?"

"Well, you must understand that in the battle you were in a year ago that we were just as willing to offer you a contract if you had won. And I must say that the difference between winner and loser was not grossly overwhelming. That being the case, I sent my scouts out to keep an eye on . . ." he then made quotations with his fingers, ". . .'second best.' And as such, I have watched you go from selling your CDs from the hood to the colleges to the Web. . . . And now I am aware that major stores have begun to beckon you for your product. Which, I assume, according to my latest findings, you have moved close to ninety thousand units of."

Suddenly Hannibal felt naked. He felt flattered that someone took so much interest in him, but disturbed that Jennessy knew so exactly his every move. He played his concerns off with a straight face. "Actually we are over a hundred grand now. But I gotta say that I am impressed with your research."

"No, Bull, I am impressed: with your energy, your tenacity, your performance; which is why we would like to have you join the family here at Crown Records. I have already had a contract made up for your signing. I have big plans for you here."

Jennessy took a contract from his drawer and passed it to Hannibal. Hannibal took the document and began to peruse. How much things change in a year. A year ago he would have almost killed to hold this document in his hands; now he questioned it.

Jennessy, taking note of Hannibal's meticulous eye, interjected, "Don't strain your vision. I'll break it down for you. It is a five-year deal. You put out three albums. You get a five hundred thousand signing advance. We're giving you the extra cash because we want you to be able to get the best production. You get fifty thousand dollars every time you go gold and another one hundred thousand every time you go platinum."

"What about publishing and royalties?" Hannibal asked as soon as Jennessy had put a period to his thought. Jennessy seemed a bit surprised by the question and the quickness and the straightforwardness in which it was delivered.

"Hmm, smart boy. Okay, we spilt publishing seventy-five–twenty-five, and you get fifteen cents off of every dollar. And when you consider the millions that you are going to be selling, that's a lot of money."

"Now, you said that we split publishing seventy-five–twenty-five. I'm assuming that's seventy-five percent mine?" Hannibal asked.

"Of course," Jennessy answered, though not feeling comfortable with being questioned.

"Now, were you planning on doing any of the production?"

"No, no, no. I'm just an overseer. I try not to get my hands dirty."

"So then, I'm also assuming that I will be splitting the publishing credits fifty-fifty, with whoever produces whatever tracks?"

"It will most likely be Noah. We want you to have the best. But yes, that's usually how it goes."

"So then, if I am correct, you would be getting twenty-five percent off of my fifty percent, for doing nothing. Because I know that you wouldn't be helping me write my rhymes."

Jennessy, realizing that he had allowed himself to fall into a trap, had no other recourse but to say, "Yes."

Terrence stood there and smiled to himself, watching Hannibal work.

"Well, Jennessy, I am not so sure about that," Hannibal remarked.

He played his card and waited to see how Jennessy would play his.

"Okay, okay, no big thing. You get one hundred percent of your publishing rights." It was a nice quarterly check to give up but he had no choice. "So that's the deal."

"Okay, well, now it all sounds very good."

"Great, great. Then we can get to work."

"That's all cool but I don't want a record deal."

Jennessy was beyond surprised. No one had sat in that chair and said that to him before. He was in virgin territory. "Really?"

"Yes, really. What I do want from you is distribution."

"You're not serious?" Jennessy replied. He was not shouting, though a part of him wanted to.

"Why white folk always think we not serious?" an annoyed Terrence interrupted. Hannibal did a short wave of his hand. Terrence said no more.

"I am very serious. I already have a record label."

"Cannibal Records," Jennessy replied with tacit mockery.

"Yes. So you see, I'm not looking for a label. What I do want is a distributor; which is where you come in."

"Interesting, but let's keep this real. You've moved a hundred thousand units, which is outstanding for a CD done in your basement; but I am sure as you know, in real terms it is not even humble. Next, I have listened to your CD. There was some good stuff there but it is raw, unpolished, mastered poorly and your production is garbage. Speaking of garbage: your packaging, there is nothing attractive about it. It is just a name and a title. You have a grassroots following but without a professional promotional effort no one else will have the slightest idea who you are. As it stands, this album won't sell."

After Jennessy's speech, Hannibal remained silent.

"Hate to burst your bubble but this is the big time. And I know you, Bull. You're just like me; you're about making money. So I know that you see the big picture. You see the picture, don't you?"

"Always."

"Exactly. So you must see that Crown is the best place for you. We got the best team in the game and we know and love hip-hop. We have a great record of platinum artists and we have debuted many at number one on *Billboard*. Just look at what we have done for Flawless." For Hannibal, Flawless's name was like a nail scratch on a chalkboard. "Flawless is the number one hip-hop act out right now and he didn't get there on his talent alone, nor will you. And I see number one in your future, Bull. I see it clearly. You wanna own a label, cool. But get yourself established first. Then a couple years from now, start it up, and I promise you that you will be saying to someone else what I am saying to you right now. And you will look at yourself as a millionaire and you will say, 'Jennessy was right.' Sign the deal, Bull, and let's get to work."

"You're a very interesting guy, Jennessy. But now let me keep it real with you. I have moved one hundred thousand copies on my own, which in the scheme of big music is a humble figure. But I get one hundred percent profit off that, in comparison with the fifteen cents off the dollar that you were offering. Now, I sell those at ten dollars per copy, which means that I have already brought in over a million in revenues; add to that my side profession and I am already a millionaire. Now, this is what I have done in my basement. Imagine what happens when I reinvest that money into real production and real studio time. And like you said, I am already in talks with record stores about housing my product. As for promotions, have you looked in a bus or a train lately; nigga, I'm all over the place. So you see, I don't need a record contract. What I need is a distribution deal; and only because right now, at this level, I can't get my product into all of the hands that you can."

"Tell me, Bull, you're an artist, why would you want to trouble yourself with all of the worries of business? We all have to learn to play our roles in this game."

"C'mon, Jenn, you said that we were just alike, remember? So you should know the answer to that. It's simple. The more control you have, the more money you make. I learnt that a long time ago. And I'm the god of this game. I write the play and I play every position. Now, you and I both know that this album is going to sell. Whether Crown is a part of that movement or someone else, I leave up to you." Hannibal then gave a look over to Mook and Terrence. "With that, I think that it's time to go. But you got my number, call me when you're ready to talk."

Hannibal had said everything that he needed to say. It was all in Jennessy's court now. He wanted the deal from Crown because of the brand name appeal that it carried, but they were far from the only players in the game.

Jennessy remained seated with palms clasped before his lips as Hannibal first and then Mook rose; then with Terrence, all three left the office without a good-bye or a look behind the shoulder.

All three men walked down the hall leaving Jennessy's office, heading toward the elevator. Jennessy's secretary was somewhat surprised to see them leave so soon and in the manner in which they did. People usually left Jennessy's office either very happy or very upset, sometimes being escorted by armed guard.

They walked quietly for a few feet down the long hallway when Terrence broke the silence. "That was a pretty good act you just put on. Sure you did the right thing?" he asked Hannibal.

"Everybody always trying to pigeonhole a nigga," Hannibal replied, more so talking to himself.

"Fuck, I don't even know why we're here. We should just stick to doing what we do best," Mook commented.

"Damn, nigga, can't you see the big picture? This is where we can make some real money and we don't have to worry about bullets or jail." Hannibal was irritated that even at this level Mook failed to see the vision. It had taken a lot of coaxing to get him this far. They wouldn't have told him, save for the fact that the operation had gotten too big. Mook was against it but in the end he took the title and the money, though he felt completely out of place. He wanted to give all of this up and wanted Hannibal to do so as well.

"But you ain't hear the cracker. He ain't gon' give you no

distribution. And like you said, with what he's offering, we make more just by hustling."

They arrived at the elevator and Terrence pushed the button. He felt like responding to Mook but at the time he knew that it wasn't his place, though it was largely due to his efforts that Cannibal Records was a success. He was the true president of the label. Mook only took top billing because his was a precedent relationship.

"Don't worry, it'll happen," Hannibal quietly replied.

"You're a fucking dreamer, man!"

Hannibal bit his tongue out of extreme respect for their friendship; more so because he was in a place of business and he would be damned if he lost his cool and came off like just another idiot thug on the street. Cannibal was not going to look divided, not in Jennessy's house. The elevator arrived and all three entered.

Once inside, Hannibal said quietly, "Everything starts with a dream." They all remained quiet in the ride down. They exited the elevator and were about to leave the building when Hannibal felt a buzz in his pocket. He pulled out his pager to find that he had a message.

> *You drive a hard bargain, but I like your*
> *style. Have your lawyer call our lawyer*
> *and let's work out a deal. Under conditions,*
> *however. I wanna take care of packaging*
> *and promotions. Now let's get to work.*
> *Jennessy.*

If there was ever a definitive moment in which one knew that one's dream had begun, for Hannibal this was it as a huge grin came across his face.

"Ma niggas, it is on."

BOOK THREE

FiFTEEN

It was bedlam in JAH. The staff of the small record store was pushed to its limits as it tried to cater to the demands of the mob. The store could only hold one hundred or so at a time. This left the cold curb for the other two thousand. Nine months later it was winter again and again the weather was unforgiving. Yet the fanatics were here, lined up in Harlem with all manner of Hannibal banners and posters to see the devourer in person.

Hannibal, Terrence and Reaper sat behind a table, signing records. Reaper was a new hard-core rapper; slim, dark-skinned with a wild 'fro and an aquiline nose. He was the only artist beside himself that Hannibal had signed to the Cannibal label. He was for the most part a wannabe Hannibal, emulating his raw sound inflection for inflection, but he was no Bull. Hannibal knew that Reaper sounded like him but he didn't mind. He knew that everyone in the game sounded like everyone else so why promote the style of another rapper?

Behind them Mook leaned against the wall, looking as if he would rather be anywhere else. The other boys either played back up to the security at JAH or peppered the crowd outside and the passing traffic with flyers. The entire store was packed, making it very hard to move and even harder to hear at times as "The Silence" was being played loudly over the store speakers. If the lights were off it might have seemed like a club. There was even a DJ. RA was doing an in-store interview with Hannibal.

"Yup, dis is yo' main dog RA, here in Harlem at JAH Records, in total pandemonium! Yo, as everybody out there knows, it is Bloody Tuesday, and that means ma god Hannibal the Cannibal's debut effort is out today, today, today. He is signing records up here in One twenty-fifth. And it is crazy." RA turned his attention toward Hannibal. "Ma god, what is going on?" he asked.

"Nothin' man, just lovely, just feeling the love."

"I say you are. There is mad folk up in here to see you. How does it feel?"

"It feels good, it was long in coming but now we here."

"C'mon, it wasn't that long. A year ago no one knew you and now you the biggest buzz in music. Tell me how you did it."

"Just hard work and a lot of hustle."

That wasn't the answer RA wanted but he had learned in his tenure never to push. "Aw'ight, aw'ight. I see we ain't getting nowhere wit' dat. So Bull, you here at JAH Records, just a local small-name store, we wanna know why you ain't choose to be at one of the bigger chains today?"

"Well, y'know we gon' do dem eventually but I'ma hustler, always have been, forever will be; so I respect and support hustle. My man Enoch here been runnin' the shop for a minute. And you know, it's hard for the small cats to keep up with the big heads so I'm just showing my support. So we in Harlem today, tomorrow we gon' hit Brooklyn."

"Damn, that's ma man Bull, keeping it real. Giving back to the community. So now alla y'all keep it real wit' him and go get the CD. Yo, I heard it and it's the sickest thing in the game. Now Bull, you ain't here by yo'self, why don't you tell us about the fellas to your side?"

"Well, right next to me here is ma man Reaper, as in grim reaper. Y'know, he bring the death. He's new to the fam, but he is Cannibal at heart. Brooklyn born, and cat's crazier and more hard-core than me."

"More hard-core than Bull? That's hard to believe. Let me hear from this guy." RA now addressed Reaper: "Yo, what's going on, son?" he asked.

"Nothin'. Reaps just in it, lovin' it, doin' ma thing."

"Aw'ight, aw'ight. Holdin' it down, I hear you." Noticing that Reaper was going to give him the typical rapper rapport, RA quickly turned his focus back to Hannibal, to Reaper's disappointment. "Gotta 'gree, Bull, heard him on your album. The cat's nice."

"Well, of course, only the best eaters roll wit' Bull."

"Now, who is this guy?" RA asked Hannibal while eyeing Terrence.

"Well, this is ma family, Terrence. T is the VP of Cannibal Records, and just about anything else; he do it all."

Terrence then interjected himself, "Well, god, I'm just all about cannibalism, son. So whatever is good for the Can', I make it happen."

"Well, I see dat you brothers got this on lock, and we gon' take a break and be back in about five, here at JAH wit' Bull. But again, for alla y'all out there who don't know, this is Bloody Tuesday, so go get that CD. *Hannibal: The Silence of the Lambs.*"

It was evening, although in January in winter, 6:00 P.M. appeared much more like midnight than dusk. A Black Lexus SUV, windows tinted, drove down Harlem's streets. Inside, Terrence steered, Reaper rode shotgun and Hannibal and Mook were seated in the back. The other boys took the A train home. They were just now leaving the signing after being there for over four hours. Hannibal should have been exhausted but his mind was still all about business as he looked out the window and saw a huge billboard for the album with him wearing the same mask as Lecter did in the movies, running alongside the Apollo Theatre.

"So T, what were you saying about all of the reviews?" he asked Terrence.

"Niggas playa-hating hard. They gave us some fucked-up reviews. They say dat you a homophobe and a misogynist," he replied.

"I bet you it was either a faggot or a bitch who wrote that. They just saying that, they ain't saying nothin' else?" Hannibal questioned.

"Well, beyond the controversy, they said there was some good shit there. People feelin' yo' voice. I got a call earlier today that says that we might get three and a half mics in *The Source.*"

"We might get three and a half," Hannibal repeated. "Not the four and a half that Flawless got." He said the last statement lower, more so talking to himself. "What about radio, beyond RA, what's everybody else saying?"

"Well, a few stations won't play da shit, even though it's getting the most requests. Faggots run the shit, and we black so they wanna fuck us. Plus some a the shit's too raw; when they edit it up all you hear is a lot of blank space."

"Shit is like dat?"

"Just like dat."

"Well, what about projections, what kinda figures we looking at for the first week?" Hannibal was now fiending to hear some good news.

"We ain't got no real comp; we should have number one. It was a good idea coming out in the first quarter."

"What about the numbers, we got enough to top Flaw's first week?" Hannibal related everything he did on par with Flawless. He forever felt like he was playing catch up. He couldn't wait for the day when he surpassed him.

"I don't know. That's some pretty impressive numbers and wit' no strong radio, to be real, I don't see it. But either way we gon' make way more money; he's under contract, remember." Terrence had become very apt at his new role. He ran the business with the same efficiency and gully mentality in which he ran the streets.

"Yeah, the next step is to figure out how to distribute the shit ourselves and keep all the money. It fucks with me every time I know that Crown is getting four dollars off of every disc sold."

"Dat's the move, cut crackers out and keep all the green black," Terrence remarked.

"Yeah, but we still under da thumb and if we wanna keep the deal we need to get another artist. Me and Reap alone ain't enough."

"Well, god, y'know I spit too."

"Forget that; I heard you, nigga, the only thing you spit is saliva."

Reaper began to chuckle. This was the first utterance he had made all ride. He was new to the game but he already knew protocol.

"Naw, we need somebody else, somebody nice," Hannibal added.

"Well I do know this other kid. Muthafucka is sick," Terrence said to Hannibal while looking back at him through the rearview mirror.

"Yeah, who is he?"

"He's ma boy."

"Oh shit!" Mook blurted out, breaking his silence.

"What was that for; niggas got shit to say about my peoples?" Terrence replied to Mook's reaction with rancor.

"Yeah, motherfucker, I do," Mook said, surprised and angered that Terrence spoke back.

"Everybody shut the fuck up," Hannibal intervened. "Now, T, I thought I seen all yuh people; have I met him?"

"Naw, I just met him the other day too. I saw him spittin' on the street. He ate this one kid up. Then we just started buildin' afterwards. Kid's real cool, got good energy and he's boroughs too, I think. But nigga is a college cat, he don't hustle. Smart as fuck but he can rhyme better than any nigga on the street."

"College cat. You ain't fucking wit' me, are you? Don't waste my time, T."

"Yo, I know I got a big mouth and I talk a lot of shit but I ain't bullshitting you on this one," Terrence said with a sincerity rarely present in his speech.

Hearing the austerity in his voice, Hannibal responded, "All right, I'll take your word for it . . . let's meet him."

"Good shit."

"What's the cat's name anyway?"

"It's Micah," Terrence replied.

"Micah . . . hmm; interesting."

SiXTEEN

It was nightfall in Manhattan, somewhere between Broadway and the Village. The area had an artsy flair, though not being blatantly bohemian. A line of about four hundred extended down the block as the people waited outside in the winter cold to get inside the Spit Café. The Spit was the haven of underground hip-hop in the city. They had an open mic and frequently held emcee battles. It was here that the young and the aspiring came to hone their skills, taking their best lyrics from the street corner and putting it on a stage. The battles here were known to be fierce.

Flawless and Hannibal had both already been here. It was only two years ago now when they were regulars; but so much had changed since. It almost seemed like a lifetime ago. Their battles here were legendary. Now that both of them had taken off, the establishment had taken up the habit of selling the tapes of their freestyle battles that they recorded. Who knew that they would one day become so valuable? Someone did. Decadent, the robust, light-skinned thirty-five-year-old owner of the Spit did. He had the foresight and the vision to see talent. So he saved the tapes and now he was making a killing.

Tonight was Friday. Pablo, the stocky, medium-tanned thirty-year-old doorman, was cropped upon his customary stool outside of the café, collecting fees as he let people in with an attitude of smug indifference. From the Spit's external appearance it looked no different from a hole in the wall. The name of the café was plainly written in graffiti on a wooden board atop the door. Once inside, the interior did nothing to make one rethink one's initial position. This *was* a hole in the wall and it was packed to capacity. Virgins to the Spit always wondered why anyone would come here. Then after the show began they found out. It wasn't for the ambiance: it was for the mic, it was for the stage, it was for the lyrics. The fact that it looked like a hole in the wall added to its raw, underground appeal.

The people came out in masses, especially on a Friday night. Friday was when they had their infamous emcee battles. Only the best of the best flowed on Friday. The people came from all the other boroughs and Jersey and Connecticut to see who would win, cramming themselves into any crux and crevice. By fire code only two hundred people should be in there at any one time. Decadent always topped this number. It was so tight that everyone, without a choice, became very friendly and at times intimate.

It was now half past midnight. The show had been hot to this point. The DJ began to lower the volume, signaling that the intermission was over. The host, Liu Kang, squeezed his way to the stage. Liu was the host of the Friday night battles. Within the world of the underground his title offered him a measure of respect. The Mortal Kombat buff was a tall mulatto with a curly red Afro and cocky as a result of his shine in the sun. He got onstage and took hold of the mic.

"Yo, we back from the intermish here at Spit, an' we 'bout to start it, wit' the sickest lyrics. This is it, folks, main event, main event, main event, main event. We need ma man 'Cah and Serious Flowz onstage right now."

Serious Flowz quickly crammed his way to the stage. Flowz, a tall, brown-skinned brother with locks in his early twenties, knowing that he would be going on, had not strayed far from the stage.

"All right, we got one, now we need two. Where 'Cah at?" Liu inquired. When he said *'Cah,* he was speaking of Micah;

however, Micah was not in sight and there was no shuffling of people to suggest that he was coming.

But Micah was there. He was seated at the back stairway, as was his custom; he kept away from the crowd whenever he had to perform. The twenty-two-year-old sat with headphones on, concentrating on the task at hand, ignorant to the noise around and the fact that his name had been called. He was handsome, dark-skinned, with a slim muscular build; a pretty boy of sorts, but not overtly so, with his hair neatly cornrowed.

A young brother who knew who he was came and tapped Micah on his knee.

"What's going on?" Micah asked him.

"They calling yo' name, son," the young man replied.

"Cool."

Micah calmly began to make his way to the stage. It was far away and it would be an effort squeezing by everyone. After about a minute, he arrived.

"Here he is finally. Let's get this shit started. Now, normally this would be a three-round battle. But my man 'Cah here has waved two of his rounds. So he'll flow only once. Yeah, I know, crazy shit, right? But the cat thinks he can take it in one round. Serious Flowz, however, has wisely chosen not to do that. Normally we wouldn't do this shit. There is only one other cat I've known to pull this off so I am interested in seeing what this nigga is gon' pull outta his ass. Flowz lost the toss and so he goes first."

As the beat came on, Liu stepped back and handed the mic to Flowz. His rhyming was good but he was typical, not very creative. Micah threw back on his headphones. While Flowz was in his face, close enough to spit at him, throwing every known aspersion in the book, Micah was far away. He seemed almost sad as he meditated on what he was going to say.

After two and a half minutes and over one hundred bars, Flowz had finished. After his applause, Liu handed the mic to Micah. Micah took off his headphones and reentered the real world. He took the mic, licked his lips and began, slow at first.

Yo, yo, yo, yo
Yo, I'm too cerebral
For yo' feeble cerebellum
So I'ma fuck wit' yo' system
Like my man Akenaton
Hack yo' noggin
Play possum like Bin Laden
Ma posse's lodged in
Yo' medulla oblon-gaden
You hock-tooing
But you ain't spittin' nothin'
Serious, why you frontin'?
Yo' flow's a joke cousin

He begins to go faster now.

You say you the hardest nigga
'Cause you kill the most niggas
Now show me yo' gangsta
An' go kill some crackers

Flowz seems a bit shaken and surprised by the remark.

Um, you lookin' kinda shook
Son, what's wrong?
Um, you ain't hard enough
To put that shit in yo' song
Well, um, fuck it I did it
I guess I'm too dumb too stupid
Too fucking hard headed
To know that I should be scared of it
So I'ma leave you livid
'Cause my rhymes I live it
Ma flows is fluid
So I spit the truest

While is you just a satyr
Fucked on yo' lower nature
Fiending, to be greater
Kid, you just a hater
Now you encroach, like a roach
To out the torch, of a God
Yo, ma nigga, I say you must be mod
I don't know if you is a demagogue
Or just semi-odd, but like a Seminole
I'll scalp you
Believe son I'm too powerful
Too damn metaphysical
Paralyze an' baffle you.
You blind pupil
Battling me is futile
'Cause verily I say yo' rhyming
Is beyond pathetic
For yo' words have no path
And even yo' etic lacks ethics.

At the close of Micah's last line the crowd exploded. The profusion of *oh shits* seemed to come in unison. Micah exited the stage to be greeted with pounds and hugs, and faces of disbelief.

Liu responded with downplayed enthusiasm, "No doubt, no doubt. Cat did his thing. Don't know what the fuck he was saying, but now, is it enough to win? To the panel of judges, what's the deal, what's the fate?" The three preselected judges sitting in the audience showed their cards. "Aw'ight, this is the way it's going down." Liu began to strain his eyes, using his hand as a blinder from the glare of the light. He read the judges' decision. "We got one for Flowz, one for 'Cah, and the third . . . for Flowz. Flowz is the winner. Ah guess showboatin' don't always pay off, at least not for everybody. What do you expect when you just a reflection?"

There were some boos in the audience. Micah seemed calm and unfazed. He put on his headphones and began to make his way out of the club. He came with no one and there was no other reason to stay.

He stepped out and fixed his black coat and threw his lavender scarf around his neck. The difference between the heat of the packed café and the cold night wind was like a sharp stab to his system. He began to make his way down the block when he heard a voice shout out: "Yo, Micah!"

Micah turned around to see Terrence running toward him. The two friends greeted each other with a pound and a lot of love.

"Yo, what's up, T? What you doing here?" Micah asked.

"I'm here to see you, nigga," Terrence greeted with a smile. "Yo, you know you was robbed, right?" Micah didn't say anything, merely smiling. "Yeah, you know, you know. I don't give a fuck; you burnt that nigga's whole shit in three lines as far as I'm concerned. Where you get all dem words from, son?"

"Just life, just living and reading."

"That's a lot of fucking reading. I can't do that shit. Nigga, I can't do that shit. That shit be hurtin' ma head too much."

"You funny."

"Yo, I'm serious. I'm better at on-the-job training. Still, I be reading the dictionary every now and then, learnin' a word here and there, keepin' ma *lexicon* tight. It ain't like yo' shit though. I just like droppin' words every now an' again to keep niggas on their toes so they never see you comin', y'know what I'm sayin'?"

"I hear you, man."

"But yo, check this shit. I brought someone to see you."

Bull began to make his way out, leaving through the back door so as to not draw too much attention. Beyond Decadent hardly anyone else knew that he was there. Hannibal turned around and headed toward Micah and Terrence's position.

Micah looked over at Terrence.

"Whoa, you actually did it. You brought Bull to see me."

"What I told you? I'm VP at Cannibal. Muthafucka listens to me."

Hannibal walked over with an almost proud look on his face, bopping his head. When he arrived he patted Terrence on the shoulder.

"T, I must say that you did not disappoint."

"Fuck yeah. I told you, I told you," Terrence spoke, feeling extremely proud of himself. Micah, somewhat in awe, didn't know exactly how to address the man.

"Mr. Hannibal . . . It's a . . ."

"Just Bull, god. Just Bull." Hannibal calmed Micah's temper. He then walked over and gave him a strong pound.

"Bull, nigga is nice, right? Give it up, give it up."

"You right," Hannibal agreed.

"Cat got some shit like Flawless," Terrence added.

There went Flawless's name again. For some reason it did not irk Hannibal as much when he heard it in this context. "Better than, I think," he responded. "You shoulda won tonight," he said to Micah.

"I know," Micah replied.

"Your shit is good man, real good."

"Thank you."

This was all too much for Micah. He had just lost the battle and now he was getting praise from Hannibal himself.

"You do have more than one rhyme though?" Hannibal asked.

"I got hundreds."

"So why did you only do one round?"

"He wasn't worth it and I didn't feel like wasting my breath."

Hannibal smiled to himself, thinking: Cocky motherfucker, he *is* like that nigga. "I like your style, what are you doing tonight?" he asked.

"Nothing. Why?"

"We got a lot to talk about."

"Really, about what?" Micah wasn't quite sure why he asked the question. He was ready to go anywhere with Hannibal.

"Nigga, what else . . . cannibalism. C'mon."

SEVENTEEN

"*Tell me Clarice; you would never tell me to stop, say that if you love me, stop?*" The voice of Lecter reverberated through the room in his distinctive, eerie British accent.

"*Not in a thousand years,*" Clarice Starling replied, while Lecter had her trapped; her hair stuck in the refrigerator door.

"*Not in a thousand years,*" he repeated. He then made an aggressive motion forward, as if to bite her, but then pulled back. "*That's my girl.*"

Hannibal and Micah sat on the sofa in the expanse of the room lit only by the light of the immense television. Hannibal sat with an excited look on his face. This was one of his favorite scenes in the movie. Micah watched with likewise excitement. He loved the movie, and enjoyed watching it even more with Bull as his company.

"Now, watch this, this is the shit right here," Hannibal remarked almost on the edge of his seat.

"*What's it to be, Clarice: above the wrist or below? . . . This is really going to hurt.*"

Lecter then went about apparently hacking off Starling's hand with a butcher knife, but as would be revealed in a few more shots of the film, he had truly cut off his own. Hannibal could no longer control himself.

"I just don't get it! Y'know, I've watched this movie a hundred times and every time I get to this point, I keep hoping the shit changes and he hacks off the bitch's hand instead. That's the one thing that doesn't make any sense," Hannibal raved with uncustomary emotion. There were few people who got to see a more playful side of him, in whom he could intimate and share his inner feelings. He used to with Mook. But recently he hadn't found Mook to be trustworthy company and, more than that, they just didn't see eye to eye anymore. Mook had been his boy since forever, it seemed. Now it seemed they remained friends out of mutual respect for the time already put into the relationship. For some reason with Micah, though Bull didn't know him, he felt as if he was able to let himself out.

"But c'mon, you don't get it?" Micah asked.

"Get what?"

"It's because he loved her, why he did it."

"Love. Loved who?" For some reason that word seemed aberrant and completely out of place in the conversation.

"Who else: Starling."

"Naw, nigga; Lecter too cold to love any bitch."

"But he did, trust me, just look at it. And even better, look at the book."

"You read the book?" Hannibal asked. He knew that a book existed but he never paid it any attention. He was surprised to be in the company of someone who had actually read it.

"Yeah. I saw the movie, loved it and so I got the book. Y'know, they usually say that the book is better so I wanted to see how."

"Good shit, man."

Hannibal was impressed. Very few people he knew actually read, and none of them loved Lecter enough to read the book after watching the movie.

"But believe me, if you don't like this ending, you gotta hate the book's ending. I mean . . ." Micah was set to tell the book's close but Hannibal stopped him.

"Don't tell me. I'ma read it for myself."

Hannibal rarely read. He always thought that it was a fault

of his character. He wanted to read more; now this was his chance, and what better book to start with than his namesake. He was happy that Micah brought this new interest to him.

"Lecter fan like you, I'm surprised that you haven't already," Micah said to him.

"C'mon, god, in this world niggas only got time to hustle and eat; reading is a luxury. But I'm gon' make time though. I'm gonna read it. So you sayin' that he loved her?" Hannibal asked, showing deference to Micah. Micah had read the book. He was now more of an authority on Lecter than Bull was.

"Yep, he loved her. But cat wouldn't go to jail either."

"That's true, man. Never go to jail, no matter what. He did the right thing. Prison fucks niggas up worse than war."

Hannibal didn't know that many people who had been in war. He, however, knew too many who had been in jail. To him they always came back worse off for the experience. He had long ago vowed that he would never go to jail, and if he did, it would never be for anything stupid.

"All right. Movie's over. Let's take a walk."

The credits were rolling. Hannibal felt safe to turn the TV off. He had just completed count 106. His pace had slowed in the last year. His new hectic schedule left him little time to sit home and watch. Given that, he enjoyed his off moments when he was able to catch up with what was real. Lecter seemed even sweeter when watched after a hiatus. It was like having sex again for the first time in months. He felt like a born-again virgin.

After Hannibal turned the television off, the entire room was in darkness. He then pronounced *lights* and the room lit up. Only this was not Hannibal's apartment in the projects. He had recently moved into this million-dollar house in Englewood, New Jersey. It was a common practice of rappers at the time to go from the hood to the suburbs, though Hannibal didn't move because of fashion. He had no real aversion to the projects; he received a lot of love there. But his dream was bigger. Unfortunately, not everyone there shared his vision. Many of them couldn't see past the ghetto; he knew that they were doomed to stay there, accepting their place in the world. Hannibal accepted nothing: He would make his place and it would be at the top. Despite how he was written into existence, he would write how he was to leave it. He moved because he knew that regardless of how much everyone there respected him it was not wise to stay fed amongst the hungry. A hungry man held no allegiances but to his stomach. He had to leave, because like crabs in a bucket, eventually they would try to pull him down. He couldn't have that. He would get out of the bucket first and then throw a rope back. But he was well prepared to be the top crab and step on as many heads in order to get out.

"What do you think of the house?" he asked Micah.

"It's nice," Micah answered, looking around at the great white empty room with columns that extended up to the very high ceiling. There was no furniture, save for a divan and the immense television.

"Empty, I know. I just got it, haven't had the time to set it up yet. But as long as I have my TV and Lecter, I'm at peace, y'know. But tell me, Micah, how do you feel about cannibalism?"

"I love it."

"Good, because I only eat with the best. I like your work but better than that, I like your style."

"Thank you."

"Tell me something else . . . do you see the big picture?"

This was the key question that Hannibal asked everyone. Based on the answer, Hannibal would determine how to class Micah. Micah was not exactly sure what Hannibal meant, but he knew not to ask. He answered instinctively, "Yeah, I see it."

"I know you do. Welcome to the family." Hannibal gave him a very strong pound.

"Thank you," Micah said humbly while in the midst of the embrace.

"Now on to family business. the *Source* Awards are tonight. We're gonna roll through."

"Good. I'm ready for whatever. Maybe even something special."

"And so he loved her?" Hannibal asked one more time. The abhorrence of the thing still irked him. He just didn't see where love played a part.

"Yeah, he loved her."

"Bullshit."

EiGHTEEN

What is death? What truly happens after you die? Flawless thought this as he looked above at the evening sky. He stood at one of the balconies of his huge Bergen County home, looking down at the pool below and all that he had accomplished. You have come far, Flawless. You have done a lot. And if I died now, what would be remembered? Will anyone remember me? What will they say about me, about what I have done? Where will my place be in all of this? Flawless stood asking himself these questions. For the first time ever, his thoughts began to run the range of eschatology. He had thought about the end before, much the same way that everyone else did. They thought about it but they never penetrated it, because the thought was all too depressing. Such thoughts were left up to others to define. So many walked by faith, or better yet, by ignorance, in a grand purple bliss, though there were some who wished to know the crimson reality. Those who desired to tackle the question. The question tackled Flawless now. Really, what is death? Can it be that there will come a time when I will not exist? What would that be like? As much as he tried, he could not fathom that. He could not fathom his nonexistence. But he had to come to grips with it; the fact that one day, like it or not, he was going to die. To die, what was that really? Then it came to him. Thinking, thinking was what made him what he was. In truth, he wasn't the flesh he saw in the mirror. He was the thought that brought him to the mirror. It was his thoughts that made him who he was and he was merely their manifestation. Thinking, that was life and that was death. So when I die, my thoughts die, I won't think anymore. The thought of that brought a tear to his eye. He had been thinking for as long as he could remember. The thought of not thinking saddened him. Not thinking, that is death. And as there will come a day when I will die, there will come a time when I will no longer think. Would there? he thought. He wasn't quite sure. All he knew was that there was something called death. And to him, death could only truly be not thinking. He loved his form but if he had to be separated from his flesh, but was aware of this fact, he would still be alive. I could live with that, he thought. But this was all speculative. He didn't know. And no one else did either. So as he stood there on the balcony of his new beautiful home, he came to the realization that he knew nothing.

Erika sat before her mirror, getting ready for the night. She didn't have to put in any extra effort than she usually would for any other occasion. She was going to an awards show, yes, but this was *The Source* Awards; this was hip-hop, no stress. She dipped her head for a moment and was unable to see Flawless's reflection in the mirror. And likewise, Flawless's image could no longer be seen when Erika raised her head once again; her face filling the mirror, permitting no other reflection but that of her own. A hand then came from behind and landed gently on her shoulder.

Flawless had come to speak with her. All of his thoughts of the macabre had put him in bad spirits. He sought to hear her words, to suck on her energy, to be imbued in all of her life and feel alive again. But standing there behind her, he couldn't help but notice. "You look beautiful, Erika."

"Thank you," she replied.

"You're all grown up."

"You sound like a father."

"Sometimes I feel like I am." He truly felt this way and beyond. He had long since elected himself her protector.

"But you're not, Michael," she said, tilting her head so that she could see him. As she looked up at him, for a second she almost looked like a child again.

"I know, I know," he said to her.

"And I'm not a child anymore. I'm twenty years old."

Say that to my perspective, he thought. "I know, but you my little sis . . . I been watching out for you since we were young."

"I know, and I thank you for everything you've done, but I don't need you to protect me anymore."

"Understood," he said. He didn't really but he would try to make himself. Erika, sensing that his acquiescence came too easily, pressed further. "No, Michael, really understand. You've done this for a while and it is really getting tired. Every time a guy comes around me, either you or Tommy breaks it up. Please stop that. It has gotten beyond annoying." During her speech, Flawless began to look away. "Michael, I am serious. Why is it that you are supposed to live your life and find love and I cannot?"

"Listen, I know niggas, and I know how they treat these girls. And you are the one clean thing I see in this world. I am not about to have anyone turn you into his bitch."

"No one can turn you into something that you are not. I am not an idiot. I may not be the most experienced person but I do know men. But if I lived my life the way you see it, I would never trust anyone. I would never find love. And I wanna find it, Michael; I want to love."

"I thought you already did . . . but I understand, believe me I do. No more stress." For a moment he believed what he said. Erika believed it as well.

"Thank you." She felt as if she had just had a big weight lifted from her shoulder. She hugged and kissed him on the cheek. Morose thoughts still filled Flawless's consciousness but this wasn't the time to share them. Perhaps Erika was telling him that she wasn't the one to share them with. But if not with Erika, who? He would grow mad if left to tackle these thoughts alone. "Now, let's go to this show. This is going to be your night, you're going to win it all."

Trish then walked by the open door. "There you two are. I've been looking all over for you. Wow, Erika, you really look beautiful."

"No, girl, you look beautiful. Doesn't she look beautiful, Michael?"

Flawless stood there looking at both of them glowing, wondering for a second if he were looking at twins. Did they look exactly like each other? No: one had locks, the other had braids; but they resembled each other very much so in their features and they were familiars in spirit.

"She's all right, but she's not real," Flawless coyly responded. Trish gave him a wry look. Flawless then walked over and hugged her. "I'm just playing, girl. You look good, you look beautiful." Erika looked at the two of them, feeling very happy for her brother. She liked Trish a lot and felt that they were good for each other. She also felt jealous in some respects. She wanted the relationship that they had. She wanted love. Beyond her brother, she had never felt love for another man and she hungered for it, she dreamed of it.

"So are you ready for tonight?" Trish asked Flawless while in his arms.

"Definitely," he said defiantly.

NiNETEEN

Flawless stood eyes closed, meditating. He wasn't praying; he rarely did that, though he was tapping into his deeper spirit. It was his custom before performing. Then he opened his eyes and saw crewmen, sound engineers and electricians abounding. They were all running behind a maze of poles, wires and board fixtures. Amid the unionized workers, Flawless could see the sprinkle of celebrity. They were backstage for the reason that they had recently given an award, received an award or were about to announce one. In true hip-hop fashion, each person was a party in and of himself. Every man had at least four other inconsequentials to aid him in doing a job that one person was more than capable of handling. Flawless smiled at this and then he looked over at Tommy, ready and waiting to back him up. That's all the friend that I'll ever need.

"Are you ready?" Tommy approached and asked him.

"Yeah, I am."

"Good, because Ebony is just about to call your name."

Ebony was a female rapper. She was arguably the best female in the game and in the top echelons of her male counterparts. She was beautiful and she was conscious. She rapped with substance, a trait lacking in most of the music at the time. This made Ebony something of an oddity; the dark-skinned beauty was nevertheless highly respected for it.

She announced his name and the beat to the fourth release

of his now diamond-selling album came on. The two friends came onto the stage. There were about ten thousand people in attendance. The vast majority were industry players. This made Flawless's job more difficult. He hated performing in front of an industry crowd. He knew that while they were smiling at him in their seats, they were cursing him in their thoughts. Everyone wanted to see the king of the hill fall.

At the time Flawless was on top of Everest and he had scaled it in record time. It took most artists at least three albums before they arrived at that level; very rarely did any of them sell ten million records. It was an extreme accomplishment for a lifetime's work. To do it all with one album was rare and to do it on your debut effort was all but impossible. For this feat, Flawless was guaranteed at least a paragraph in the history books. Flawless knew this, and many in attendance knew it as well; for that, many of them hated him.

Flawless had to put those thoughts to the back. No time for a slip of the tongue. Every slip would be more fuel to the critics. Fuck 'em. Let's take over the world, Flawless, c'mon, he thought as Tommy proceeded to hype the crowd. The beat came around and then with a deep fire from within, he let loose "The Method of Madness."

> *This is the method of madness*
> *The mode of illness*
> *A motherfucker's movement*
> *Lucrative and looted*
> *It's too hopeless to loop it*
> *So there ain't no hooks to it*
> *Too moot to be muted*
> *So like a boot I'ma kick it*
> *Yo, sick wit' it*
> *Whenever I spit it*
> *Stay flippin' the script*
> *So you can never get it*

Ma endo is heavy mental
Mo' addictive than menthol
I'm yo' endocrine
Niggas, I'm indoctrin'ed
The doctor is in
Flawless is the physician
The madness is in
The mind of this mad mathematician
I see numbers in everything
And it numbs me to everything
Sometimes I think I'm a king
And sometimes I'm just a thing
So I stay wondering
While I stay wandering
Whether a thinking thing
Can exist beyond thinking
But they tell me that that's not the thing
For me to be thinking
I'm just supposed to bling-bling
And give shoutouts to Sing Sing
And I'm just a single man
So I just sing along
So I just play along
But this shit is played out, son
So now I'm mad vexed
This world makes no sense
It's all just nonsense
An' this madness, I'm trying to fence
But every sentence is a sentence
Binds me to the page
It's a contract I can't change
Even when I try to change my ways
I stay a ward to the state
Whether I'm in Penn State
Or the state pen

Words an' wardens got me boxed in
'Cause this world is mad to niggas
Want us disrespectin' each other
Pimping our women
An' pullin' the triggers
When we do, they got mad laws
An' mad bars
Always, mad ways
To keep mad cats as slaves
So on mad days
Mad niggas, get mad blazed
Wantin' mad dreams
Of mad things unseen
Mad cream, an' mo' moets
Mad love, an' no projects
We mad prophets, wit' no profits
Mad paupers, an' poets
Off the plantation, yet we still three-fifths
A free slave, a man born into madness . . .

Smile pretty for the cameras, he thought. No, this is hip-hop, it's always good to look hard. I ain't gon' smile; I'ma look upset. But he didn't feel like making up his face. He gave up . . . hell with it. I'm just gonna look. A series of rapid flashes came from a myriad of cameras. Flawless was in the backroom press area of the awards. There were so many flashes he felt he would throw up as a result of the blinding. It could not be helped. Flawless had been the big winner of the night. He was going home with four awards, including Record of the Year and the most coveted, Lyrist of the Year. He had to buck it up; he didn't want to upset the media. If there was ever a group of people who knew how to player-hate, it was them. They got their degrees in it, he thought. So he had to smile pretty for the cameras, or front on a frown or do whatever. Whatever he did, he had to have his picture taken.

● ● ●

The reception for the awards was being held at the Goldstein Ballroom. Flawless remembered the ballroom very well. This was where the first party that Jennessy had invited him to was held. So much had changed since then. He first walked this hall fascinated, with the eye of a peeping Tom. Now everyone was peeping him. Everyone wanted to be around him, to hug him, to touch him, to take pictures with him. A lot had changed, indeed, but he had already known that it would. He knew all along that he would be here.

Just about everyone else was there with him. Anyone who had any link to the business, from record executives, to artists, to producers, to video directors, to video girls, to photographers, to reporters, they were all in attendance; throughout it all, Flawless was the main attraction.

While being consumed by reporters, Tommy approached from behind and spoke to his ear, "You've come far man, you did your thing. Lyricist of the Year, I am mad proud of you, brother." Tommy congratulated him.

"Thank you, man. I appreciate that," Flawless replied. He then turned around and gave his best friend not a handshake, not a pound, but instead a profound hug.

"Y'know, you almost tripped me up during the show. You changed up 'Method.' "

"Yeah, I know. Sorry about that."

"Why didn't you tell me you was gonna do that."

"I didn't know. It wasn't planned. The words just flowed out of me."

"Damn, that's tight, that's tight. I think I like it better this way."

"Yeah, man. Me too."

"Ma god, Flawless. You got talent. I love you, man. You got talent," Tommy said.

"I love you too, brother."

He called his friend brother, not merely in the loose Afrocentric applicability of the word, but rather with the profound intimacy of blood. Flawless had been feeling down all night. His brother's affections did much to lighten his somber.

A few feet away Erika and Trish smiled while looking on. It was a rare thing for men to show each other affection. Whenever it happened it was always beautiful. Beautiful, is what Erika thought of her brother. He had accomplished so much and she was so proud of him.

Then there came a shuffle and a change in the direction of the melee. Many abandoned their original positions in Flawless's circumference and spliced their way through the crowd to see the man who was now entering the ballroom. There was a new epicenter of attraction.

Hannibal entered like a magnet to all. They were looking at him, the man with the number one hip-hop album in the country; doing 250,000 in his first week despite weak radio play. *The Silence* wasn't the most commercial album but it had a core grassroots following. The album was roughly underground in content, where Hannibal remained. He was hardly heard from and rarely seen. He had no penchant for the media and never gave interviews. The interview with RA was an exception. Even Bull had to acquiesce to the God of hip-hop radio. Given all that, the sight of the enigmatic recluse was a feast for media eyes.

Hannibal walked with Micah to his left and Terrence and Reaper carrying the rear. The rest of the boys were left home tonight; Mook opted to do the same. Hannibal admired the view. Decadence was always sweet to the vision. He found the experience even more satisfying, vicariously seen, through Micah's eyes. "This is something, ain't it?" he asked Micah.

"Yeah, it sure is," Micah replied, downplaying his elation.

"Well, this is ma first time to something like this as well. So I guess we're both virgins to this."

"Ready to pop your cherry?" Micah asked, surprised that he was able to speak so loosely with Hannibal.

"Fuck yeah, and I see some cherries that I would love to get into over there." Hannibal pointed to three very attractive girls in the distance: supple and overflowing in their raiment.

"Whoo, now that's sweet," Micah said, speaking in hormones. Terrence in back overheard the conversation and got an eye at what they were looking at.

"Don't get no cavities just yet. That one in the middle is mine. That's the ass of my dreams right there."

"Wait, hold up . . . you mean that's the one from BET that you be jerking off to?" After Hannibal said this, Micah looked over at him quizzically. Hannibal looked back to suggest that Micah had heard right. Terrence looked at both men, being aware of the unspoken conversation.

"Yes, yes, Negro. I do it. Shit, again—like I'm the only nigga that jacks off." Terrence's admission resulted in an explosion of laughter from the other two. Terrence merely curled his lips in sarcasm as Hannibal used his shoulder as a brace.

"Aw'ight, aw'ight, stay laughing. But I'll tell you this. She's gon' be jerking me off tonight. Now if you'll excuse me, gentlemen, I got some ass to get to."

Terrence cut through and headed toward the girls. Hannibal and Micah continued to laugh. Hannibal was really laughing. It was a type of stomach-bending laughter. This was a rare thing for him. He hadn't laughed like this in, he couldn't remember how long or if he ever had. He was always so serious, so business-minded that he never gave himself the time to laugh. There was no one in his life he felt comfortable laughing around. Not Mook, not anymore; not even Terrence. He knew that when you laugh too much people didn't take you seriously. Then before you knew it, they started disrespecting you. Bull would never allow that. He didn't know why he allowed himself to laugh like this now but he couldn't help it. He was drawn to him.

Micah couldn't help it as well. He laughed, feeling a younger brother's comfort toward Hannibal. It was a relationship that he had always wanted but had never known. Then from the corner of his eye, across the room, he beheld something quite exquisite; all at once he believed that she was the most precious thing that he had ever seen. His laughter turned into enamored fascination.

A slew of media personalities then came, besieging Hannibal with questions.

"Bull, how does it feel to have the top album in the country?" the reporter asked.

"It feels good," Hannibal replied, not showing his true annoyance that the reporter had broken in on his laughter.

"What did you think of the awards and the winners?"

"Listen, I didn't go to no awards, because I wasn't gon' win no awards, because I wasn't nominated for no awards. So on that, I ain't got nothing to say. In fact, tonight I got nothing to say about nothing. That's it." Hannibal tapped Micah on his shoulder. "You ready?" he asked.

"Yeah," Micah answered with divided attention.

"Let's walk."

Hannibal and Micah began to walk through the crowd, Micah staying vigilant of the beautiful figure across the room.

On the other side of the ballroom Erika and Trish were laughing to themselves about a group of men who stood some distance away, staring them down with a sniper's intensity. Their eyes never wavered, licking their chops as they analyzed the girls scientifically. Trish and Erika felt almost violated by the stares. Still, in their experience as women, they had learned to laugh off such attention. It happened too often to get upset. They were just happy that they were together. In the last year and a half, since Flawless's introduction, they had grown close. They shared much in common and Trish had a world of experience that Erika was now open to. She loved talking to her; she was like the older sister that she always wanted.

While Erika continued to laugh, something peripheral began to draw her in. She noticed someone eyeing her from across the floor. She felt the intensity in her teeth and turned in its direction to get a better view. There he was, dark-skinned and handsome. Wow, she thought, looking back at the man who looked at her.

Micah turned away sharply as the girl he stared at across the floor now stared back at him, but not being able to help it, within seconds he looked back at her. She was still staring. Again he turned away, finding this surprising and trying to orchestrate his next course of action. He looked back again and again she was looking at him. To this, he finally smiled. She returned his favor and what a smile it was. Even at this distance it was mesmerizing. At times Micah had to remind himself of his initial purpose for being there. He would then look over to his right at Hannibal and was brought back to reality.

Erika played the game, looking back and smiling at the handsome man that looked at her across the floor. She liked it; she liked him, not solely for the fact that he was handsome but because there was something singular about him. In the way he looked at her. It wasn't like the way of the other men. There was something special about his eye. She liked the way he saw her. It made her want to be seen. And so throughout the night, while accompanied by their separate parties, they foreplayed with eye play.

This went on for an hour. Though it was diverting, Micah began to grow nervous. She could leave at anytime and he would not have spoken to her. If he didn't speak to her he wouldn't be able to live with himself. This was more than not talking to the pretty girl he saw walking down the street. This girl was too much to let pass with simple dalliance. He had to talk to her.

He waited for Hannibal to become distracted. He didn't know why he didn't tell Hannibal straight out that he was going to kick it with the girl across the floor. Maybe it was because he wasn't going to kick it with her. You didn't just "kick it" with this girl. He didn't know her but he knew that he didn't want to do that. He wanted to talk to her on a profound level. It meant something to him. For that reason he didn't feel like sharing his thoughts with anyone. So when Hannibal became involved in a group flirt with Terrence, Reaper and three girls, Micah made his move.

Erika noticed that the guy she had played with all night was moving and he appeared to be coming toward her. She became nervous. Would she talk to him? Of course she would. She wanted to talk to him. But what would she say? She didn't know exactly. The only thing she did know was that she wanted to be alone when she did. She had to separate from Trish. Not that she didn't feel that Trish would understand but merely because she wanted to talk to him alone. She wouldn't feel free to express herself fully in Trish's company.

"I'm going to the bathroom," she said to Trish.

"Do you want me to come with you?" Trish asked.

"No, I'm okay."

"Are you sure?"

"Yeah, it's just right there."

"Well, make sure you walk with your cell just in case you get lost in the shuffle."

Erika pulled out her mobile and shook it in the air. "I have it." She then walked off and proceeded toward the ladies' room. Flawless saw her walk away. He was a bit annoyed that she was walking alone. He, however, did nothing, being mindful of their earlier conversation.

Micah saw that the beautiful girl had walked away from her original position. He didn't know how to take this. He knew that she had seen him. Did she walk away to avoid him? He didn't know. He watched her walk past the bar and head into the ladies' room. Maybe she was just going to the bathroom? Not sure of what to do next, he halted in the middle of his movement, waiting.

Erika stayed in the bathroom for five minutes, squeezing her way through an assortment of artificial women, all cackling about which rapper they had already been with, which one they wanted to get with and which one they were going home with that night. Throughout it all, her brother's name was thrown about many times. Erika tried not to pay attention to that or to them. She didn't need to use the bathroom, really. She merely used it as an excuse to separate from Trish. But she did use the time to freshen herself up with a dab of water to the corner of her eyes, after which she left the ladies' room and the cackling women behind.

Micah stood there for a while, feeling a bit stupid. Maybe she didn't want to talk to him and this was a signal. Maybe he should just go back over to Hannibal. He and the others were talking to three girls in the distance and they were all but sure things. He continued to debate the issue when he saw the beautiful girl reenter the floor. Instead of going back to her prior spot she stopped short at the bar. She then gave a slight look over to his direction. This was a sign if ever he had seen one. He continued his drive but then he was stalled by a shuffle of people moving in the opposite direction. The mass of the crowd halted him like perpendicular traffic.

Erika laughed to herself at the exploits of the handsome guy. Then she stopped smiling. She had lost sight of him in the mix of the traffic. Other than when she went into the bathroom she hadn't lost sight of him all night. Losing him now made her sad. She twisted her head looking for him, when a big hulk of mass came and blocked her perspective. He was about six feet to her five feet, eight inches in heels, and he was broad, fat but not obese. All Erika could see was the thick leather jacket he was wearing. It was a biker jacket, the one that guys spent $2,000 on. By the smell of it, it was brand new. The leather was so pungent that it made her want to throw up. Even more nauseating was the thick, heavy platinum cross that hung over his neck, glistening blindingly, inches from her brow. By the weight of the chain and the diamonds imbedded inside, Erika knew that it was valued upward of $20,000. This man was wearing an average man's yearly salary about his neck as an accessory.

"Yo, Ma, you all right? You lookin' kinda lost here." he asked.

"I'm fine," she replied, while continuing to look for that handsome guy with a measure of discretion. In her attempts, she looked up and recognized the mountain of a man that stood before her. She knew him. He was a famous rapper. It was Stalin.

"I would say that," he remarked to her statement, looking her up and down like a piece of tender meat. "Damn, you sweet, Ma. Best thing I seen all night."

"Thanks."

From a distance Flawless saw this. It irritated him but he fought his urges. Then someone approached. He was a light-skinned man in his midtwenties, garbed in his hip-hop uniform: Timberland boots, sweatpants, a leather jacket, a scarf, his hat to the back and ice, lots of ice. It was Bin Laden and he was drunk. Flawless could smell the stink of liquor on his breath. He came onto the precipice and stood by Flawless's side, looking down at the people below.

"What's goin' on, Flawless, how you livin'?" he asked.

"Yo Bin, I'm good. How 'bout you?"

"Cool," Bin sharply retorted. "Nigga a the hour, huh? Well, enjoy that shit while you can. This business is as fickle as a fuck." He never looked directly at Flawless, more so keeping his eye on the people below. "One minute you do platinum, the next . . . they act like they don't even remember your fucking name."

"So Ma, whatchu doin' here all by yo'self?"

Across the floor Stalin continued to question Erika. Erika was trying her best to remain calm while becoming more and more annoyed by Stalin's presence. Then during the rapper's probing, an incredible calm came over her body. To her left she could feel the heat and the slight presence of a hand. Not wanting to look directly, Erika looked down at her feet. She was reminded that she was wearing her boots, the black ones that extended up to the calf and gave her three more inches of height. She noticed the pair of shoes to the left of hers. They were tan work boots. They were a bit scuffed at the toe but they weren't old and ragged. She started at the shoes and then roved upward: from the cuff of his blue denim, leading up to the manufactured fading at his knee, to the brown of his hand, and then she stopped herself from looking any farther. She didn't have to; she knew who it was. The man standing beside her now was the same man that she had been eyeing all night.

Both Micah and Erika looked forward, sensing but never directly looking at each other. They did this out of the sake of nerves and the eerie feel of the moment. The oblivious Stalin continued his harangue.

"So yo, listen, I'm already bored of all this shit. Ma Hummer is outside and my hotel is not too far away; how 'bout you roll wit' me and we get outta here?" Stalin asked, believing he already knew the answer to his question. He was going to sleep with this girl. Well, not exactly sleep. He would enjoy her for an hour or two and then kick her out. Well, maybe not. This girl was really fine; she could spend the night. For him her saying yes was only a formality. Why wouldn't she say yes? They always said yes. As such he paid no attention to the fact that Erika paid him no attention. However, after five minutes and entreaty after entreaty, the annoyed rapper got the message and walked off cursing her all the way. Erika was unaware of all this.

Erika and Micah stood looking away in silent fascination, both playing the game, neither one wanting to say a word. The attraction between them was intense; neither wanted to break the beauty of their silence.

Micah raised his hand to his forehead, wiping something from his brow, and then freely hung it down to his side when it came in contact with . . . something. At first he wasn't quite sure what it was but then it came to him. It was her hand. He was touching her. He knew this, and he knew that she knew this; after a moment he wondered why she didn't move her hand. It was the custom for strangers to immediately pull away at the chance of any accidental bodily contact. Erika wondered all of this also, as she realized that Micah was not moving his hand and that neither was she. Then it happened. As if functioning as sentient agents of their own: their fingers found each other.

His pinky finger made a slight motion downward. It was a tingle that sent shivers all over her body. His pinky, noticing that her pinky had not retracted, proceeded farther. It went down deeper and deeper, until it was in the slit between fingers and felt the moisture of her lotion. Her pinky reacted to his presence and moved closer to his. They touched, they rubbed, they embraced; then the other fingers in like suit, one by one, became involved. In silence they held and massaged hands. It was sweetly erotic, as they rubbed each other intensely under the cover of the crowd. The friction created a fever that flowed all through their bodies. Micah's nature rose and Erika's moistened. At this point everything and everyone else in the room became a blurred purple haze. They turned around and faced each other.

Erika looked at him with enamored eyes. The bit of water inside of hers only added to the glisten and the profundity of their brown.

"Who are you?" she asked him.

"I am whoever you want me to be," he resonated with a subtle smile.

She squeezed his hand playfully. "Stop playing. Who are you?"

"Hello, I'm Micah."

"Hmm . . . my handsome Micah."

"And who are you?"

"Hi, I'm Erika."

"My beautiful Erika."

"Do you really think that I am beautiful?"

"Girl, I think that you are . . . beyond."

Erika blushed and a braid of her hair fell to her face. Micah gently moved the strand to the side and Erika placed her face in his palm. Her face was so smooth to the touch; she felt so warm and safe in his hand as if she was folded in his arms, as she now wanted to be.

Back in the real world, Bin Laden was still talking to Flawless. Flawless heard Bin Laden's words, though he never looked at him.

"Yeah, man, all this shit, the cars, the girls, the money. Yep, the money, all the fucking money you think that you making, but . . . but you really not. You think you making millions, right. Nigga, I thought so too." A slur had developed in Bin's speech. His inebriation was beginning to take over his faculties. "The reality, the reality is a pale fucking fraction. The way they set up that contract, they earn millions off yo' shit . . . and you only see . . . shit. I couldn't fucking believe it when I looked at my contract. I almost fucking killed Jennessy; coulda fucking did it. Still could. Still would, if I could get away with the shit. Fuck it; might do it anyway. Fucking contract, man. Shit. That's what they do. They train you; they set you up and send you out there. And when something else comes along, they turn against you and leave yo' ass out to dry. That's why I turn against moth- erfuckers. Fuck them, fuck they whole shit. I'ma start ma own shit and make better bombs than they do. So dem an' they con- tract can go kiss ma ass. Contracts. Nigga, have you checked out your contract?"

Bin Laden's last question stuck Flawless like a needle. He faced Bin for the first time.

"Yeah, man, yeah," Bin continued, realizing that he had pricked a nerve. He then began to sniff something. "What's that smell?" he asked. "Shit, what's that smell?" he repeated more frantically. He looked down and saw his pants drenched. "What the hell is this?" he wondered out loud. "Shit. I pissed myself. I pissed myself. Now, how the hell, did that happen? Yo, I'ma holla at you later." Bin then walked off in drunken dismay.

"Yeah," Flawless said to himself.

Tommy then approached.

"What was that all about?" he asked.

"Just piss, just a lot of piss."

"What?"

"Forget about it."

"Forgotten." Tommy then changed the subject. "Yo, you see Erika over there?"

Erika's name all but wiped away all of Flawless's thoughts of Bin Laden and contracts. "Yeah I do."

"I am surprised that you haven't broken it up."

"Well, we spoke and I promised her that I wouldn't do that anymore. So I guess she's on her own."

"All right, that's cool, that's cool." Tommy wasn't going to say it but something in him couldn't help it. He knew that if Flawless found out from someone else, knowing that Tommy had known, he would be upset. "Still, I just thought you should know that the dude she's talking to is one of Bull's boys."

"Really?" Those words combined together were like a check to the abdomen.

"Yeah, I saw them come in together."

"Hmmm."

Across the floor Micah and Erika were still trapped in a purple haze.

"I really don't even know what to say," she said to him.

"I don't understand, why?"

"Well, I wasn't expecting to find someone like you . . . here."

"Someone like me?"

"Yes, someone different."

This room was filled with Stalins, all of them thinking they had everything and could have any girl they desired. Different for her was the divergence of thought. That she found to be extremely attractive. And he was handsome too, with a smile that lit up his entire face and made her weak in the knees.

"How do you know that I'm different?" he asked her.

"I can see it in your eyes. They tell me something."

"Yeah, what do they tell you?"

"They tell me something different."

They laughed while holding hands; their fingers couldn't see fit to separating.

"Hello, sister," Erika heard a voice coming out of the dark, pricking at her ear. It was as if she was in a wonderful dream and her alarm clock in the real world began to ring. At first she tried to ignore it. Then it came again. "Hello, sister." Trying desperately to hold on to her dream, she incorporated the ring of the clock. The words seemed to come out of Micah's mouth. But wait, that's not right. Micah wouldn't call me sister. And that is not his voice. The alarm came again, "Erika!" The words shouted out of Micah's mouth. She knew better than to react. It wasn't Micah who was speaking. It was someone else. She was waking up, or so she thought. She did a slow turn around to find Flawless standing behind her. Upon seeing him the purple haze was broken; all of the noise of the party came crashing back into consciousness. Never before had she not wanted to see her brother as much as she did in that moment.

"Michael. What are you doing here?" she asked, still dazed.

"We all came here together . . . remember?"

She had forgotten all of that, as to how and why she was there. All she remembered was seeing Micah and feeling the warmth of his hand. "I know, I know. I just meant . . ." she said fumbling her words.

"Yeah," Flawless replied, feeling that she didn't want him around. He had never seen his sister act like this before. "So who is your friend?" he asked.

Micah, noticing that Erika seemed a bit confused, introduced himself. "Hi, I'm Micah." Micah also wanted to meet Flawless. Flawless was his hero on the mic. He had studied

Flawless' CD much the same way that Hannibal had studied Lecter. He wondered how Erika knew him exactly. He hadn't heard when Flawless called her from before. He hoped that she wasn't his girlfriend.

"I got your album, man. I am seriously a fan. I really love and respect your work."

"Thanks," Flawless replied.

"So you're Erika's . . . ?"

"Brother . . . yes."

"Oh, that's cool."

"Yeah it is. So Micah, how you came here? You rhyme, who you with?"

"Oh yeah, I'm with Cannibal. I came with . . ."

Before Micah could finish his sentence he heard a distinctive growl coming from the back.

"He is with me," Hannibal said. "What's up, Flawless, how you livin'?"

These words were the first shared between the two in almost two years. It was only three months shy since they last faced each other; now they were both here. Micah and Erika stood caught in the middle of the intensity.

"I'm good, Bull. Read the papers. I'm doing fine."

"Yeah, that's cool. You should read the latest editions. I'm doing pretty good myself."

Tit for tat, they tacitly poked each other and then stared in silence, not knowing what else to say. Micah thought to interject when Jennessy came into the circle.

"My boys, my boys, together again. The two princes of Crown." Jennessy had brought the media and their flashes with him. He hugged and brought the two of them together, standing to either side of him with his arms around their shoulders, in the classic politician's pose. Behind them, Erika and Micah were caught within the frenzy, never letting go of each other's hands. They felt as if they had to hold on even tighter now so that one of them would not be pulled away in the mix.

"My boys, I have an idea. It just came to me. How about the two of you doing a single together? The two Princes of rap, it would be historic. What do you boys say?"

"I got no problems with it," Flawless quickly replied. If there was one thing that Flawless was confident about, it was his work. He would enjoy a duet with Hannibal. He knew that he would eat him alive. There was no other form of music but hip-hop in which collaborations were as popular or as competitive.

"Yo, I'm for whatever earns dollars," Hannibal announced.

"Believe me, my boy, it will. So it is settled then. You boys get your best stuff together and I'll get the best production. At the end of the day, it will all be brilliant. Now, smile pretty for the cameras."

Again, all three men engaged themselves in the politician's pose; Jennessy with a Kool-aid smile sandwiched between two grimaces.

"Well, that's my night," Flawless announced as soon as the last flash came. "Erika, let's go."

Erika looked confused. She did not want to leave Micah's side but she would have to go. She saw the stubbornness in Flawless. He would not be bargained with, at least not without a scene. So she let go of Micah's hand for the first time since they had touched. The detachment wasn't easy; their hands seemed as if they had to be ripped apart.

"Give me a minute, I'll be right there," Erika said to Flawless.

"Erika," he persisted.

"I'll be right there!" There was a sharpness in her voice. She was angry and was doing her best not to show it. Angered but contained, Flawless stepped off to the side.

Erika turned to Micah.

"I gotta go."

"Why?" he asked.

"I just do." She pulled out her pager. "Quick, zap me your information."

Feeling a bit out of place, Micah responded, "I'm sorry, girl, but I don't have any of those things."

Erika smiled. "Wow, a normal person. I knew you were different. Give me your hand." She took his hand and wrote her number in his palm. There was something so seductive about how the pen strokes graced across the patterns in his hand. When she was finished, she curled his hand into a fist and then let it go.

"Call me."

"Erika, we gotta roll," Flawless pressed from the side.

"Call me," she repeated.

"Definitely," Micah answered.

She walked over and joined Flawless; without saying a word to each other they made their way through the crowd. Hannibal then came over to Micah.

"What was that all about?" he asked.

"I am not quite sure."

"Who was the girl?"

"She's Flawless's sister."

"Didn't know ole Flaw had a sister that looked like that. Chick is hot. You gon' have fun blazin' that."

"Yeah. I guess so," Micah answered, not really paying any mind to what Hannibal said, looking down at the number in his palm. "I guess so."

TWENTY

A black Mercedes Benz limousine drove across Forty-second Street and pulled onto Broadway. The limo was driving aimlessly, circling the city. At three in the morning it made for enjoyable driving. Streets that would be congested in a few hours were now sparse enough to maneuver about with a measure of liberty.

The limo was deep with a carrying capacity of nine. It had an exquisite leather interior, a minibar, a television, DVD player, an X-box and a PlayStation 3 with games already preprogrammed inside. Also in a side compartment there was a laptop with wireless Internet access. The vehicle was fully loaded with all of the conveniences of modernity. These were all compliments of Crown Records, and Hannibal was enjoying it.

He didn't enjoy it by himself. Terrence, Reaper, Micah and three girls joined him. The girls were the same ones who Terrence had eyed earlier at the party. The one that he was fond of was among them. Now she appeared to be very fond of him: she sat there, with a contortionist's control of her anatomy, giving him the grind of a lap dance. The second of the three did the same for Reaper. She sat on his lap and arched her back so that their mouths could meet, wrestling each other with their tongues. The third sat facing Hannibal, taking his hands all over her form. Hannibal looked at her with subtle amusement. Micah sat to himself, engrossed in his palm.

The number had already been etched into his brain. He already knew it backward and forward. He looked at it now out of fascination, admiring her handwriting. Her penmanship was as immaculate as her touch. She had written her name above the digits, as if it was necessary. As if he needed any reminder that it was her number. Her number. He couldn't wait to call her, but when to call? He wanted to call right now. No, he couldn't do that, that would be too much. She would think he was crazy, and perhaps would regret having given him her number, but then again, perhaps not.

"Mic', you all right? You lookin' kinda lonely over there," Terrence called to him.

"Naw, I'm all right," he replied, looking up from his hand.

"You sure? 'Cause y'know, we boys. Gotta look out for each other. And she could do us both."

This evoked an immediate response from the girl on his lap. "Hey, what do you mean, do you both? What do you think I am, some sort of cheap ho?"

"Naw, Ma, fuck no. I don't think that. Classy girl like you, you ain't no ho; a chickenhead maybe, but a ho, no."

"Hey, fuck you!" she responded with rancor. She removed herself from his lap.

"Damn, girl, I'm just fucking with you," Terrence said and then grabbed hold of her waist and pulled her back down to his bulge. "Now, sit your ass down and don't move off again." She looked at him like a sourpuss and he mocked her grimace. Then he smiled and she smiled in return and pecked him on the lips. She soon preoccupied herself again with her lap dance and while she wasn't looking, Terrence looked over to Micah and silently mouthed the word, *ho*. Micah smiled to himself, while feeling a bit sad for the girl.

"Girl, you know what I want you to do for me?"

"What's that, baby?" she replied to Terrence's question.

"I want you to do that thing that y'all be doin' when y'all make ya ass cheeks move by themselves. Can you do that?"

"What do you mean? Like this." She stood up and bent over slightly so that her entire rear all but covered Terrence's face, she hiked up her tight dress and began, through an act of precise muscle control, gyrating the cheeks of her rear all by themselves. It was a spectacular act and Terrence was very appreciative.

"Oh shit. Oh shit! That's it, that's what I'm talking about. That's talent. I think that's the best talent that God ever gave to a woman." The girl seemed to be turned on by Terrence's exuberance and continued her act with gusto. This girl, whose name Terrence could not remember but merely referred to as "that ass from BET," put on a show worthy of the best strip clubs. She had been in many videos for many rappers and had done comparable things, the things at least that they were able to show on camera, but she was not a stripper and had never been. However, the nature of the stripper had become a fascination in the recent era. Many girls had taken to the vogue, if not the profession.

The other nameless girl who sat next to Reaper joined in on the act. Her show was even more spectacular. She planted herself on the floor of the vehicle and hiked her legs into the air. Her dress fell over, revealing a well-shaped rear end with a string as its only cover, which now gyrated feverishly in front of Micah's face. He was turned on by this and fought the urge to grab hold of the firm before his eyes. In between his internal debate between gratification and restraint, he thought it was sad that these girls didn't even think to be offended by all this. Reaper then did what Micah had refrained from doing. He poured a bottle of champagne from thigh to center and following the flow, drove his head into her canal. She reacted with a screech and a giggle and locked her legs reflexively around his head.

Amid all of this, Hannibal remained stoic, smiling only occasionally. He gestured with his hand for his girl to get off. She did so and snuggled next to his side.

"So Micah, what did you think of tonight?" Hannibal asked him.

Micah turned his head away from the ass before his eyes and answered, "It was cool."

"Interesting world, isn't it?" Hannibal asked while nodding to Micah to look at the trick that Terrence's girl was performing. She was in the midst of a wine that would put the best belly dancer out of business.

"Yeah, it sure is," Micah replied. "What do you think about that single with Flawless?"

"I'm thinking about it."

Hannibal wasn't merely thinking of it. He was strategizing with the methodicalness of a general. It was the number one thing on his mind.

"You and Flawless; that should be something."

"I know, gotta be on my best game for that. Can't let him eat me on that shit."

"You're right. He's gonna come hard."

"I think maybe we should work on that one together. What do you think?"

"Cool, love to," Micah replied, not being sure in what capacity he would be working. He didn't really care. He was down for whatever.

"All right, we start working shit out tomorrow."

Hannibal gestured over to his nameless girl to go over to Micah. Terrence had asked the girls for their names earlier in the night and in a minute he had forgotten them. Hannibal never bothered to ask. She went over to Micah and then began to give him a lap dance. Micah looked at her in slight fascination and touched the parts of her body where she placed his hands. In doing so, he caught a view of his palm and Erika's number. All at once the scantily dressed girl gyrating herself in front of him didn't seem to matter.

TWENTY-ONE

Erika sat feeling like a princess on her queen-size bed, sunken into her soft feather pillows, surveying her sovereignty. Her new room was thrice the size of her old and came with its own bathroom, as did all of the rooms in Flawless's new house. She looked across her lavender carpet at her reflection, which came off of her closet. It took up the entire wall and was mirrored from ceiling to floor. The wall opened and inside was her deep walk-in closet, filled with Italian names from the fabrics to the shoes. To the right of her closet was her bathroom, also done in lavender with gold fixtures and with a separate bath and shower. This was her new life; she loved it and she owed it all to her brother.

She sat there imbued in the glow from earlier, when it came to her that the semester would soon begin again. For the last month she hadn't given it a thought. Now that she did, she didn't want to anymore. It was not that she hated school; for the most part she enjoyed it. She just didn't know what she wanted to do with her life. Approaching the second semester of her sophomore year at NYU, she was still without a major. Should I major in business or law? And if I studied law, which field? There were as many fields of law as there were denominations of Christianity, it seemed. And then again, how about fashion design? I've always liked clothes. What about history? I've always loved to read and research. Erika thought of everything and still came to no resolution; for some reason she didn't feel pressed to do so. This lifestyle was beginning to make her lazy. It was her brother's fault. He had made things too easy for her.

Michael, Michael, Michael. Ever since she could recall he had been there for her. He took care of her. Flawless would help her with her homework and whenever the girls bullied her at school, he would go down there and confront whoever it was, no matter the numbers and no matter when they brought their brothers and their gang affiliations with them. He seemed fearless in front of the odds. He was never a thug but he could act that way, whenever it concerned her. He never allowed anyone to touch his sister. He wouldn't let anyone get close to her as well. Only now she wanted to feel close, she wanted to be touched.

She thought of Micah and she glowed. She really liked him. She hadn't wanted to leave his side earlier but Michael had persisted. That had to stop. He went too far this time. His overprotection had gone unchecked for too long. But how strong could her argument be while she sat there in the perks of his labor? She didn't know. She wouldn't think of that now. For now, she would just glow in the insanity of the moment. She had rubbed hands with a complete stranger; she would have kissed him too if he had asked her, or if he had let her. That was crazy.

She then heard a voice: "You are glowing," it said. Erika looked to her side to see Trish standing at the door.

"No, I am not."

"Yes, you are."

"Okay, yes I am."

"The guy you met tonight is doing all of that to you?"

"I don't know. I don't know if it's him or just the sweet possibility of something more."

"What's more?"

"I don't know. More is just more."

The girls began to laugh. Erika's laughter simpered as Flawless joined Trish at the door. "Really," he remarked.

"Yes, really," Erika said with a fight brewing on her tongue.

"And what was that tonight, Michael? I thought you said that you weren't going to pull that overprotective shit anymore." There was anger in her contralto.

"I'm not, but I am not going to let you jump off of a bridge either."

"What are you talking about?"

"That nigga you were talking to is in Bull's camp."

"And so what? Your beef with Bull has nothing to do with me, or him."

"Maybe not but I know Bull, and I know the type that rolls with him."

"And what type is that? 'Same type as all the other niggas,' " Erika said in frustration; she had heard this argument a million times before.

"You keep being naïve but I ain't about to see you turn into some gangbang whore. That's how it starts, you know? You start to like one guy. Then he takes you back to his room. You think it's him alone. But then six other niggas jump out and all you can do is cry and scream."

"You are so fucking dramatic. That shit would never happen. Give me some fucking credit." She had never spoken this forcefully to her brother before. Flawless was taken aback by the fury. Regardless, he continued, still retaining his calm.

"Why, it can happen to other girls but it can't happen to you? Or maybe that guy wouldn't do that because he's different?"

"Yes, exactly. He's different."

"And you know this because you spoke to him for all of five minutes."

"Yep, exactly," she affirmed with a twist and a pout of her lips.

"Oh, fucking grow up, Erika, and stop being so naïve," Flawless shot back in anger. This was the first time he could remember cursing at his sister. They had shared profanities before but always in a joking manner; now he was pissed. It hurt him that she spoke to him in the manner in which she did. And deeper down in the recesses of his thoughts it troubled him that she seemed to be truly taken with this name; more so than she did with all the other names that he had run off. He knew that this day would come sooner or later; none would have been good enough but, of all of the prospects, why someone allied with Bull? That made it even worse.

"I am grown, Michael, whether you choose to see it or not. And I am going to go out with whoever I want and you're not going to stop it. So *you* fucking grow up and deal with that."

He shook his head and walked away from the door. Trish stood in the portal for a moment after, not knowing what to do. She didn't know what to say to Erika and she wouldn't know what to say to Flawless when she walked back to him. She merely stood there, conflicted in the middle of everything, and then silently retired.

The room was dark. Erika was a half of an hour into her sleep. She had stayed up for another hour, debating whether or not she should apologize to Michael for all that she had said. She meant all of it. She just didn't mean it the way in which she had said it. It wasn't natural for her and her brother to be on bad terms. She didn't like it. She wanted things to be the way they were, they way they always had been. She loved him but she had grown up and things needed to change. So she debated the issue until she fell asleep. She wasn't asleep for too long when the phone began to ring.

Erika groggily leaned over to her bed-end dresser and picked up her room phone. "Hello, hello," sounding half-dead, she said into the receiver. She was surprised to only hear the dial tone as the ringing continued. Then it came to her. It was her mobile. For a moment she thought it might be the person who she had thought of all night. The thought shot her out of bed. She ran to her coat pocket and feverishly searched for the phone in the dark. But it wasn't there. But then where could it be? Her pocketbook, she remembered. She rushed over and grabbed it and ferreted the phone out.

"Hello, hello!" she said in a frantic haste.

There was an uncertain pause and then Micah's voice came over, "Hello, Erika."

"Micah . . . hi." An immediate ease came over her body.

"I am not sure, am I calling too late?" he asked, his voice coming over like honey along with the filtered sounds of the phone line.

"No, no."

"It's four-thirty in the morning."

"Yeah, yeah," she replied, looking over at the glaring red digits of her alarm clock for confirmation.

"And it's not too late?"

"For you, no."

He paused in the glow of her words. He had been nervous about calling, dialing the number four times before he allowed it to ring. He didn't know if this was the right time, and he didn't know how she would react. He followed his heart and allowed the ringing to continue until a voice picked up. Now he was happier that he did.

"Y'know at first I wasn't going to call for about two days."

"Why?"

"Didn't want to seem too eager."

"Really."

"But you know what, I don't care. In fact, I want you to know that I want you."

"You do." She was melting inside to hear him say what she was feeling as well.

"Yeah, girl. I am digging you bad. You have been in my thoughts all night and it feels good to have you, even if only mentally."

"I can't stop thinking about you as well. And I don't know what but something happened to me tonight, and I can't explain it, but it feels . . . really good." It felt even better to express these feelings to him.

"Yeah it does," he affirmed, and then words like autonomous agents of their own, flowed through him.

Girl, you leave me speechless
And feverish, I'm amorous
And anemic, 'cause my blood
Gets weak, with every thought of you
To reminisce on the smell of you
You make whole the hollow
In my heart, you give roots to my bark
Of my existence, you are the spark
And mark, that I would barter my soul
And live infinitum, as an unholy whole
Just for a moment
Just for another moment, to hold you.

At the end of his speech, she remained silent, hoping that it wasn't finished. He had done it, he had her now; she was wet. "Wow, did you just write that?"

"Actually, it just flowed out of me."

"Whoa, that was so beautiful."

"No, girl, you're beautiful."

"So tell me, what's happening here?" she asked, feeling the butterflies in her stomach. It was that beautiful feeling of a new relationship on the horizon.

"I don't know, I really don't. But whatever it is, I like it."

TWENTY-TWO

He danced dark inside of the tightness of her wet, back and forth always in rhythm. With a beat so precise and in sync that he could rhyme to it. So he rhymed to the lines of her cavern, back and forth like the equivalent of an aneurysm. Taking care to always look down in his motions. The motions much like the lunar pull on the tides. It was the semblance between violence and calm, a sweet balance. Then the beat and her body kicked in, with such a fury that he lost all mind of his will. The depth willed him now, pulled him in and arched his frame, throwing his body into an angle and opened his eyes to the light. Then the light from her brow struck him and woke him from his slumber.

Flawless awoke that night to a quickened heart. It beat so hard and so fast that it seemed to lift the fabric from off his chest. He placed his hand before it in an attempt to temper its pace. All his actions seemed to do was send the reverberations throughout the rest of his body, as upon his thigh, he could feel now, a stickiness. What was the meaning of this? he questioned as he looked down at the sheets with a sick disposition. Then his eyes carried him forward. There at the edge of the bed he saw her, a little girl, a precious thing, very pretty, but not just any. It was Erika, at about age eight. The age she was when their father left. With sullen eyes, she looked back at him, in a still pose, saying nothing. The sight brought chills and raised the hair and bumps across his body, as he watched, watched her in her translucence, then watched her fade away into nothingness. He then looked up and saw images and figures floating around into and out of the room, the likes of which he could not explain. He was instantly terrified. He looked over to Trish, sleeping calmly. He wanted to wake her but the fear had gripped his vocal cords. In his mind he screamed and screamed, though in reality nothing came out save for strained air. He fought his fear and kept on screaming, "Trish, Trish!"

"Trish!" The word finally came out as he woke in a cold sweat. Trish woke up with him.

"What, what?" she shouted, jumping up out of her sleep.

He replied only with heaving breaths.

"Baby, what is it, what's wrong?" she asked while reaching out for his shoulder. Again, he didn't reply, not knowing what to say to her. How would he explain the things that he had just felt, that he had just seen? He couldn't. He wouldn't, at least not now, not tonight. For now he merely reached over and hugged her, tightly.

"Baby, baby. What's wrong?" she asked him, being almost moved to tears by Flawless's gesture. He just continued to hold her tighter, shivering. She got the message and silently held him back.

After a few minutes the pace of his heartbeat had slowed back to normal. He let her go and pulled away. She looked at him now with tears in her eyes. The tears in his eyes had evoked an empathetic response. She had never seen him cry before. She saw real fear in him and it scared her.

Without a word he got up from the bed and walked over to stand by the doors that led to his bedroom balcony. He stood by the ghostly, flowing white curtains, looking out into the night sky; the brilliance of the full moon shined upon him and threw a shadow, which stretched across the length of the large room into its dark corners. Trish, feeling beyond confused, reached for the lamp switch. "No lights," he said, before her hand could reach it.

"Okay," she replied. At least he was talking. "Are you ready to talk?"

"No, it's nothing. Don't worry about it. I'm sorry I woke you."

"Baby, that wasn't nothing."

"It was. It was only . . . only images, dreams. It was nothing."

She couldn't stand it anymore. She got up and walked over to his position. She hugged him from behind and he took her hand to his heart. For a minute nothing was said between them. They merely stood there in their moonlight embrace. And then . . . "I'm dying, Trish," he calmly said to her.

"What?" she sharply replied. "What are you talking about? Dying. Dying from what?" Her mind ran the gamut: from AIDS, to all manner of lesser venereal diseases.

"I'm dying from death."

"Dying from death. What? Baby, I don't understand."

"I didn't expect you to."

Though she was confused, she felt hurt that he had expected her to be confused. She wanted to know what was going on but he seemed to be speaking in riddles. "It's nothing, Trish. I have just come to grips with my mortality. Death walks with me now."

"Baby, talk plain, please. You are throwing me all over the place."

"Calm down, Trish. It's all right. It's cool." He spoke with familiarity, his tenor tamed of the eerie ethereal.

"What do you mean by calm down, that it's cool? No, it's not cool, Michael. It's not. You wake me up in the middle of the night screaming my name and shivering. Then you won't tell me what's wrong. Now you tell me that you're dying and you want me to calm down. No Michael, I can't do it. I can't do it," she said, shaking her head no.

Flawless, realizing the disturbance that he had caused her, hugged her tightly and quieted her rant. He looked into her eyes and thought to tell her everything that he had seen. Then he looked across the room and saw the images again, floating around. He held her, trying his best not to scream and keep her ignorant of what he was seeing. At this point, Flawless no longer knew whether he was awake or still dreaming, but he did know one thing: he didn't have much more time.

BOOK FOUR

TWENTY-THREE

It was summer in Brooklyn and it was as hot as hell. As the young man got off the bus and headed up Utica Avenue, preparing to make his way across Empire Boulevard, the sun weighed down upon him like oppression. He quickly threw on his sunglasses, doing this as much for style as for protection; the nineteen-year-old thought it made him look cool. Along with the sunglasses: his ribbed white tank top, fitting tightly to his muscular form; his baggy jeans, worn below the waist and just above the crack so that the brand name at the top of his boxers was visible; his messenger backpack, hanging over which was a white gold crucifix (he couldn't afford platinum but that didn't mean that he couldn't bling-bling); and his Timberland boots, which as a result of the heat made his feet burn a bit, but he could deal with a little moisture for the sake of style.

He stood by the intersection waiting for the green. He pulled out his Discman and in a moment the beat came on . . . loud. It deafened him to everything else around. The light changed and he crossed the street with an extra bop in his step. The rhythm was intense, the hottest thing in the clubs all over the country.

Crown criminals
Flawless and Hannibal

Brooklyn's own cannibal
An' QB's king lyrical
Shuttin' down the show, yo
Taxin' Crown for that dough dough
Goin' pow pow to the Po Po
Fuckin' wit' us is a no-no

By the time he had crossed the street, Hannibal's distinctive growl came over.

Now, Bull is the first to bat
An' I'ma kill this shit right here
Because this beat is fat
I'ma eat this track
When I'm done, nothin' left
No leftovers for leftovers
Eating the beef
And the hors d'oeuvres
I got no table manners
I was raised by panthers
Born and bred in the boroughs
Where you got rivers, we got gutters
So we stay rippin' shit
Niggas take what we can get
Get rich quick
And die with our gats.

He was entranced in the sync of the beat and the words as he walked up the avenue, cutting through the downward traffic of people, passing the department store and the Plexiglas bus stand. And then . . . he saw her: She walked down the block seemingly in slow motion, giving him the opportunity to examine her form from toe to head. She wore platform sandals, and beyond that all he saw was a flawless sheet of ebony, brown skin that seemed to shimmer in the light of the sun. He followed her well-shaped calves past her slightly knocked knees, watching her figure widen and thicken at the hips, until he had reached her deep thighs where he saw another stitch of fabric; denim cutoffs, neatly fit to the cuteness of her hips; ribbed midriff, which bulged out at the chest, holding up her endowments well. Endowed she also was with a pretty face, dimpled cheeks, thickened lips and hair worn naturally with a mop-like appeal. She was beautiful; if his eyes permitted he would have analyzed the DNA in her bloodstream. She walked by him and gave a flirting eye as she passed. He saw her figure swing from the back and he was gone. The beat was sick but her body was sicker.

Just then a Beige Toyota Camry came onto the avenue. A heavy beat came through its speakers, resonating throughout the streets. Like a tremor, Hannibal's voice shook the earth with its passing.

But we got ambition
Got mad intuition
Fuck goin' to prison
I'm heading for the mansion
Bull in the palace
Princess Dying for me to stab her
Fucked Buffy
Now they call Hannibal the cracker slayer
Crack the whip, yo
Push the stick, though
Do seventy in six
I'm out the back quick
Wit' the Crown jewels
Queen singin' the blues
Blues skies turn red
As I'm blazin' at feds
An' they fed up and down
'Cause I'm gunning them down

Bucking at Buckingham
And ducking the clowns
I'm back in the house
Fucking with royalty
This for yo' ass, boss
Now I'm pimpin' that Crown pussy.

The Camry's driver gave an eye to the beautiful girl walking down the avenue and the young man pursuing her. It was a subtle glance but enough for his girlfriend, who sat in the passenger seat. He began to explain his position but she had no ear for it. Then Flawless's voice came on and consumed her with its tacit suave. She forgot her argument and simply bopped her head.

I'ma Crown criminal
Flaw flow subliminal
Sublime and lyrical
Scalp heads like Seminoles
No man can hold me
I'm whole and unholy
Schooled and unruly
Rule rap, absolutely
Cats pay me homage
Cats cop ma image
Niggas stay coppin' ma flow
Like Popeye do spinach
But I don't love that chicken
Y'all spineless, I'm spittin'
The flippant, I'm flippin'
The cons, I'm connin'.

The Camry continued up Utica to pull over outside of a beauty salon. The girlfriend exited the car, wearing her tight jeans, which appeared even tighter on her wide figure; her *I Love Flawless*

T-shirt, which was pushed out at the top by her large chest; and her intricate and complex weaving of hair, which made it hard for her to sleep at night. She stepped onto the sidewalk and all at once the oppressive heat hit her. She hurried into the beauty salon, and as she opened the glass door, she could feel the immediate change in temperature.

Beyond the dryers and chairs filled with customers there was a stereo system and all over there were speakers. The beat that was being played in the car was played in the salon as well. Everyone was bopping their heads to it, even the older women.

> *Coming through the compound*
> *Gunning for the big crown*
> *Checkmate ma friend*
> *Nigga crown me king*
> *'Cause I come to rip shit*
> *Fuck you and your rhetoric*
> *It's time to get rich*
> *This is for reparations, bitch*
> *So I shot the sheriff*
> *And the fucking deputy*
> *And the mayor*
> *And the nigga in Albany*
> *I ain't partial to parliaments*
> *I ain't pulling for presidents*
> *While y'all niggas pantomime*
> *Yo, I'm panting for mine*

The girlfriend approached her friend, who was busy with a client. All three women began to comment on the weather and, as Flawless's voice rang through, they all spoke on it with fondness, and a bit more.

While they continued to swoon, the barber of the shop walked by them wearing his locks wrapped neatly in a scarf, a T-shirt with Haile Selassie on the fore and a lion to the rear, genuinely worn-out jeans, and flat-footed sandals. And as the slim man was leaving the salon, he spoke to the women up front, flirting in his Jamaican twang.

He stepped into the heat and the rhythm's continuance, bopping his head and giving greetings to the brother behind the wheel of the Camry. He held his arms out, taking a deep breath and smiling to the sun. The young vegetarian then made his way up the block.

As he proceeded the beat faded to an almost null; then it began to come from in front of him, getting louder and louder until he reached its epicenter: a ministereo system set upon the sidewalk. The young vegetarian stopped by the stand and looked at the bootleg CDs laid on the mat. He surveyed but did not see the disc he was looking for. He made his inquiry and the vendor quickly reached down and handed him a CD labeled: *DJ RA's Wicked Mixes Vol. 3*. He nodded his head in agreement.

He looked at the disc in his hand, feeling extremely pleased with his purchase, and with his head down he didn't notice the black Lexus SUV that drove with the same beat thumping down the avenue. But then he looked up to see a riot of people running toward him. There were about fifteen of them, ranging in ages from ten to twenty, both male and female. They ran past him in a fury, causing him to turn around, look down the block and see where they ran to. Then came the shouting, "Bull, Bull!" "That's Bull in that Jeep!"

Hannibal? the vegetarian thought. Could it be that the devourer was driving down Utica?

The light at Empire turned red. Hannibal slowed the Jeep to a halt. The lull was all the people on the street needed. They rushed to his car as if he were the ice-cream man. Some were fascinated just to see him; others took time to admire his ride. The black exterior burned hot in the summer heat and his rims shined brilliantly, enough to blind whosoever was inclined to look too close. At seeing the crowd that had gathered outside, Hannibal rolled down his window and let in the hot air.

The most daring of the group pushed to the front. "Yo, Bull, Bull! Can I get your 'graph, man?" he asked.

Hannibal looked up at the light about to change and then back with a smile.

"Seriously, little man, I would love to. But we in the middle of the road right now. And I would park up but I'm in a mad rush. But, yo, don't take it no way, you know I'm always around."

The light turned green and Hannibal was set to pull off. While everyone in the crowd said good-bye, a teenage girl shouted out, "Bull, I love you. I want you to be my baby daddy!" Everyone reacted with shock and laughter. She herself was surprised at what she had said. She crashed into her girl-friend's arms, covered her head and laughed. Hannibal laughed as well as he drove away.

That was crazy. I want you to be my baby daddy. The words still sung in Hannibal's thoughts. The girl could not have been more than fourteen; still, she was already well developed. He would not have been surprised if she had already started having sex. He would have expected her to: She, who didn't want him to be her boyfriend or her husband, but rather her baby daddy, wanting him to lay with her, breed her and then leave her with child. Her comment made Hannibal smile, and a bit curious. But he quickly threw such thoughts away. He knew too well that a miscellaneous tryst, in a pubescent playground, had been known to cost men far more than spent seed.

"Y'know, I don't think that I'll ever get tired of this," he said to Mook, who sat in the passenger seat.

"Tired of what? The money, I hear that," Mook flatly replied.

"Naw. I'm not just talking about the money. I'm talking about this: niggas playing yo' music on the street, chasing you down the block. All this."

"So it's the attention you love."

"Shit sure as hell beats slinging rocks, don't it?"

"Well, I guess that's all on how you see shit."

"And how do you see shit?"

"It's all the same shit to me."

"You know what, I ain't got time for your negativity right now."

To tune Mook out, Hannibal switched on the radio. It was 4:30. DJ RA would be into his second segment on HRU. He turned it up to hear the God of hip-hop radio speak.

"All right y'all, you heard it here. Off of ma new hot joint, *Wicked Mixes Vol. 3*. That was 'Hannibal and Flawless: Crown Criminals.' Everybody holla back and let me know what you think. But right now, to talk about this and a lot more, we are honored, we got ma man Flawless in the house."

"Interesting," Hannibal responded. He hadn't heard Flawless's voice or anything else about him since the *Source* Awards. They didn't even meet together to do the single. Flawless did his verses in his own studio and likewise Hannibal did his. However, it was not only Hannibal who had not heard from Flawless. No one outside of his immediate circle had. Hannibal was curious to hear what the newborn recluse was going to say.

"Yo, Flaw, what's going on?"

"Nothin' and everything, man. I'm just here," Flawless calmly replied.

"Just played that new joint with you and Bull. An' like I told you before, the track's bananas, the production is off the chains; it's tough, it's tough."

"Well, Noah is the beats man, an' he did his thing again." Flawless was speaking with an almost lifeless stillness.

"That he did. But it ain't the production alone. The flows, man, the flows. It's too much. You and Bull, the styles mixing like salt and pepper. I don't know what could be better. Now, Flaw, I gotta know how was it working with the main cannibal himself?"

"It was cool. It was cool."

RA, knowing that controversy was a good brew for ratings, went for the jugular. "Aw'ight, aw'ight. Now, you know that there is a big debate goin' as to who ate who on this track. How you weigh in on this, if you even do?"

"Well, I'm not going to get into that. I don't feel I need to state the obvious."

"Oh, so it's like that," RA added.

"Just like that."

"You hear this nigga right here?" Mook commented to Hannibal.

"Yeah, I hear him," Hannibal replied calmly, while he continued to listen.

"So god, if I hear you right, if you and Bull was to have a battle, you sayin' . . ." RA continued to try to get fuel to the fire.

"Well, you already know what I'm saying. And as for a battle, we already did that, and we already know who won. I mean, cat's respectable an' all. In fact, he is one of the few I do respect out there but he ain't par to me. I can't see anyone who is par to me in this game right now. I think I might have to battle myself or die and go to heaven and battle God to find some competition."

"Oh damn, that's cold, son. But I might have to agree with you. Even though there are a lot of hot cats in the game right now."

"I know."

"Speaking of other cats. What's all this talk going on about beefs between you and Bin Laden? I even heard something going on between you and Stalin."

"Ah, man, who you talking about? You mean, 'has-Bin' Laden." The play of words on Bin Laden's name brought forth a chuckle from RA. "Bin should keep his mind on getting his career back in check and stop worrying about me. As for Stalin, I have nothing with the guy. So why he is choosing to call my name out in his freestyles, I don't know. And speaking of meetings, Bin don't want me to talk about when I first met him."

"Do tell, do tell," RA urged, seeing a bonfire on the horizon.

"Naw. It's not necessary. I'm just gon' keep that between me and him for now."

"Well, you know, sometimes the speculatin' mind can be even more damaging."

"I know, I know. That's why I'm gon' leave it like that."

"I hear you, god, I hear you. Ma man Flawless laying down the law. But tell me, can we expect to hear you laying any of this down on wax?"

"I don't see it. That's not where my mind is right now. Right now I'm on some outta-this-world, next-level *beep*. I'm doing things that right now I don't think I can put out for at least another five years. I don't think y'all are ready for these thoughts yet. And you know, anything can happen, but me coming back is what they want. When you on top, everyone wanna pop shots at you. They wanna knock you down, to bring themselves up. But every knock is a boost, y'know what I'm saying."

"Yo, I'm right here loving all of it. I hear you, and you right, you at the mountaintop right now, you king of New York. But I don't wanna be waitin' five years to hear the new joints."

"Well you won't have to. The new LP is coming out in about three months."

"Can't wait. It's gonna be just like the first?" RA asked.

"Way better than. This is all about evolution. I have been doing a lot of writing in the past few months. I have been literally living in the studio. I have enough material for about nine albums."

"Whoa, you killing it. So what you did? You just narrowed it down to the fifteen hottest?"

"Well, naw. For one, there're gonna be thirteen, just because I think that's a lucky number. And secondly they're all hot, every one. These are just the thirteen that I believe the people will best be able to handle coming from me at this time."

"Stop it, man. You teasing me and getting me wet, now I'm dying to hear it. But now, quickly before I let you go. Since you're now such an evolved man, I wanna get your take on the current state of hip-hop. What you feel is coming out of the different coasts? What you feel about white rappers? Are they a trend or are they here to stay? You know, stuff like that. I just wanna hear your thoughts. I wanna hear you."

Flawless could tell that RA only wanted to pull him into something sticky but he didn't care. He didn't care about a lot of things these days. He was speaking his mind without thoughts of repercussions. "Well, I think that there isn't anyone out there who can argue that hip-hop is an East Coast invention, and for the most part the East Coast has been the vanguard of the movement. Now, I'm not only saying this because I am from New York. This is just what's real."

The bonfire was beginning to blaze and RA wanted to make sure that it stayed fed. "So whatchu sayin', is there any work from the other regions you respect?"

"Well, now when we speak of other regions, we are mainly just talking about the South and the West. And for each of them there is some decent stuff that is put out. But to be honest, most of it is garbage. For the West to survive they had to import East Coast rappers so you don't even know what their sound is now. And I feel that most of the South just does what the East does, with all of this bling-bling an' *beep,* but only they do it worst."

"Now, with the South, are you talkin' 'bout cats like Lil' Hitler and the Gestapo?"

Lil' Hitler was the king of down south rap at the time.

"I'm not into naming names but we all know the sound, and I think it's sad because there is some real talent in the South. Only thing is it's underground. That's how it usually goes. It is sad but most of the mainstream stuff is garbage."

"Well, y'know, you sell over ten million records and you are considered mainstream."

"I know, that's why I said most."

"Now, what you feel about this whole thing of every producer getting themselves a white rapper?"

"Well, as for me, if you can write and you can flow I'm gonna listen to you, regardless of whatever. Now, out of all of them there is only one wit' some real profound talent, an' I don't think that anybody can deny that. Most of the others are . . . all right. Let's be real about it. And now all of them are being blown up because they're white. I mean, a white cat only has to be as good as the average black rapper in order to get respect. I think that cats readily give them props because they are surprised that it is a white cat who's just flowing decently. Now, is it a trend? I hope that it only is. Because forgetting all of this reverse racism bull, I don't wanna see hip-hop turn out like rock'n'roll. If you don't watch out, it could get so bad that the next generation of black kids won't even see it as black music anymore."

"Whoa, Flaw. I'm blown away, man. I am sensing a change in you. I have never heard you speak so open before. You dropping dimes on me here."

"Like I said, man, it's all about evolution. We all gotta grow. And we gotta see the big picture." After Flawless said this, Hannibal, listening in, felt as if his words were coming out of Flawless's mouth. "There are a lot of things going on in the world beyond cars, girls and ice. I mean, ma man Mumia is still on death row right now for something everyone knows he didn't commit. Then we look at cats like Rap Brown and Peltier. Now, speaking of prison, there are too many of us in there and we just keep on filling it up more and more everyday. Africa is dying of AIDS, cops are gunning us down and getting away with it, and religion got people all messed up all over, fighting over terrorism. It is the same old story: the innocent die so that the innocent have to suffer. And America is quick to go on a crusade fighting terrorism all over the world, talkin' about an evil empire, when this is the real evil empire. Why doesn't it fight terrorism right here? An' I'm talkin' about the

Klan, in and out of uniforms, and its centuries of terrorizing black people. But people don't wanna talk about that. Naw, naw. They shut their brains off as soon as you mention it. Same way they don't wanna talk about reparations. I mean, every other people have gotten it, from the Jews to the Japanese to even the Native Americans to a degree. When is it gon' be our turn? We been suffering for too long, for too little. Things gotta change and we gotta talk about it. We just gotta speak, man."

After Flawless's speech, RA was truly taken in. He had been probing him but he hadn't expected to get all of that. Most rappers at the time never spoke on issues. Those who did were not in heavy rotation. RA was impressed and a bit scared, his ebullience tamed; a part of him wanted to get Flawless off the air as soon as possible. "I hear you, brother. You talking about some real issues right there."

"The thing about all this is, some already have, but one day history books will be written about this movement, about hip-hop and its key players. Now, the thing is, how will you be remembered? Will you only be a footnote or will you get a chapter? That is something every cat has to think about before he picks up the mic. Me, I will be a chapter. I have no doubt about that. I will even have books of my own. Even if I am the one who has to write them."

"So you sayin' that years from now cats gon' be studying hip-hop in schools?"

"Exactly, just like Shakespeare. Studying the rhymes for lifetimes."

"And when it is all said and done, what will you be in all of this?"

"Well, I don't know. I guess you can say that I am the Michael Jackson of this."

The response surprised RA as an extremely odd thing to say. "Michael Jackson? I don't get it. What you sayin', god, you pop?" he asked.

"Naw, man. I'm king. And there ain't no Bull about that."

"I hear you, Flaw, I hear you. And as my engineer is telling me that we went over time, I gotta go. But Flaw, ma man, thanks for coming in. This was a great interview. I can't wait to do it again."

"Yeah, RA, it was cool. Thanks for having me."

"Always, Flaw, always. Now we gotta take a break. This is RA, y'all, HRU, y'all, I'll see y'all in a few."

Hannibal turned off the radio.

"Now, ain't that something," Mook remarked. " 'There ain't no Bull about that.' " Flawless's last statement was a definite jab to Hannibal. Mook didn't have to repeat it. Hannibal had heard it and it was now seething in his thoughts, along with the other interjected seeds. He drove forward in silence.

"Cat's calling for some shit," Hannibal said after a minute. "Let's see if he can handle it."

Flawless left the studios of WHRU and stepped into the oppressive heat. He couldn't wait to get into his limo; still, there was a group of about thirty fans that had bore the intense humidity in order to see him. Flawless decided to sign a few autographs before leaving. Among them, Flawless took note of a man who appeared to be his peer in many ways approaching him, wearing a brightly crimson-colored shirt and dirty blue jeans.

"Yo, Flaw, I'm seriously a fan. I don't want a 'graph, man; can I just get a pound?" he asked. Flawless agreed to the request and the two came together. In the midst of the embrace his peer impressed himself closer than Flawless would have liked and brought his mouth directly to Flawless's ear, where he then whispered: "Tell me, Flawless, are you now, or have you ever been a terrorist?"

At hearing this, Flawless quickly broke loose of the hold. To that, his peer remarked with a smile. "I'm just playing with you, man." It all seemed too weird and Flawless all at once felt unsafe. He got into the limo and as it was driving off, his peer shouted, "Words are a very powerful thing. You should be careful how you use them. Never know what you might create."

TWENTY-FOUR

Flawless stood in Jennessy's office, arms folded behind him, looking out at the New York City evening skyline; it had a tinge of fuchsia. There was a sea of buildings as far as the eye could fathom. And there in the center, like the eye of a whirlpool, there was a vacuum. A white hole where towering citadels of steel and capitalism once stood.

Like an eparch, Flawless imbibed all of this from on top of the Seventy-second Street floor, mumbling the words, *Take over the world.*

"So what's the deal, Flawless? You called this meeting," Jennessy called from behind his desk. Flawless did not respond as he continued to stare out into oblivion.

"Flawless, anytime now?"

"Take over the world, that's what I was supposed to do, right?"

"Some would say that you already have," Jennessy replied. "Like the new look, by the way." Jennessy made a terse reference to the change in Flawless' appearance. In the past few months he had allowed his hair to grow and was now showing the signs of locking. Also gone was his clean-cut image. He had developed a slight afternoon shadow. He carried himself very well but was no longer overly particular about his appearance.

"No, but I thought that I was edging close though. And then I looked at my bank account for the first time in a year and saw that even though I had sold close to eleven million records, going the way I was going, in nine months I would be bankrupt. To say the least, I was . . . *perturbed*. And then I looked at my contract and I knew why. You fucked me, Jennessy. I only got fifteen cents off of every album, you're taking fifty percent of my publishing and I have no rights whatsoever to my masters. I have earned you millions and I have made shit in respect . . . and I'm still under contract for seven more records. I feel like a slave."

From the moment Flawless had signed the deal he wanted to put it behind him. Over the two years the money was flowing in, more than he could have imagined. Everything was being paid for, so he paid no mind to how it was coming and how much of a lot he should have been getting. Even after he had spoken to Bin Laden, he still was not inspired to investigate matters. It was his accountant who informed him of the potential situation. Looking at the units he had moved, he thought it was impossible. Then he finally read the ten-page document; he was almost brought to tears at what he had signed.

"Always dramatic, aren't you, Flawless?" Jennessy remarked.

"I wish that it was a drama."

"But it is not. It is reality . . . and in reality, you did not make 'shit'—you have made millions."

"And you have made hundreds of millions. On my work."

"That's the business. You made millions and you spent millions. The promotions behind you didn't come cheap. Every top ten single you had cost about a million dollars to get. DJs aren't free; you think in the beginning they were all playing your music off the bat because of your charm? Then look at your three big-budget videos, all of the promotional events. It all cost and it is all recoupable. And quiet as it is kept, you did not sell close to eleven million records. In truth, you sold close to ten-point-five. Crown bought your first gold plaque. It is not a common practice and just about never done for a new artist. But I had faith in you and I know people. I knew that all your album needed was an initial boost and it would sell tenfold. And I was right, it did."

The words struck Flawless deeply. Selling platinum in a week was to him one of his greatest accomplishments. He remembered just how happy he had been when he saw the mounted platinum plaque with his name on it. It was a stab to his heart to know that all that wasn't real. What was real anymore?

"Then look at the house you've bought, look at all of your cars, your limo rides, your five-thousand-dollar-a-night hotel rooms and all the parties. All of it adds up, Flawless."

Flawless remained silent; as much as he hated it, much of what Jennessy said made sense. The Bergen County house he bought had cost him a little over two million. It took another $100,000 to have it furnished and set up properly. The kitchen had been redone with furniture-grade cabinetry, all to his mother's specifications. His mother didn't even cook anymore. Then there were the seven cars that he had. He couldn't drive any of them. People had to drive him around. When they couldn't, he took the limo. He never learned how to drive when he was younger; poverty and lack of opportunity prohibited him from learning, and when he did have the opportunity, he felt that he was too old and would be too embarrassed to make the attempt. Now it seemed that he had only bought the cars in an attempt to fill his nine-car garage. He had been fickle with his fortunes.

"As much as you would like to demonize me, the truth is, the deal I gave you was the standard. It is more favorable toward the label because with a new artist, there are no guarantees on anything. It costs a lot to break a new artist into the industry. All of the hype created behind you costs. I am sorry but we have to protect our investments."

"Protecting your investment, that's what you call taking fifty percent of my publishing? You're not supposed to have any rights to that. I never sold it to you."

"Well, yeah, yeah. But that's business. But I am not insensitive to your plight. You're one of the biggest-selling artists in the world right now. We know that you're going to sell. I don't see why we can't work out a more favorable arrangement."

"Really," Flawless replied tersely.

Jennessy walked over to him and placed his hand on his shoulder. "Really, Flawless, you are not just an artist to me. You're like a son." Flawless couldn't contain himself; he had to laugh. Jennessy's bullshit was too much. Jennessy, like all murine creatures, had a pliable vertebrae, which allowed him to squeeze in and out of situations. "Have I not done for you all that I said that I would? Done more for you than all the others, cared for you more. I made you number one."

"Yeah, you did that for Bin Laden and Bull as well."

"Bin Laden!" Jennessy said his name with contempt. "Don't even talk to me about that nig—" He swallowed the last word before spitting it out, corrected himself, and then continued, ". . . Don't talk to me about that guy. You know what he did? You had a problem with your contract so you came to me and spoke with civility. We spoke like men and like men we are going to work things out. This guy barged into my office with fifteen other . . . guys, all pointing guns at me. NYPD had to come and take them out. That's Bin Laden for you. That's why his career is the way it is right now. And that's why 'star or no star,' everybody gets run through security downstairs now before they come up."

The anecdote was amusing. Flawless could literally imagine Bin Laden doing that. In truth, if he were a man of the gun, he would have been inclined to do the same.

"As for Bull, that was all business. I couldn't care less what happens to him. He was never my top priority. You are."

"Whatever, Jennessy."

"You don't believe me. Well, all right, this is what I am going to do for you. You wanna make money. Do what everybody else does. Tour, and tour heavy, more than you have.

You're commanding one hundred thousand dollars a gig, at least."

"I know this, Jennessy. What new thing are you doing for me?"

"Well, this is it. I will work out a deal with you. I'll sell you your album for only five dollars per unit. You can then sell those at your shows for whatever you want. You can sell it for fifteen, even twenty. If you presign all of them, you could probably sell them for thirty. You'll make a healthy profit."

"You want me to buy my own work from you," Flawless remarked. The thought of it was abhorrent to the core. Was this his only choice? Was the business that dirty? Unbeknownst to Flawless, Jennessy was being dirtier. It was his plan to sell the records to Flawless independent of Crown's knowledge and embezzle the monies straight to his bank account.

"Hey, Flaw, it's a good deal, man. And your new album is coming out soon." There was a break in Jennessy's speech, an uncomfortable pause, as he allowed his proposal to simmer for a minute.

"Oh yeah, there is also something else I meant to talk to you about," Jennessy said, breaking the silence.

"What's that?" Flawless asked.

"It's nothing big; nothing at all. It's just a little thing about some of your word choices on the new album."

"Word choices? What do you mean?"

"Well, up in marketing, some people believe that some of the things that you have said, might be construed as being . . . insensitive . . . to certain people."

"Insensitive? What the hell are you talkin' about? This is hip-hop; we all but fucking invented the parental advisory sticker." Flawless was now confused as to what Jennessy was getting at; he wanted clarity. "Spit out what you're saying Jennessy."

"Well, blatantly put: you used the word *kike* or derogatorily made references to Jews about seven times in the album and we need you to change it."

"Are you fucking kidding me?" Flawless retorted in disbelief.

"No," Jennessy calmly replied.

"Because I used the word *kike?*"

"Yes."

"Jennessy, I must have used *nigga* like a hundred times."

"We didn't count. But you could have."

"I even used *cracker* a couple of times."

"Twelve, to be exact. We didn't like it but that can pass."

"This is bullshit, Jennessy; this is fucking bullshit. Fuck them. I ain't changin' shit."

"Flawless, listen to me." Jennessy then placed his hand on Flawless's shoulder and in a fatherly way looked him directly in the eye. "You have to learn to see the big picture in this. You're not rapping on the street corner anymore. This is the big time. You're selling millions of records. Things are run differently at this level. Do you think that if you were some low-level rapper, who's barely begging to go gold, that I wouldn't care less what you say: cracker, kike, spick, chink, turban head, faggot, bitch, whore; whatever, who cares. Trust me, I wouldn't give a fuck. But you are not, Flawless. You are who you are. You are who we made you. Trust me, Flawless, you're a creative guy, this is just a small thing to change that will save you a big headache. Change it."

"I don't give a fuck, Jennessy. I'm not changin' it. If they don't care about me changing anything else, fuck 'em." Flawless asserted.

"All right, all right; fuck 'em. No stress. I'll leave you to think about it. But remember this. I'm not the one who took the sting out of the word. You did that; it's not an accident that that word is the most commonly repeated in your album." There was another uncomfortable pause between the two, at which time Jennessy felt it best to change the subject completely. "Tell me, did you look at the latest *XXL?*"

"No."

"You should, there is an article on Bull in it."

"So."

"Well, he had some very interesting things to say about you in it."

Jennessy walked back to his desk, picked up the issue of *XXL*, flipped it to the article in question and handed it to Flawless. Flawless read a bit and then remarked:

"Is this nigga for real?"

"Apparently so. Tell me, is your album completely finished; every track is set?" Jennessy asked.

"Just about, we only need to do the photo shoot."

"Before you send it off, might I suggest one more track?"

"What do you mean?"

"Nothing new, just something in the effect of a response. As edgy as you want it, whatever you feel is appropriate; knowing you, I think that it is all going to be beautiful."

Flawless became silent. He returned to the window and again peered out into the evening sky. He knew what Jennessy meant, he knew what Hannibal had meant, he knew full well the war that was about to brew. "Beautiful."

TWENTY-FIVE

It was beautiful; it was winter in July. At least it was for Micah, as he stood there leaning over the railing at the ice skating rink at Chelsea Piers. It was an odd thing to do in the summer, but the people were trying to get a break from the heat any which way that they could. In the last month the mercury had risen to over 100 or at least the high nineties. It had become so hot that the waters at the beaches began to boil; as Micah looked across the Hudson he could see the people like the walking dead, sweltering, glowing like embers.

The skyrink was as packed as if it were the week before Christmas. There were about two hundred people on the ice at any given time and at this time Erika was one of them. Wearing cutoff denim shorts and a T-shirt, with her braids to the wind, she dallied in and out of the crowd of people with an Olympian's grace, or at the least that's how Micah saw her. He saw her and saw no one else. Engulfed in the loud music being played over the sound system, he heard nothing but the scrape of her blades on the ice. She was without a doubt, in all facets: "Beautiful, so beautiful."

> Beautiful Erika, amorous and esoteric
> Puts mind in hysterics
> Thoughts of form and flesh
> Warm to the touch

Sweet to the taste
I'd abdicate a vegan's fate
To diet on your lips
Flow with your hips
Be lost in your eclipse
Hapless in happy pursuits
Like a perfect suit we fit
An angel incarnate
Love reincarnate
Soul mate for lifetimes
Searched lifetimes for your light
Sun to my solemnity
The profundity in purpose
Makes me nervous, these thoughts of us
Emotions in green season
Beyond reasonable reason
How an arrow shot in the dark
Healed a bleeding heart
And now, whatever the weather
Be I an Arawak
Or arrogant resident
Of the equator
I'll forever equate her
With beauty, truly
Girl, be mine completely, my beautiful Erika
And here now she comes before me.

Erika cut through the traffic and slid to a halt at the railing behind which Micah stood with pen and pad, bleeding on the page until the very moment she arrived; before he could pronounce a word, she kissed him, swallowing his tongue; and their tongues danced, he could taste her taste buds, feel the pores of her speech: it was a palatable palate, coupled with her scent, he fell deep into her and didn't want to come out. But . . . eventually, like all mammals, they had to come up for air.

"What are you doing here all by yourself?" she inquired.

"Nothing, just writing about you," he replied.

Reflexively she kissed him again, not as long but just as profoundly.

"That's so sweet, can I see it?"

"Of course. I wrote it for you."

"Good, but later, okay?"

"Why?"

"Because now I want you to skate with me," she implored him with her eyes.

"Girl, you crazy. I ain't going out there."

"C'mon, *please*," she sang on the last syllable. He had told her before that he had no intentions of getting on the ice. She agreed but had also convinced him to rent blades, telling him that if he wanted to get to rink side he had to wear them. He didn't contest her point. And though he possessed no real desire to skate, he figured that sooner or later he would have found himself out there. He knew that if she had asked that he could not refuse her anything; nevertheless, he would put up the front.

"Naw, girl, I'm a black man. What I look like skating on a big block of ice?"

"Well, I'm black too. So how did I look skating?"

"You looked good but you like some kinda anomaly or something. Plus, girl, you gon' look good doing just about anything."

"You're cute. But you're wrong, it's not only me, I know a lot of black people who skate."

"Yeah, right, like who?" he asked, and gestured for her to look at their company. There were other Africans about, but they were few and far between.

"Okay, maybe this place is not a good example. But nevertheless, a lot do. I mean, Michael does."

The name Michael seemed oddly familiar. He knew he had heard it before but could not recall to whom it referred. "Who's Michael?" he asked.

"Michael, Flawless," she replied.

"Oh, oh, okay. Flawless ice skates?"

"He did up until he was fifteen."

"You have pictures of that?"

She replied with an implicit *of course* in her speech.

"Well, you better not let any of those get out."

"Why?" she asked with naïve confusion.

"Just don't."

Erika, recognizing that they had strayed from her request, began to pull him onto the ice. He reluctantly followed.

"Erika, you gon' have me fall on my ass out here in front of all of these people. Girl, I'ma thug. How's that gonna look?"

"You're not a thug," she said laughing.

"Yes, I am."

"No. If you were, I wouldn't be with you."

In her twenty-one years, from prepubescence to present, she had been courted and coveted by all makes of man, from the clown to the criminal. For her it was a daily annoyance to be propositioned at least ten times. This was so, in whatever the weather and whether her garb was loose or form fitted. The thug for the most part tended to be the grossest offender and over the years she had grown an aversion to the wannabe criminal bravado.

"Micah, guess what," she said to him.

"What?"

"You're skating."

Micah looked down and realized that they were in the center of the ice.

"What do you say to that now, black man?"

"Oh shit," he blurted. At the recognition he instantly lost governance of his legs. He fell to the ice, taking Erika with him. It reminded him of when he was younger when his uncle had first taught him to ride a bicycle, how he had duped him into riding by himself. He had ridden an entire block thinking that his uncle balanced his steering from behind. When he finally gave in and looked back, he saw his uncle as a shadowy figure fading away into the distance. The consciousness of solitude hit and he fell instantly. This experience engendered the same feeling. Only this was much better. Erika fell on top; her chest impressed itself upon him.

He thought to apologize but he couldn't get a word in past her laughter. With her smile, the light shining from above created an aura about her. On the cold ice, in the hot summer, she appeared angelic; she spoke heavenly, "Oh, I love you, Micah," which she uttered without forethought.

They were both silent at the realization of what was said. They had been talking to each other almost every day ever since they had met. They had, however, seen each other rarely. She was in school and he had been on tour with Hannibal. Now the tour had ended, her semester complete, and they had spent the last three days together. They were aware that their attraction was more profound than lustful. Until now no one had uttered it but they had both played with the emotion in their thoughts.

Micah needed to know if she had meant what she had said or if it was just the unfortunate byproduct of gaiety. "Say that again?" he asked her. Erika licked her lips and considered the gravity of what she was about to say, twice. Did she truly mean it? "I love you, Micah." The words came out before she could have answered the question. As soon as the words left her lungs, she knew them to be true. And before he could respond she kissed him, softly and with her entire being.

She kissed him because in a way she didn't want to hear his response. To hear him say he loved her as well would have been English's sweetest pronouncement. But to hear differently or, even worse, to hear the dead silence as he thought of a considerate rejection, that would have been a lifelong torture. Ignorance was bliss, so she kissed him and remained blissful. But if she listened keenly, she would have been able to feel his love in his touch as they embraced each other freely on the cold ice, in the hot summer, with two hundred people skating around them, in a haze of purple.

TWENTY-SIX

The room was nice. It was far from being the presidential suite but nice nonetheless. It was sufficient and seeing her in it now only went to expand its proportions. She stood there before him both wanting and nervous, not wanting to show the latter. It was now the latter of that hot summer day, which was an untamed hot summer night. The AC did much to cool the room but not their temperament. Their natures rose higher than the mercury. They knew why they'd come here.

His eyes guided him to her lips. His right hand with inadvertent purpose found her respective breast. The supple was divine as he massaged gently around the fabric. When he had gotten mind of his will, he began to will his hand away; she, however, placed her hand before it and fastened it to its place. It sank deeper in and arched her disposition. Their nerves eased and they fell into each other.

Within minutes and pauses in their kissing, they had disrobed. They embraced each other standing bare flesh to flesh. They maneuvered themselves until the back of her knee aligned itself with the bed's edge. They fell over, he on top of her, her legs naturally opening, inviting him in. Then he paused in his approach and pulled away from her. She reacted longingly, not wanting to let him go. But he raised himself regardless, to her confusion.

"What's wrong?" she asked.

"Nothing," he replied. "I just wanted to look at you."

He had always admired her figure and fantasized about its naked form. He could not help himself now. He had to look. For a moment she felt like a specimen on a petri dish. Modesty made her feel to take cover. It was not that she had a low esteem when it came to her body. She rather liked her frame; still, there were things that she perceived as faults that were a persistent irritant to her quietude. She pondered all of this now as his eyes surfed her surface. It terrified her almost. His opinion mattered too much.

"Girl, you are beyond a doubt the most beautiful thing I have ever seen."

She saw the love and the sincerity in his eyes and lost all thoughts of faults and stretch marks. Now she liked the way he looked at her. She never wanted him to stop. He could feel the humidity thicken between her thighs; he knew that she was ready. He began to better position himself for his approach and then she stopped him.

"Micah, I have something to tell you," she quietly stated.

"What?"

"Um . . . it's my first time."

"Yeah?"

Her pronouncement pulled him back a bit. It was surprising to him but not disbelievingly so. She was twenty-one and had never committed her heart or her body to another before. She had been with others but she had always stopped them whenever desires extended beyond fondling. She now had no thoughts to stop Micah. She wanted him, wanted him to be her first, and wanted him to know so.

"Yeah. Are you scared?" she asked, somewhat on edge at his response.

"Why would I be?"

"Well, you know how we virgins get: Always remember the first; I'm gonna love you forever now."

She was truly terrified as to what his response would be.

Micah himself was not a virgin and had not been for a long time. He didn't date virgins, for the very same reason she'd said. But Erika was a thing of another matter. He felt honored that he would be her first.

"I love you, Erika," he said; the words she was so afraid not to hear before.

"I love you too, Micah," she replied, not being able to hold back her tears.

"Well, then . . . I guess we are both virgins."

With that, he entered her and felt as if he had dived into the deepest ocean cavern. He drowned himself in her being, losing himself in her sweet profound, fitting to her like a hand to a glove; her body, calling to him, clinging tightly to him, sweating with him, breathing him in, never wanting to let him go.

TWENTY-SEVEN

She sat on the bed's edge. He sat on the floor with his head set between open thighs. It was a pleasurable experience for both parties. She was braiding his hair, cornrowing the year's worth that he had accumulated. She was half-done and half of his hair stuck out liberated.

They sat there watching the television. Micah scanned through channels during the intervals of hollering. Erika had to comb out the kinks and locks that had grown into his hair. Most times she tried to be gentle, though she at times would tug on it a bit more forcefully, just so that she could laugh at his grimace. He was cute. If this was how love truly felt, she now knew why all of those love songs were written.

He lay his head affectionately by her exposed knee, taking in the sweetest of her smell. The lotion she wore had the scent of apples. It made him want to bite into her, again. He fell in love with the smell as he had fallen in love with the woman.

"This is so funny," she said.

"What?" he remarked.

"The only other person I have ever done this for is my brother."

"Yeah, that's cool. You still do?"

"No, I can't. He's been locking his hair lately."

"Flawless, really?" he remarked with surprise. Flawless had always seemed to be the perennial pretty boy. It would be hard to see him with locks. He began to wonder how he himself would look with his hair twisted.

"Yeah, I know, it surprised me too, but he has been going through some changes lately. Y'know, you kinda remind me of him."

"In what way?" he asked.

"In your styles; the way you carry yourselves, the way you write. You know, in just ways I can't really explain."

"Well, as long as you don't think of me as a brother, we're okay. So the two of you are close?" He already knew the answer to this. He could tell from the fact that she always spoke his name with fondness and so often. As he thought of it, he didn't think that they had gone through a single conversation where his name didn't come up once. Sometimes he felt as if Flawless was the other man in the relationship.

"Yes, very," she answered. "Only we've been arguing a lot lately."

"About what?"

"You, mainly."

"Me? Why?"

"Doesn't think that we should be together. Something about you and Bull."

Now the trinity had turned into a quadity: Micah was completely confused. He knew that there was something between Hannibal and Flawless, but he didn't know much about the relationship. Being new to the family, he didn't feel it was his place to ask. Now that it concerned Erika and himself, he felt he needed to know.

"What about Bull?" he inquired.

"Where to begin." The legacy of Flawless and Hannibal had been going on for so long now. It had only been five years but it seemed like lifetimes. "He and Michael have been battling for years. It was always a big thing on the streets whenever they battled. Kids used to be talking about it in schools for weeks afterward. Most times Michael won but it was always a battle. And

Bull always came back. Each of them has been trying to get past the other. Michael thought he did that when he won the championship battle. But then Bull came out and got a deal too. And now it seems like the whole thing is starting up again."

"So what does that have to do with me?"

"Well, he doesn't like Bull or anyone with him. But it's not that. He doesn't like seeing me with any guy. He is really protective. Always been like that. It's getting on my nerves."

Micah had known stories about overprotective older brothers. Ofttimes they were more fanatical than fathers. He had been fortunate that most of the women he had dealt with before were older than him by one or two years; they had all already gone through their battles with siblings and parents. He was curious of this thing called the older brother. He was the second to last child of four. He had a younger brother and two older sisters. The disparities in their ages were so great that he didn't know if he was to be the brute when potential suitors came to the door with erections beckoning. Also they were his family but he wasn't that close to them; there was a distance, it was almost as if he didn't even know them at all. They were just there, it seemed, to pretty the picture. So he had to ask, "Why do you think that he's like that?"

"Well, growing up, we only really had each other. He had to protect me. He just can't see that I am not a little girl anymore. Sounds like a dad, doesn't he?"

"That and something else." Their relationship seemed sweet, though he didn't know that many brothers and sisters who were close. He always seemed to argue with his, but perhaps that was wrong.

"Yeah, but y'know, for all his shit, I still love him to death."

"And he loves you," Micah remarked. "Everybody loves Erika."

"Do you love me?" Erika asked. She had heard him say it earlier. It gave her such a high that like an addict, she craved to hear it again.

"Girl, I love you beyond," he replied, glad to see the conversation brought back to its focus. He had begun to grow sick of all of the talk of Flawless. He was feeling jealous of their relationship. He knew it seemed ill conceived but he couldn't deal with the fact that someone else was that close to her, even if it was her brother.

"You know, for a long time, I would walk by and see couples together, see them happy, and I wanted that for myself. Y'know, I have been with girls before. But it was never profound, never meaningful. So even when I was with someone, I always felt alone. So then I started talking to the Creator, and I would say: 'Give her to me, just give her to me.' Let me feel that thing that others do. But then I stopped saying it because sometimes it sounded like I was saying: 'Give hurt to me.' And you know what they say about being careful what you wish for; because sometimes you can bring things to life without even knowing it and when it comes to you, you might actually hate it. And so I stopped wishing. And then one day, I saw this beautiful girl in a crowd and she made everything else disappear."

"That's me, right?" Erika cut into his intimation with humor. She was smiling and overflowing inside to hear him express the thoughts that she had for so long harbored. To have a dream come true was all too beautiful.

"Yeah, that's you," Micah replied. "And you know, I knew then that the wish had come true. I just don't know which one." Micah knew that he loved her. He knew this because if the condom had popped and she was for some reason to become fat with his child, he knew that he would be happy. He had never thought that of any other woman before. With everyone else he had been overprotective of his sperm. He had always had the fear of getting the wrong girl pregnant. He knew that beyond a wedding, childbirth was truly when marriage began. With everyone else, the prospect terrified him but not with Erika.

"I could never hurt you, Micah." Her voice came through

his thoughts. "I could never, because I have had the same wish for a long time now. But I wasn't sure if those things were real. But you have made me a believer." She then leaned over and kissed him and knew why she had waited all of these years. For a long time she thought it to be excessive. All of her girlfriends had long since given in to the invasion. Many times she had thought to let it go capriciously as well. She now knew that everything was right. She truly loved this man that she kissed, and he had kissed all of her lips with kind emotions. He had been gentle; even though it had hurt at times, she could not help but to pull him in, deeper and deeper. It was a symbiotic experience. They were in unison: with breast to chest, pelvis to waist, nails to back, hands to ass, face-to-face and tears in her eyes; now she recognized that she had been incomplete for the first half of her life. At the realization she finally felt whole. "Hold me, Micah. Don't let go. Just hold me, never let go."

TWENTY-EiGHT

Flawless stood outside of the hard oak door and knocked softly. As he waited he admired the quality and texture of the wood. It was pure and it had been expensive. Everything in this house was. Two years ago, things he would have thought of flittingly now irritated him. He didn't need all of this. It had to stop. Then again, he knew that if she had asked, he could not refuse her anything. He knocked again and again there had been no response. Perhaps she was sleeping. He called a bit harder this time. The extra force opened the door. Her bed was empty. Erika was not in.

He walked inside and admired the splendor of her room. He remembered how it was when he first bought the nine-bedroom house. How happy she had been when she picked this room for herself. She had hugged him with pride. He would never forget how she looked at him. They rarely looked at each other anymore. In the past few months, since the night the visions first came, they had rarely spoken. This had never happened before. Before they could have only gone simple hours without speaking to each other. Now they had grown up and things had changed. He came to speak to her tonight; about what, he didn't know.

He was about to leave but then something drew him to sit by her mirror. It was an old browning picture of the two of them when they were younger: he was twelve, she was eight, with her head to his stomach and her arms wrapped tightly around his waist. He looked at it and began to smile. He was surprised that she had it out where she was forced to see it everyday. He then looked up to see a woman's reflection in the mirror. Erika, he thought. "Erika," he said; he turned around to face her and saw that he was wrong.

"It's me, Michael," Trish replied, feeling somewhat disappointed that he thought she was someone else.

"Hey, how are you doing?" he said to her, feeling disappointed that she wasn't someone else.

"Nothing, as usual, just looking for you."

"I was just looking at this picture of us when we were younger."

She walked over to him, wearing a fuchsia tank top over her blue jeans, and examined the photo. "It's beautiful," she said. "You were so cute when you were younger."

"We both were. Things were harder but seemed so much simpler then."

"They always are."

"Yep. You know, I remember when we were younger and Erika was learning to talk, how she had a hard time pronouncing my name. It was cute; she could never pronounce the 'el.' I used to love the way she said it though. I remember it still. Hmmm, it makes me think. 'El' means God and I got mic in my name: I guess I was born to rhyme."

"You really love your sister, don't you, Michael?"

"Of course, shouldn't I?"

"Of course . . . of course."

"Y'know, my father left us when we were real young and my mom had to work two jobs at a time sometimes. So we just basically had each other. We had to take care of each other."

"Why did your father leave?"

"I guess for the same reason why all other men leave." There was a break in his speech; and then he continued, "Y'know, he did stuff, and Mom told him to leave." The vagueness of the response made Trish want to question more. Then she realized that he had been vague on purpose.

"What would you do if you saw him now?" she asked.

"I don't know . . . I'd probably kill him," he said flatly, without any change in inflection and then remained quiet, making it seem as if it would be odd if she reacted. So she didn't react to that statement. She waited a moment and then she reacted to another.

"You know, Erika is grown, Michael. You don't have to take care of her anymore."

"Yeah, that's what they all say. And what about me?"

"Let me take care of you."

"You want to?" he asked.

"I would love to," she replied.

Ever since the night the visions came there had been a chasm between them. He still had not explained it all to her and she had gotten tired of asking. Now she was tired of the distance. He was changing. He was going through something and he wouldn't tell her any of it. In fact, they didn't really speak anymore. When they did, it was always miscellaneous discourse, nothing profound. That was one of the things she loved most about him. They used to be able to speak on everything from philosophy to hip-hop. She confided in him more than she had ever done with anyone else. She now felt as if she was losing her best friend.

She walked over and stood directly in front of him. He pulled her close and planted his head into her stomach; it felt good, feeling his breath on her navel.

"What are we waiting for, Michael? It has been over two years. Let's get married." Fearing rejection, she had not brought this issue up in over a year. But it had now been two years and she was twenty-seven to his twenty-five. She was two years older and three years closer to thirty. And if there was ever a number that forever represented adulthood, it was thirty. The prospect of it scared her. She needed to move on with her life. Just shacking up wasn't cool anymore. She wanted to start having children. Though they made love without hindrance, Flawless was always in the practice of pulling out. She hated it. She wanted him to stay inside of her. She would always hope that he would lose his guard and fully give in. Many times, though she knew very well that it didn't work that way, she would ingest him, just so that a bit of him would fester longer inside. Perhaps through osmosis one of them would find their way to the Promised Land.

Flawless looked up at her with his chin in her stomach. "What's the rush?" he plainly asked.

Trish, not believing that he was still using a year-old argument, had to restrain her frustration. "There is no rush, but if there is love, what's the wait? Is there love, Michael?"

"There is love, but there is also confusion and strife and demons."

"When is there never confusion and strife?" she asked. She didn't understand the demons part so she paid no attention to it. But perhaps if she did, she would understand what it was that he was going through.

He saw them almost daily now. They walked with him. Many times he had to keep himself from screaming in good company. Surprisingly, he never revealed his torment though it began to puzzle him as to why he now saw the things that he saw. He saw doctors, many doctors. He took a thorough eye exam, a spinal tap, full blood work, an MRI and a CAT scan. The doctors all thought this to be gross excess. Time and time again, everything came back fine. He had twenty/twenty vision and was as healthy as an ox. He had hoped that the doctors would have come back with some scientific malady; that perhaps he had popped an optic nerve of some sort. Anything. Let it be anything, but nothing. And so the nothing plagued him, though what he saw wasn't nothing. He was left to question, which led him to read more than he ever had, on a multitude of issues, on things that he had long since ignored, from politics to metaphysics. Nevertheless, the question persisted unanswered. Then the question brought him to other questions, and then others. Then the questions turned into words, then they began to rhyme and then he had to write. He killed a good many pens on a good many more pages. He bled and he bled and he bled. At times he would grow cuts upon his fingers and his own blood began to mix in with the solution. As it did before, DNA gave the text a special font. After he had written he knew that he had to record. He put a bed and a fridge in his home studio. He recorded with an unnatural urgency. He felt that he didn't have that much time and he was so alone. He couldn't speak to Tommy, because he would have to be soft and intimate before his boy. He wanted to talk to Erika but she was hardly ever there. For some reason he didn't want to talk to Trish. He felt as if she couldn't understand what he saw and out of love would be left to pity him. He didn't want pity. He wanted understanding. It seemed now that the demons were the only ones that did, because they were the only other ones who shared in his experience.

He could see lines floating all about Trish. They were like wavelengths moving up and down; like the cilia of a cell. Flawless thought they were the vibrations of the universe. It was the only conjecture that held reason. He felt as if they brought him closer in tune with the question. He began to appreciate them for his awakening, though it seemed no matter how far he had gotten his old self kept dragging him back.

"Have you seen the new *XXL*?" he asked her, diverting completely from their original topic. Seeing that he had done that, Trish felt that she could quarrel no more.

"Yes, I have . . . what are you going to do?" she asked disinterestedly.

"What else? Hit the wax."

"I was hoping that you might just let it go."

"You know better than that."

Trish, having been Bin Laden's publicist and then Flawless's, knew very well the etiquette of hip-hop. It was born and bred on competition.

"I know," she replied. "But I was hoping that you would let it go anyway."

"Can't. When a cat calls you out, you gotta go," he replied, sounding much like his old self again. "Otherwise niggas won't respect you anymore. And if they don't respect you, they won't listen to you. And then it's all over. He's saying I got soft. It's time I reminded these people that I got to where I am through battling. Maybe this time I will finally be able to get past Bull. I just have to tackle it, finish it and move on." This was all because of Hannibal. If it had been anyone else, he would have been more inclined to let it pass. He had let Stalin's and Bin Laden's remarks go. He was even aware that Lil' Hitler and his Gestapo were calling his name. Everyone wanted him. His new sense of being shrugged them all off. But Bull was a thug of a different matter.

"All of these thoughts toward hate; what about love?"

"What do you mean?" he asked.

"What is this thing between you and Hannibal, Michael?" This was a question that she had waited two years to ask. Now she needed to know and so he told her.

It had been six years now that Flawless had begun to etch his name in the annals of hip-hop legacy. From the beginning of the 1990s he had been a lover and a follower of hip-hop; before then he paid it little mind. He didn't like most old school rap: for him it had either been too slow or too fast, and for the most part always too simple. So unlike all of his friends at the time, he was no herald for the movement, and would have never thought then that he would be where he was now, doing what he was doing.

Then the renaissance came. There was a revolution in lyricism and flow. He became enamored with the likes of Hakim, RSK-9 and Nemisis to Society. Their wielding of the verb was beyond par. It was food for inspiration. He remembered the first day that he picked up the pen and the first time he rhymed over a beat. Something in it rang true in his soul.

He remembered the first time he battled. It was the custom for a few of the boys to hang back after school and start a cipher. Most times they just freestyled over the radio, talking about any and everything: from what was in fashion to what was in the news, a ghetto CNN of sorts. Then there were the times when they'd battled. The one who was the most apt and creative in his degradation of his opponent won. In high school, the hip-hop heads, as they were called, were a new click in and of themselves.

High school beyond all other institutions was arguably the most segmented. Just about everyone fitted into a category. There were the popular ones, more often than not the athletes and their respective cheerleaders. Then there were the so-called geeks, the ones on the debate team and the chess club, those who had valedictorian prewritten in their DNA. Then there were the loners, the ones who were either chastised or feared for their reclusivity. The majority of the student body was moderate, having the tendency to waver in and out of these categories. With the advent of hip-hop there arose a new category, being the DJs and the emcees. In the beginning there had also been the break dancers, but break dancing had begun to wane in popularity as hip-hop came into the nineties. Though as all things are cyclical, it was seeing a resurgence with the birth of the millennium. Hip-hop created a shift in the high school dynamic, because it drew its members from all different frontiers. A geek could become a well-known and respected DJ, irrespective of whether or not he could catch a basketball. If he was skilled on the ones and twos and knew how to keep the party moving, he was the man. It was the same for the emcees. It was only here where both jocks and loners were considered equals, equal until the beat came on and one of them fell victim to the word.

In high school, Flawless was average and tended toward being a loner. For weeks he would sit back and just watch them, running rhymes in his head but never spitting them out. Then measure for measure he began to edge himself closer to the circle; first as a spectator, then as an attendant, and then, before he knew it, the words were coming out. The silence and nodding of the heads confirmed to him that he was good. So good, in fact, that as soon as he had finished, one of the members unleashed a preemptory strike. He was harsh, and soon those who cheered Flawless now goaded his aggressor. Flawless thought to back down, but he knew that if he did he could never open his mouth before them again. While his consciousness debated the issue, his subconscious took over. The words began to flow freely. By the time he had taken reigns of his speech, he had won and garnered his name. "Yo, man, this kid is nice, his shit is sick. This cat's flawless," they said of him. Tommy was the first to dub him Flawless, and so they met and became instant friends. Tommy had been heralding him ever since, from street corner to street corner, to the World Trade Center, to Forty-second and Broadway, to the Spit Café. Flawless had been unparalleled, winning battle after battle. Daily he practiced on how to turn his tongue into a razor. He would cut throats and leave the membranes of the fallen as a mass of crimson pulp at his feet. He had slayed more men than had reddened the fields of Magenta. He was the king of Queens; his hegemony, however, extended beyond his borders. All of the boroughs paid homage. It was even rumored that as far away as the West, the hip-hop folk of the land sang his praises. Flawless became the underground king of New York.

Then he met Hannibal. It was at the Spit Café. Flawless saw him as he walked with a phalanx of sixteen. He could smell the criminal on his brow. He had encountered many a thug who thought to put their might beyond the muzzle of their gun. Many were afraid to challenge them. The fear of repercussions bit their tongue. Flawless had no such inhibitions. The fears that he held as Michael were shorn as soon as he took the stage. Here he was truly Flawless.

Flawless grunted at Hannibal's growl-and-gravel approach to flowing; he watched as he ascended round after round with what he thought was simple rhyming, until only two were left and Hannibal did the unprecedented: he lasted three rounds until Flawless finally put him down. It was a pyrrhic victory. For the first time ever, Flawless seemed beatable. And the next time he met with Hannibal, he was beaten. The news of the king's dethronement echoed throughout all of the hollows of the hip-hop underground. With one defeat, in one moment, Flawless went from king to jester. Those who he had done away with easily now looked back at him with mockery. All did, save for Tommy. This was why to this day Tommy was still his only true friend.

Flawless would meet Hannibal again, this time as a challenger. As before they had been the only ones to ascend to the final round, and again it was a battle. This time Flawless was the winner. And he would continue to win, for eight other meetings. And it seemed it had taken him that many times to regain what he had lost. But then on the tenth, Hannibal came back, and he had to rebuild all over again. So it went. Flawless would win the lion's share but Hannibal was always there to filibuster his reign.

Throughout his years performing at the Spit, he had always hoped that some agent, some producer, some executive or A&R thereof, would see him onstage, see him for his talent and present him the deal he worked so hard for. His time was coming.

Flawless moved on and had been the first since its inception to win nine battles on 106. He had been the sole member of its hall of fame until three months later, when Hannibal matched his efforts. Then there was the championship battle where he finally got the deal he had battled for years to attain. He felt as if he finally surpassed the Bull. But Hannibal kept on coming back. Now they were here and the battle had begun again.

•   •   •

Trish listened attentively to the tale and the obsession. For her, it was all nothing but testicular tongue play.

"I won't wait in the wind forever, Michael," she said to him.

"I know that you won't. I wouldn't expect you to," he replied.

"Good. At least we are on the same page with that."

TWENTY-NiNE

It was on a Thursday that Terrence, Hannibal, Mook and Reaper entered the main floor of Peaches nightclub. Peaches was a warehouse turned into a chic ultraexclusive nest bed for celebrities. In former days the club DJs played a plethora of sounds, from pop to house to techno. Now hip-hop ruled the day and likewise hip-hop acts carried the swing. They were the new rock stars.

The men of Cannibal looked about the melee and then went to the VIP section. Many were in attendance. Hannibal eyed Trujillo, a big man in the likes of Stalin, in the corner coupled with the rest of the Latin Mafia, every *papi* with a *mami* on his lap. Pinochet was across the floor sipping Cristal with Batista. All of the terrorists were there and the fans flocked about them looking for a pound, a hug, a picture or a deal. Many times they were harangued from the minute their pinky toe touched the dance floor by the starving, all hungry to flow for them. On rare occasions they acquiesced to a young'un's desires; however, they were usually shunned with an emphatic "Naw!"

Hannibal and the others took their seats amid the raucous. His reputation, as always, had preceded him. Many had known of Bull before he had even made a record. A few had put him in their rhymes. Most rappers talked crime and violence, few actually lived it to the extent that they professed. All knew the genuine article when they saw it. Given that, they paid homage to the Bull and kept their distance.

"Why we here?" Mook asked Hannibal.

"What's wrong, you don't like looking at all of this fine ass?" Terrence answered.

"Nigga, was I talking to you?" Mook snapped back. Terrence had taken up the habit of talking out of protocol. Mook noticed that Hannibal rarely checked him. He resented the fact that Terrence had been little by little edging his way into his enclave. He saw him with a bird's eye and longed to step on this worm.

"It's all part of the business," Hannibal answered. "Gotta show your face at these things, keep your name in the press." Hannibal was no media junkie but he understood the business of hype.

"Plus, besides all of the faggots, there is mad bitches in here," Reaper added.

"An' we all 'bout the bitches ain't we?" Terrence said, playing off Reaper's emotions.

"Fho sho. There ain't nothin' like a firm ass." After Reaper said this, Mook gave him a wry smile. Terrence then marked a pretty girl mere feet away.

"Yo, Reaps, see dat one over there? Damn, she look good."

"No doubt, cuz, no doubt." Although Reaper said *cuz* with a southern twang, he was as Brooklyn as the rest. His speech was due to the diffusion of down-south slang into the North, due largely to the movements of Lil' Hitler. The tiny Napoleon and his Gestapo Boyz had all but secured martial law in the South. Having saturated the southern market, he was now seeking lebensraum in the North. The proliferation of slang was the first signal of his coming.

Hannibal began to think of Micah. He wasn't there and ever since the close of the tour, he had hardly seen him. "Yo, Terrence, where is your boy?" Hannibal inquired.

"I don't know, nigga probably messing with sister again, as

usual," Terrence replied with his mind on the rear end in front of him. Terrence, like most members of an entourage, enjoyed the perks of company. Given that Hannibal found more interest in making money than in women, there was a lot of surplus to go around.

"Hmm, whatever make a nigga happy, I suppose," Hannibal commented.

"I don't like that nigga," Mook uttered, seemingly out of nowhere.

"Why the fuck not?" Terrence barked back out of his gaze.

"Same reason why I don't like you," Mook replied with an intimidating calm. It stayed Terrence for a moment. He could see a deeper brood in Mook's eyes, though he did not know that under the table Mook had taken to stroking his steel barrel and fingering the trigger. Security at these clubs was infamous for making high-profile rappers and their crews go in unchecked. And now the hard, cold steel running across Mook's fingerprints felt good as he went in and out of the hole. He teased himself, took his time, smiling all the while; he would suck of this to the fullest, not erupting prematurely. Though beyond patience, if it were not for Hannibal, he would have killed Terrence already.

"Gonna have to do better than that, Mook," Hannibal remarked, sensing something, still not knowing the extent to the evil that brewed in the man's thoughts.

Hannibal's voice calmed Mook a bit. "I don't know, I don't trust him. He ain't like us; he don't know shit about hustling."

"Well, then maybe he's exactly what we need. Help get us out of the shit we been in."

"Whatever, but I don't trust him. I don't see any good coming from this."

"Nigga, you never see any good anyway, pessimistic motherfucker!" Terrence blurted, not being able to refrain himself any longer. Mook's pessimism had been a pungent stank since the first day he met him. Why Hannibal still kept him around, he didn't know. Terrence had co-founded and helped to build Cannibal, yet Mook had the bigger title and the bigger check for doing nothing.

Terrence's words pressured Mook's blood. He massaged the barrel with rhythm. He could almost feel the taste of the coming. "I am so close, so close, nigga," he said while licking his lips in anticipation.

Terrence saw the look in his eyes. He had been on the streets long enough to know what it all meant but felt impotent. There was no metal in his waist to add weight to his argument. He had become soft in latter months. This was what happens when you live without the ever-present fear of having your brains blown back. He would not make that mistake again; for now, he had to put up the good front.

"Then bring that shit, then," he retorted.

"Shut the fuck up, both of you. Tired of your shit now!"

The respect for Hannibal's raised tenor quieted all moods. They became silent. In truth the entire club had become silent. And then it was heard:

"All right y'all, I got a gem for y'all tonight," the club DJ's voice registered crystal clear through the speakers. "Fresh off the wax, off ma man Flawless's new LP. This is it, hot like fire, 'Bullshit.' "

Hearing the title, Hannibal could only imagine what the song would be about. What played over the speakers of Peaches that night was far beyond. Flawless had hit back, or hit first, depending upon how one saw things. He stated his dominance and took Lil' Hitler down in the first verse.

This is that bombshit
To dead all that dumbshit
The shit you can't fuck wit'
Because shit comes too quick
For all you clit critics
Thinkin' Flaw got soft wit' it

Well now I'm briningin' it
For you bitches talkin' bullshit
I'm the champion of Shangri-La
Got cherubims in every corner
Shellac any challenger
Che Guevara of this motherfucker
Flaw is king
Jus' doin' ma thing
But now everyman, from China man
To chi chi man wanna chagrin
But y'all gon' grin an' bear it
'Cause I'm here to claim it
Ma style, you tame it, neva
Flo' raw forever
Ain't fettered by the feeble-minded
Neva blinded by the nearsighted
I see the future, fuck Lil' Hitler
I'm the new fuhrer
Got mo' fury than the first
Quick to put yo' ass in a hearse
'Cause I verse without rehearsal
Not kiddin', son, shit's personal
Don' doin' the dozens
'Bout puttin' characters in ovens
Built concentration camps
For all you cats in rival camps
So all who got beef wit' Flawless
'Bout's to end up in Auschwitz
Ouch it hurts, don't it
When yo' bones sear from yo' flesh
Betta steer far from the best
If you kno' what's best for you
Sling so many syllables
Leave yo' ass a vegetable
Sorry fools can't understand me

Because I stand over you
An' I'ma laugh at you
As I paralyze with parable.

Bin Laden and Stalin took theirs in the second.

"Has-been" Laden
Where you been Laden?
Bin been hidin'
Bin been laden
Bin been hidin' in caves
Bin been laid up for days
Been thought you was dead
Nigga what? Bin been afraid?
Now Bin is back
Bin in Bentleys, Bin's the mack
An' Bin's quick to draw
But Bin flow tight, hell naw!
Flippant fool, why you wanna fuck wit' Flaw
How you forget, how you
Pissed yo' drawers
When you saw me at the Source Awards
Sorry boss, but you jus' like Stalin
Big fat boss of nothing
But for grubbin'
I see you hoverin'
You want some attention
Player-hatin' so hard
You got anal retention
Though trust me on this one
Son, you don't want it wit' Flaw
Ask Bull
He don't want it wit Flaw
Naw!

However, the focus and the mantra of the song was Hannibal, who he saved for the last verse. He ripped into him tacitly with a pitchfork.

Negro Neanderthal
Why you so mad at the world?
Is it 'cause all you poppin'
Is blanks
An' I don' fucked yo' girl
Don't act like you don't know me
I'll unfurl a fury
What is this you obsessed with Flaw
Nigga, you in love with me
Bull, you a shallow fellow
Everywhere I go you follow
While I'm shadow boxing
You stay boxin' ma shadow
You stay in ma dark
While I'm the spark
Nigga you just an afterthought
With a bad aftertaste
How's the aftertaste?
You be suckin' on the semen
'Cause you wanna see me more clearly
Clearly, I'm sick of this shit
Been beatin' beef, from the Spit
To the championship
What Cannibal can't do nothin'
But suck on dick?
You can silence the lambs
But you can't step to a god
I been lecturing before Lecter
I slay Bulls like Mithra
Burn you like ether

'Cause you can't rhyme with ma meter
An' don't send a clone to do a man's jobs
I'm too grim for yo' Reaper
Son, I'm the sunum bonum
The son of man
While you jus' a lost black boy
Who wanna be an' old white man
Callin' yo'self a cannibal
'Cause you don't know yo' history
Some cats see you as Bull
But nigga, you jus' shit to me.

Of the four who were attacked, Hannibal was the only one in attendance. He alone had to bear the eyes and the mumblings of the crowd. Batista, Pinochet, Trujillo, all were looking at him. Hannibal's anger swelled but he wore his embarrassment well. As the song ended the DJ's voice came over:

"You heard it here, heard it first, first strike. Blazin', ain't it?"

Mook smiled to himself while the others were stunned. Bull remained silent. He watched the crowd watching him, trying to appear as if they were not watching him. Then a new beat came and again they lost themselves to the rhythm. Terrence would not let it go that easily.

"That motherfucker! That bitch want a war, don't he? 'Cannibal can only suck dick.' Naw, *you* suck dick, motherfucker!"

"Calm down." Hannibal cut into Terrence's rant. "It's all right, tit for tat. I understand. It's on now."

The club DJ, Sebek, stood high above in his booth, surveying the lay of the land and taking a break between mixes. He had the turntables before him, surrounded by crates of vinyl from old school to funk. Bes, another Peaches DJ, approached with an unnatural look of fear.

"Yo, y' know Bull is here, right?" he said.

"Yeah, for how long?" Sebek asked, playing cool, although already a twinge of fear was ebbing at his feet.

"Long enough, he heard you play that 'Bullshit' track."

What Sebek had feared had occurred. He had received no announcement of Hannibal's presence. If he had, he wouldn't have played the song. He had only received the vinyl today and wanted desperately to be the first to play it. He, however, did not want this. But now that he had it, he had to play it off. "Oh well, fuck it, so? Whether he heard from me or somewhere else, he was gon' hear it."

Bes heard his friend's bravado and knew it was pretense. "Well, yeah, fuck it. You know that Bull is the new Deacon of hip-hop."

The Deacon was a onetime Mob hitman who had learned the business and had founded a hip-hop record label. Using the same method of intimidation that worked in the streets, he created a rap dynasty that had lasted five years until his incarceration. Though it had been years since he had been sent away, his name was still considered the barometer for gangster in the business.

"Whatever, I don't care about that shit," Sebek remarked. Then suddenly he recalled the pork chops he had ingested earlier. "Take over for me a minute?" he asked his friend as he took his time and went to the facilities.

Three hours later, it was four in the morning and the party was over. Sebek collected his check from the club manager and began to make his way downstairs toward the back entrance. The load that he released earlier lightened his step and his heart. After a while he had stopped thinking about Bull. Yes, he had heard the song. So what? He heard and he left and that's that, he thought as he said good-bye to the big fellow holding the heavy iron door open for him. It was amazing how the front of the club opened to one of the better-looking strips in the city and the back looked like a back alley war zone. He stepped into the war and heard the loud clank of the iron door behind him. He always dreaded its bellowing echo.

He could feel the chill in the September air. He smelled that autumn was on its way. Wearing a T-shirt alone, he began to shiver and curse himself for not carrying a jacket. He would be okay though. A subway station was only three blocks up. He knew that it would be sweltering in the nether of the city.

He then heard something coming from his left: "Yo, I'm telling you, it wasn't me. I ain't play shit tonight," Bes frantically pleaded as both Terrence and Mook held him up to the chipped brick wall. With his nose bloodied, Bes tried to reason with them.

"Hey, what the hell is going on?" Sebek reflexively shouted. This had been his second mistake of the night. His voice registered in Terrence's ears. Suddenly Terrence realized that he had been beating the wrong man.

"Naw, I know that voice. It's this big-head nigga right here," he said to Mook. They dropped Bes and began their approach. Seeing them coming, Sebek thought to run but his feet became jelly; vestiges of the load he had released earlier now began to revisit his intestines.

"What the fuck?" was all he could say as Terrence and Mook attacked him like wild dogs. He could hold it no longer. The load fought through the weakened will of his rectum and began to amass itself as a two-pound weight in the base of his briefs, to flow over its continents, sliding down his inner thigh, at times sticking itself to the thick of his denim and finally lodging itself at the base of his shoes as a muddy mess.

If he had had the time he would have felt ashamed. Terrence's fist came too quick. Though Terrence was slim, he punched heavy. Mook's fist followed with a convict's brutality. The combined force brought the DJ on his back. As he lay there on hard concrete, they stomped him viciously. The last thing he saw clearly were the ridges on the soles of the boots before they hit. The first hit brought his head to the back and opened his skull. While still holding on to consciousness, he used his hands as a guard. Terrence continued to stomp upon him regardless. This broke the DJ's arms and wrists and created a loud ring in his ear. After that he heard and felt nothing else, but he could see through a bloodied eye the kicks that Mook delivered to his midsection with such force that he broke four ribs and almost punctured his lungs. The disgorging of blood was so much that he had to be careful not to suffocate on his own throw up. The beating had lasted for at the most a minute. To the DJ it all seemed like a lifetime, as if the kicking would never stop.

"I bet yo' ass never play another Flawless track again, mother-fucker!" Terrence's words echoed down the alleyway. Terrence and Mook were in the process of walking away, when Terrence smelled something. In his fury the thick foulness that had usurped the quality of the air hadn't reached him. Now the stench came off with added repugnance.

"Oh shit," he remarked. "Yo, I think this nigger shit on him-self. Did you just shit on yo'self, motherfucker?" he asked Sebek, who could respond only by shaking. "Yes you did, you did shit on yourself." He was about to walk away with just a story to tell the boys afterward, but then he looked down on his shoes and saw the smeared remnants of fecal matter. "Oh, hell no. Hell no, this motherfucker didn't just get shit on my brand new Tims!" In his rage Terrence delivered one final stomp to the DJ's face. The force of the delivery knocked out the DJ's teeth. Swallowing them was the last thing he remembered before he passed out.

While Terrence continued to curse the unconscious DJ, Mook meditated on just how Terrence's brains would look stained against the wall. He wanted to kill Terrence so badly that it had given him an erection and his preejaculation had stained itself to the inside of his boxers. He was seconds away from pulling his glock out when Hannibal's voice called from up the block. He and Reaper had been waiting in the SUV. Mook wanted to kill Terrence but it would have to wait.

The two men walked defiantly away, not even giving an eye to Bes. They knew that they didn't have to. Bes had seen what they were capable of. He knew to keep his mouth shut. As they proceeded up the alley, Terrence strode four steps ahead of Mook. From behind, Mook licked his lips, watching Terrence's head bob up and down in rhythm. The rounded protuberance of his scalp aroused him and again he began to foreplay his trigger. No, not now, he said to himself. He then quickened his pace and overtook Terrence's position. The back of the man's head was too tempting a target.

Back down the alley a bewildered Bes walked over to his friend. The DJ was lying in a bloody puddle. His face had become an ambiguous mess. Bes was brought to immediate tears. He went to knock on the back door but it opened before he could reach it, almost as if it had been waiting for everything to be over.

"Call an ambulance," he shouted.

"It was already on the way," they replied. He knew then that they had seen the entire event and had done nothing. He felt disgusted. For that he would quit his job the next day. For now he attended to his friend. "Oh fuck, this shit is serious."

THIRTY

Micah made his way up the three marble steps, passing the ceiling-high marble columns, which led to the marble plateau that was the living room. The room appeared to be very different than it had months past. It was now furnished somewhat, with a divan and its complements; still, it seemed empty amid the great white expanse. It was a house and not a home and had the hard, testosterone reek of bachelordom. As always the immense television encapsulated the vacant space; its sound reaching the outskirts its mass could not, bringing Lecter's distinctive British proper to ubiquity.

He approached Hannibal at one with his favorite pastime. This was somewhere around count 110. Being respectful, Micah stayed to the side.

"What's going on, Bull? I heard that you wanted to see me," he said to him. Terrence had been the relayer of Bull's desires. There was a sense of urgency in his voice, which made Micah feel as if he had been errant in some manner. Though he knew that this reasonably couldn't be, nonetheless, he walked into the house with the feeling of going to the principal's office.

For a minute Hannibal gave no response. He heard him but his focus was on Lecter, and for the first time he looked at Lecter with a subtle sense of disdain. "You were right, you know," he finally said.

"About what?" Micah asked.

"I hated the book's ending." Hannibal's still austerity made Micah believe that there was something dread on the horizon.

"Yeah, me too," Micah responded.

"He fucking loved her. Shit don't make no sense," Hannibal remarked. Micah found the impact that this was having on him humorous but kept his observation to himself.

"So where have you been lately?" Hannibal inquired.

"Just livin', man."

"Flawless's sister," Hannibal noted without posing a question. Micah responded in the affirmative, feeling uncomfortable with her name being brought to the floor. Hannibal never said it but it was felt that he was not the most supportive of their relationship. "Interesting. Let's talk."

Hannibal turned off the television midway into the picture. He had never done this before. Then for the first time in the conversation he gave Micah his full attention. "I gotta put out a new album and I'm gonna need your help with it."

"In what way?" Micah asked.

"In a big way. I got too much shit on my mind: running the business, trying to expand, set up our own distribution network so we can say fuck off to Crown and run things ourselves. Y'know what I'm saying?"

"I hear you."

"Thing is, with all this shit on ma plate, I don't have time to write. I mean, it's comin', but it's the same old thing, and now I need some next-level shit. Something that niggas are not expecting. That's where you come in."

Micah intuited the rest. He was asking him to become a ghostwriter. Though it was a taboo and not respected in the industry, the phenomenon of ghostwriting was more common than admitted. Micah knew that unlike any other form of music, hip-hop looked down upon one man penning another man's vocals. This was not the case in the other genres; for the most, it was expected that someone other than the vocalist would write the lyrics. This was another matter altogether in hip-hop. It was music born in the gullies and prided itself on its dirt realism.

"We're going to write it together," Hannibal added.

"All right," Micah said.

"Cool. But I don't want you to get too crazy with it. Remember, this is Bull you're writing for. It gotta still sound like me. I know how you get. You like to get creative and rhyme yo' shit all over the place. But niggas ain't ready for that. So just keep it simple."

"All right."

"Okay, now that we got that settled, let's talk business. I like you, Micah, you a cool kid." Hannibal said this as if to suggest that he were his elder. Being only two years older, he was far from that. Hannibal, though, appeared to have already accumulated a lifetime of wealth of knowledge. "I am going to give you basically the artist's share of the album. So let's say you get about fifteen points and I take the credits but we split our share of the publishing fifty-fifty."

"It sounds real good," Micah replied. "But what does that all mean?" he had to ask. Hannibal smiled at his naïveté.

"Okay, let's break it down. Now, for the most part, a point breaks down to a percent. Now, as our agreement goes, dem motherfuckers at Crown get about thirty percent of the cake for distributing the CDs. Now we basically do the rest. So now, that's roughly seventy percent that we have left. Cannibal is an independent label, of which I am the sole proprietor." As Hannibal continued to break down the logistics, Micah took note of how strictly Hannibal adhered to the jargon of business in his speech. Hearing him now there would be no differentiating him from a fortune 500 mogul. He supposed that business talk was a slang in and of itself. "Which means that roughly all of that seventy percent comes back to me of which I have to use for paying these producers, paying employees, paying for promotions, packaging and manufacturing, not to mention that cocksucker Uncle Sam." At this point he went off on a tangent and with it went his business proper. "Every time I think about how much that dick took from me last year, it makes me wanna shoot somebody." Hannibal's eruption sparked a chuckle from Micah. Then he began to wonder if Hannibal had ever shot anyone. He knew little about Hannibal; what he knew bred reason to speculate. "I tell you, that's the one thing better about the drug game, I didn't have to worry about any accountants and taxes. But I did have to worry about lawyers. I tell you, dem niggas get their hands dirty in everything. You know how many lawsuits I got pending? Remember dem bitches from the limo after the *Source* Awards . . . yeah, dem. They comin' back now lookin' for some money. Tryin' to say we raped them."

"Get the fuck outta here!" Micah blurted in disbelief.

"Don't worry about shit though. Bitches gon' drop the charges."

"How do you know that?"

"One, they ain't got no case. And two, I'ma send some people to pay them a visit."

"Pay them a visit. What do you mean?"

"Let's just say that no matter how big you get, always make sure that you have some friends in low places. The shit comes in handy." Micah was a bit taken aback by Hannibal's last statement as he intuited what Hannibal implied.

"That's how the system is: they give a nigga a little bit a money to eat, then they take it back, to feed themselves." Hannibal then stopped himself, realizing that he had strayed from the original topic. "Now, back to the point. Think of that seventy percent as one hundred percent, of which you get fifteen percent. How does that sound?"

"Um, it sounds good," Micah replied, although he had lost his way in the diversion. No worries, he figured he would learn the rest on the job.

"I know it seems like a little, but it adds up to a lot. Especially when we add in the publishing rights, you lookin' at a lot of money from all of the radio play we gon' be getting. This time around we have a better relationship with radio and they're gonna be more set to playing our shit. So we cool?"

"Yeah, we cool."

"Then let's get to work. I figured we would do roughly twenty, twenty-five tracks, and pick the best thirteen." Hannibal was enamored with the number thirteen as well. There was something about a number that everyone feared that intrigued him.

"Cool, but I have a thought."

"Go ahead."

"About your image."

"Whatchu mean?"

"I mean, the whole Lecter cannibalism thing is cool but why don't we go deeper with the name Hannibal?" Micah felt he had to be delicate, being respectful of Bull's fanaticism.

"I'm hearing you," Hannibal replied.

"Well, you know the name Hannibal really comes from this guy from North Africa back in the days. He was a Carthaginian general, he fought against the Romans in the Second Punic Wars, crossed the Alps with war elephants and almost sacked Rome. Any of this sounds familiar?" Micah asked, noticing the blankness in Hannibal's expression.

"Vaguely," he replied. He had heard that the name existed before Lecter but had never explored it any deeper. Micah recognized that he was now teaching Hannibal something. It was a comfortable change; Hannibal was an adept listener.

"Well, for what he did, he is considered one of the greatest generals and military geniuses in history. And he was a brother." Micah had saved the latter statement for the punchline.

"And he was black, I like that!"

"Yep, he was. Some idiots try to tell you different, like they do with the Egyptians and Jesus, as if everything great that happened in this world had to come from a white man."

"I know exactly what you mean. Exactly what you mean, everybody always tryin' to limit a nigga. General Bull, I like the sound of that. Micah, you a smart motherfucker."

All he had told him were general facts; nevertheless, Micah smiled at the emphatic compliment. "It fits you. And even better, the title of the album," which suddenly came to him.

"What's that?"

"*Elephant Warfare.*" As he said it, he knew it was right. It evoked such a sense of power and grace, along with ominous dread.

"Oh shit. That's it. That's it right there. That's the motherfucker." Hannibal's reaction showed that it had had the same impact on him. It also brought prior thoughts back to fore. "Now, speaking of warfare, we got a war on our hands."

"What do you mean?"

"Well, Flawless has started some shit and we're gonna finish it. So we gonna work on an extraspecial comeback."

"Really." A comeback for Flawless, he knew what was meant by this. He had heard "Bullshit" over the radio; it was harsh. Hannibal would expect no less in the rebuttal. But why must it be Flawless? Let it be anyone else, Stalin, Bush, Batista, anyone but Flawless. But Micah knew not to question; Hannibal's mind was set. It was Flawless who had attacked him. The wrath would fall on no one else.

"What's wrong . . . feel conflicted 'cause you fuckin' his sister?" Hannibal interrupted Micah's thoughts.

"Something like that."

"That's an easy fix. Break up with the bitch and let's get to work. General Bull: *Elephant Warfare*. I like the sound of that." And that was that.

BOOK FiVE

THiRTY-ONE

The day the city stood still came that mid-December. It had been planned to perfection and executed masterfully. On the evening of the eve, Terrence arrived at the studios of WHRU with a package in hand. Upon telling the receptionist of his purpose, he was hurried through security, walked down bending gray-carpeted halls, escorted with the eyes of the envious all around, and brought directly to RA's engineer. He opened the package. It glowed before the engineer's eyes with golden luminescence. Almost salivating, he asked Terrence, "Is that what I think it is?" Terrence nodded his affirmation. The confirmation was almost too much to bear. With a beating heart he held it up to the window so that the God of radio might see.

At glimpsing the glow, RA went to an impromptu commercial break. Seeing Terrence, RA also asked the question, "Is that what I think it is?" The engineer, with an ear-to-ear grin, nodded his head in the affirmative. RA clasped his hands, thanking the Creator for life. Seeing this, Terrence silently made his way back down the bending gray-carpeted hallways, past security, past the receptionist, into the elevator and out of WHRU studios. His feet touched the Manhattan concrete and saw the black SUV with the door open, waiting for him. The second Terrence was in the vehicle, RA was making the announcement. He looked over at Reaper and smiled. Mission accomplished. They drove off.

"New York, New York, I got it. I got it here in my hand," RA announced. "The thing that we all been waiting for. We all knew it was coming but we didn't know when. But when is now. Now I got it. I have the comeback." The comeback that he spoke of was Hannibal's rebuttal to Flawless's "Bullshit." It would arguably be one of the most hyped and anticipated singles in hip-hop history.

Flawless's second album had been released at the eve of autumn. *Poorman's Philosophe* garnered critical acclaim and moderate sales. To date it had only moved close to 2 million units, most of which came in the first week. Many artists would kill for these numbers. However, they were grossly incomparable to Flawless's previous effort. In the same time *Flawless Victory* had almost tripled that number. *Philosophe* was a deeply introspective album: It was more political, darker, at times disturbing, always thought provoking, but it was not commercial. There were no party songs in this batch. Flawless abandoned Noah. With an ASR-10 as his weapon of choice, he did much of the production himself, and looked to European and Caribbean talents for the rest. In his travels abroad, Flawless had become impressed with some of the offerings in the UK and Germany. He had also made links with Jamaican producers to create mellow reggae melodies. *Poorman's Philosophe* was a truly profound collection, which was ultimately ahead of its time.

In the aftermath of my afterlife
I'm half the man I need to be
Half the god I used to be
Used to be, about booties and Bentleys
Now I'm all about bending realities
Debunkin' fallacies
Changin' philosophies
Spittin' heresies, an' crashin' hierarchies

See, I was given choices
But the truth must be told
For I was born of a free will
But on a straight and narrow road.

With no penchant for violence
No palate for war
No purse for blood
Yo I pawn for peace
In the milieu of the millennium
I am one in a million
In the muck of monuments
In the muck of arrogance
Ambivalent ambulance driver
Victim and vampire
Adversary and beneficiary
A fish out of water
A merman dressed in
Brand-new worn-out denim
Jeans: blue and tanned
Stonewashed by sweatshop hands
Handicapped capitalist
Conflicted by my selflessness
Hip-hop hypocrite
Yet in balance it makes sense
And yet all so senseless
So many deaths
For so many debts
And in all this
Where is all the profits?
But I had left town
And prophecy found the prophet
With his hands down
As Y2K came in 2001.

At the time, the average man wasn't feeling it, except for one track and it was a bonus: this was "Bullshit."

It was found at the end of the album, thirteen seconds after the thirteenth track. It was not a Noah-type beat but Elijah's production was equally as impressive. This was the Flawless that people knew and loved. It was this bonus track that sold the album. Every DJ played it in every club at least twice every night. This was so even after the news had hit about what happened to the DJ outside of Peaches nightclub. That was an event that had been played down and not followed up. With no witnesses to come forward, there were no charges to bear. The DJ would live but he would forget that night. He had received so many blows to the cranium that he had lost a portion of his memories and had developed a permanent speech impediment. Regardless of this, the song was played on the radio, in the beauty salons, in the cars and in the mind. People had heard it so much they found themselves involuntarily reciting it. Flawless had denigrated all four men and they had become the laughingstocks of the city, indeed the nation; in truth, the lore of "Bullshit" had taken on international proportions. It was a career-ending strike. Every man had to come back.

Lil' Hitler had done nothing so far but make threats of violence in the magazines and on the radio. The situation had brewed so badly that Flawless was told not to travel to the southern basin. Lil' Hitler was their fuhrer and the Gestapo had strong gang affiliations. Stalin and Bin Laden had gone to the studios and made their respective rebuttals. Stalin's was a case of another matter. The attack upon him had not been as blatant so the fact that his retaliation was subpar was made to pass.

Bin Laden's career had been in a downward spiral. After getting out of his contract with Crown at gunpoint, Jennesy had made it his point to see to Bin Laden's destruction. It was a little-known fact that Crown was a major benefactor of WHRU; from Jennessy's takeover he saw to this. He knew that having the top hip-hop radio station in pocket would come in handy. There had been a time when one of the regular DJs was waging his own personal war against Crown. Soon others began to question Crown practices as well. Jennessy used his leverage and squashed a roach. DJ Anpu had to seek work outside of New York, effactually being banned. He would later return years after and take back up his tirade at a rival New York radio station, WASR; as such, the radio wars began.

The same was happening to Bin Laden. He had been signed to another label, but WHRU would not play his music. Though there were other outlets WHRU, for the most part, held the monopoly on hip-hop radio in the city. They were the trendsetters and other radio stations followed their lead. Bin Laden and everyone in his Al Qaeda network had been whitelisted. Jennessy had created a coalition against him; no one would listen to what he had to say. With no way to feed his lifestyle he fell back to his old roots. The Taliban took him in. It was here, while watching his existence fall to pieces, that Bin Laden, feeling bushwhacked, found his resolve. He would kill Jennessy and likewise wanted all things Jennessy-related dead.

Then came Hannibal, upon whom the true charge fell. "Bullshit" was an attack against him. The others were merely the opening act. Everyone knew this. The full weight of the comeback was on his shoulders. Hannibal understood the magnitude of the undertaking. He waited, allowed it to eat into him from late summer into late fall. His second album was not to be released until January of the next year. "Warfare" was the first single and was given to radio early that December. It was a commercial hit despite its blatant militancy. It called for the people to fight back and take up arms militia style. It was also critically acclaimed. "Hannibal has evolved," they said. "The words are profound, the delivery energetic and Noah's beat outstanding." With "Warfare," Hannibal came onto a new plateau. Though they loved "Warfare," it was not what the people hungered for. The city yearned for the comeback. They all knew it was coming, but when? Now, it was here . . . in God's hands.

Yet RA would not play it that night. He chose to tease instead. He would delay the pleasure and sweeten the climax. He played a snippet of the song and announced that it would be played in its entirety the very next day at 5:40 P.M. exactly. The announcement went through all of the barrios of the boroughs like wildfire. This conflagration was a herpes in the ear of the entire city and so the city went to sleep that December night in antsy anticipation.

It was the talk: in the schoolyards, cafeterias, playgrounds, on the basketball courts, on the construction site, at the office cooler, barbershops, in the taxicabs and movie theaters. It seemed that everywhere within a minute at least one person was talking about it. On this day there existed no one in hip-hop save for Flawless, Hannibal and RA. The people listened to WHRU all day. All day the station had been playing the snippet. All day it had been teasing; soon everything would come to a crescendo. When RA took to the air at four o'clock, the entire city was listening. He sat for moments smiling at his omnipotence. Was this what power truly felt like? The eye of RA glowed as he looked about him. His studio was filled with rappers and fellow Kemites who all wanted to be there, just so that they could say that they were a part of history, if even just a footnote. Trujillo was in attendance, as were Batista and Pinochet. Even the revolutionary Guevara had stayed back after his own interview to have a ringside to the fete. RA had done a prepoll from the night before. Though his new album had not sold as much, with "Bullshit," Flawless was still considered the king of New York. The decision had come down and Flawless was expected to win seven to three. The people were dying to hear the comeback but most had no faith in Hannibal to win.

The clock struck 5:39 and the engineer cued the CD. "All

right New York, this is it. Are y'all ready? The comeback is here. An' I heard it. I gotta tell ya, I think that there might be a new king. But I ain't made up my mind yet, an' I leave it to y'all to make up yours. But whatever, ready or not, it is here. Hannibal: 'Coup d'etat,' " and with that said, the prurient finally entered.

THiRTY-TWO

The A train came to a familiar screeching halt at the Forty-second Street subway station. Micah and Erika, coated and hand in hand, entered, headed to Harlem. Micah was going to look at a brownstone he found in an ad. Erika was coming along to give her opinion of the space, which she planned to be spending a lot of time in.

They entered the middle car in the midst of the melee and surprisingly they were able to find a seat together. It was evening time, late rush hour; at this stop the train should be brimming. It was not empty by any account; nevertheless, sardines would have begged for this comfort. Today was a colder day than it had been in recent weeks. They had dressed warmer for protection. They were fashionable in their wool overcoats but heavier and more cumbersome for it. Once in the heated car they took the chance to undo their bindings. Once his coat had been opened, she placed her head to his chest and he placed his arm about her shoulder. There they sat as young lovers layered in cloth and comfortable in their skins.

With her ear to his heart she listened attentively for its beat. Through the thick fabric she was not able to hear one.

"I can't hear your heartbeat," she looked up and said to him.

"Don't worry, it's there," he replied.

"I don't know, I can't hear it, I think you're dead," she remarked playfully.

"If I were, how would I be able to talk to you now?"

"Well, maybe you're dead and you just don't know it yet."

"So then, you're saying that we only die if we acknowledge death?"

"Maybe. And maybe we only live if we acknowledge life, but I'm not quite sure."

"Well, then, I will never acknowledge death and I will live forever."

"And what would you do if you could live forever?" she asked him.

"I would stay here, with you, in this moment, in love."

"But I won't live forever. What will you do when I die?"

"Girl, you will never die. I'm not sure about a lot of things, but of that I am."

"So then, we will both live and love forever," she stated and asked him at the same time.

"Why not, why not."

In like vein the two lovers found each other's lips there in the crowd of the not-so-packed train. They kissed, eyes closed, hearts entwined and minds miles away, in a haze of purple.

When they had come up for air the train had come to a stop at Fifty-ninth Street. Many of the passengers got off and were readily replaced. A young man came on and sat himself directly across. In his hands he held a periodical. He opened it spread-eagle before him. It covered him from stomach to brow and brought the full picture on the cover of the publication within eyeshot. There they were shown profiled head to head, Flawless and Hannibal, and above them were the words *Crown Warfare*. The airbrushed tableau stood before them like a hanging harbinger, as if they had needed any reminder of war.

"Do you see that?" he asked her in reference to the glare of the *XXL*.

"I'm trying not to. But it's hard when it's like on the cover of every magazine. It's even in the newspapers. It's like it's all the press wants to talk about these days."

"Not just the press. Everybody, it seems."

"Not everybody. Do you want to talk about it?"

"Nope."

"Then not everybody. There are some people who don't care."

Erika spoke in frustration. The battle had deeply affected her. It had been going on for months and she wanted it all to stop. Why Flawless felt the need to do what he did, she did not know. But to read article after article, with all types of rappers who were calling threats out, deeply troubled her. Micah, sensing the disturbance in Erika's mood, held her tightly. He kissed her brow and in his arms, for a moment, she felt safe.

Three young men in their late teenage years entered the car from the other end by way of the intracar passage. They were wearing heavy goose-down coats, their jeans well below the crack, do-rags over their cornrows and a skull cap over their do-rags. They came in loud and took their seats, sprawling their legs defiantly. One of them was especially raucous. He was wearing headphones and the music was played loud enough that it carried throughout the car. He drew the attention and disdain of the entire body. To add to this annoyance, he recited word for word the exact lyrics of the song being played.

Both Micah and Erika looked down at them with fascination at first but then more as an irritation. They never understood why certain people felt the need to turn their every action into a spectacle. As Headphones began to recite, Micah knew right away what it was. It was "Coup d'etat." The teenager had recorded it when it first aired on RA's show the evening before, after which he quickly placed it into his Walkman and had been playing it ever since, though he didn't have to. If he had remained listening to WHRU, he would have heard it played ten times that night and another ten times so far today. It was the hottest single on radio and Micah had written it. There was a strange satisfaction that came from hearing others recite your words, even if they credited it to someone else. He felt pleased and then he looked to the girl in his arm.

"That's Bull's comeback, huh? It's really harsh."

"Yeah. So was Flawless's."

Erika turned about and looked at him. "Never knew why they had to get into this mess in the first place." The way she gazed made him feel as if she already knew something that he hadn't told her.

"It's just hip-hop. It's all part of the game," he remarked.

Erika listened attentively.

"That doesn't sound like a game . . . it sounds personal."

As his friend continued to rant Hannibal's lyrics, another of the three teenage boys had grown tired of all the noise. "Yo, why don't you shut the fuck up with that shit? Everybody don't wan' hear that," he shouted loudly. In response, his friend pulled his headphones down.

"Yo, nigga, what was that?"

"I said shut the fuck up with that. I don't wanna hear that shit."

"Why, 'cause Bull buss yo' boy ass with this track here."

"Get the fuck outta here. I see you was listenin' to RA just long enough to tape the song but you was too scared to wait for the results. Flaw buss Bull by four points, nigga."

"Naw, nope. That whole fuckin' voting was rigged."

Whether it was or not was a matter of debate. But as it stood, after six hours of telephone voting and email tallies, the decision had come down fifty-two to forty-eight percent. Flawless had retained his title—barely.

"That shit was rigged," Hannibal's advocate continued. "One, there was a two percent margin of error. Yo' boy only won by four points and we all know that HRU is mad biased toward Crown niggas."

"What that got to do wit' shit? Both Flawless and Bull is under Crown."

"Naw, Bull ain't. Cannibal is an independent label; they only do distribution through Crown. Flawless is under contract so of course they want him to win more."

Hearing all this at the other end of the car, it was amazing to Micah how much they knew about the business.

"Naw, that's Bullshit," Flawless's advocate remarked.

"Just deal wit' it. Yo' boy sucks and now everybody knows it."

"Sucks, what the fuck you talkin' about? Bull can't even write. Nigga rhymes like a kid in kindergarten."

"Kindergarten. Nigga, you blunted or something? Did you hear 'Warfare'?"

"I did, so what?"

"Well, then, that's all I gotta say." He didn't need to argue further, "Warfare" could lyrically stand on its own. Silenced for a moment, Flawless's advocate could do nothing but shake his head, until saying, "I don't think he wrote it."

This statement struck both Hannibal's advocate and Micah.

"What the fuck you talkin' about?"

"I'm serious. I don't think he wrote that shit. And I don't think he wrote 'Coup' either. Comparing to the shit he did before, shit don't add up."

"Now you goin' too far. Can't admit that your man got his ass *buss* . . ." he placed extra emphasis on the last word, ". . . so now you bitchin', tryin' to say he ain't write shit. Nigga, you just a little *bitch* like Flawless." With this he laid an insult to his friend and the entire train had heard. The rage began to swell within. Hannibal's advocate, sensing that he hit a nerve, decided to push it even further. "That Flawless is a pussy. I don't even know what the hell he be talkin' 'bout nowadays. Talkin' 'bout 'matter matters but only in the makeup of the mind.' I'm like, what the fuck? What kinda shit is that?"

"That's 'cause niggas like you too stupid to understand shit."

"Whatever, man, I don't get it. I liked a nigga better when he was talkin' 'bout bitches and Bentleys. But since he ain't talkin' 'bout dat, or no real street shit, that bitch can go suck dick." He threw back on his headphones and continued to sing along, louder than before. He was giving extra emphasis to the more insulting lines. It appeared as if he had won the argument. His friend, feeling embarrassed, yanked the headphones off.

"I told you to shut the fuck up with that shit."

"Nigga, you fucking crazy?" Hannibal's advocate shouted, before pushing his friend with enough force that he went hurling backward to the floor. Both men seemed surprised at the ferocity of the thrust but they didn't think of that for long. The fallen quickly got to his feet and the two began to banter with blows. The people on that side of the car abandoned their seats and ran to the other end. Micah and Erika looked on in shock as the third of the three attempted to break up the quarrel.

"Yo, what the fuck are y'all doin'? Y'all are stupid or what; fightin' over this shit? Both a dem niggas is rich. An y'all ain't seeing a dime a dat shit." His words went unheard and he was merely thrown about in their fury.

"This is so crazy. I can't believe this is happening," Erika commented.

"Yo, let's get outta here before they bring that shit down here," Micah added.

The train finally came to a stop at 125th Street. All of the passengers exited the car; many because it was truly their stop, while others hurried over to the adjacent car, trying to make it before the doors closed again.

"C'mon, Erika, let's go," Micah said. They exited just before the doors closed. As the train was pulling off, they looked on in amazement when, from the other end of the car, transit police rushed in with batons and tended to the fight . . . violently.

The train had left the platform for almost a minute before either Micah or Erika could speak. "This is too much. This is too much," Erika said as they looked at the vacant tracks where the train used to be, feeling their purple haze dimming around them.

THiRTY-THREE

Cannibal Records was located on the ninth floor of a sixteen-story Harlem office building. Hannibal had chosen Harlem to be the location because, for one, Brooklyn was too familiar to be a workplace; two, New Jersey was too far away from the scene and three, Lower Manhattan was too contrived and typical. But Harlem was perfect. There was something in the plain pronunciation of the noun that evoked history. Hannibal was no buff but for as long as he could remember it had been synonymous with blackness. This was a connection common not only to him. Throughout the planet it seemed that Harlem had been dubbed the New World's black Mecca.

As Micah walked the streets of Harlem that day, passing by the HMV, the CVS, the Disney Store, the Popeyes and the McDonald's, he felt no Mecca about him. Harlem peered out as a remnant of its former self. Many of the prominent buildings on the strip were no longer home-owned. The infamous Apollo Theatre, which now jutted out like a sore amidst the canker, stood as the greatest testament of that. There was a new movement in the air.

As Micah was making his way into the building, he looked across the way and was reminded that a former American president had set up office in the building on the adjacent block. Oh, how things change, he thought.

As he passed the chatty, gum-chewing receptionist and

approached the door leading to the offices he noticed the banner for Cannibal Records, scripted in blood red on a black background. How far Hannibal has come, he said to himself, though he was saying this not knowing from whence Hannibal truly came. Everything he knew of the man was peripheral.

Micah pulled open the wooden door and entered the office. All at once he felt that he had entered Cannabis Records instead. There was no Cannabis Records that he knew of but he imagined that if there was it would be like this. The smell of the burnt plant hit him like Epsom salt, with a thick fog that could rival the worst London night. Through the fog he was able to see nine of the boys sitting about the lounge, playing dice. Reaper and Mook sat to the side looking on.

Once he entered, Reaper called him over. He made the rounds giving pounds to everyone, trying his best not to cough up a lung or get high in the process. He had done the numbers, all save for one. Mook. He had met Mook before but he had never spoken to him. Mook wasn't one for talking as he saw him and Terrence had never spoken favorably of the man. Speaking of Terrence, as he approached to give Mook a pound, he wondered where exactly Terrence was. Without Terrence as his guide he felt like an alien in the mélange.

Mook grabbed hold of his hand and pulled him in. It was a strong pound of intimate intimidation. In their embrace Micah felt something hard jutting out at him.

"Sorry 'bout that," Mook said, sensing that Micah had felt it. Mook then removed from his waist what appeared to Micah to be a small hand-held cannon, which he laid flat on the table before him. It was a black .45 Glock 30. Micah didn't know this. All he knew was that it was big. In his years Micah was fortunate to have never been so close to a gun. This was a real-life weapon with no other purpose other than to kill and maim. It was an uncomfortable situation. Mook could smell the fear in him and he relished it.

"Where's T at?" Micah asked Reaper, trying to take his

mind off the cannon lying on the table; while Mook stood to the side staring at him, his eyes gnawing through Micah's cranium.

"He went out for a minute," Reaper answered. Micah looked around and saw that no one else took the slightest notice of the cannon on the table. It was as if it was natural for a gun to be there, much the same as the magazines. This feeling was confirmed when another of the boys removed his gun and landed it on the table.

"Shit, that's better," he remarked. "Now I can whop yo' ass without worrying about shooting ma dick off."

Damn, did everyone in here have a gun? Micah began to think. Perhaps not, he calmed himself, thinking that it might be just the two. But even if it were, he still felt uncomfortable. "Is the man in?" he asked Reaper in reference to Hannibal.

"Yeah, he's in the office."

"Cool."

Micah began to make his way toward Hannibal's office when Mook called to him: "Micah, here. Can't leave ma man out. Here, take a drag of this," Mook said to him, holding out the burnt blunt like an olive branch with a needle in it.

"Naw, that's all right. I'm cool," Micah calmly rejected. He had no particular aversion to weed but he had no intention of getting blunted there. After refusing, he politely turned and continued on his way, when Mook called out to him again:

"I am being nice. When someone is nice to you, you should be nice back. Otherwise, it is considered rude," Mook said in a plain, dry draconian manner, expressing the breaks between his words with an added pause. His voice cut through the meaningless chatter and brought the room to silence. All eyes were on Micah. This was the worst part of an already uncomfortable situation.

"That's all right," Micah replied, while weighing his words. "Thank you anyway but I'm straight."

After a pensive lull Mook flatly replied, "Cool."

Micah nodded in respect and walked away, turning the corner from the lounge, toward Hannibal's office. With a quickened heart he knocked at the door.

"Who dat?" Hannibal called from within.

"It's Micah."

"Roll through."

Hannibal's office was not what Micah expected, given where he'd just come from, but was much the way he thought it should have been. The carpeted smoke-free room was modest in comparison to Jennessy's. Still it was functional, and better yet it was professional; the first good sign that Micah had seen since entering the offices.

Hannibal was on the phone and signaled that he would be with him in a minute. Micah took the time to further survey the room. Hannibal sat behind a large desk, before an even larger window, which gave a view of greater Harlem. On the wall there were framed posters, all with the Cannibal letters and logo. In the corners there were stacks of cardboard boxes, all containing CDs or some other form of Cannibal paraphernalia. Micah was about to take a seat when he noticed that there was no chair. That's strange. Why was that, he wondered? Whatever the reason for this, those who called on Hannibal either stood in his seated presence or sat on the floor, either way never being directly eye-to-eye with the man. Micah stood and took note of another oddity, which was the impersonality of his desk. Alongside the computer there were no small-framed pictures of family or friends or a girlfriend. Did Hannibal have a girlfriend? Did he have a family? Micah didn't know. In the months that he had known him, he had never heard him speak of one. In fact, he spoke of nothing personal as it pertained to himself.

"All right, all right, thanks for the notice . . . then I should be receiving that plaque any day now . . . Good shit." Having finished his conversation he turned his attentions squarely on Micah. "Yuh hear that, ma boy? The 'Warfare' single is already certified platinum."

"That's good, man. That's real good."

"Ma man Micah, gon' be a millionaire. An' a lot sooner than you think too."

"What do you mean?"

"Well, we gonna have to move up the release date of the album by a week or two."

"Why is that? What for?"

"Motherfuckers already bootlegging the shit."

"Are you fuckin' kidding me? How are they doing that? How did they get a hold of it?"

"Well, I gave it to them," Hannibal replied nonchalantly.

This caught Micah off-guard. "What . . . what? *You* gave it to them? What do you mean . . . you bootlegging your own shit? Why would you do that?"

"Well, I figured, with the way the fucking Internet is, niggas was gonna be bootlegging shit anyway. So I might as well distribute it to them myself and get a cut off that side action. An' this way Crown don't get shit. It's just profits for us all around. You get what I'm saying?"

"Yeah, yeah . . . but then again, naw, naw."

"Don't worry about it, you'll get it when you grow up."

"Yeah, whatever." Then while Micah tried to understand the numbers behind what Hannibal was doing, it suddenly hit. "Oh yeah, I wanted to talk to you about something," he said, recalling the purpose of his visit.

"We can talk about it on the way," Hannibal answered while reaching for his coat.

"On the way . . . where are we going?"

"We are going to see . . . my parents."

"You have parents?" Micah blurted.

"Fuck yeah, what you think? I sprung from immaculate conception, or something?"

"Naw, that came out wrong. I'm just saying that I never heard you speak of them before."

"Yeah, well, there are reasons for that. But I'm glad that you're here, so you can roll through."

"All right," Micah nodded as he and Hannibal made their way out of the office. He did not believe that Hannibal was the product of immaculate conception but he was curious about the man's parentage. Without a doubt, Hannibal was the most independent person that he had ever met. It was as if he was born big, without a history, and had left the womb walking and self-sufficient. The thought of Hannibal with parents struck him as odd, coming from a man who never spoke of or seemed to have need of anyone.

With Hannibal in the lead they cut the corner into the smoke-filled lounge. Every man, upon seeing Bull, sat at attention, except for Mook, who remained unmoved. Hannibal walked through saying nothing, restraining himself. He didn't have to act; he knew that a purge was coming.

Micah kept in step behind him as Hannibal shepherded him through the wolves, while Mook eyed him from behind with an air of antipathy.

"Where you headed, Bull?" Mook asked.

"We just gotta take care of some business," Hannibal replied with his back to the question.

"Cool. I'll roll through."

"Naw, that's okay, god. It's cool: we'll handle it," Hannibal retorted, giving Mook his full attention.

After a cumbersome silence, Mook replied as he had before, "Cool." Hannibal gave him a nod of the brow to quiet the matter and he and Micah headed out the door, leaving Mook behind, in a fog of weed and an odium festering.

THiRTY-FOUR

The black SUV turned onto the residential block in Brownsville, Brooklyn, and parked before a modest-looking house, which was attached to all of the other modest-looking houses that aligned the block. It was only after 5:00 P.M., but dusk had already set. A gray shadow coddled the concrete. Hannibal threw his hood tightly overhead and the two men stepped out of the vehicle. Hannibal was hooded to mask himself as he went to the house. With his picture on the cover of every hip-hop publication and billboards and flyers in abundance, he was finding it difficult to walk about without being recognized. Today, he had no desire to be known, at least not here.

He made an aggressive move up the steps. Micah followed at a slower pace. When he had arrived he was able to see the white-stained-yellow, aluminum-sided exterior of the house and the storm shutter hanging off its hinges with its ripped meshed window. Hannibal rang the bell. In the time that they waited, Micah wondered if this truly was where Hannibal's parents lived.

"Who's there?" an older female voice finally called from within.

"Mama, it's me," Hannibal answered with a measure of humility in his tenor. They waited but there was no further response. "Mama, it's Gavin." Gavin . . . who is Gavin? Micah wondered. No, it couldn't be, Hannibal? But if it wasn't why would he say it, and to his mother at that. Hannibal's given name seemed like an unnatural thing that had no relation to the man standing outside of the door. It came not only as a shock to Micah but likewise to its bearer. It had been more than ten years that he had been going by the name Hannibal; he no longer felt like a Gavin, in fact, he never believed that the name fit him. Now he was at the doorstep of his parents and they would acknowledge him in no other manner.

"What do you want?" his mother curtly replied.

"I came to see you, Mama. You and Dad." There was another sustained pause. Micah could feel the tension in the air. Before the door opened it was proceeded by the sound of multiple locks from top to bottom being aggressively undone. A slim woman in her late forties, of a stern figure with an erect carriage and a drawn face upon which sat bifocal frames, now stood in the doorway. Today was Thursday but she was dressed in church wear: clogs with white stockings; a long white skirt; sensible matching white blazer; a white shirt, buttoned to the neck; and a white hat with a matching plume. She was a scary figure as Micah perceived her.

"Come in," she said uninvitingly.

Hannibal respectfully removed his hood and both men softly crossed the threshold into the grips of a small living room, narrow and claustrophobic, beyond which there was a small kitchen and dining area. It was a humble dwelling and ornately Christian. On every inch of every wall there were framed pictures of a white Jesus and quoted psalms and proverbs. There were also seemingly innumerable porcelain religious figurines. They were everywhere, from the coffee table, to the old wood-framed television, to the dining table, to the stovetop, to the glass unit. There was also a two-foot mock-up of Jesus standing by the side of the door. It shocked Micah in the shin as he entered. Hannibal had not been here in years, yet nothing had changed, not even the music. The songs of gospel played through with the welcome of a funeral dirge.

"Hello, Mama," he said. He thought to hug her but seeing the stern expression on her face he chose not to.

"Hello, it is very nice to meet, you Mrs. . . ." Micah had begun a sentence without realizing that he didn't know how to finish it.

"Scott," Hannibal added.

"Mrs. Scott," Micah said, completing the greeting and the picture. Gavin Scott, that's his name.

"And who is this, Gavin? Another one of your drug-dealing friends?" In her voice Micah heard what seemed to him to be a repressed accent; from where it came exactly, he could not tell. Nevertheless, an accent was definitely there. "No, Mother. I told you, I don't do that anymore," Hannibal answered respectfully. He was prostrating himself. It was a strange thing. Micah had never seen him show deference to anyone before.

"No. Now you do that rap . . . whatever. As if that's any better," his mother responded to her son's humility. "Go ahead, take a seat." She gestured to the sofa. Across the brown, worn-out carpeting there lay a plastic path that led to the couch, which was set against the wall and equally dressed in plastic. Hannibal walked ahead and seated himself. Micah followed, knowing not to make a step outside of the borders. He sat down gently and could hear the ripples in the plastic as his weight settled. Mrs. Scott sat in the opposing and equally dressed loveseat.

"So tell me, young man," she said to Micah, "what church do you go to?" There was an interrogatory manner in her question that made Micah feel as if he were back in the 1950s and he was on trial at the senate subcommittee for un-American activities, and McCarthy had just asked if he was or had he ever been a communist?

"No, ma'am, I don't have one. I don't go to church."

"Hmm," she replied with the sharpness of a dagger.

"You have a very nice home, Mrs. Scott," Micah commented, feeling that he had to say something nice to ease her distemper.

"Thank you."

"No it's not," Hannibal interrupted, speaking more forcefully, but nevertheless with obvious restraint.

"Excuse me?"

"It's not, Mother. You've been living in this same . . . place all of my life. It's falling apart."

"Falling apart but not fallen. The Lord keeps it up," Mrs. Scott rebutted.

"Oh God, always the same thing."

"Oh God, indeed. Something you seem to have lost all sight of."

Hannibal was going to say something when he heard the sound of keys at the door. The other occupant of this house had come home. Everyone sat in an awkward silence, waiting for all of the locks to be undone and for the door to be opened. Hannibal's father was a dark-skinned older man in his fifties, of an average height, with a stout frame, carrying a lunch box and wearing a bus driver's uniform. He had a sour demeanor as he entered the house, which quickly grew bitter as he caught eye of his company.

"What are you doing here? I thought I told you never to come to this house again," his father greeted.

"Hello, Father, how are you?"

"You have not answered the question. Why have you soiled the grace of my home?" The insults came with an unnatural aggression. It made Micah wonder what had happened to erode their relationship to such an extent. Hannibal shook his head to keep his calm. "I came to see you, Father. I am your son, after all."

"No, you are not. I buried my son a long time ago." Micah had heard it in his mother but in Hannibal's father it was confirmed. They spoke with a Jamaican accent; it was repressed heavily, nonetheless it was there.

"I understand," Hannibal calmly replied with little reaction to his father's statement. Still it was true that they had buried him. Straight ahead in the glass unit, Micah was able to see a framed picture of a younger Hannibal with candles burning about him in the manner in which they would eulogize the dead.

"But I told you, I don't deal drugs anymore, Father."

Oh, so that was it. So then Hannibal truly had been a drug dealer. "Good for you, good for you. But what are you doing now?" Mrs. Scott asked.

"I am making music."

"You call that music," she said with a scoff. She then pointed upward, referring to the canticle that was being played. "Now this, this is music."

"Gospel, can't argue with that," Hannibal replied, returning the sarcasm. He was still restraining himself but his deference was waning.

"You have still not answered the question. Why are you here?" his father pressed.

"Well, Father, I am here because I wanna move you out of this place."

"And how do you propose to do that?"

"Well, Father, I have been doing all right for myself. So I would like to buy you a house. It could be anywhere you want. I remember you always talked about moving to Florida. Well, now you can."

"Boy, you must be crazy if you think that I would take any of your drug money."

"I told you that I don't deal drugs anymore. Everything I do is legal now." Listening in, Micah could sense the strain that having to repeat himself was putting on Hannibal.

"Well, just because it is legal don't make it right. Not in God's eyes," his mother added. "The Lord sees what you are doing, Gavin. What difference does it make if you sell drugs or make music about selling drugs?"

"I can't make it right with you, can I?"

"No, Gavin. You need to make yourself right with Jesus."

"And here I thought Christianity was the religion of forgiveness."

"Without any remission of sins, there can be no forgiveness," Mr. Scott responded.

"I understand. But please, Father. I can't stand to see you live like this." He went into his pocket and took out a large roll of bills. Hannibal didn't sell drugs anymore but he still carried his money like a dealer. "Please, Father, take this."

"Boy, have you not heard a word that I have said that you would so insult me?"

"How do I insult you? I am trying to take care of you. Doesn't it say to honor thy mother and father?"

"Is this how you honor us?" his mother asked.

"Listen hear, Gavin. I have heard your music." His father began to speak to his son for the first time without being on the offensive. "I have heard your voice and I must tell you that there is something in it. You have a gift, child, a way to motivate and inspire people. With that gift you were meant to be a minister." Hannibal shook his head in disbelief. "I have something to share with you, something that we have never shared with you before; just for the fear of speaking it out loud we wouldn't dare. However, now I feel that it is time that you knew. But it was that when you were born, that you were born with a veil of fat over your face. It was a very odd thing to occur and the doctors thought that it was strange. Though, thank the Lord, you were healthy and dismissed from the hospital without delay. But your mother and I being spiritual people sought spiritual counsel. The spiritualist that we brought you to took a fright when he held you. He said to us that this child is born special and meant for greatness: that the child had a mind greater than all of the politicians of the island put together. He said that you would be great but if you were to be for great evil or great good, he did not know. All he knew was that you were going to be great. And the thought that you may be evil frightened him. Your mother and I visited other spiritualists and they all said the same thing, more or less. Given the task set before us, we saw to making sure that you would be of great good. And the Lord knows that we tried. We tried, boy, but the devil would not be undone, he had his grips in you. When we saw that he had fully taken you, we had no choice but to let you go. You are gifted, Gavin. There is a force and a power in your tongue. Unfortunately, you have chosen to use your voice and your gifts in Satan's ministry. And I have no welcome for the devil or any in allegiance with him even if they are of my seed. So you are dead to me, Gavin. Leave my home, and heed my words well this time: never return."

"Mother," Hannibal said, turning to the womb for his final appeal.

"Do as your father said."

"Fine."

Hannibal gave a look to Micah and both men then slowly rose, peeling themselves from the plastic sofa. Micah had been quiet through it all. Now that it was time to leave he had no thought of what to say exactly. "Good night, it was very nice meeting you both."

"Child, I can see it in your eyes that you are a good boy, you have a good soul. Do yourself a favor and leave that one alone, he will bring you nothing but trouble. I bore him, and for that reason I chose to bear no more," Mrs. Scott said to Micah.

To his wife's words, Mr. Scott shook his head slightly. His eyes spoke of the frustration that his mouth didn't. Hannibal had been restraining himself for the entire visit, but now the final straw had fallen.

"Y'know what, I may have been a drug dealer, but y'all are worse. You are nothing but addicts. Religion has got you more doped up than any drug could ever do. You are high off of your superstitions. Worse thing is, you don't even know it. You bury me. Well, I bury you too. Don't worry, this is the last time that I am coming here. You make me sick. But you are right. I am great. Evil? I laugh when I look at the fear in your eyes: old and pathetic."

"I pray for you, Gavin."

"Don't pray for me, Mother!" he roared loudly. "I have done fine so far without your prayers. Hell knows what your prayers will do for me now. I'm out. Let's go, god; there ain't no heaven here."

Hannibal and Micah crossed the threshold and the door closed quickly behind them. With his hood off, Hannibal quickly descended the steps and headed toward the Jeep. Before he arrived he was stopped and recognized by two teenage girls, who fawned in his presence. Micah was prepared to step down from the landing himself when he looked up and saw a billboard in the distance. It was one of the ads for the new album. It featured Hannibal in ancient armor, sitting atop a great African elephant with an army in back of him with the words *Elephant Warfare* scripted across. Micah began to think of Hannibal's parents. They may have wanted to bury their son but they would have to look at his image everyday as they went into and out of their house.

THiRTY-FiVE

In the beginning was the Word
And the word was with God,
And the word was God.
The same was in the beginning
With God.
All things were made by him;
And without him was not
Anything made that was made.
In him was life; and the life was
The light of men.
And the light shineth in the darkness;
And the darkness comprehended it not.

In the light of the rectory, in a dark church suit, young Gavin comprehended nothing but that he had been sitting on the hard wooden bench for hours. His ass had fallen asleep and he felt that if he had remained there for a minute longer the other members of his anatomy would likewise begin to atrophy.

It was the dead of winter and inside it was as hot as hell. Outside a coat of ice covered the naked branches and sheeted the roads. This was Brownsville, Brooklyn, and like all the other poor areas of the world it was neglected. Snowplows all but never came that way. The people had to wait for the spring and nature to thaw the ice. By that time, it had eroded the streets and fattened the potholes. So it was on ice that Mr.

Scott drove his family as his old Lincoln Town Car coughed and skidded its way to the nearby church. It was a small church set in the middle of the block between a liquor store and a burned-out Brooklyn public library. Young Gavin entered coated, scarfed and hooded, and after thirty seconds he felt like stripping.

It was hell in the church. The old radiator was a fickle thing. At times it didn't work and the parishioners would have to suffer through the freezing hours. On other days, as it did on that day, it shot out burning steam with a loud clank. It was as hot as summer, when the women went about fanning themselves with any makeshift fan that they could find. The men sat pulling and gnawing at their upright shirt collars, while the children sat in a constant fidget. Everyone wanted to at least unbutton their shirts and take off their shoes. But they wouldn't; church propriety would not allow it.

Eleven-year-old Gavin sat there in silent misery, listening to the rector wail on and on, quoting scripture after scripture, expressing every comma of his speech with a gargle. Froths of saliva had begun collecting in the corners of his mouth. The microphone, which appeared to be the only thing that worked well in the church, reverberated every breath to gross proportions. Seeing the wads of spit sling forth, Gavin began to pity the parishioners up front. He pitied the microphone even more, which he now suspected had to smell like a mix of cheap cologne and a septic tank. Add to this Mrs. Brown's constant cheerleading, jumping up and down in a bawl with the pastor's every inflection, and one had a subtle understanding of Gavin's torment. *I am missing Transformers for this? If God was good, why would he torture me so?*

As he pondered these questions he fell into a trance and was taken away by his reveries. He began to believe that he was Galvatron, the purple-clad leader of the Decepticons, and that he was able to transform into a cannon and make fodder out of all who stood in his path. As he daydreamed, his head nodded back and forth and for the first time since he had been there a smile took over his face. But then it suddenly went away. He felt an unnaturally cruel shooting pain in his abdomen. He was awakened to a scream but a gloved hand was set before his mouth ready to muffle his outcry. The hand belonged to his mother, as did the source of his pain. She had pinched him back into reality.

A pinch: If ever there was a more cruel way of administering pain, young Gavin did not know. He would have preferred that she had punched him, slapped him, kicked him, even whipped him. If she had done any of that, that still would not have equaled the immense pain brought on by one pinch; especially the way his mother did it. She would dig in deep and grab hold of a chunk of skin and flesh and twist it about. When she had let go, his brown skin had turned bloodshot red and the sting to his side would last him for a day, perhaps two.

"Now you will know how better to act in the house of the Lord," she said to him. This was her reasoning for the pain. God. It seemed to Gavin that God was the root of all pain. He was the cause that made him suffer so. Born into this cold world alone, with two Christian parents and no siblings; oh, how he longed for a younger brother, someone to pass the torment with, to play with, to talk to. "Speak when spoken to," she always demanded. So he rarely spoke and damned he was if he spoke with an accent. His mother would never tolerate that. He wanted someone to laugh with. There was little laughter in his house, nothing but the strict adherence to gospel. His only relief came when he slept, when he could dream. He used to love dreaming and he used to hate that he had to break his sleep and be up for school at the dawn of every weekday. He hated even more that he had to give up his somnolence and his cartoons on a Sunday as well. By nightfall every Saturday, his mood would turn sour as he would consider the great torment he would have to endure the next day.

At first he folded his hands and pouted his lips in anger. His mother gave him an unforgiving look, and he knew to let go of his pose. He laid his hand flat on the wooden bench under his coat. The splinters in the old wood were beginning to prick his rear but he knew not to fidget, lest his mother pinch him again. He limited his fidgeting to his hand under his coat. He moved his hand back and forth aimlessly until it met up with something inadvertent and warm. He pushed it in, to then look up and find Mariana Reyes amiably smiling at him.

She was a pretty little Cuban girl, with a smooth deep brown complexion, accentuated by her rich black hair, who at thirteen was already well into showing the signs of puberty. She was a precious thing to the eyes and she was smiling at him.

Why was this pretty girl smiling at me? he thought. He didn't know the answer to this but he liked it. He also didn't realize that his hand had pursued the solid warmth even farther and had landed itself upon her exposed knee. When he became aware, he thought to move it. But another softer hand fixed his hand to its place. He didn't know the exact meaning of this but it excited him. So with her hand on top of his, he massaged her kneecap. She began to incline herself closer to his position. This induced him to do the same with discretion. Under the watchful eye of his mother, he edged closer to her as did his hand, under the coat, toward her thigh. It began to move slowly up and under the ruffles of the fine church frock, all unbeknownst to her older brother and mother and father, who sat to her right.

The two enjoyed themselves that day in silence and within a minute Gavin's hand was in her underwear, in between thighs, in between flesh, warm and wet; he lost himself and before he knew it the service was over. It was time to go. The two youngsters without a word left with their separate parties, and young Gavin savored the smell on his fingertips.

That turned out to be the best service Gavin had ever been to, and so the services remained to be week after week. Whenever they were able to sit together they would fondle each other, at times with her hand in his pants, under the cover of all of the noise and rancor of church. When chance did not allow, they suffered in their longing. Either way, it made Sundays far more interesting, and a reason to go to bed early on Saturday night. This pious affair went on for two years.

Until one Sunday when Mariana had excused herself to go to the bathroom, teenage Gavin followed her and did the same. Unplanned, the two met in the rectory hallway and as she walked by, he grabbed hold of her hand and she willingly went with him as they hid in the unlocked janitor's closet. Within seconds his trousers were down and her dress was lifted up high. They found each other there for the first time in callow untamed fury. And they were so engrossed that they paid no mind to the noise of the people moving about. It was not until the janitor had pulled open the curtain and they were given an audience of fifty . . .

The shame was too much; within a month Mariana and her family had fully moved from Brownsville to Bronx. Mrs. Scott had to abandon the church she had been attending for the past eight years and seek God in another, miles away where no one knew her. For this, she thanked her son by whipping him. Only slaves had been beaten as badly. Throughout it all, the thirteen-year-old did not shed a tear and felt no shame for his actions. Sundays in church without Mariana were never the same. She was the closest thing to intimacy that he had ever felt with a woman. He had never felt that way again.

In high school Gavin was a quiet, brooding young man. With the no-name apparel that his parents bought him, in this vain world, he should have been a great target. Strangely he was never picked on. There was so much ember in his eyes that the other boys feared him, though his quiet intensity was an attraction to girls; he didn't even have to talk to them, they would always come to him. He was especially a target for older women and at a time when he was in the apartment of one such, she told him that he gave off a particular pheromone, like musk. It was a natural scent that gnawed at the estrogen in women. He took heed of what she said that day, before he entered her with a dispassionate fury.

As he walked to school one day, a car pulled up to him. Two strange older men were inside. The one in the passenger seat called Gavin forward. He told him that he would pay him $100 to make a delivery. Gavin accepted, never questioning what was in the package. He didn't have to. No one would pay so much to deliver anything other than drugs. He had no problems with it. Drugs were as pandemic in the community as poverty and the crisp bills aroused him like nothing else ever did. He cut school and took the train to Harlem to deliver the goods.

A week later the very same car caught Gavin as he was leaving school. It was another package and another $100. This time the delivery was in Jamaica, Queens. And so he became intimate with the game of drugs. He began to make regular deliveries for Rodigan. He was the slim, light-skinned man who always rode shotgun and, as Gavin would learn, was one of the biggest dealers in Brooklyn. He trafficked in everything, from crack cocaine to weed, with a slew of young boys, much like Gavin, working for him. They would hit the streets, from barrio to barrio, from Crown Heights to Bed-Stuy, pushing the weight, as it were.

Rodigan took a liking to the young man for the simple fact that he was silent and never asked questions. He decided to promote him into dealing. There was to be a meeting at the base in the Cypress Hill projects; young Gavin was invited to meet the rest of the crew. Rodigan and his Latino counterpart, Bolívar, were there along with fifteen other teenage boys. When it came time to introduce himself to the others, he clearly pronounced *Hannibal*; this was the first time that he had ever referred to himself as such. The name shook everyone in attendance. The weight of the name and the conviction in which he pronounced it could evoke no other emotion but respect. At this time, Rodigan began to look at him differently from the rest.

All of the boys were paired together, each team taking a certain area of a certain neighborhood. It was at this time that Hannibal met and became friends with Mook. Mook was an impressionable young man who was always seeking to make an impression. Like the rest, he was born into poverty and he saw drugs and the lifestyle as the path of salvation. In school he had been a bully and a thief and had gotten into enough fights to make him a staple in the juvenile facilities. He did all of these things to receive the respect that he believed he deserved. He admired and envied Hannibal for the respect that he gained effortlessly. Mook began emulating his friend; they became good friends, they had become brothers, it seemed, and Hannibal was able to laugh for a time, as they also grew to be well-matched partners. Their teamwork made for the most lucrative pairing of Rodigan's eight.

In those years young Hannibal looked at the world around him and he was disgusted by the state his people were living in. He saw that the true difference between black and white was green. In this capitalist world, green was the only color that mattered. "The white folks had it and they wanted to make sure that black folk never got it." He saw ascension through the steps of dollar signs. So he saved his money, unlike his counterparts. While they ran to buy the latest Jordans he kept his old ones and stored his money in a shoebox. His modesty was, for one, due to the fact that he was always one for substance rather than flash, and also the fact that new clothes and sneakers would have to be explained to his parents. He kept the material benefits of his side profession limited; an after-school job, which he never went to, explained his late evenings.

Two well-dressed Italian men, both walking with an overseer's disposition, came to visit Rodigan one day. The manner in which they surveyed the apartment clued Hannibal in that these were the true bosses of the operation. That was the first time that he saw Jersey and Jacobin. He liked the calm and control he saw in Jersey, likening it to that which he saw or would like to see in himself. And likewise, Hannibal was of particular interest to the gangster. Jersey was unmistakably drawn to the young man, for many reasons, the most apparent of which was the fact that unlike all of the rest, he was the only one not blunted at the time. Jersey asked that the young man travel back with Rodigan to Jersey's office. Hannibal was set to leave, at which time Mook became visibly disappointed; at his urging and Hannibal's request, he was permitted to go as well. And so it began that through his company, whatever doors were opened for Hannibal were opened for Mook.

In the drive to Jersey's Bay Ridge office, Hannibal quietly listened in. He began to learn the intricacies of the business, the dealings with the Colombians and the Peruvians, the connections in Boston and L.A., and the wholesale and the market value of the trafficked contraband. He became inspired as to how he could set up his own operations, irrespective of Rodigan.

At sixteen Hannibal had been working for Rodigan for two years. In that time he had saved just about all of his money. He had accumulated a little over $50,000. It was an incredible feat for any teenager but Hannibal, even at that age, had already begun to see the big picture. He knew that there was far more money out there. What he had was only a fraction. So it was that he and Mook made a trip to Jersey's office. The young men, under a watchful Jacobin, were allowed into the underground enclave where Hannibal requested to be made Jersey's Brooklyn provost. Jersey laughed at the teenager's ambition but was impressed by his courage and vision. Having already taken a liking to him, Jersey allowed Hannibal to set up a small operation of his own and introduced him to the contacts that he would be dealing with in Boston.

Hannibal did set up shop and, through his efficacy of management, within a year was nibbling away at Rodigan's business. He attracted other dealers: one, because of his age, and two, because he offered a larger share of the profits than Rodigan afforded them. It was here that he met Terrence. Terrence was a skinny kid, who at thirteen had been in enough fistfights to last thirteen lifetimes. He was gully and rough around the edges but he was also quite possibly the best salesman Hannibal had ever met. The boy could talk and when his voluble pitch had ended, the prospect had bought tenfold what he originally desired. Hannibal liked Terrence in the beginning because he made him money. He would grow to love him for his energy and loyalty. Terrence loved Hannibal off the bat because he was always in control. Terrence didn't know much but he could sense that there was something greater in the man, and he knew that all he needed to do was walk in his path and greatness would come his way as well.

Rodigan became a problem. Young Hannibal had encroached upon his domain too much. Thoughts of killing Hannibal began to brew. Jersey informed him of this, as Rodigan had informed Jersey of his plan. The vision would not be curtailed. So it was that Hannibal and Mook, masked, with shotguns in hand, came upon Rodigan and Bolívar as they sat getting high in the living room of Rodigan's apartment and without words stained the walls and carpets. Hannibal left the room after the blind of the shot; Mook stayed to watch the life ebb away and the blood stains stick. This had been the first time that either had ever done such a thing. Mook enjoyed it and would enjoy it more in the future. Hannibal was unmoved. He broke the killing down in logical terms. He killed Rodigan because Rodigan was going to kill him, because he meant to stifle his vision. Hannibal had seen the big picture now and now he would be a slave to no man; he wouldn't even be a slave to God.

At seventeen, Hannibal was kicked out of his parents' home. It came about when he had started operations on his own. Being the boss was not merely an after-school activity, there were now far greater taxes on his time. Within the last two years Hannibal had been discrete as his parents saw things. Now the excessive truancy became questioned. His mother had hints but no concrete proof. The proof came on a Sunday. His mother came to Gavin's room early that morning to tell him that the Lord beckoned; on that morning Hannibal defied his mother for the first time. She did not take to disobedience lightly. She beat him until she grew tired. Hannibal stood still and bore it; still, to this date, he bore a mark on his back as a reminder. His parents left him alone that day, his mother cursing him in true Christian fashion, his father acquiescing to whatever his wife said. When they returned that Sunday their son was not home, and Mrs. Scott took the liberty of searching his room. She found packed deeply in the back of a large trunk a shoebox, neatly layered with hundred-dollar bills, all having the stink of weed. She called his father to attest to what she had found. They had a discussion, she made the decision and then both parents awaited their son's homecoming. There were no beatings this time; nor choices, as the decision had been made and it was final. "Leave our home." So it was that Hannibal was diswombed for a second time. He took up residence in Cypress and had been on his own ever since.

It was in the late nineties that Hannibal came into hip-hop. He had always been conscious of the movement that had been spawned in the South Bronx some twenty years ago. He had grown with it, watched it as it developed from underground parties to a seedling, to a fad, to mainstream recognition. He appreciated the movement for what it had accomplished. And there came a time when Hannibal saw a newspaper that detailed all of the major moguls of hip-hop. He read about men who had made hundreds of millions of dollars upon the backbone of the beat. He watched videos and saw how they flaunted their excess. Many had made their wealth upon a myth that was truly his life.

Bull knew that his affair with drugs could be exploited for only so long before a jail cell or a bullet found him. Mook at the time was already doing two years in Sing Sing after being found with a nickel bag. His prior offenses and stiffer antidrug laws were enough to get him fitted in an orange jumpsuit. Mook's incarceration was a turning point for Hannibal. His dream would not stand confinement. The word came to him out of necessity.

He listened to rap more now than he ever had. He studied it and recognized that those who had been successful had been so not only for their lyricism but also for the distinctiveness of their sound. He practiced and practiced in private until he had created an animalistic furor of his own. Terrence was the first to notice the talent. Terrence, who had been a graffiti artist and an overall lover of hip-hop, encouraged him to move forward.

But hip-hop was not only about the voice; it was also about the creativity of freestyle. One had to prove himself on the streets. So Hannibal began watching the kids on the corner, analyzing their mode of battle. It then came to him what exactly most freestyling was. It was not always the spontaneous birth of a witty rhyme. Much of it was planned. Freestyle, as it became to him, was the art of ad-libbing. Most rappers had hundreds of rehearsed witty lines, much like a script. The art came into play in how the rapper made these lines fit to whomever he was battling. This would be the ad-libbed line. The ad-lib and the old had to fit smoothly together and delivered almost without thought. It was not an easy skill to master; however, Hannibal, after three months of practicing believed that he was ready to be heard.

He remembered the night that he'd first met Flawless. He was twenty years old and it was at the Spit Café in a four-round emcee battle. He was a virgin to this world but he had already heard of the legacy of the great whore that had taken in man after man and dispatched them all. Hannibal went into battle accompanied by the sixteen. He saw the man, who he perceived to be a cocky pretty boy, sitting quietly in a corner in the back stairway, as was his custom. He had already won so many times that winning had become routine. He was even known to handicap himself at times and flow once to his opponents three in order to make things fair. All in attendance expected him to win. The others fought among themselves merely to see who would be his final competition.

Hannibal had his plan well laid out. He had over three hundred rehearsed lines roaming through his thoughts. He observed all of the contestants, from how they looked to how they walked. He prepared what he could say to belittle their appearance. He watched and listened to each man carefully, and made assumptions as to their possible line of attack against him. He knew that they all knew him or had heard of him. He knew that the fear factor would play a part. Most rappers talked violence; all knew who the real killers were. Hannibal had only killed one man in his life, in what he believed was an act of self-defense. His legend had far surmounted that figure.

Hannibal's planning paid off. He ascended round after round by mixing in his ad-libs with already well-practiced lines. The virgin flowed like a pro until only the great whore was left. Hannibal had not planned for the extent of Flawless's arsenal: he lost but it had been a close battle; so close that he was cheered even in defeat. To have lasted the rounds with Flawless was an extreme accomplishment. The name Hannibal became the murmur in underground hip-hop in the city. Then two weeks later when he defeated Flawless, by following like strategies with new lines crafted especially for Flawless, his name became etched in stone. He was king for a time and he saw his path paved clearly before him. Hip-hop: it was by way of the beat and the word that he would attain his vision.

It would not be accomplished so easily. With a vengeance, Flawless came back and it seemed like battle after battle Hannibal fell before his word. The defeats weighed heavily. He saw Flawless as an obstacle that he had to surpass. Many times he wondered what it would be like if he and Flawless were to join forces; the feats that could be accomplished if he had Flawless's talent within arm span. But he abandoned such fancies. He knew that Flawless would never join him of his own will and he was too proud to make the offer. They remained enemies, battling each other from the Spit to 106 to the championship. Now he was battling Flawless once again, out of house, out of church, under the word of God, with a life of drugs and violence seemingly behind him.

THiRTY-SiX

The car drove through the tollbooth of the New Jersey Turn-pike. Hannibal was going home; Micah was riding along with him. Hannibal seemed visibly upset. It had been an hour since they had left Brownsville and neither one had spoken a word in the entire time. Micah thought to break the intense silence.

"You all right?" he asked.

"I'm cool. I'm cool," Hannibal replied, sternly looking straight ahead at the white line in the middle of the road. After another uncomfortable silence his body eased and he released his tensions. "I'm sorry 'bout that shit back there. I don't know why I'm letting shit fuck with me. It's what I expected. Thanks for being there tonight though. Now you know how I grew up to be as fucked-up as I am."

"No, man, anytime. I was glad to be there. It was kinda crazy though."

"Yep."

"Yo, Bull, there is something that I been wondering and wanting to ask all night; yo, are you Jamaican?"

"Yep."

"Yeah, I know I was picking up something from your parents. But I wasn't too sure. But how come I never hear you speak it? I don't hear an accent in you in the least."

"Well, y'know, I was born there but we came up when I was mad young and I never been back. Plus my mother would never let us speak it in the house. She was born in the gully but she like to act like she was one of dem hill people. So she looked down on it. So we couldn't speak it. So that's a part of my life I don't know. So it's hard for me to really claim it, y'nuh."

"So, I guess, you're more Brooklyn than anything else then?"

"Yeah, yeah. But we all Africans; you taught me that, right?"

"Yeah, yeah, I guess so." At that moment Micah recalled the reason why he had come to Cannibal earlier that day. "But, um yeah, there was something else that I wanted to talk to you about."

"What's that?"

"Yo, man, I think we should cool it down with the whole beef between you and Flawless."

"Really, why is that?" Hannibal asked, already sensing the root of the argument.

"Yo, me and Erika was on the train the other day and these two guys got into an argument and then started beatin' the hell out of each other because of it."

"Who won?" Bull quickly asked him. Not expecting such a question, Micah was silent and Hannibal was forced to ask again, "Who won? The guy fighting for me or the one for Flawless."

"I don't know. We left while the fight was still going on. Plus the cops broke it up. Why do you ask?"

"It's just a question."

"Well, whatever. The point is, cats was beating each other to a pulp over the shit."

"Now, Erika . . . that's Flawless's sister, right?" Hannibal asked. Micah replied in the affirmative, again feeling uncomfortable with her name being brought up, even though he was the first one to mention it. "So you was with Flawless's sister and the two of you saw two niggas fightin' and y'all got spooked, and now you wanna change up our plans?"

"That's not it exactly," Micah said, feeling as if Hannibal had distorted his point.

"Actually it is. Let me explain everything to you, right. Dem niggas weren't fightin' because of the music. They was fightin' 'cause they stupid niggas. And that's what stupid niggas do. And now if they fighting, it means that they listening to the music, and if they listening to the music, it means that they will be buying the shit, and if not them, we know the white kids who idolize them will be buying it, which is good for business. And that works for both me and Flawless; and we are all businessmen."

"So it's all good if it makes us money?"

"C'mon, stop being naïve. This is America, the fucking capitalist capital of the world. And hip-hop is the most capitalistic shit out there. All this shit is about money. And you know this. Don't write the shit and then get weak on me now. But I know what this is, this ain't about me and Flawless, it's about that ho you fucking. It is, isn't it?" Hannibal had said the insult arbitrarily and had not meant it to be truly insulting. For him it was merely a manner of speaking. Nevertheless, it struck Micah deeply.

"Yo, I don't appreciate the disrespect. Don't call her a ho."

Such lines coming from a man to Hannibal was a funny sorrow. "Oh, god, you're gone. You lost. You don't think she's a ho? That's the sure sign of a lost nigga. Yo, get this shit straight: They are all hos, every last one of them."

"Even your mother?" Micah retorted, knowing that despite how men usually felt toward other women, there was always an innate reverence toward Mother.

"Fuck yeah. Jus' 'cause she gave birth to me don't change that," Hannibal stated flatly and Micah was left silent. "That's where niggas get it twisted. She might be Mom to me but she just a ho to another man." After a pause in his speech, and a shake of Micah's head, he continued. "Yeah, she's a ho. She's a ho for Jesus. She an' all the rest a dem church bitches, saving that shit for the afterlife so they can join Jesus' harem and run tricks in heaven. Y'know, for years she ain't been giving the old man none. That's why his weak ass is so bent up and frustrated." There was another break in which all Micah could do was hold his head in his palm and wait for the punchline that never came. "You hear what they said. Bury me. I'm their only child and they wanna bury me without bullets. Bury me and praise their white Jesus. Naw, hell naw; I'ma bury you! Damn right, she's a ho." Hannibal had rambled all of that out aimlessly, more so speaking to himself than Micah. Then he brought his attack Micah's way. "You know what you sound like, you sound like one of them people who's all about, 'why do we disrespect women in our music,' an' all that bullshit."

"Why do we?" Micah simply asked, posing a question that he had many times wondered himself.

"C'mon, nigga, don't tell me you're this lost. Can't nobody disrespect anybody who don't wanna be disrespected. We disrespect them, right? So then why a thousand bitches fucking fightin' to get into a nigga's video? Listen, I've seen bitches suck up to three dicks just to suck mine. And this was happening before I got into music. Tell me, is it disrespect to call a roach a roach or am I just stating a fact and calling a thing by its name?"

"I'm sorry, man, I just don't see everything the way you do."

"Yes you do. You just don't want to admit. You a man, why you make how women are treated trouble you? Listen, I'm tired of people telling me shit. It ain't my job to fucking uplift the woman! Same way it ain't white folks' job to uplift niggas. Why should a cracker care if you respect yourself? It's better for him if you don't, right? All the better for him to stick it to you. Same way it's better for you that the woman is a ho. Because don't fool yourself, all you really want is the pussy. And the easier she gives it up, quicker you can leave that bitch and move on to another hole. Shit is, sometimes pussy get good and niggas get stupid. Which is where you're at right now."

"Yo, man, you sick."

"Naw, nigga, I'm real, and I'm right and you know it. Go ahead smile, laugh to yourself and then say, 'Bull is right.' "

His remarks did bring a smile to Micah's face, though still no sympathy for the argument. "You're funny, I will give you that. Let me ask you something seriously though. You ever felt any kind of love for a girl?"

"God, you're killing me. Where you coming from with all this shit?" he asked while laughing.

"Just answer the question!" Micah pressed in an attempt to cut through the mockery.

For a moment Hannibal thought of the girl in church. "Fuck no, I ain't got time for that shit."

"That's sad, man. You don't know what you're missing. That's really sad."

"No it's not. It's real. I'm a hustler; all I got time to do is hustle. Look around, man. Look at the shit that we living in. Cat wakes up everyday to roaches in the cereal box, no heat in the house, piss in the elevator, garbage in the streets, rundown school, fucked-up teacher, no textbooks. Go home to either get harassed by the police or robbed or shot by gangs. Shit is fucked-up all over. And all you wanna do is get out of it. So you hustle. If you can ball, you ball everyday. If you can flow, you flow everyday. If you can't, you push weight and sometimes you do all three. Shit, man, you do anything just to get the hell outta this . . . hell."

"And you don't see nothing for love in all of it."

"Naw. It's all money. There is mad niggas in love and broke in the ghetto. Look at my father. That ain't me. I see the big picture."

The big picture, that great concept which was the thesis of Hannibal's life; Micah had avoided asking before, but now for once and for all, to better understand the man, he needed clarity. "And so what's the big picture?"

"Bill Gates money and beyond. Total, complete world domination," he retorted, as if the answer had been on the tip of his tongue waiting to be unleashed.

"World domination. C'mon, man, that's an immature European concept."

"We all Africans, right? So they ain't shit they know that we ain't teach them. Watch me, I'ma take over this bitch. This whole fucking thing."

Micah had no immediate rebuttal; at the time he could only think to say, "So then money is all that matters to you?"

"Yep."

With that answer Micah didn't know whether to laugh at him, laugh with him or to feel sad for him. He knew now that Hannibal would never feel love for a woman in the way he did for Erika. He would never experience that terrestrial heaven, the divinity of loving and being truly loved in return. It was happiness without a dollar sign. They had not fathomed a denomination large enough for it. It could not be bought or traded on any market for there was no price tag for peace. It was as free as the intangible and as fantastic as the surreal. Hannibal may indeed take over the world but he would never know this, and no argument or trick of sophism at the time could bring him to it. Micah did not know what to say so he said nothing—and they drove on again in silence.

THiRTY-SEVEN

Flawless sat around the table in his large and rather exquisite kitchen. As his cook went about fixing him a snack, he looked past the island in the center at the custom-made cabinets and remembered just how much they had cost. They were made of real oak and wreaked of excess as everything else in the house did. He had become so annoyed by all this that he had sold three of his seven cars and had plans to sell a fourth. He was not on the brink of bankruptcy—intervention had saved him and the planned international tour would handle the rest—but after halting at the promontory he had resolved to expunge the disease, one cut at a time. He would keep his cook, however. In the past two years he had fallen in love with Maria's touch. The things she could do to a plain tuna fish on rye with extra lettuce. His mouth watered at the thought and he couldn't wait for her to place the sandwich before him. He bit into it and, with a full mouth and a smile, thanked her for her care and services.

"Will there be anything else?" she asked him.

After a swallow he answered, "No, that will be it, thank you."

"Okay, Mr. Flawless, have a good night," she said before leaving the kitchen and returning to her quarters. Mr. Flawless, she called him. She had done this for two years, and for two years it never failed to amuse him. He placed the sandwich down on the saucer and returned his mind to his thoughts before hunger. He had laid out on the table numerous applications for different colleges across the eastern seaboard. Recently the bug to go back to school had bitten. He wasn't quite sure how he would be able to, given his schedule with the new album. Still, free time would come in months and he thought that if he were still alive that he would like to sit in a classroom again and talk of philosophy, literature, science and history. There was so much to be learned.

While Maria was leaving, Mrs. Williams entered with the clank of excess jewelry and the thundering of heels. She was set to go to a club, with her dress, black and fitted, and her wig, blonde and molded to her scalp. His mother, with a lot of free time and a personal trainer, had returned her figure to some semblance of old. She entered from behind and kissed her son on the cheek and left with him the richness of her perfume. "Hello, son, how are you?" she greeted in jubilance.

"I'm fine, Mommy. How are you? All dressed up, I see." Her attire came as no surprise. Within the last year his mother had grown into new company and had begun going out.

"Yes, my dear, me and the girls are going to hit the town. So tell me, honestly. How does your mother look?"

At this point Erika walked into the kitchen toward the refrigerator, in front of which her mother stood. "Beautiful," Flawless replied.

"Yeah, Mommy, you look so good," Erika said, concurring with her brother.

"Thank you, thank you," answered Mrs. Williams with a diva's bow. "So what are you looking at there, Michael?"

"Nothing, just some college applications. I was thinking of going back to school."

"Really, and what for?" she inquired.

The question was like an electric jolt to the elbow for both brother and sister.

"Wow, Mom. I thought you would be all for it . . . y'know, education and responsibilities and all that."

"Yes, Michael, all that was relevant before you were a success. That's what school is for. But you already are a success, and you already are responsible. So what's the point in going now?"

"I guess there isn't any," he replied, feeling too weird to argue what used to be his mother's point.

"But it is all up to you. Sweetheart, you do whatever makes you happy. But now I have to go. So you say I look good, right?"

"Yes, Mommy; you look great."

"Great, so I am off. You be good and don't wait up."

With that she left with the same thunder in which she came.

"That was weird," Erika remarked.

"Yeah, I guess things change."

"Yeah, but they shouldn't change that much."

"But still, if there is anyone who deserves to live it up, it's her."

They both smiled at each other and both of them recognized that it had been a while since they had shared such a moment. He felt as if he had his old sister again; someone who he could talk to, and he needed so desperately to speak to someone on the issue of visions. Perhaps now was the time.

"Michael, we have to talk."

"Yes we do, but you first," he replied. He couldn't wait to tell her but he was happy that she also had something to impart. He thought that it would likewise be about the fact that they had not been speaking.

"Okay, I think that you should squash the whole thing you have with Bull."

"I didn't start it," he said, confused and curious to see where this came from.

"Well, then, you finish it," she replied.

"Why are you bringing this to me now? I battled Bull for years, it never bothered you before."

"Well, because now it's bigger than before. This is bigger

than you think. It affects more people than just you and Bull. I mean, Micah and I were on the train the other day and these two guys just started beating each other up over it."

"You and Micah." He tried not to show it but he had just swallowed the name as if it were undiluted sulfur bitters. "The nigga you been seeing . . . the one in Hannibal's camp?"

She hated him using the word *nigger*. She hated it even more in reference to Micah. *Micah*. He hated the name just for being and even more for its affiliations. In the past three months Erika had returned home late many nights and many nights she did not return at all. She was gone; lost herself to this name. And it had seen all of her and touched her in places where no one should. Like the soil with a fixation for dirt she returned to it again and again. Her purity and sweetness were forever gone as she stood before him now, a remnant of her former self. He shielded his feelings and looked upon the waning beautiful.

"Yes, what does that have to do with anything?" she asked with irritation in her voice.

"Why don't you ask . . . Micah to stop it?" he replied. It was such a disgusting name. What kind of mother bore such a name? It should have been aborted, miscarried or otherwise forcibly ripped from uterus.

"Why would I do that?" Erika asked, not following his line of argument.

"Because he is the one who's been writing it."

"What are you talking about?"

"Always so naïve. What do you think he does there at Cannibal? Huh, you never asked?"

"He is waiting for his album to come out."

"And in the meantime, he wrote Bull's last three songs. Including the one against me."

All of this came upon Erika with the suddenness of a gut check. "How do you know this?" she asked after a protracted lull.

"One, I know things, and two, I know Bull. I know what he is capable of. He didn't write those songs. And no one else in his camp did; they're too stupid. That only leaves your boy." Flawless had no hard core proof for his theory but it was a well-argued one. He had battled Hannibal for so many years that he was very familiar with his style and range. Hannibal's banter was a signature, unique like a fingerprint, and his prints were not on those songs. "Listen, Hannibal wants to be some old shriveled-up white man. That's where he got all that cannibal shit from. What the hell does he know about Carthage and Rome and history and politics? For years I thought he would get on the ball but he never did, until now." The more Flawless said it to himself, the more it made sense. Hannibal could not have written those songs. And he was thinking this not only because many were saying that with "Coup d'etat" Hannibal had dethroned him. Even though recount after revote he was still leading in percentages, it was a slim lead. Though many had looked forward to the fight, they had expected him to win by a greater margin. The fact that it had been close had thrown everything up in the air. He felt as if he had lost, and had thought to do a rebuttal to a rebuttal but if he did that that, would only entice his foes to come again and this war could wage unto infinitum.

Erika had remained silent. She did not know what to believe. Had Micah lied to her or was it Michael who was lying to her now? Either way, she would be angry with one of the two men in this world who she loved. She left the kitchen without a word. As she walked away he turned and watched her leave. When she had left his view he returned to his neglected tuna fish on rye. It did not taste as good this time. And no matter how much he tried to soil and sully it, she was still beautiful.

THIRTY-EiGHT

It was late and they were already in Jersey. Micah would sleep in one of the large rooms tonight. He had no aversion to sleeping in Hannibal's house and was growing tired of hotels. He had no plans to meet with Erika that night and Hannibal didn't seem in the mood to deviate on the ride over, the latter parts of which were not as tense as they were in the beginning. The mood of both men had eased and they began to joke and laugh again as brothers, in a manner Hannibal would have done with no one else.

Hannibal kept the jokes coming as they entered the house and headed up the large stairway to the second floor.

"Don't worry though, I like you. You're green as fuck but I like your optimism."

"Thanks," Micah returned with dry sarcasm.

They arrived at the second level to a great white hall aligned with a series of rooms. Micah halted at the second door from the stairway. He would rest in this room for the night, as this was the one he usually stayed in when he slept over. Hannibal induced him to do otherwise. It was only 9:00 P.M., much too early to go to bed. Hannibal suggested, and both men agreed, to play video games or watch a movie until fatigue had set in. So they both headed to the last room down the hall, which was Hannibal's.

"Yo, I'm tellin' you, shit don't make any sense. It's like a, like a . . . fuckin' oxymoron, or something," Hannibal raved.

"What' s up with you, man? You against everything tonight?"

"Naw, naw, hear me out. I'm telling you, it don't make no sense. Christian hip-hop is like, like one big fuckin' contradiction. Hip-hop is supposed to be rebellious. It's supposed to be fightin' against the system. Shit ain't supposed to be praising some white Jesus and promoting the quo. What the fuck is that about?"

To all this Micah merely shook his head in exasperation.

"What, you ain't got nothin' to say?" Hannibal commented on his silence.

"Bull, I am learning not to argue with you and not to take you too serious."

"You're right, you can't argue with me. But believe me when I tell you, you better take me seriously."

"Yo, man, I'm not even listening to you."

"Naw, but you are hearing me though."

Micah just followed behind, trying to ignore Hannibal, as they came to his door. The room opened to darkness and Hannibal, being consumed with his conversation, paid no mind to the subtle sounds of sex coming from inside of the room. He had begun to pronounce *lig . . . ,* when a voice from inside the room cut him off. "Yo, Bull, that's you. Don't turn on the lights, don't turn on the lights, just give me a minute."

"Nigga, why you still fuckin' in my room?" Hannibal barked after realizing that Mook was in there. "There are about a thousand rooms in this house and you always gotta be fucking in mine! Yo, hurry up and get out!" This had gone too far, for too many years. What was before only a fraternal annoyance had gone beyond exasperating. Hannibal closed the door. Outside, Micah began to ask him what was going on . . . when something hit him. There in the darkness, there was a shadow of something that struck Hannibal as being odd. On primal intuition alone, without giving it a second thought, Hannibal quickly reentered the room.

"Lights!" he said loudly. The room came alive to him like

never before and as it never would again. "Oh shit, get the fuck outta here!" he replied in complete astonishment at what the light had revealed. Hearing Hannibal's reaction, Micah rushed in to see what was going on. "What is it?" he asked before looking. Then he turned forward: "Oh . . . shit!"

Both men stood at the doorway in silent disbelief as they looked at both Mook and Reaper naked in bed together. They were in the act and Reaper was the apparent recipient. All parties seemed too stunned to move or talk.

"Bull, it ain't what you think," ashamed Mook said, breaking the silence.

"What . . . what . . . what the hell is this?" Hannibal remarked.

"Yo, just give me a chance to explain."

Mook and Reaper then began to separate themselves from each other.

"Explain what? The fact that you're fucking a dude?"

"Yo, you don't understand."

"Understand what? The fact that you a faggot?"

"Yo, I ain't no faggot!" Mook stated boldly.

Hannibal found this hard to believe.

"What? You was just fucking a dude, weren't you?"

"Yeah, I fuck ass sometimes but I ain't no faggot."

"What?" Hannibal reacted dumbfoundedly at what he was hearing. He looked back to Micah. "Yo, you understand that shit?" Micah answered by putting both hands up in a look of confusion.

It shamed Mook that Hannibal had found him like this. It shamed him even more that Micah was there. "Yo, just send everybody out, I'll get dressed and I'll explain it," Mook said to his friend, almost pleading. Hannibal would hear none of it.

"You know what, you and homo thug there get out. 'Cause you, we done—you ain't got shit to explain to me," he said to him with a certainty that had forgotten years of friendship. At this point Reaper hurriedly began getting dressed. Mook did the same but at a slower pace.

"C'mon, Bull. Just send everybody out and I'll explain it," Mook repeated. He was in fact pleading now. Micah began to feel sorry for the man and to having been a witness to this.

"Explain what? You a faggot, and I don't keep company with faggots, so get the hell out," Hannibal barked, punctuating the word with exclamation.

Angered Mook responded, "Yo, I told you, I ain't no faggot. I fuck ass but I ain't no faggot!" This was a logic beyond Hannibal's reasoning.

"What! Are you crazy? Y'know what, I don't care. Chi chi man, fudge packer, pillow biter, whatever you prefer, get the hell out!"

Reaper was fully dressed and in a timid hurry exited the room. Hannibal gave him a look of indignation as he walked by. Micah tried not to look at him at all; he in fact wanted to excuse himself.

Half-dressed, Mook continued his plea. "Yo, listen. You know I did two years in Sing. And y'know . . ."

"So what, you went and lost your manhood." Again he turned back to Micah. "See, I told you about prison, it fucks niggas up." For Mook, having Micah there to share in his shame was the worst part of the matter. "Prison? Yo, man, that shit ain't no excuse. We done, I don't know you."

"That's it. After all these years and the shit we been through. You gon' play me over some shit like this?"

" 'Some shit like this?' Listen, I'm traumatized. That was the most fucked-up thing that I have ever seen. That image just wiped away everything we been through."

"I made you, god."

"Whatever, nigga. Ain't nobody made Bull, not no parents, and no God. I made me. I came by my own and made everything else around me. I made you the president of Cannibal and paid you more than what you was making hustling and you ain't do shit but complain. I been waitin' for a chance to drop your ass. And this just did it. You dead to me, nigga."

"Fuck you. You bury me. At least I am real with myself about what I am. I ain't trying to put cologne on ma shit. You think that you can do all the dirt you did and then just walk away?"

"Yep. And that's it. I'm done talking to you."

No more words were said. Mook grabbed his shirt from the floor, picked up his boots and went to the corner for his coat. As he picked up the heavy leather, he felt the extra weight and remembered that he had his gun. He looked back at Hannibal and put away thoughts of homicide. At the time he couldn't kill Hannibal, he couldn't even think of it. He threw his coat over his arm and walked out with his head as high as he could raise it above the shame. He stopped at the doorway to look at Hannibal but Bull would not look at him. After a second, he turned away and caught Micah in his periphery as he walked out. He, however, could kill him.

It was almost a minute before the two men left alone in the room could say anything to each other.

"You all right?" Hannibal asked Micah.

"Yeah, I'm cool man. I'm okay . . . Um, what about Reaper?" Micah asked.

"What about him?"

"Are you dropping him as well?" He was curious to know.

"Fuck no. That nigga earns for me. I could care less who he fucks. Mook was my boy; he's supposed to watch my back. How's he gonna do that if he's looking at my ass? You tell me?"

Micah felt a buzz in his pocket. He pulled out his pager and checked the message.

I need to see you now.
Call me back as soon as
you get this.
Erika

"Yo, I gotta go," he said to Hannibal. Though he did not like the sense of urgency in the message, he was glad to have received it. He wanted any excuse to get away. This day had been too much. It had started with him knowing nothing about Hannibal. Now he had had his fill of him and all the creatures in his menagerie.

"Pussy calling, huh?" Hannibal asked.

"Whatever."

Hannibal alone was left in the huge house. He walked deeper into his room and sniffed a scent of disgust. He found a can of disinfectant atop the bureau and began to spray the room out. He also removed the sheets from the king-size bed. To distract his mind he turned on the immense television. While flipping through the channels he came upon Player. It was something of a twenty-four-hour fete of pornography. There was a strip show on and Hannibal took an eye to the girl who came on camera. She was beautiful and very good at her craft. Through the immense television her eyes pierced through and it seemed as if she was looking directly at him. As he stared at the screen he felt as if he knew her or had seen her before. He had not but she held a resemblance to someone in the past and as the beautiful Spanish girl danced about, he at once knew that he wanted her.

"Yeah . . . pussy calling."

He made a call. The phone rang thrice and then someone picked up.

"Yo, Terrence."

"Wha' gawn?" Terrence replied over the line.

"Turn your TV to Player."

"Already there."

"See the girl onscreen?"

"Yeah, she sweet. I'm enjoying her right now."

"That's a little bit more information than I needed to know. But what I do need from you is to find out who she is. Get her number and call me back."

"In the mood for love, huh? I'm not sure if I can get it at this time though."

"I understand, but see what you can do."

"Aw'ight."

Terrence fixed his pants and began his search by looking in the cable guide to find the name of the program. Then he went online to the official Player site and did a search for the particular show. The show came up, along with a link. He clicked on this and before the site came he was bombarded by a slew of other nonrelated pornographic sites. It was a bazaar of bizarre proportions in which everything was on sale.

Though intrigued, there was no time to delay. Terrence went straight to the site at hand. He searched until he found the girl. He found her bio, at the bottom of which was the number for the agency that represented her. He called the number. It was too late and no one was in the office but there was a message and a cell phone number was given. He called that number and asked for Mr. Goldstein. Terrence explained to him who he represented and he called Hannibal back after twenty minutes.

"What's the deal?" Hannibal answered.

"Took a few calls but I got her name and number. You in luck, she lives in New York. Believe me, your name goes a long way. You gon' call her?"

"No, you call her. Tell her I wanna see her. Tonight."

Hannibal hung up the phone and continued cleaning his room. Ten minutes later the phone rang again.

"She is excited to see you. I sent a limo for her. She'll be at your place in about two hours."

"Good shit. Talk to you later. And much love for everything."

"Yo, General, always love. And yo, don't hurt her too bad."

Hannibal hung up the phone. Two hours later the doorbell sounded. Hannibal opened the door to reveal the same figure from the television, looking strikingly stunning at his doorstep.

"Hello," she said.

"Come in," he replied.

She stepped into the house and better revealed herself to

him. She wore a well-tailored, three-quarter-length black leather coat. Underneath she wore a mini skirt, which could not be seen given the coat's length and its brevity. Beneath that was pure skin: a beautiful mocha brown, a seemingly flawless coat. He admired her form. She was more attractive than the camera had alluded and taller, in fact. The heels she wore added three inches to her five-foot, six-inch frame; altogether with her disheveled black mane, she was a precious thing to the eyes with her full lips and her deep brown eyes. The past seemed present in her resemblance.

"I have to tell you that it is a real pleasure to meet you. I am a really big fan." Her voice was subtle and had the slightness of an accent. It was Cuban, but he didn't know that; he only knew that it was Spanish and it sounded sweet to his ears.

"Thanks," he replied blandly. "Why don't we go upstairs?" he asked her, more as a command rather than a request.

"Sure. But, um, you didn't want to go out?"

Terrence had invited her over under the pretense that the two were to go on a date.

"Yeah, yeah, but we can do that later," Hannibal replied. Though he had no intentions of going anywhere. He had never gone on a date with a woman before. He had never courted a woman before. He had never spent a dime of his own earnings on any woman; before tonight, other than his mother, he would have never thought to. He never had to. They would always just come to him. There was an unmistakable attraction about his quiet intensity. The pheromones were strong in him. There was a thing about the embers that grabbed hold of the heart and wet the thighs, as it now did for Rosa. That was her name. Hannibal did not know it because he had not bothered to ask. Terrence had. It was his sweet words that got this pretty girl from her house and the company of her friends into an unknown limo to drive two hours until they reached an unknown house in Englewood, New Jersey.

"Okay," she replied. Not being exactly sure. Though she

comforted herself in the presence of his attraction. To have his eyes look upon her now as she had looked at him through television screens and magazine covers was thrilling. He silently pointed the way upstairs, gesturing for her to go first. As she walked ahead he watched her from behind as she ascended the stairs. He examined the firm shape of her bare thighs as they flexed and released with every step of ascension. He thought of putting his hand to the calf of her stem and following it all the way up to the root and fixing itself to the cleavage of her ass.

When they reached the second level she halted for further directions. He again gestured her in front, pointing the way down the long hall to the last room. He allowed her to walk a distance ahead of him so that he could enjoy her stride. She would in turn look back intermittently, smiling to see where he was. She entered the room at his prompting and the devourer came in after. She stood still in the center, in front of the immense television, twirling the belt of her coat. He walked deeper into the enclave and sat in an armchair facing her.

Rosa, feeling the need to break the silence, spoke, "You know, when my agent called and said that Hannibal wanted to see me, I was really shocked. I mean, I had just seen your video on BET and I was thinking about just how hot you are—how handsome you are, and then I get the call. And it was all, like, so weird."

"It was weird for me too," he replied without emotion, with his hands clasped before his lips.

"Really?"

"Really."

"So where are we going tonight?"

"Wherever you would like to."

"Well, I know this really great restaurant in the city. It's on the expensive side, but . . . y'know." After she said that, she knocked herself in her mind. She was in a mansion with Hannibal. He wouldn't care about the expense. Though in truth she would have gone anywhere with him, to a McDonald's or a pizza parlor. It would have all been sweet just to be out in his company.

"It's not a problem, we can do that. But do me a favor first," he said to her slowly.

"What's that?"

"Take off your clothes. I want to see you."

There was such an abruptness in the request that it shook her and made her uncomfortable. It was not that she had a problem taking off her clothes. It was her profession, after all. It also was not that she didn't want to for him. In fact she had fantasized about it many times before and many times on the ride over. But for her this would happen later, after a good talk and a good meal, in those petty moments when people got to know each other. After that, on this first night, she had planned to give of herself willingly. But to arrive here without a prelude was discomforting.

She, however, complied. She had no will to deny or argue the embers. So piece by piece she revealed herself: going from coat to boots to shirt to skirt to bra until finally nothing, nothing but bare beautiful skin. Her confidence had not been with her as she disrobed. For the first time in a long time she felt naked.

"Turn around. Let me see you from behind," he said to her with a piercingly cold methodical. She did as he asked slowly and then returned back to her original position. She felt like covering up but she didn't; she merely played with her thumbs to the side.

"You know, I am really not that comfortable with all this," she found the courage to say.

"Now, that's funny," Hannibal remarked to himself. But noticing the change in her temperament, he spoke to her more soothingly. "It's okay, believe me, it's all right. Come here." At the request she walked over and stood in front of him. He called her down and she bent over to him with the scent of cucumber melon.

"What's your name?" he asked her.

"Rosa," she replied with a quiver. She found it unsettling that she had come so far and he didn't even know her name.

"No, that's not your name; at least not for tonight."

"Then what is my name?"

"Starling. Your name is Starling."

"I don't understand—why Starling?"

"Because you are a being from a star. You're like celestial an' shit."

"Oh, well, okay. Thank you."

She had no idea of what he meant but she took comfort in her ignorance and in what appeared to be a compliment. They began to kiss, or more so she kissed him and he let her. In this tiny display of intimacy she was able to get some ease out of all the awkwardness. "Wow, I always wondered how you would taste," she said to him. To that Hannibal brought his index to her lips. "Shhh, don't talk." They began to kiss again and Hannibal finally indulged himself guiding his hands about her flesh: her breast full and supple; her waist, narrow and smooth; her ass, round and firm; her vagina, neatly shaved and wet, and was getting even wetter as his finger probed in and out of her. Then he stopped her, stared into her eyes and with the guidance of his hand brought her brow to his waist.

There was a bulge in her mouth to the side of her cheek. It appeared as if she had gulped a ball or perhaps an egg or perhaps some small animal and it was moving about, palpitating from side to side. It fascinated him as her hair did a tickle to his abdomen. The sight of it all was the most fascinating part of the experience. In that moment he recalled a concept in economics known as the Law of Diminishing Marginal Utility. It stated roughly that the more one takes of something, no matter how great it is the first time, after each successive turn, one will enjoy it less and less, until they enjoy it none at all and it leads to repulsion.

He thought of this law now as his muscles began to tighten, constrict and then came to an ease. She rose from bended knee, fully dressed in a black mini and a floral blouse, with a smiling face. She ran her fingers through her hair and pulled the blonde mane to the other side. She looked at him now with her blues, and a sense of pleasing; and he looked back at her with a façade behind nothing. He was too busy thinking of the Law of Diminishing Marginal Utility. At that point Flawless had come to a resolution: After the tour, if he were still alive, he would go back to school.

He fixed himself there in one of the studios of Crown Records. He had come to the Manhattan studio to do some recordings and more so to get out of his house. The pretty girl standing before him came by way of a page that she had spent many months, while in the company of many other rappers, waiting for. Now Flawless was thinking of a nice way to tell her to leave. Then a knock came at the door. Flawless asked her to answer it. When the door opened Tommy was surprised and fronted a smile at the blonde before him. "Is Flawless here?" he asked her. She stepped out of the way and revealed Flawless, seated by the big mixing board.

"Tommy!" he shouted with joy to see his good friend. The two friends met and gave each other a strong hug. "What's up, god?" Tommy said to him.

"I'm cool, man. What's up with you, how you been doing?"

"I been doing good. I am doing great actually," Tommy replied. There was a different tone in which Tommy was speaking. Flawless couldn't put his finger on it exactly but the voice seemed stronger to him and distant. The distance was to be expected. It had been months since the good friends had truly spoken like good friends.

"So what you doing here?"

"Well, I was in the house and then someone else told me that you were in the studio. So I just came by to check on you."

"Cool, man, cool." Then there was a break in the conversation in which the good friends had nothing to say to each other. It was a strange thing that they both noticed but did not comment on.

"But, um, we need to talk," Tommy said, breaking the silence.

"Okay."

Tommy gave a nod of the head, to mean he wished to speak in private. Flawless got the message and spoke to the neglected pretty girl in the corner. He was glad that Tommy brought the issue up. Now he had an easy way of telling her to leave. She left the room with some sense of disappointment and the feeling that she would not be getting back into that room or any other, as it pertained to Flawless.

"So what was that about?" Tommy asked.

"Nothing . . . just perks of the job."

"Yeah, she looked like she could do a lot of perking. So what's going on? You and Trish not working out?"

"Naw, I wouldn't say that. It's just—y'know. I don't know, we just . . . just . . ."

"She's a beautiful girl man. She is a really good sister. You don't need to be messing with all of these girls."

Beautiful. It had been a while since he had used that word to refer to her in his thoughts or his speech. Now he hardly thought of her. Even while he spoke to her he was thinking of something else. She wasn't stunning anymore. He did not know why exactly he came to think less of her. He just did.

"I know, I know," Flawless replied. "But let's not talk about that. Let's talk about what you wanted to talk about. You excited about the tour?"

"Actually, Flaw, that's what I came to talk to you about. I'm not going."

"Really, why not?"

"Well, man, I got a deal. I got signed to Regal. And it's a really good deal too. I am gon' be working on my stuff, plus I'm also gonna be doing production for some of their other artists. That's good shit, right?"

"So you're not coming on the tour?" Flawless replied, almost oblivious to all that his friend had told him. Tommy shook his head, taking a slight offense.

"Flaw, you haven't heard me. I told you, I can't. I'm gonna be working on my album."

"No, I heard you. I heard you," Flawless replied. "That's real good, man, that's really good." Flawless was finding it very hard to be happy for his friend.

Tommy could sense it. "Yeah, thanks."

"I'm sorry if it's all coming out the wrong way. I'm happy for you. It was just that I thought you were coming on the tour. You know, I really need you there with me."

"C'mon, Flaw, you don't need me. You never did and especially not now."

"What are you talking about? You're my best friend, of course I need you."

"I'm your best friend, right? Then tell me, Flaw, how many times have we really talked to each other in the last year and I mean really talked to each other?"

Flawless threw his hands up, wondering where this argument was going. "I don't know, man, I don't know."

"Well, you know what, I don't know either. But I bet you, you can count it."

Flawless began to think about how many times he had spoken to his friend in the last year. He knew that it hadn't been as it had been before. Since the images came he had not given much thought to anything else.

"We haven't spoken, Flaw. And we supposed to be boys. You going through some changes like I never seen before. I try to reach out but you don't tell me shit. And you ain't sayin' shit to Trish either, 'cause I asked her and she don't know."

For a second Flawless felt betrayed. As if his friends had been conspiring behind his back. Then he realized that he had not spoken to them and they had each inquired out of concern. "You're right, man. And I understand. I have been going through a lot. There are these things that have been happening, shit that I have been seeing," Flawless said, feeling that he was almost about to break down.

"Like what?" Tommy asked, hoping that his friend was about to open up.

"I can't tell you. I want to but I just can't."

"Then, Flaw, I can't help you. I can't. But beyond that, I'm leaving and I signed the deal because I gotta do this for me."

"I don't get all that, Tommy. What do you mean, do this for you? I thought we were doing this together?"

And here it was that Tommy let out what he had been thinking for the past few months, for the past few years, in fact. "C'mon, Flaw—together? There ain't been no together. I been playing backup to you ever since high school. I have always been there for you. I have always been pushing you."

"Naw, that's not true. You ain't been no backup to nobody."

"Yes, I have been, yes I have. And for real, man, you don't really respect me."

"Ah, get the fuck outta here! You gone too far. I don't know what the hell you talkin' about now," Flawless retorted with angry inflection and slight condescension.

"Don't you fucking patronize me, Flaw! I been there for you and now you gonna listen." There was a tear that was building in the corner of Tommy's eye. There was pain in the words of long-grown, festering thoughts. Flawless saw it and it quelled his quarrel. After a deep breath Tommy continued, "You don't respect me, god. Listen, man, I am the one who produced your demo. Me. And when you got signed, you got hooked up with cats like Noah and Elijah and you didn't even look at me to produce shit. You didn't even think to give me a chance. I woulda been cool just to try something, even if the shit didn't make it onto the album. Just to get the chance. Then, Flaw, you had sixteen tracks on that album . . . sixteen, and you didn't even think to put me on as a feature on a single one. Now, I know I ain't the nicest nigga in the world. I ain't you, Flaw. I ain't got

your gifts, but I'm all right, man. I can do a little something.
And you know what, you know this, you been knowin' this and
I'm your boy, man. I'm your fucking boy and you didn't even
see me. You couldn't even think to put me on a single one. Fuck
it, Flaw, you wouldn't even have to give me a whole verse. I
woulda been cool with eight bars."

After his speech, Flawless could visibly see the tears welling
up in both eyes. It was too much to bear, too much to look at.
He looked away and placed his head in his palms with his
elbows braced atop the padding of the board.

After a sigh, Tommy continued, "Then we get to this album.
You going through some serious shit and you ain't even telling
me. You know how I find out shit about you now . . . it's
through your lyrics, man. I love the new work and I hear it in
your words. That's how I gotta find out how my best friend is
doing. I wish you would talk to me but you're not."

"I wish I could too," Flawless said to himself. Tell him about
the months of tortured sleep. He felt he couldn't tell him that
he walked about quiet because he feared that when he opened
his mouth he would not speak but rather scream. Flawless
could not bring himself to tell him that, not yet. Tommy stood
there silently, almost begging to hear something, but nothing
came. So he continued.

"Now, with the first one, I excused shit. I said maybe ma
man is just nervous. He just got into this thing, he don't wanna
push it. So I'm like cool, just being pleased to be there wit'
Jennessy and all them other big heads, gettin' coffee and order-
ing food for niggas an' shit. But now when it came time to do
the second joint, I didn't even get a call. I wasn't even invited
into the studio. Shit, I didn't know who was working on the
album until I read the insert. This time you went all over the
world, gettin' shit from niggas in Germany and Timbuktu an'
shit while I'm right here, and I bet you never thought of me
once. That shit hurts, man. That really hurts. You ma boy and I
love you but you don't respect me for shit."

His words were too heavy for Flawless. Like daggers, they were pricking at his heart. It was all true. Flawless couldn't stand it, he couldn't sit it; he couldn't even look at him. If he did he would see the welling in his eyes and he would have broken down.

"You don't respect me, man. For you, Tommy is just always supposed to be in the background. I am just there to be your boy and nothing else. I am just a footnote in your book. If I didn't take charge and say something, I would have never even gotten into this chapter. You would have just skipped right through me, not seeing me but just expecting me to be there. You're paying me about forty thousand dollars a year just to hang out with you. I ain't ungrateful for nothing but I need to do more with my life than just being your boy and making sure that nobody don't talk to Erika. I mean, that shit is crazy. I used to think it was funny but now that shit is just crazy. I heard about being overprotective but I got two older sisters of ma own and I know we don't really get along. But still, me and my little brother don't be acting like that. That shit is too much."

Flawless had been softened by Tommy's words. Then he heard a name and something in him grew hard again. For a minute he heard nothing else that his friend was saying and the tear that was making its way down his face defied gravity and rewound itself back into his tear duct.

"So I got the deal and I took it because now I gotta do for me and live my life, make my choices and be my own book."

"Fine." Flawless finally spoke, still keeping his face in his palms and not looking at his friend. "I understand. It's cool. I am happy for you. I hope everything works out over at Regal."

"Look at me, man!"

Flawless turned and looked his friend in the eye. Tommy thought to say something else but after seeing the now-cold look of indifference, he decided not to. The talk was over. There was nothing left to argue.

"So that's it?" Tommy asked him.

"Yeah, that's it."

"Cool."

Tommy walked out. He never wanted it to come to this. He walked out hurt and disappointed, feeling as if he had just given up a lifelong friend—more than a friend, rather a brother. But he also left Crown with his head up, a record deal and a promise for a future for himself.

As the door closed Flawless felt immediate solitude, more alone now than he had ever felt in his life. There was no Tommy to watch his back anymore or drive him around. How would he go on? Who could he look to for support? He held his head down. Then it hit him. Why throw away friendship over nothing? He had decided to call Tommy back.

He raised his head to leave . . . and then there they were, all around him. Demons of a sort he called them, amorphous figures phasing in and out of walls and furniture. He thought to scream but realized that he had seen them too many times now to be afraid. So he sat there alone and accepted them as friends. He closed his eyes and pondered seriously about his sanity. Then he opened his eyes again and they were gone. He breathed a wry breath of relief and looked across the room onto the adjacent wall, where he noticed a small crack in the finish that he had not seen before. It was an odd thing. This was a new studio; there should have been no cracks there. It intrigued him. He got up and walked over to the wall and reached for the crack, but for some reason he could not touch it. He felt the wall and it was smooth, crackless. Nevertheless the crack was there. He saw it plainly but now it was over his hand. It was apparent and intangible. The weirdness of it raised his goose bumps on end. He felt the sudden urge to leave the room. He turned his eyes away from the crack, grabbed his coat and scarf and went out the door. Without focusing his vision on anything, he hurried to the elevator, went downstairs, got into the limo and instructed the driver to take him home. As the car drove, he sighed and for a moment his thoughts were able to wander. But then . . . he looked across the way . . . and noticed . . . that there was a crack in the window.

Hannibal got up from the bed. With one motion he pulled the sheet covers off the bed with him. The sheets pulled away to reveal Rosa lying there naked in a semifetal position. Her back was to him as he sat on the edge of the bed, putting on his boxers and jeans, all the while ignorant to the fact that Rosa lay there on the bed shivering. She shivered not due to any real reproach of the cold, as the room was well heated; she shivered because she didn't know what else to do, lying there feeling as if she had been invaded. In that twenty-minute meeting of flesh, she had given herself to him and he had ripped into her sovereignty, her sensibility, and left her there a shell of herself. There was a burning feeling between her thighs that burned her throughout her soul. She felt soulless and without solace, empty and shallow, knowing not what else to do but shiver.

The room was in darkness. Only a sprinkling of moonshine crept into the crevice. Hannibal looked toward the engulfing black hole, which was the immense television, and pronounced: "Hannibal." With that, the television came on and in seconds the movie began to play. The light from the screen engulfed the room with an oppressive brilliance. With that he had taken away her last sheet of cover. She was now truly naked, and to find discomfort in nudity was a discomfort for a stripper.

"I guess we're not going out," she said to him, shielding her eyes from the light.

"I don't think so. But you can still go by yourself, if you would like."

"Y'know what, I can't believe I did this. I can't believe I left my house to do this to myself. Fuck you, fuck you."

She began to get up and to fish for her clothes. She then recalled that she had taken them off on the floor by the television. She had to pull herself together and walk toward the

almost blinding light, into the immense ugliness of Mason
Verger, kneel down and regroup her clothes. Hannibal sat
watching the movie unmoved as she dressed in the shadows
cast behind the TV. She was set to go when he called to her.

"Wait up, don't go."

"What the fuck do you want now?" she barked back. He got
up, undid the sheets from his feet and walked to her position.
She felt both uneasy and eerily attracted to his proximity. She
cast her eyes away, not wanting to feel the embers.

"What the fuck do you want?"

"I don't want you to go," he replied.

"Why the hell not?"

"You can't leave—you can't leave; because I haven't eaten
you yet."

"What?" For a moment she thought that this might have
been a sick proposal for foreplay as he began to back her into a
corner there in the dark shadows. He came closer and made an
aggressive motion forward as if to bite her nose off. He came
within a terrified inch and then pulled back and broke into
a smile.

"Just fucking with you," he said to her.

"What?"

"Don't. You don't have to go. I don't want you to. I like you.
We can do that restaurant thing another time. I got no mind to
go out tonight. Plus my cook can prepare anything you want.
Stay; watch a movie with me. I didn't mean to frighten you."

She was confused, perhaps more than she had ever been
before in her life. She had never seen such a sudden turnabout
in behavior. He was now acting the most human that he had
been the entire night. *Get out. Leave. Run away.* All these
words harangued her thoughts. But she did not listen. He led
her to the bed, where they sat and watched the movie amiably
together. She wanted to leave but his will had hypnotized her.
He had already torn down her esteem and she felt as if she had
no mind to refuse him.

So they sat and watched the movie and he spoke freely of his enthusiasm. She smiled and at times became engrossed in the film; within an hour she had let herself go and did not think of what had occurred earlier in the night. This was how she had hoped the night would have been from the beginning. So she ignored the past and enjoyed the present while presently Hannibal baited thoughts of ripping into her once again, once the movie was over. This was count 112.

THiRTY-NiNE

Erika sat alone at the bright fuchsia booth with a view to the street, twirling an empty teacup around and around. She had been waiting there in the Manhattan diner for almost thirty minutes now. She was tired, so much so that she paid little mind to the waitress when she came and placed before her a well-formed blueberry muffin.

As the waitress walked off Erika looked out at the passing traffic while a figure comfortably approached from behind and kissed her on the cheek. She smiled tacitly at her lover's greeting as he sat himself across from her, his settled weight creating a lavender imprint in the booth.

"So what's up, why did you want to meet here?" he asked her.

"I like their blueberry muffins."

"Okay," Micah replied. "Well, whatever the reason, it's always good to see you."

She did not respond and for moments merely sat quietly.

"Micah, have you been writing Bull's rhymes?" she asked forthrightly. She said it all at once because she believed that it would have came out all mumbled and dismembered if she had tried beating about the bush. Perhaps she would have convinced herself into not posing the question at all, and that would not do. She needed to know.

"Yes," Micah, after a pensive moment, answered. He was

curious to know how she knew to ask. But he knew that if she knew to ask, then she already knew the answer.

"And the one against Flawless as well."

"We worked on them together . . . but for the most part, yes."

"Maybe we should be talking to you about squashing the rift then. You've been a part of this whole thing while you sat there on the train with me, looking just as caught up in this as I am. How could you do that, Micah?"

"Do what? I mean, nothing said was personal, at least not on my part. It's just rhetoric; you know how the game is."

"C'mon, Micah, do better than that. Tell me something else."

"Tell you what? I mean, one minute I'm battling cats on the stage just to get a voice over a mic. The next, Bull is telling me he likes my work and he is paying me more money than I have ever seen in my life to write for him. I'm a writer, so I'm like, I'll write whatever. What did I do that was wrong?"

"So you can't see the wrong in any of this?"

"Girl, believe me, in the past few days I have seen a wrong in a lot of it. But that's how it is; it's just hip-hop. It's competitive."

"Listen, both of us were on that train and saw what just hip-hop was leading to."

"I know that. I saw it and it had an effect on me too and I tried talking to the man about cooling shit down. He wasn't hearing me. So what am I going to do?"

"You can stop writing for him," she said flatly.

"And why don't you stop being Flawless's sister."

"What?" she retorted.

"I mean, c'mon, Erika, don't be naïve." There was only one other person who ever said that to her. She hated when he said it: she hated it even more coming from Micah.

"You know, I really hate when people say that to me."

"All right, I am sorry. But it is not that easy. I mean, a lot of times you sit there so hungry for a deal that you'll take whatever comes to you. Then when you're in there they tell you to write this, which is not really what you want to be writing but you do it anyway because this is your big break and you don't want to blow it. You do it to a point where you figure that you'll get established and then you can write what you really want. So yes, I wrote 'Coup,' but I also wrote 'Elephant Warfare.' "

"So then everyone just turns a blind eye and the cycle continues."

"What blind eye, what cycle? I am just doing what I have to, to eat."

"Eating, bling-bling, cheddar; money is all anyone ever cares about."

"No, I don't," he calmly came back, though he felt offended that she was putting him in the class of the average materialist. "But love, you're coming down hard on me and being very hypocritical."

"How so?"

"Well, love, it's because of all of this bling-bling and cheddar why your life has changed as much as it has. And I know you, Erika, as much as all this may bother you, you like your new life. You like living in a big house, not having to worry about where your next meal is coming from and how you're going to pay the rent. Think about it."

She did not have to think long. She only had to think of her room, her closet and the brand-new BMW she was driving. She was in school and taking classes without purpose. Her entire life seemed capricious and this flitting disposition was based wholly on her brother's affluent affections.

"You're right. You're right. And maybe I have been wrong about a lot of things in how I saw the world and myself. But you know what? The other day on the train opened my eyes a whole lot and something has got to stop. We can't just let things keep going this way. This is bigger than us. We might only see the business of it but there are a lot of people out there, some dumber than the guys on the train, who do take it personally. But I understand, trust me, I understand what you are saying."

"Believe me, Erika, I could care less about writing this shit. I would much rather sit here and write poems about you."

"Really. And what would you write?"

"I would write about how I feel whenever I'm with you."

"And how is that?"

"Complete, whole, at peace. But they tell me that peace don't sell," he replied.

"Yes it does. You just have to pitch it right."

She stretched her hand across the table, calling for his. He answered and brought their hands together. The love could be felt through the fingertips as their hands embraced, their hearts raced and their minds gave way to a haze of purple.

BOOK SiX

FORTY

There was stillness in the air, in an air of confusion. It was cold but not chilling, and there was no wind to be seen. In this late January eve there was an ambiance to augur the unanticipated on the crimson carpet as the portentous went about from limo to rug in characteristic gaud. It was a who's who of the entertainment world, from movie stars to pop stars, all signifying that big rap had juxtaposed itself with popular culture. There was a plethora of media with enough flash of the cameras to put the sun on hiatus. The mass of artificial lights all but made up for the gray skies at the epicenter of the rug. On the outskirts, however, thousands of fans bore the gray while barricaded in, looking on along the street to the Radio City Music Hall. Among them was a young man who carried a banner that read: *Hip-hop stand up and speak out against the war on terrorism, for reparations, for AIDS in Africa, the power of truth is final, fight the future.* He walked about hollering, though few paid him any mind. The *Source* Awards were back again and at home in the hall for the first time. That was all that mattered.

Flawless, however, did see the young man who hollered across the way as he stood hand in hand with Trish, a handsome couple, being interviewed for the preshow jam.

"Well, Flawless, you're nominated for four awards tonight, like you were last year. Last year you came out with four out of four. You think you can pull that off or better tonight, given that your second album had all the critical acclaim but not the same sales as your first?"

"There is a crack on your forehead," Flawless flatly replied with an odd smile.

"What?" the reporter retorted at the oddity of the remark.

"Nothing," Flawless corrected himself. "It doesn't matter. You're asking me about the present. The work didn't write itself for the present. This was written for the generations, for lifetimes to come. So whatever happens now, happens; what is going to happen, that's what's important. As for now, just take care of that crack on your head."

The reporter had no idea what Flawless was talking about. There was an eerie tone in his speech. This was very different from the Flawless this same reporter interviewed just a year ago. His yesteryear jubilance was replaced with a new philosophic morbidity. He understood nothing that the man said but nonetheless found himself discreetly grazing his forehead ever so often, feeling for a crevice or some form of indentation.

"Well, okay, Flawless. Thanks for the view—and, and that's that." The reporter was set to walk away when he noticed a dark figure coming through the gray. "Whoa, and look who has just come to our cameras, our resident cannibal himself, Hannibal."

"What's up, Flawless?" Hannibal greeted, standing behind with Rosa at his side, looking beautiful with her hair disheveled, her smile radiant and her eyes obsequious.

"Nothin', Bull. Nothin' at all," Flawless replied.

"Whoa, Bull, does this meeting mean a reconciliation between your two camps? And Bull, how do you feel about performing tonight?" The reporter rolled off a series of questions all in one drag.

"I got nothin' to say right now," Hannibal replied with a stern look, which told the reporter not to press the matter further.

"Well, okay, that's my segment right here. Back to you up there, Carson."

The disappointed reporter then left the couples alone.

"Let's talk. Ladies, why don't you give us a minute?"

At Hannibal's prompting, Rosa walked off without an argument. She hadn't known Bull for long but she already knew not to debate the point. Trish was more reluctant to leave. Flawless comforted her with his eyes and then she also walked away, but never out of view.

"What do you want to talk about, Bull?" For the years that they had known and battled each other this would mark only their second conversation. Both men knew this.

"Nothing, just regular shit, about life and business—family," Hannibal responded.

"Nigga, you funny. We ain't got shit to talk about. You said enough on wax."

"So did you."

"That's jus' 'cause I'm trying to end it. Believe me, man, there are crazier things in this world than beef with Bull."

"And for that you wanna end it. Why?"

"Because I am tired of this shit. We been battling each other for years and every time I thought I beat you, you just kept coming back. Sometimes I wished that I could just rhyme you out of existence."

"But you can't. That's me, god, unstoppable Bull."

"Whatever. Ain't you tired of it; you don't wanna move on?"

"I am moving on, doing big things. And stop your complaining, man, don't you see the big picture?"

"And what's that, the story?" Flawless replied.

"Yep. See, always knew you was a smart nigga: the big picture. The truth is, none of us would be where we are without each other, if it wasn't for the story of our battles. Think about it."

"Don't have to. I know, story or no story, I don't need you, Bull."

"Fine, you can lie to yourself. That's why your reality is falling apart all around you." Hannibal's last remark struck

Flawless. What was he talking about? Could he see the untouchable crack as well?

"What do you mean?" Flawless asked him. But Hannibal ignored the question.

"You say you're tired; well, I'm tired too. You wanna end all of this shit?"

"Yeah, let's end it."

"Cool. I was getting tired of rapping anyway."

"Why? Is it 'cause you can't write anymore?"

"Don't have to, this shit is writing itself now; plus the money in it is limited. I wanna do bigger things now. Movies. Y'know what I'm saying. Fuck *Billboard*, I want that box office. Then after that we going for Dow Jones and get that Bill Gates money. Then you just gon' see Carthage up all over the place. Elephants everywhere."

"You do that," Flawless said to him, finding it humorous that Hannibal wasn't speaking of cannibalism anymore.

"I will. And don't act like you don't wanna take over the world as well."

"Oh, I will. The words will be here forever."

"Well, then, I guess this thing between me and you will never be over as long as we both have the same dream."

FORTY-ONE

The assistant to the assistant artist coordinator stood in the dell of the backstage area with her index finger tapping the face of her watch, looking across at Micah, while he stood in the busy of the business, wondering just where the Carthaginian was. Rome was waiting and they were only ten minutes before being called to stage. He was forced to stand, surrounded by gaffers, engineers and the miscellaneous rapper, bouncing into and out of him as if he wasn't there. He could not hear her but felt her frustration as the assistant to the assistant artist-coordinator shouted into her mouthpiece from across the floor, intermittently throwing him the evil eye.

"Why that bitch eyein' you like that?" a voice called from behind. Micah turned around and found the devourer standing there.

"Yo, you know we gotta go on in a minute. Where you been?" Micah asked him.

"Just rapping with a good friend. Plus, Bull don't rush for nobody. Dem crackers can wait. So you ready?" Hannibal asked and Micah answered in the affirmative. To that, Hannibal remarked, "Trust me, you ain't ready for this."

Hannibal walked away from Micah, ignored the approaching assistant to the assistant artist coordinator and went to his DJ, Amra. He spoke directly into his ear, imparting instructions in length. What was being said Micah could not hear, nor did he pay it any mind. He felt at ease now that Hannibal had appeared. Now his nerves had only the roar of the stage to contend with.

Guevara, the hip-hop revolutionary, a Colombian brother in his mid-twenties, took to the podium donning a T-shirt with the words *Free Palestine* scripted across his torso. Before this majestic house of thousands, tonight he was not a winner, nor a loser, nor a performer. He stood there as a herald; a dreadlocked Silver Surfer pleased to be chanting the coming of warfare, the coming of Galactus and the trumpeting of the elephants. Before the completion of his announcement, the horns of the pachyderm could be heard from the speakers echoing throughout hallowed halls.

The lights came on and there again stood the Carthaginian at the gates of Rome, surveying his prospects. With burning embers he sniffed through the fat and found Flawless seven rows within. Good shit, he thought. His plans would only work half as well if Flawless weren't there.

The beat came on as a thunderous stampede. Hannibal grunted his lyrics to the trumpeting, parading about the stage like a man in the midst of a war dance. He performed the first verse of the song with Micah at his side inflecting every punch line.

From the Alps of Albany
To the blocks of Normandy
We bringin' D day to the devil
Burnin' Babylon and the Bible
Carthage to Brooklyn
Hannibal the general of every land
Flip it like Farrakhan
Keep Khalid alive in ma lung
So I spit more fire
To ignite the choir
Givin' a passion to the passive

And mad gats to the massive
We marchin' in madness
For the years of anguish
For the centuries of bondage
We bomb streets and precincts
For when you sacked us, sold us
Bought us, chained us
Cracker, worked us, raped us
Lynched us, fooled us
We been emancipated
To be incarcerated
Debated, hated, castrated
An' drug addicted
You declared war on us
Now it's all war for us
No more time to cuss
Jus' pull out yo' gats an' buss.

And as Micah went into the cadence of the hook, he was ignorant of and unprepared for Hannibal's true intentions.

"Yo, DJ, cut that," he shouted, his voice cutting through the furor and bringing everything to a halt. "Run that new hot shit like we planned and let's give the people a real show."

Amra abruptly closed the rhythm and began a series of frantic scratches. The people in the audience believed that this was part of the performance. The director in the control room knew better and ran about in a frenzy, cursing everyone around him. The cameramen looked around directionless. Micah likewise appeared surprised and confused only he was forced to play off his ignorance; the show was live and he was onstage. He improvised. He followed Hannibal's lead, saying, "yeah, yeah" and giving miscellaneous shouts to Brooklyn. Hannibal skipped back to the DJ and Micah took the opportunity to get a frantic word in.

"What are you doing? This wasn't what we planned. I thought they told you that you couldn't do this."

"Fuck 'em, new plan; just follow my lead, you already know the song." Micah got a sick feeling of what was coming. When he heard what Amra played next, his fear was confirmed. The rhythm to "Coup d'etat" came over and a slew of profanities ran through his mind.

In response to hearing the now-familiar dirge, half of the audience shot up out of their seats, while the other half sat quietly. Among the funerary quiet was Flawless, seated with Erika and Trish. The bubble of anger was beginning to boil before a word was even uttered. Hannibal couldn't see him now but he could taste the fury. He began:

Bull pull a coup d'etat
Run up in yo' area
Gun up in yo' area
Lickin' shots rat-tat-taw
Hannibal's raw an' rowdy
Born ruff an' ready
Pass on the confetti
Jus' gimme the key to the city
An' I pity the fool
Who wanna pity the Bull
I'm at the pinnacle
Y'all niggas is jus' pitiful
But let's kill all the drama
An' get to the meat of the matter
I'ma dead you now, nigga
Fuck saving the rebut for later
Flaw, you just an error
An yo' era is over
I'm over your over
Save the ovations for later
Player, think you a king
You just a kid with a pen
The pendulum swings

Yo' reign has come to an end
King of New York, please
Nigga, you the kings of Queens
You queer as folk
Went from a rapper to a philosophe
Now you feelin' dumb
So you pull "Bullshit"
Well, I got mine
Now I hope you got yourself a gun
An' you know I never bluff
I rebut wit' head butts
Shit dat make yo' head buss
An' what the fuck?
You say I wanna be some old white man
But damn, Flaw, you wanna be
A black man who wanna be a white woman
An' woo, man
You go too far, man
I know you lost yo' faith, man
But get shit straight, man
I don't come to play cracker
I come to play crackers
Hannibal come to conquer
Elephant's ma moniker
Used to run wit' the Mafia
Now I run the Mafia
So run yo' shit, bitch
'Cause this is the takeover.

The reaction to the performance was as mixed and as divided as the audience. The "Hannibal cheering" goaded their man in barbarous fashion. The folk for Flawless felt that this was not the place for such an attack. The director in the control room, after getting his wits about him, rolled with the riot, getting audience reactions and close-ups of the performance.

Micah, like the conflicted fool, was left with no resort but to rap along. As he heard the words he had written flowing off the stage, they began to sicken him. Never before had he despised a creation of his own as much as he did now. If he knew this was to come he would never have wished for it at all. As he looked over at Hannibal, relishing in the sickness, all respect he had for the man oozed out of his pores like his free-flowing sweat. He wanted to abandon him there to face the stage alone. Some force, however, held him to his position. In disgust he played out his role.

Everything was flowing to Hannibal's design. Whether they hated or loved him, they were all listening. He held their heart-strings by the testicles. And then . . .

I'm the nigga you love to hate
Hate to debate, you know
I'm undebatable; I'm unbeatable
The unstoppable Bull
That's what your sister was sayin'
Last night, "Don't stop, Bull, don't stop, Bull"
While I'm ramming her like an elephant
Almost made her faint
But she stayed up on it
Like she was an addict for the dick
Damn Flaw, surprised me too
Little sis, turned out to be a regular bitch.

The words had the desired effect. Like sabers to the esophagus it left Flawless gasping for air. The anger was too much, though for the moment he had to swallow his rage. The cameramen assailed him with a close-up. His embarrassment was exploited on the big screen from every angle. He had to remain calm and still concentrate on performing later. Erika could do nothing herself but feign stoicism.

Micah stood in disbelief. The only thing that ran through his thoughts was I didn't write that, I didn't write that. The last verse was a remix purely of Hannibal's making, distorting Micah's words and experiences for his own purposes. Micah was fortunate that the performance had ended because he would not have been able to go on. He could taste Erika's pain through the bantering of the crowd. It grabbed hold of his vertebrae and denied him voluntary motion. He just prayed she knew that the pen had been taken out of his hand.

There was mixed applause from the divided audience. An immediate commercial break was taken. Micah walked off the stage in a daze; Hannibal appeared as if nothing had occurred. As they descended the steps into the dell, the assistant to the assistant artist coordinator wasted no time in coming at him. "You, you're fucking done, it's over. You were specifically told not to do that song. You'll never perform for the *Source* again. Fuck it, you'll never even be in *The Source* again."

Hannibal then turned and looked at her and, intimidated and angry, she walked away.

"Yo, good show," he said to Micah.

"Good show, what the hell you talkin' about? Why the fuck did you do that?" Micah shouted at him.

"Y'all wanted me to squash the drama with Flawless, right? Well, I just did. I squashed it with a sledgehammer."

"Naw, you crazy. You fucking crazy. I'm done; I'm out. Since you love ad-libbing, you can stay writing your own shit."

"You know what, I don't know what I ever saw in you. You just a weak-ass pussy. You got your head so far up in that fat ass that you can't see the light from the day."

"Whatever. You sick bastard, I feel sorry for you, man."

"Feel sorry for yourself, nigga. You don't even exist! You just a part of the fucking periphery. This shit is all about Bull. Never feel sorry for me, nigga. Bull a survivor, always gon' be on top."

With that, there was nothing left to be said. Micah pulled loose his mic and Hannibal watched his little brother walk away.

FORTY-TWO

The show was over but the night was still young. Winners and losers, industry insiders, spectators and radio contestants were all here: all drinking, all flirting, all gossiping. It was the Crown after party. It was just one of many postshow events taking place that night but it was the highest attended. It seemed as if everyone was there. Stalin was seated with crew in corner. Guevara chatted with Ebony about doing a possible collaboration. Lil' Hitler and the Gestapo had come from the South in numbers. Trujillo and the Latin Mafia were also about. They all rapped about their own affairs but all, somewhere throughout the night, brought the issue of Flawless and Hannibal to the floor.

As Flawless sat off to the side with his bodyguard and Jennessy, he could feel the chattering. Hannibal had made him a spectacle but Bull was not to bear the blame alone. He was not the one who had written the rhyme. It was the name; that repulsive name that embittered his thoughts as absinthe does the tongue. It was the name that had defiled her while Flawless could do nothing but sit and watch her being raped in silence, like slaves in the past. Some protector he had been. Now he was regretting not coming back at Hannibal during his performance.

These thoughts burned holes into his membrane while the untouchable crack floated before him. In actuality, it had now become a hole, a small hole in his vision, a black gape visible in every direction. It had been weeks since he had seen the images. They had not come to him ever since the crack, now a hole, had appeared. He had hated the images when they first came: amorphous transluscent figures, morphing from semblances of man to beast to amoeba, of all manners of shapes and back again. Now he would gladly receive them in place of this hole: this unreachable and untouchable hole, seemingly a growing void in existence.

"Congratulations, you got three more awards to add to the collection," Jennessy said, awakening him from the depths of his funk.

Flawless could find no other words to say but, "That motherfucker!"

"Upset, I see. Why . . . now people are dying for your comeback? They can't wait to hear what you'll do next. It'll sell like hotcakes. And believe me, right now, you could use the sales."

"Are two million records sold not good enough for you?"

"It's good, but it's not ten."

"This is all about money isn't it?"

"Always."

"And it seems, like it or not, as long as I am under contract, I will always be a slave to you. Well, who knows, maybe I'll die soon and freedom will come in death."

"I don't understand your meaning, Flawless. Slavery has been abolished in this country for a long time now. But let me impart this tiny bit of knowledge to you. We are all slaves here, Flawless. All of us, whether we are black or white, or whatever else; we are slaves to our fate, whether we have faith in it or not. Freedom comes in the acceptance of our bondage, our definition and purpose. I have accepted that I am a businessman and I am freer for it. You must accept that you are an artist."

"That's a crock, Jennessy!" Flawless fired back. "That's the shit they tell slaves to keep them in line, keep them passive. Plus I thought that you were a deist. You don't believe in fate, remember. Isn't that what you told me? Pen it the way I want to."

"Okay, Flawless, go ahead. Believe what you want. But tell me, how free will you be if you always call yourself a slave? Think about that. And you know what, Flawless? I figured it out with you. I am the villain in your book, aren't I? And why, because I'm white, I'm an executive and I love making money? I make no apologies for who and what I am. I never have and I never will. But remember this: Your story began with our meeting. I made you, Flawless. I made you my top priority. I made you number one. I helped you take over the world. It is because of me that books upon books will be written about you. Without me, you would just be another kid spitting on the street corner like all the rest. What kind of book would that have made?"

"I don't know. I don't know."

There was weight in Jennessy's words. It was the first time since he had known him that he felt any real emotion from the man. But though he was being sincere, Flawless still felt as if he was trying to sell him something. He was trying to sell him himself. Beyond all of his attempts, Flawless could not see the man outside of the quagmire of bullshit. Jennessy's intimation did do one thing for Flawless: It took his mind off of Hannibal and the intangible hole for a minute, but only a minute, during which time he saw Lil' Hitler from across the floor in a VIP booth. Hitler raised a bottle of Cristal and nodded his head with a smile. Seeing this, Flawless looked at the diminutive demagogue and tipped his glass in return. In that moment, he noticed in the distant corner a man who appeared to be his peer in many ways, smiling back at him in crimson. Flawless believed that he remembered this man from a moment before but he wasn't sure, it was hard to distinguish; in this room he had many peers. Though with the Cristal running through his system he was sure of one thing.

"I need to take a piss," he said to Jennessy.

Flawless looked down at the smooth, hard white porcelain surface as his urine shot out against the wall, trickled down the stem, came to the untouchable hole, disappeared from sight and then reentered his visual field, to then flow out into the grated sink of the base. He didn't know whether to be amused or saddened by the experience so he just continued on peeing, alone in the restroom, in silence.

He then heard the opening of the restroom door and the footsteps of another entering, bringing with him the beat and the noise from outside. His footsteps resounded through the floor as he came forward step by step and rested himself by the urinal adjacent to Flawless's. Flawless did not look up to acknowledge him, though he felt the intensity of his presence, with his shirt giving off a glare of burning red. As the man began to undo his pants and relieve himself, for some reason Flawless's heart began to race. He didn't know why but he knew he wanted to leave there at once. He could hear the attack of the man's pee against the wall. It rushed out with a fury and overpowered the sound of Flawless's flow. Having finished, Flawless fixed himself and went to the counter to wash his hands. There was a mirror above the counter, Flawless could see the back of the man in red as he relished in his overflow, grunting audibly with his release.

"Ahhh, uhhh. Now that's the shit." The man began to speak. "That's it right there. This shit feels almost as good as fucking. Whooweee . . . damn! Life's jus' like a bitch, ain't it? It's God's joke on man . . . dammmm . . . gives you what you want but never the way you want it. Y'know what I'm sayin', god? . . . Oh shit, this feels bad and good all at the same time. . . . Yo, man, you sure you want this shit?"

To the man's gestures, Flawless made no response. He merely allowed the water from the faucet to wash over his hands, looking at the back of the man through the reflection. He didn't know exactly why this man was talking to him but then again, he did.

"Hmmm?" The man gestured again, pricking for a response.

To that Flawless answered, "It's too late to turn back now." He then turned off the faucet, turned away and left the restroom.

Some distance away Erika and Trish stood by the bar. The shame of the night's events was still fresh but they tried not to speak of them. They had only been there twenty minutes and already they could not wait to leave. In fact, they hadn't wanted to come at all. But it had been agreed that a nonappearance would give credence to Hannibal's words, the words that Micah had written. Just as Erika thought of Micah, he came through the crowd and appeared behind her. Trish made his presence known and Erika turned around and faced her sullen lover.

"Yo, girl, I am so sorry. You gotta believe me when I tell you I had nothing to do with tonight. I was just as lost. He threw me off like he did everybody else. I would have never agreed to do that song tonight. And yeah, I wrote the song but he threw in that last line just to fuck with all of us. You gotta believe me." He blurted it all out with one exhale. He stopped and looked at her face for a reaction. She only reflected her solemnity. His chest began to burn, feeling as if he would fall apart; for if she did not believe him, if she didn't love him anymore, he would not know how to go on. For some reason, without her love, he felt as if he would fade into nonexistence.

"C'mon, girl, say something. You're killing me here," he implored.

"I believe you. I know you wouldn't do something like that. I knew all along."

He smiled a breath of relief. The burning in his chest eased.

"If you knew, then why did you make me go through all of that just now?"

"I just wanted to see you squirm. I thought it was cute," she replied.

"You're funny. Tell me, you wanna get out of here? This whole scene is beginning to make me sick."

"Yeah, me too," Erika concurred, and then turned toward Trish. "Tell Michael that I left, okay."

"Okay, but he won't be happy."

"I don't care."

The two girls hugged. "Go ahead, do your thing," Trish said to her during their embrace. And as Erika was pulling off she said to her, "I envy you." Erika looked back at her confusingly. "I do," Trish repeated. She saw in Micah the love for Erika that she had always hoped to receive from Flawless. She believed at a time in the beginning that she might have seen it. But whatever it had been, it had been over a year since he had looked at her in any such way. The dream was over. "Now get out of here." Erika didn't understand but, then again, she did and for that she hugged her friend and the closest thing she ever had to a sister once again.

Erika and Micah cut through the crowd with a sense of urgency. Why? They did not know. They just felt as if they had to leave there as soon as possible. Micah held her hand and Erika followed. Then as she squeezed through, another hand reached for hers and forcibly grabbed hold of her forearm. It was such a violent hold that it completely broke her stride and pulled her loose of Micah's grip. She was dragged backward and a shuffle of people came in between them.

"What the hell are you doing? Where are you going?" Flawless shouted, as he stood infuriated, with his bodyguard in tow.

"Michael, you're squeezing my hand."

"Pay no attention to that. Where are you going?"

"I'm leaving," she said, while trying to break free.

"You're leaving, with him. After what this motherfucker did to us tonight?"

Micah came and saw the fury in the man. He tried his best to quell the quarrel. "Listen, I was just as surprised about tonight as you were. I had nothing to do with it. I swear to you."

"Nothing to do with it, except write the song and be on stage and play backup."

"You don't understand."

"Nigga, shut the fuck up!" Flawless barked, almost cutting the oxygen away from everyone in circumference. If it were not for the proliferation of noise and the darkness in the club, this would have been a fantastic scene. Her brother's last remark angered Erika and she broke loose of his grip.

"Let go of me. He is telling you the truth, Michael. He had nothing to do with it."

"And you believe this because he told you."

"Yes!" she asserted.

"Always so fucking naïve."

"Well, then, you let me be naïve. I'm leaving." She held onto Micah's hand again, turning to leave.

"No you're not!" Flawless barked back.

"Listen, why does it have to be this way? C'mon, man, this is not necessary at all," Micah remarked with a voice of reason.

"Nigga, it is this way because I am not going to make some name turn her into some whore."

"Listen, I would never do that. I could never do that. I love her, I really love her."

For Flawless, those were the most offensive words he had heard all night. "No, motherfucker, I love her! And if you think that I am going to let you fuck up the one thing that I care about in this world, you got another thing coming."

"I understand, Michael. I understand completely. I love you too. But I love him and I am grown and I am leaving," Erika stated.

Again, Erika and Micah began to make their way out and again Flawless grabbed hold of her hand. "No, you're not."

"Let go of me, Michael!" Erika shouted in a fury, ripping her hand free. The words hit Flawless to the core. He looked at her now and watched the little girl fade away. He felt as if all the love he had in the world was gone, all being sucked up into the untouchable hole.

"Fine. Leave. I don't fucking know you anymore. You're just

another whore, chickenhead, bitch like all of the rest." Flawless pronounced the curse from in a daze, straight, without inflection or emotion.

The words stung Erika profoundly, far greater than any rhetoric of Hannibal's had earlier on. She could not think of what to do or what else to say, except, "Fine" and swallowed her pride and her shame together.

Again, Micah and Erika began to make their way out of the club. Flawless allowed her to walk a few yards this time before he went after her, when he was stalled from behind. It was Tommy.

"Let it go, Flaw, she's gone. The more you push, the more you're going to push her away," his friend said to him.

Seeing his friend by his side once again, his temper subsided enough to let her leave. "Tommy, what are you doing here?" he asked.

"C'mon, man, you my boy. I'm always gon' have your back." His words were needed reassurance in a time when everything seemed to be falling apart.

"Shit, nigga, as fine as she looks, I would wanna fuck her too," a voice pricked at the back of his ear. Flawless did a sharp turn around to see Hannibal, Terrence and Reaper. "I hate to rub it in but that was it. That was the best shit that I have ever seen. They should put that shit in a movie." Angered, Flawless clenched his fists and made toward Hannibal with a checked motion to swing.

"What's this, nigga, you gon' swing at Bull," Hannibal said, almost laughing. "That ain't yo' style, Flaw. You know what, let's do like the old days. Let's battle for it. Hottest flow takes it."

Flawless recomposed himself. "I'm done battling you."

Flawless then saw the untouchable hole hanging over Hannibal like a black hole in his forehead. It was the first time since he had begun to see the hole that its presence actually pleased him.

"Yo, Bull, let me pop this nigga for you," Reaper impetuously interjected, raising the shirt above his waist to reveal the gun lying by his pelvis. Hannibal looked over at him wryly, laughing to himself.

With Reaper's attempt at intimidation, Flawless's bodyguard raised his shirt and revealed the glock by his side. "You better keep that shit under your waist."

"Whoo," Hannibal reacted, smiling at the standoff. Tommy, seeing the great probability for the stupid to happen, stepped in, almost shielding Flawless. "Yo, everybody, just chill the fuck out!"

"Guns, guns, guns," Terrence remarked and then brandished his own weapon, cocking it before everyone and holding it to his side. "Now, I know you niggas don't want me to set this shit off." Within the past few months Terrence had taken back up the habit of wearing the tool wherever he went but this was the first time in years that he had it unsheathed. It felt heavier in his hand now than it ever had.

They stared at each other, none truly wanting a confrontation. Flawless's bodyguard was the first to step down. Reaper decided to punctuate the point: "Yeah, you better step down, faggot-ass nigga."

"Whatchu say to me?" the bodyguard said, gripping the handle of his pistol. The tension rose to another octave and every man became keen to all the sounds and motions about them. Then loud and crisp, sounds of gunshots came over the club speakers. It was a sound effect being played by the DJ from one of Hannibal's songs. In all of the confusion it was taken to be a real shot. Reaper and Flawless's bodyguard fired off in response.

Flawless saw the flash of light and closed his eyes. Damn, God, is this it? Is this the end? Is this the way how I'm gonna die? Now will all the questions be answered? Give it to me. I am ready to learn. No, I'm not, he admitted to himself. No, not like this. I wanna live; I wanna love. I don't wanna die. Then he heard a series of shots and a force took him in the darkness, lifted him off his feet and down with a crashing thud.

Still in darkness, he flayed his arms around until he came to a body. He felt a warm liquid washing over his hands like water. Oh shit, I been shot, he thought. He could not stand the curiosity. He opened his eyes and with his heart racing he looked up to the ceiling. He could see the disco ball spinning, casting a psychedelic madness in the dark. He could hear the screams and cries crashing through the pounding beat. Then the beat came to an abrupt halt. He tried to move but felt a heaviness upon him.

He would not give in to death so easily. He moved about frantically and in his motions he discovered that a body lay on top of his. He pushed the body off. He then needed to blink twice to realize that the body was Tommy's and he was not just a body yet. He held onto life as the dark warm liquid flowed freely from his punctured stomach and coughed up in gargles out of his mouth. Flawless realized that it had been Tommy's blood that he had felt. He himself had been unharmed. "Tommy, Tommy," he said, gripping hold of his friend's hand. Tommy marshaled all of his strength to grab hold of Flawless's. Tommy forced words out in a strained whisper. Seeing that his friend was mouthing something, Flawless brought his ear directly to his bloody lips. Flawless could not understand and he strained his ears to make sense of it. Then it came out, more clear and precise than Flawless had ever heard anything in his life. "I love you—brother." With those final words Tommy gave way to the ghost. "No, god. Not like that. Don't fucking say that shit to me. Don't go like that. Tommy, don't fucking do that to me. Don't leave me to live with that shit. Not like that," Flawless pleaded but it was too late. Tommy was gone. And left alone in the chaos the tears ran down Flawless's face in a deluge; he teared, he cried, he wept, with his friend dead on the floor.

Jennessy stood on high with his bodyguard and watched hell break loose below. It was a fantastic tableau as like ants everyone ran headless, searching for an exit. "Get me out of here," he said, and his bodyguard began to escort him through the back exit.

People pushed, shoved and stampeded in an attempt to get out. Within the madness a man walked about as if inebriated. In a drunken dance he staggered with his cocked gun unused, and his blood flowing freely from his torso. In his dance he flayed his arm about wildly with indiscriminate purpose. Terrence swung his arm until he came before Hannibal. At seeing him, Terrence walked forward with his gun pointed. Closer and closer the macabre figure crept until he collapsed in Hannibal's arms. The tool fell from his hand and landed in a bloody puddle. He then looked at his general. "I'm sorry, Bull. I fucked up. I fucked up." The weight of his body, once so light and filled with vim, took hold of him. Hannibal guided him to the floor. Crying, Terrence recited, "Shit, nigga, I am sorry that I can't help you anymore. But it's all right; I see it, man. I can see it clear as fuck now. I see the big picture, man. I see that shit." Everything else that came out of Terrence's mouth was a series of mad ramblings. Hannibal reached over and gave his soldier and his friend one final pound. In doing so, he looked across the floor and saw Flawless holding onto Tommy. The eyes of both men met across the club through all the confusion in a quiet moment of intensity. Hannibal released his gaze of Flawless as he did Terrence's hand. He rose to his feet and walked away, as Terrence lay dying, and Trish ran crying toward Flawless.

Hannibal walked slowly through the chaos. He came to the exit when he saw Rosa in the corner. He had been so consumed with the affairs of the night that he had forgotten that he came with her. In fact, he couldn't recall why he had brought her. Perhaps he liked her or perhaps something else. Whatever the reason, he called for her hand and she took his, and together the odd couple squeezed their way through the chaos.

FORTY-THREE

From the balcony outside of his bedroom Flawless looked at the immense property that he had acquired. Standing alone in the naked January air wearing a T-shirt and jeans, the country property appeared before him like a forlorn forest, decadent and decrepit. The continuous gray skies did nothing to beautify the gaud. The rich land appeared godless and infertile. What right does man have over land, to have such avarice while so many suffer? Those thoughts ran through the mind of man as he floated in a sea of bad tidings. The tidal drag of death had pulled him into the deep unknown. He had never known death so personally before. He had never felt the perishing of one so direct to his circumference. Before death was just a concept, intangible and distant. Despite all of his recent philosophical ponderings he never came to the reality of this feeling. To feel the soul of his friend ebb slowly away. Death was real and it had touched him and nothing else came to bear but Tommy and his final words. Words said to him only twelve hours ago now, most of which he spent in a Manhattan police precinct. He was interrogated, browbeaten and harangued and then finally let go. Throughout it all he sat in a daze penetrated only by his friend's last words and those words he spoke the night that the crack came. Heavy was the love of his brother and he had been a bad friend.

"Take over the world, huh? I am sorry, brother. You died for my fucked-up ambition," Flawless said aloud to himself.

"Michael," Trish called from behind. Flawless turned to see her standing half of the length of the room away. She was dressed to leave, in a crimson overcoat, with heavy bags to her side.

"Where are you going?" Flawless inquired.

"Um . . . I'm going back to my place for a while," Trish spoke tentatively. "Um, I feel that it's the best thing to do."

Flawless, in disbelief, returned to his repose, shaking his head.

"Just like a fucking woman. You leave me now, of all of the times."

"I'll be there for you whenever you need me. But I feel that it would be best if we took a break for a while." It took strength to get the words past the barrier of her heart.

He turned back to look at her. "I need you now. Here. Why are you doing this? What is this, because you wanna get married? Believe me, this is not the time for that."

"It's never the time for that. And that's not what this is about. Truth is, you don't love me, Michael. I don't believe you ever did, and after last night, I don't believe you ever will."

"I have told you a thousand times."

"Just words."

"What do you want from me, blood?"

"No, just your heart."

"My best friend just died and you're coming to me with this shit? You know what? Fuck you, leave."

"Okay, Michael," she replied and began to motion herself to leave. She looked down at her bags and they looked like two-ton anchors. Leaving was the last thing she wanted to do. What she wanted most of all was for him to hold her—hold her again as he once did, giving of himself wholly as she had always done. He had never done that; before she had believed that he would. In the beginning he played with her, dallied with her, teased her before entering. Now he would stay in his studio with the door closed, sometimes never coming up to bed. He did, only when the urges overtook him. Then he would creep from behind, aiming straight for between thighs, and she, hungering for any bit of affection, always welcomed him wet. Then they would dance a little, wine a little, his body would tense a little, ease and then he would turn his back to her and go to sleep. This was not what she wanted. She wanted mutual love and passion. She needed it like oxygen. She found herself suffocating here in this big house with all of the fresh country air.

Within the past few months, in his distance, she had been inclined to give up hope. After last night it had been squashed immutably. "Y'know, I loved you from the start," she said to him. "I never really knew why. There was just something about you. Something in your eyes that just spoke to me. And I knew that what I felt was right. And I loved you, Michael. I loved you so completely, as if the Creator had written me with the sole purpose of loving you. I knew it from the first time I saw you walk through the revolving door. I knew it, Michael, and every cell in my body was drawn to you. And you have always distrusted me for it. You would never fully let me in. You have been inside of me on every level, every time, but you never fully let me inside of you. Once partially, mostly, but never fully, not even once. In the beginning it was okay, it sufficed, because it came with promises, but in the last year you have completely shut me out. You are going through what, I do not know. But I do know that you don't trust or love me enough to tell me because I am not the one you want; and no matter how much in likeness I may be fashioned, I will never be her and you will never be him."

"Trust and love. Funny. You wanna know what you are, Trish? I had my guesses in the beginning but now it has been confirmed more than ever. You're a fair weather ho. You saw a big check coming from the beginning and you jumped on it. And now when you see a glimpse of rain, you jump ship. You didn't see love walking through the door. You saw a potential payday. And you got it, Trish. You shook your ass and I fell for you. And ever since you been trying to lock in the deal. 'Marry me, Flawless, marry me,' is all I heard from the beginning. One time I actually thought about it. Tommy and I went looking at rings." The thought of Tommy brought the image of the moribund to fore and caused a break in Flawless's speech. "Now . . . now I'm glad that I didn't. Now when you walk out, you leave with your bags and not the house. You're leaving me now. You just watched me watch my boy die and you're leaving me. That's your love for me."

Perhaps this was very bad timing, to leave so soon after. But then, would it have made a difference a week later or perhaps a month? Perhaps it would have but in her mind it was not his life she wished to walk out of, it was his bed. She wanted to be there for him, only now as a friend. It made sense and she had been listening to her heart for too long now. Being a doormat had grown tiresome.

"And you know what? You wanna know real love? I only got head from all the other girls I have been with since we been together. That's real love for you," he said to her with the cold intent of returning the dagger.

Practicality should have tamed the sting. She knew that he was a rapper. She knew women. It would have been idiocy to think of the relationship in terms of linear fidelity. She knew better. And perhaps there was a measure of solace to be gained from knowing that his cheating was limited to fellatio. But to throw this at her now when she had just opened her heart to him was confirmation for why she was leaving. Those were the last words that he said to her. "Thank you, Michael. Good-bye," were the last words that she said to him. She picked up her bags. They didn't seem like such monsters now and left walking through the hole and out of his life.

FORTY-FOUR

Hannibal sat alone in a daze in his bedroom, watching his favorite movie for the one hundredth-and-whatever time. He was not enjoying or paying attention to the screen. He watched it now out of habit. Actually, it had begun playing inadvertently. After he came home from the police station, beaten and too tired even to sleep, he arbitrarily pronounced his own name. As the program was set to his particular voice, the system began playing the movie and he didn't have the energy to say *stop*.

He had been in the precinct for hours. Surprisingly, for all of the dirt and deeds done in his prior life this was the first time that he had ever been in a police station. The cops knew who he was and it was not because of his celebrity. He had no record, not even a parking violation; there were, however, junkets of files like fan letters dedicated to him. Hannibal had always been smart and Jersey had been influential. With all the paperwork collected, it was all circumstantial, nothing worthy of taking to court. So he sat in the precinct feeling as if he was in the middle of a bad police drama, answering every question. He knew they had nothing. They hadn't found him with a gun and there were too many witnesses to the affair who said clearly that he had not been one of the shooters.

As for the shooters, Reaper (Jason Armstrong) and Rahim Muhammad (Flawless's bodyguard) were taken into custody but they were not the ones the police really wanted. They wanted Bull but they would not have him, not today, not for this. He was free to go home though he was told not to make any plans to travel.

He sat on the bed listening to Lecter with the same blank expression he had given the police. He began to hear sounds approaching. He looked over and saw Micah standing at the door. He was saying something but Hannibal couldn't hear him. His ears felt clogged. He put his fingers to his ears and then everything became clear.

"You fucking killed Terrence," Micah said to him.

"Nigga, get outta here wit' dat shit. I loved him more than you did. You hardly even knew him," Hannibal replied with his eyes still fixed to the screen.

"That's why you left him to die alone."

"No, nigga, get your shit straight. I stayed there and watched him die. Where were you? Off with some bitch? That's love for you."

"I told you about this shit, didn't I? But you wouldn't listen. You had to make it come to this."

"This . . . naw. Nothing is *this*. This ain't over yet."

"So what, now you kill Flawless?" Hannibal didn't answer. "Go ahead, I don't even have to worry about that. I know that you're not that stupid. You can't make no money in jail. Plus, you know how you hate prison; you might turn out like Mook."

Hannibal then turned about and for the first time looked Micah directly in the eye.

"You know something, Micah? I think I finally figured it out. You know what my parents said to me about when I was born and that veil of fat and shit. At first I didn't pay attention to it but then it began to weigh on me. And y'know what? I agree. I am great and I am going to be greater still. Only thing is, I don't give a fuck about being good or whatever. I'm just Bull, nigga. Hannibal. You know, I read up on that cat. Barca was running the whole Italian countryside, fucking up crackers for seven years, and he would have took over Rome too, if it wasn't for the people back home got scared and wouldn't back him up. Just like today, niggas will be niggas and can't see the big picture. They're the same ones who eventually sold him out and he had to run from Carthage and poisoned himself so that he wouldn't get captured. And for selling him out to Rome, what happened? The Romans destroyed Carthage and threw salt into the earth so that nothing would ever grow there again. That's what niggas got for being small-minded. When I read all that it finally came to me. I figured your purpose out. The movie was made to bring me the name. You came to bring me the purpose behind the name, to teach me who I truly am. And for that I thank you. See now, I see that it is not just a cool name but really who I am. When my parents told me about my birth, it all came to me. I am Hannibal, and this is Rome, and hip-hop is my elephant, and this is the takeover. 'Coup d'etat,' that's your title, remember? You brought it to me. But now you turning your back on me, just like them other small-minded niggas. I thought your mind was bigger than that but I guess I was wrong. But I learn from my mistakes. This time I'ma get rid of the niggas before they can fuck shit up. So I thank you, Micah, for showing me my purpose. Now get the fuck out of my house."

With those words he wrote Micah out of his reality. For a moment Micah just stood there, feeling a burning sensation in his chest. He was set to leave but stopped to ask Hannibal one final question.

"Tell me, Bull. What will you do after you take over the world? Will the big picture be complete then?"

"Naw. Then I'll take over heaven," Hannibal answered with cold conviction. "We need a change. That motherfucker been fucking shit up for too long."

Again, Micah was silent. He had nothing to say. There was nothing more to be said. So he merely walked out with his chest burning, leaving Hannibal all alone with his big picture.

FORTY-FiVE

Flawless looked out over his stone balcony, watching Trish put her bags into the trunk of her car. The event seemed to have been slowed somewhat, enabling him to embrace every detail of her leaving. Throughout it all he wanted to shout, *Trish stop, don't go.* Indeed, he shouted it over and over again in his mind, though something bit his tongue as the words came to his lips, as he stood alone in the cold, silently watching her drive out of his life.

Long before money came his way, Flawless spent a day walking through Times Square with Tommy. They were going to see a movie. As they proceeded upward it was quite possible that they had passed somewhere close to two thousand people in just a two-block stride; this was a number that kept on being added to. With every successive second, hundreds of people walked by, people he had never seen before. They came in throngs, going about their affairs, and from whence they came he did not know. They just kept on coming, everyone chattering away in an unintelligible mélange of nonsense, rapping to the percussion of the traffic. All these people were coming, and they were talking, but were they thinking?

He knew that he was thinking, of that he was sure, but of the thoughts of others he did not know. There were billions of people in the world, could they all be thinking—thinking, not exactly the way he thinks but rather as he thinks. Could they all be universes onto themselves? Or were they just orbits of his own consciousness, brought into being only to pretty his picture? Truly the only thing he knew of was his thoughts and his existence; he could not attest to anything else. But what of the past, what of history. There were records of thoughts and experiences of others that were there independent of his birth. But did they truly happen, or did his mind create the past in the world and in others in order to give his present meaning? And was the past a whole thing or just a patchwork of things learned, or things remembered? He didn't know. Was Tommy truly thinking, or was Tommy walking here beside him because he wanted him to? That could not be, he had spoken to Tommy on many issues, from hip-hop to women. Tommy had thoughts. But perhaps Tommy had only become real when he came into Flawless's direct world. If he had never met him he would have been just like the rest, walking by, chattering away. And if he died, it would not have been real to Flawless. It would have been just a blurb on the news, or rather just a statistic. That was what all of these people were to him, background to his foray. He was walking about in a world of nothingness where existence was created and destroyed with his every forward footstep. It was an extremely selfish thought but one at the time he could not stop himself from indulging in. Everything in this universe existed the way it did because of him. And when he died, it would all go away. He saw the world only through his senses and when he closed them everything disappeared. If it still continued to be, he didn't know, and if he didn't know, did it really matter? How did he know that the world about him wasn't all created at once with the birth of his thoughts, and when he closed his eyes forever, so too would it revert back to darkness. Could anyone successfully argue against his selfishness? He didn't know. But just then at that moment, he and Tommy beheld a very beautiful girl walking down the square and they both turned simultaneously with her passing and hollered in gregarious rapport. When the image had become an afterthought he looked over to his friend and smiled. This was confirmation enough for him at the time. Yeah, my boy is thinking, or at the least so he thought. They then crossed the congested street, almost being run over by a yellow cab, and went into the movie theater.

He never thought that way again, until just now as Trish drove away. Would she now just become a number, a blurb in the newspaper, a nameless automaton walking-chattering about, there only to give depth to his reality? He didn't know. He realized then that man could attain all of the knowledge in the world and if he could not answer that question, he truly knew nothing. "Good-bye, Trish."

Two hours later Flawless was dressed and headed to the city. He had not slept all night. Somnolence was bearing but his mind would not allow him to give in. He felt so alone there in that immense house. His mother had gone on a Caribbean cruise and would not be back for another week. Trish had just left, Tommy was dead, Erika was wherever Erika was and he was alone with the untouchable hole. The demons used to keep better company. He had to leave. He couldn't stand it. He called Tommy's parents and was on his way back to Queens, to give his condolences and cry with company. He called a limo and saw as it now pulled up downstairs. He realized then how much he had grown to detest riding in limos. He had to learn to drive; this was stupid.

He was on his way down when he felt the vibe from his pager. He hoped that it was Trish but then he saw that it was something else.

Hello, my boy. I have good news.
I have just spoken to his people
and guess who wants to do a single
with you . . . Michael Jackson himself.
Great news, huh? I told them that you
would love to do it. So get your best

work together and let's do it.
Call me back. I know that you're excited.

P.S. Sorry about your friend.
Jenn

After reading the message Flawless smiled and felt like throwing the pager against the wall and smashing it to pieces. But he didn't. He held onto it. He squeezed it tightly and then returned it to his pocket.

He stepped out of his house and walked toward the limo while looking up at the sky. The clouds were clearing. The sun was not out in full but was fighting its way through. He opened the door and was set to step in, when, "Michael!" a voice shouted from behind. He knew that it was Erika's. Her voice at that moment was the sweetest thing that he could have heard. He knew that apologies, along with other things, were in order. With a happy face he turned around to see Micah standing by her side. The sight of the name turned his stomach.

"Michael, we have to talk."

"I have nothing to say to you."

"C'mon, Michael, don't do this."

"I don't have to, you've done enough."

He got into the limo and instructed the driver to pull off. It drove a four-car length of the driveway and then stopped and the door opened. Erika and Micah ran toward it and got in.

Flawless was seated, looking out the window. They sat together on the opposite side facing him. He wouldn't directly look at them. "Drive," he instructed, and the car pulled off.

It was not until they had driven the long length of the property and had passed through the iron gates of the house that anyone said a word.

"Talk fast," Flawless said to her.

"You really hurt me last night, Michael. I really couldn't believe you said all of those things to me."

An apology was in order. It was in fact the reason why he had stopped the limo. Though the only thing that he could bring himself to say was, "Tommy is dead."

"I know, Michael, and I am very sorry. Tommy was my friend as well. I have been crying all night. But I told you, I tried telling you, that this was going too far."

"Too late now for 'I told you so's.' "

"It's not too late. You can stop it before it gets worse."

"Trish left."

"Oh God, Michael."

"And now you're gone as well. What can I tell you . . . women? They sure know when to stick it to you."

"I am not gone, I am just in love. Why is it wrong for me to be in love?"

"It's not. It's just . . ." He stopped himself. He was about to get into the usual argument of not wanting her to get hurt. Then he realized that it had grown old and he was too tired to argue it.

"Let me love, Michael. And you love as well. Go to Trish and work things out. She cares about you a lot. You gotta let me go and you gotta let go of what you have with Bull. Don't you see it's tearing everything you built apart?"

Flawless had a thousand arguments all competing to be heard. But he was too beaten to bring them forth. He thought of Bull and just how all-encompassing his hatred for the man was. It had been about six years since their first meeting. Now he could not recall just how he lived and thought before the man. It was as if his beef and competition with Hannibal was one of his reasons for being, as if he were written to battle him. But who was doing the writing? Was this story the manifest narrative of his will? Or was the pen in someone else's hand? Was there someone else rhyming his existence over a beat, putting it on wax and selling it for $13.95? Was his story being sampled and bootlegged? Was it being looped and refashioned into a novel, or perhaps a movie, so that others could read or watch and take enjoyment from his impotence? Was his life and purpose just a pawn to be played with? Was he nothing but a slave to the script?

He looked back at Erika and he looked at the name he hated so much seated beside her. Why he hated him so he could not answer. He looked at him now as a reflection of himself, as man was a reflection of God, and as God wished that he stood on man's side of the mirror.

He was in the netherworld. It was a parallel of what was real, only more distorted and exaggerated. In this inebriated state he looked at her now and a voice came out of his mouth saying, "Let her go." It was the one succinct thing amid all the purple ambiguity. He then stepped out of his reflection and back into reality, to repeat under his breath, "Let her go."

"What did you say, Michael?" Erika asked.

"You're right. You're right," he said to her. Those were hard words to say but with them he felt a weight ease its brace on his heart. His lungs filled more freely and he gave a great exhale. Again, he looked at Micah, the man who sat by his sister's side. "And you, what do you have to say?"

"I love her, man, I love her a lot. And not with any real intent could I see my way to hurt her. That's real. I respect your feelings, because I respect my own, and I understand them. I could never knock that. I can only reflect to you a mutual love. And right now my friend is dead. And now I just want to see this whole thing end."

Flawless nodded his head and smiled approvingly. He liked what he had heard. "Okay. I hear you. Go . . . live your life. Be happy. And the next time you see Hannibal, tell him he can say whatever it is he wants against me but the battles are over."

"Thank you, Michael," Erika said with such a great sense of relief.

Flawless was still not sure of everything and past arguments plagued him: Don't let her go; don't let her go; beat Hannibal; don't trust the name. He knew that it would take time to truly cool the demons. He eased back into the contours of the seat and breathed and in that moment it came to him that he did not see the untouchable hole. He searched his visual field and it was nowhere to be found. It was gone and with it came a great smile. The hole was gone. In its stead was no crack, no images but rather nothing. He laughed to himself. Erika looked at him quizzically but she did not disturb his laughter. She had not seen her brother laugh like that in a while and it was good to see.

At this point something came to Micah's throat and he began to cough in a series. It wasn't a terrible cough, because he kept it in, though it was burning his chest.

"What's wrong?" Erika asked him.

"It's nothing," he replied. "I just began to feel kinda sick."

Flawless reached into the minirefrigerator, pulled out a bottle of water and handed it to him. As Micah began to drink the water and Erika tended to him, Flawless looked over and saw the love between the two and wished that he had that. He had walked about many times before seeing lovers and wishing that he had their affections. To be so lost and naked with someone, it looked to him now as a beautiful thing. "Give her to me." He had always wished that he had that, that he had her. Then he realized that he did and he had let her go. He allowed her to drive out of his life. What a fool he had been. However, it was not too late. He was not dead yet. Flawless pulled out his pager and crafted a message. It read:

> Trish, I am sorry. I am sorry for
> everything. Let's work it out,
> I love you.
> P.S. Marry me.
> Michael

He stopped himself before sending it. Did he actually mean what he had written? He wasn't sure but it was okay. Weddings didn't happen overnight; he could have up to a year to get used to the idea. He laughed and was about to press send when he heard something cut through the air.

Flawless looked to his left and saw that there was now a small hole in the window. Was this the untouchable hole again? He looked away to see if the hole would follow him. It didn't but it did reappear as he looked at the adjacent window to his right. Shit. It was back. He stretched out his hand and reached for the aperture and, to his surprise, he touched it and it cut him. He looked at the trickle of blood and knew that this was not the same thing. He was in a daze now as he looked out the window. The tinted glass obscured his vision. He could nevertheless make out a dark image of what appeared to be a van driving alongside. Then there came a very loud crash. The glass window shattered to pieces.

The sun had come out and the light of day shined in oppressive brilliance. All things were made clear. He could see the van driving beside them, hear its motor humming, the friction its tires made against the road; while with its door open, two armed men leaned out, with the barrels of their rifles pointed at him.

"This is it," were the last words that he spoke. Everything seemed then to him to have moved in slow motion. There was an explosion of light, which caused him to blink. When he reopened his eyes he saw what could be nothing other than a bullet coming toward him, spiraling. It was moving slowly, creeping closer and closer. At this speed he should have easily been able to dodge it but for some reason he had no will to parry from its path. He felt helpless as the spiraling thing increased in perspective.

Then came the sudden depth of heaviness, as if he had dived into a body of water and was being propelled by its buoyancy. He instinctively flayed his arms. He swam frantically, doing a full turnabout. It was then that he saw, lying on the seat of the fine leather interior along with displaced shards of glass, what appeared to be a body. It was an odd thing to see. He did not recall another body being in the limo. Even more strange, the body wore his clothes. No, it couldn't be, he thought. He swam closer to see his matter lying stagnant and shivering, with a clean hole to the head and eyes wide open. In that moment he saw himself in both directions.

He looked on as the hallowed frame was being torn apart by successive shots. The resulting wounds spurted blood, which shot up like a fountain. He looked in the corner of his eye and watched the birth of a tear. It went through infancy, toddlerdom, pubescence, and as it came to adulthood it began to swell and overflow the haven of its lid. It trickled over its borders and began its journey down the topography of his face. He watched the tear and recalled his life in flesh in all of its stages: from his first step, to his first day in school, to the day he walked home crying because he had messed himself, to the day he had broken his leg while playing basketball, to when he had fallen off of the bicycle when his uncle was teaching him to ride, to the day that his father left while he stood looking on with clenched fists and an intense hatred, resolving himself that no one would ever touch his sister again. It was all here vivid before him: his first kiss, his first touch, his first time, to the first line he had ever written, "I am God." He remembered the first time he picked up the mic; how divine it felt in the grip of his hand, how his voice carried throughout the crowd and how they cheered. Flawless retraced his life as he traced the flow of his tear. It had surmounted his cheekbone and now angled down a steeper descent. The end was near and the images continued to flash on. He remembered the first time he met Hannibal and for the first time ever, he thought of the man with calm serenity and understanding of purpose. Trish, I am sorry. Tommy, forgive me. Mother, I love you. The tear was crashing and all of the images began to spiral into a crescendo. In these last thoughts one dominant icon repeated itself in abundance: Erika. The thought woke him and he wondered of her safety.

He floated to his right and saw her there in the midst of a scream, across a sea of bullets with her hand outstretched. Even in her grief she was beautiful.

The tear fell from his cheek but he didn't care anymore as he saw a bullet pierce through her abdomen and likewise pierced through the core of his being. In grievous pain he shouted, "ERIKA!" The word resonated and vibrated at an octave unchained that echoed throughout existence, creating a crack in reality. Like a crack in glass, it grew and splintered off in the design of a web, which stretched to the limits of space. He saw his sister now as a prisoner behind the gossamer. There was an abeyance in time, both minute and infinite: as the fraction, which was her left eye, ruptured out of the great design, falling, leaving a black hole in its stead. Flawless floated over and caught the eye in webbed consciousness and then everything else about him shattered. Reality came crashing down like remnants of glass to reveal an eternal blackness.

Think, Flawless. Think, think. You can't die unless you stop thinking. He felt nothing; saw nothing; he only perceived blackness. Do not give in, Flawless. Think, think. Just keep on thinking. Then came the beat: *Boom ba bom boom—ba ba boom ba bom boom*. In the senseless ubiquity of black, it was indescribable. There was no form but the thought of that which used to be man knew fear, and all the ranges of mortal emotions until he came to peace and the understanding that he was surrounded, and he was in a battle. And the beat continued, a rhythm far more infectious than any of Noah's design. It began to turn over; his goading audience awaited and his opponent was . . . think Flawless, think. You can't die if you keep on thinking. The beat is on, Flawless, think. Then a voice came and the word seemed to emanate from without and within.

I am beyond man's definitions
Beyond man's comprehensions
No borders bound me

Bigger than bounty
I kill the killers
I kill the verb
The logos loaded
I am the scourge
A demiurge to demons
Existed before semen
Before me, I see no men
Just boys without reason
Goys for the slaughter
Forgetting that I am your father
And your father's father
And it seems the more I fathered,
The farther apart we grew
And so gravity I grew
To keep you in check
Orbit of my circumference, get it.
You're just a concomitant son
I am the sunum bonum
Sum of all things
Got the whole pantheon panting on
Because ma thought's pandemic
Ma word is hectic
I'm sick wit' it
Put Hecate in fits
Because the reprobate
Can't operate on my level
I bedevil the devil
I dabble in dogma
A Dogon from Dogstar
Made man from mantra
Flawless so nice
Dropped the universe
All in one stanza
I am God.

There was no applause, no eruptions, but rather a still in the blackness as the beat faded, and then the dark gave way to a blinding light. Think Flawless, think—think, think . . . and then nothing, nothing but an eternal peace.

Erika saw no bullet, only a light, then heard a deafening sound and the image of her brother's head being blown back. "Michael!" she shouted. With no concern for her safety or the sea of bullets riddling the limousine's interior, she stretched out her hand. Bullets whizzed through the spaces in her fingers, flew an inch from her nose and pierced her side. Weakened, Micah grabbed hold of her hand and pulled her down, falling to the floor, shielding her body with his and caught a bullet in his upper left thigh. He paid no mind to it; he thought only of Erika's safety.

In reaction to the gunfire, the frightened driver dallied in a frantic zigzag. The van sped up and became parallel to the driver's window. A flurry of bullets was fired off, loudly tearing through the glass and the driver's body. Without a pilot the speeding vehicle veered off the road, skidded into a thicketed ditch and crashed into a tree.

"Erika, Erika. Are you okay? Erika, answer me!"

Erika had no answer. She only looked over at her brother's dying body, open-eyed, looking back at her, with a tear trickling down his cheek. "Michael, Michael," she cried.

"He's dead, Erika. Now, don't you die on me too."

"I'm so scared. What happened, Micah? I am so scared. I don't want to die."

"You are not going to die. You're going to live. I'm going to get you through this."

Looking at her brother's eyes she could almost hear his voice screaming her name. "Michael, Michael. Don't die, Michael."

"Erika, quiet. I hear something."

Micah covered Erika's mouth and eyes and calmed her trembling. The sound of boots cutting a path in grass could be heard coming from the outside. It all moved in rhythm with Erika's quickened heartbeat. The door to the limo opened. Erika could feel the sting of the cold and the light of day. For seconds there was nothing but silence as an armed figure threw his crimson shadow before them, swaying his rifle from side to side. Erika could feel the intensity of the light ebb and flow with every sway of the figure's body. Then as if moving involuntarily, Micah tilted his head upward and looked into the face of his killer. It took only a moment's recognition. Erika heard the cry of successive shots. The door slammed, closing out the intensity of the cold and the sting of the light.

"Micah, Micah," Erika called in darkness, attempting to move his hand.

"Don't do that, Erika. Don't look," he said to her, holding tight his bloody hand before her eyes.

"Micah, what happened?"

"Don't worry about it. Don't worry about anything. Just sleep. Can you do that for me?"

"Yes, but Micah . . ."

"No, Erika, just sleep. Please."

"Okay."

Micah continued to shield her, feeling the life ebb slowly out of his body.

"Erika, do you remember when we first met?"

"Yes," she replied at the pleasance of the thought.

"Other than small patches of memories of my childhood, I can't remember anything solid before that . . . as if everything before then never happened. It's as if my entire life began when I met you."

"Micah, don't say that."

"No, it's okay, Erika. It's true. I know it is. I think maybe I have always known."

"Why, why are you talking like that, Micah? Don't die, Micah. I couldn't live with losing you too."

"No Erika . . . you live," he said, feeling so tired, fatigue

weighed on him like the weight of the world. "Never acknowledge death, remember. Never acknowledge it and live forever."

"Okay. But you acknowledge life, remember that?"

"All right Erika, but I already did. I already did. But now I
am tired. Girl, I am so tired. I need to sleep . . . I need to sleep;
will you sleep with me, Erika?"

"Yeah . . . okay . . . let's sleep. My handsome Micah."

"My beautiful Erika . . . Let's sleep."

And so they slept in each other's arms, in their own blood,
in their purple haze.

FORTY-SiX

RA walked through the gray-carpeted sinuous halls wearing his solemnity in his stride. Each step he took came with an effort as he made his way past a sea of swollen eyes, and pushed the heavy, wooden soundproof door open into the studio. The door clanked behind him and he stood alone to dead silence. He came to the crescent-shaped table and seated himself in his padded chair, sinking his contour into the well-formed depression. On a seeming dais of death he looked upon the great black mic looming before him. It was 3:57 and he would be on in three minutes. The job of God never before seemed to be such a chore. He was chagrined at the thought of speaking when usually the jubilance would be seeping through every orifice in the anticipation of being exhaled. There was no jubilance left; the news he had heard and the news he was about to bear had sucked the mirth out of the man. Contemplative he awaited his cue.

"RA, it is time," the engineer's voice came cutting through the silence.

"Okay," RA replied. He reached over and curled the headphones on like dumbbells to his ears. The thick padding sucked all of the oxygen out of the air and suffocated the sound around him. The clean, crisp filter of the airwaves came on and he could hear every nuance of the drag as he pulled the microphone to his lips. He lathered, took a deep breath and then let it all out.

"What's up, New York? This is yo' God, RA, coming to you once again in the place to be . . ." His voice trailed off, he had no heart to finish his regular spiel. "Yo, people, I got sad tidings to report. This is a very dark day in hip-hop. Which just comes right after another dark day in hip-hop. Just a day ago I came to you and announced the shootings and the deaths that took place at the after party of the *Source* Awards. As I told you before, I was there, and to witness the shooting and the riot that resulted afterward was for me already disturbing. Now I got no energy to speak on what has happened." His speech broke as he tried to contain himself. "Look, I am just gon' say it because there ain't no good way to say it. Flawless was gunned down and killed in a drive-by shooting two miles outside of his Bergen County home. His sister, Erika Williams, was also shot and is currently in intensive care at St. Joseph's Hospital, along with his driver who was shot and killed as was another unnamed man."

Jennessy stood by the window in his office, arms folded behind him, looking out at the great expanse. He listened to RA's voice as it cracked under the pressure of his announcement. RA's delivery touched the heart of the executive, though the radio jockey was not his first bearer of the news. Jennessy had been informed within an hour of the shooting; since then he had seen gray clouds in this sunny sky.

A call came to his door. "Come in, Jane," Jennessy answered, expecting his secretary. Jane walked the length of the office and placed a file on his desk.

"Here is the file you requested, sir."

"Thank you, Jane," he replied without turning around. "So tell me, how many unreleased tracks for Flawless do we have?"

"Somewhere close to one hundred."

"Enough to do about eight or nine more albums, plus a greatest hits. What a prolific young man. Thank you, Jane. You can send our young friend in now." Jane exited the office, leaving the door open behind her.

"I loved you much, Flawless. I loved you most. You will be missed."

"Mr. Jennessy," a voice called from behind. Before turning about, Jennessy wiped the emotions from his eyes and turned off the radio, cutting RA off midspeech. The president of Crown Records then greeted the young man at the door of his office with a great smile. "Serious Flowz, the man of the hour. How are you?"

Jennessy looked at the platinum Rolex on his wrist, swaying his briefcase back and forth at his side, standing outside of his closed office door. He looked toward his secretary in exasperation. "What am I paying people for, Jane?"

"I don't know, Mr. Jennessy."

"I have been waiting for twenty minutes now. I have things to do."

"I know, sir. Security sends their apologies. They have been detained downstairs but should be coming up any minute now."

"Jane, that is what you told me ten minutes ago."

"I know and I am sorry, sir."

"You know what, fuck it. I'll walk down by myself. But believe me, when they come in tomorrow and find that they are no longer employed, they will know better to be more punctual. I will see you tomorrow, Jane."

"Good-bye, Mr. Jennessy. I'll see you tomorrow."

Then for the first time in over a year Jennessy walked the length of the Crown Records offices unescorted. He made the march to the elevator feeling naked. Many of the employees noticed the oddity of the stride; however, too many were too dismayed at the word of Flawless's passing to give the boss an eye. The boss stood by the door for exactly a minute. When security still had not arrived, he pushed the button and stepped into the elevator alone.

Instead of the usual funerary mix being played overhead,

one of Flawless's songs was the programmed croon. I am gonna have to have that changed, Jennessy thought. It is just gonna kill me to hear that over and over again everyday.

The doors to the elevator opened to the parking lot. Jennessy's Benz was parked only a few feet away. Being the president of a company gives one perks in parking, yet making the distance alone made the car seem as if it were a mile away. Yep, someone is going to get fired, the denim clad executive thought as he breathed in, breathed out and stepped off toward his car. It was a distance of about twenty steps. Jennessy trembled inside as he made the first ten, calmed a bit after fifteen and by the eighteenth he felt that he was home free. He pressed the button disabling the alarm system and made the final step with his hand outstretched toward the door.

"Turn the fuck around, Jennessy!" a familiar voice commanded. Jennessy didn't have to see him to know who it was. It was because of this voice that he had begun the practice of being escorted to his car over a year ago. Jennessy turned around slowly with his hands half-raised to look upon the last face he wanted to see in the world, as Bin Laden stood five steps away from him with a cocked Tec-9.

Yep, someone is definitely getting fired.

The rapper stood before his ex-boss, looking far different from his yesteryear opulence. There was no ice on his wrist nor around his neck and his clothes had the natural worn-out look of age. Scuffed boots and baggy jeans were covered over by an oversize, dirty, crimson goose-down coat. He was unshaven and he had allowed his coolie hair to grow wild. "I bet I am the last nigga you wanted to see," he said to him. Jennessy didn't answer. "You don't have to answer. I know, nigga, I know."

"What's up, Bin. How are you doing?"

"What's up, what's up? Don't act dumb. You should know what the fuck is up! You fucked up my life."

"No one fucked up your life, Bin. You did that."

"No I didn't, you did that. And don't you fucking talk back to me! Not anymore," the rapper barked in hysterics.

"Okay, okay, you're the boss."

"You're fucking right, I'm the boss. I'm running shit now." Bin broke off in the middle of his rant and, as if being mentally besieged, pressed the barrel of his gun to his forehead. "You screwed me, Jennessy. You put the hit out on me. I used to be selling out stadiums and now I can't even get a gig in a bar—in a fucking bar, nigga."

Jennessy made a slight step forward. Bin Laden quickly pointed the pistol back in his direction.

"Okay, it's cool. Just calm down."

"Don't tell me to be cool. You took my life away from me and you want me to calm down?"

"I gave you your life."

"And then you took it away. Who do you think you are, God? Nigga, do I look like a fucking pawn to you? You set me up, send me out and then you fucking leave me out to dry?"

"I didn't let you go, Bin. That was your choice when you came to my office with ten guys all with guns. You remember?"

"What did you expect, nigga? You was taking all of my fucking publishing."

"You sold it to me."

"You gave me an extra two hundred thousand dollars in my advance. I didn't know what I was signing."

To that argument Jennessy had no response. He just kept his hands up, his mind rummaging through a milieu of thoughts on how he was going to talk his way out of this mess: I swear to God, if I get out of this, the entire security force is going to be fired. I won't only fire them but I'll find a way to get everyone in their family fired. Heads are going to roll.

"So what do you want, Bin? You came here because you want something," Jennessy said to the mad rapper while fathoming a plan.

"I wanna blow your fucking brains out!" Bin coldly retorted.

The response was not what Jennessy wanted to hear but he kept his cool as he regurgitated his phlegm.

"No, Bin, that's not what you want. If it was, you would have done it already. What do you want, Bin?" he pressed him carefully.

"You wanna know what I want, nigga? You wanna know? I want the bitches back! The fucking big-ass bitches that I used to be fucking all the time. Bitches who used to be lining up to suck me off now be walking by me like they don't know me. I want all of my ice back. I want ma platinum watch, ma ten thousand dollar rings, ma crosses and ma teeth. Alla that shit that they repossessed. I want my rides back with the fucking hot-ass rims and the Xbox already built inside. I want ma fly-ass crib back and all of ma shit in it. You know they even took away ma platinum plaques. They didn't leave me with nothing. Nigga, I want ma life back, the life that you took from me."

Jennessy looked at the man who was close to weeping and he knew that he had him. He saw his exit out of this maze of madness very clearly now.

"I'm back in the ghetto, man; fucking projects. You know, they got roaches and rats up in dem places. I forgot how big them motherfuckers used to be. I won't even walk outta ma house in the daytime outta shame of being seen."

"I understand, I understand completely. I hear you, Bin. I hear your pain and I am sorry that you have suffered. I didn't know. But neither of us are saints; we are men and we make mistakes. And also neither of us are dead yet. Things can be rectified."

"What the hell do you mean?" the hysterical rapper asked.

"Well, Bin, you can have your whole life back, you can be back on top, king of New York once again."

"Don't bullshit me, Jennessy!" Bin shouted, jolting the gun in Jennessy's direction. Jennessy stepped back, shaking his exposed raised palms.

"No bull," he replied. "I wouldn't do that to you. I see that you're serious. But the truth is, Flawless is dead . . ."

"Don't talk to me about that nigga. Everybody talkin' 'bout him, like he was fuckin' Jesus or something. I'm glad that motherfucker is dead," Bin blurted.

"Are you admitting to something, Bin?"

"I ain't sayin' shit. I'm just sayin' I'm glad niggas is dead."

"You're absolutely right. He is dead and his throne in Crown is open. There is a void to be filled. I have a contract right here in my briefcase. Seeing you now, I realize that you are the man to fill it." Jennessy's words were far sweeter than the finest Cristal. It was what Bin wanted to hear, the promise of a rebirth, with all of the trimmings and the naked women that he could think of.

"How do I know that you won't dick me like you did before?"

"Because we live and learn, Bin. You have learned and so have I. This time you get all of your publishing and you will get twenty points off of every record. And I'll give you not just an advance but a two hundred-fifty-thousand-dollar signing bonus."

The promise of wealth was an incredible aphrodisiac. The hardened Bin began to grow soft. His anger waned as did the pallor in Jennessy's cheeks. The executive's heart began to ease as he saw the barrel of the pistol lower; death pointed toward the floor. Jennessy began to lower his arms. Then the madness retook Bin Laden and he jolted his pistol back into its erect state.

"Fuck you, Jennessy. You must think that I am the dumbest nigga. You ain't gonna bend me over and fuck me twice."

"Bin, don't do this!" Jennessy compelled.

"Don't worry. I'll be in hell just a few seconds after you." After saying this, Bin Laden smiled and nodded, and then Jennessy smiled and nodded, and then six rounds were fired off and the blood spilled all over the denim.

FORTY-SEVEN

In his latter years, Flawless had become a very philosophical man and to a degree rather spiritual. He, however, was not religious. He held no allegiances to mosque, church or synagogue. It was the metaphysics of theology rather than the application of it that he admired. So when the time came to decide how he should be buried it was debated. Erika did not agree with her mother that the funeral should be held in a church. Mrs. Williams, though not an avid parishioner, argued that the affair would be a farce if taken irrespective of God. Erika quoted from Flawless's works where he stated, "If God created everything, then every house is the house of the Lord." His reasoning was good but his mother's traditionalism would not allow it; and given that the honor of burial had been bestowed upon his mother, her voice won out.

As bequeathed in Flawless's will, his mother was also to receive the house. It was for her that he had bought it, for her long years of working. To Erika he left the rights to his entire catalogue, his works and his legacy. "I love you, now it is your time to take care of me, little sis." When the attorney read those words to her, Erika fell to her knees. She had never known anyone at almost twenty-six who had written a will. It came as a shock to everyone when they were called to the attorney. What must have plagued the man to bring him to such a state in life's prime? No one among them knew. In the last year he had rarely spoken to them or perhaps they had rarely spoken to him. His mother felt an immense culpability. In the past few years she had lived fat on the life that her son offered, never fully taking the time to see how the young man suffered.

For Tommy, Erika was left the charge of releasing Flawless's ten-track demo that he had produced. All rights and proceeds of this were to be given to Tommy, or as it was, to Tommy's family. Finally, to Trish he left a letter in which he intimated to her his love and also the fears that had stopped him from loving her fully. With this he also left a diamond engagement ring, along with the pronouncement that she had lived to hear and that he died without saying, "Will you marry me?" Only Trish was not there to accept it. She was gone and could not be reached. She had left her job at Crown and moved from New York. Her apartment was bare. Where she had gone, Erika did not know. She searched desperately for her sister but she could not find her. She never heard from Trish again. It took years before Erika came to understand the meaning behind this.

There were thousands inside of the church and thousands more looked on from the outside; later thousands upon thousands would walk the streets in the procession down the long strip of Jamaica Avenue. The guess list was a who's who of the industry, many of whom Flawless hardly knew, and of those he knew, many he hardly liked. Nonetheless they were sorrowful of his passing, and so they walked the avenue weeping and mingling to the beat of the requiem. The people walked alongside with all forms of makeshift banners and posters, expressing the gravity of their dole. Erika estimated that there were well over ten thousand people there. The strip had been shut down for the hours in which the procession was to take place. It was a great testament to the love of the man that such a commercial district would hold a Sabbath at his passing. On these streets, where his words were sold and bootlegged for profit, for a day put away all notions of dollars to pay its respects. Its message: "You were loved brother, you were loved."

Her mother would support her weight at times as Erika made the walk. The bullet had gone straight through and had ruptured no vital organs. She had been released from the hospital after a week. She walked but at times did so gingerly. She took support in her mother's shoulder and carried on through the day. How she was to carry on through the remainder of her life, she still did not know. This was only half of her grieving. "Micah." Micah had died and no one acknowledged his death because they didn't know him; to them he was just another nameless body in the car, along with the driver. His burial would also be left to her charge. The thought of her love brought with it the thought of the man upon whose doorstep many had thrown the blame, a man who was not in attendance, or if so, went unseen.

With sprawled legs and a sullen face, Hannibal watched the funeral procession on his immense television. With a screen so large it was almost like being there, though he was glad that he wasn't. His presence would have caused an unease in the proceedings. He knew that many believed that the killing was his doing. He didn't need to see the close-up of the man walking about with a poster that said *Hannibal did it* to be reminded of this. The police had been in touch every day since the shooting. They had nothing, he knew this; then again he also knew that public opinion was against him and that the police could find ways to fill in the gaps. He wouldn't be the first innocent man to see death row.

Yet and still, it was not the thought of jail that troubled him. So many had died and the sorrow hadn't spoiled. He sat there watching the funeral and in a smaller corner of the screen there was Lecter playing his part as Hannibal now played his.

Flawless, Flawless, Flawless. I guess now it's finally over. What do I do now, who to battle? Hannibal sat alone on a stage by himself feeling purposeless.

Between shots of the procession MTV inserted images of

Flawless performing. Seeing Flawless onstage made Hannibal feel as if he had experienced this moment once before. He rummaged through his memories and could find no recollection. But in his search he did come upon the night he battled Flawless for the championship. It had been a losing night but now three months shy of being three years past, it was a fond memory.

He remembered club Rampage, under the banner of BET and Bin Laden, against the glare of the light; for a man who was usually emotionally detached, Hannibal's heart raced while standing on the platform. He knew what lay ahead.

Flawless had taken the first round by audience applause. Hannibal returned the favor and had taken the second. Now they stood even for sudden death. With the roar of the crowd, a mic between them and the future at its threshold, Hannibal was to pioneer the final.

I'm a corrupt nigga
I co-op niggas
Put 'em in projects
Have 'em push weight for profits
Everybody knows I trick hos, and at times
I have even been known
To trick faggots
Whatever the market
Nigga, I'm down with it
If it's to get rich, yo I fuck with it
Because I'm a greedy motherfucker
A vegetarian motherfucker
Because if it ain't green
I don't fuck with it, motherfucker
So don't fuck with me, motherfucker
'Cause I'ma sick motherfucker
I'm the reason they got
A Rite Aid on every ghetto street corner

Got the corner on contraband
As if ma name was Greenspan
When Bull roll through the barrios
All the Latinos be like, "El capitan"
. . . Yo, you say you Flawless
Well, nigga, I'm heartless
Put two in your chest
And have no regrets
Or better yet
Send a nigga to Sing Sing
Niggas there have you
Sing singin', soprano
Turn that ass into a so-porno
When it's all over
Flawless be like, Yo
Ma ass, it's not TV
It's HBOoooooo

He ended his final verse to a roar of applause. It took two minutes for the crowd to be settled. He knew he had done well but he also knew the caliber of his opponent. He looked across the mic and saw Flawless approach with a look of cold determination.

Negro Neanderthal
Why you so mad
At the world?
Is it because all you
Poppin' is blanks
And I don' fucked your girl
Nigga, don't act like
You don't know me
On your dome I'll
unfurl a fury
Nigga you see me
Yo, I be . . .

Sicker than six wise men
Bring Vietnam to the Vatican
You think I can't
Nigga, watch me
I'm gonna can can
On your coffin.

There was a roar of applause and Hannibal cleared his throat in an attempt to play off the remark.

Ohhh, now you coughing
Ain't surprising
Because your rhyming is limited
You just a little kid
I'm the sovereign
Wisest of wisemen
Even Solomon gotta salute
Because the shit's too astute
Flow too tight for amateurs
Leave you in a rapture
I rap a rhapsody
The shit you can never parody
You best me on the mic,
Nigga, I think hardly
Even when I flow southpaw
You still subpar to me
Pardon me, when I'm done
I'ma leave y'all niggas in poverty
I'm sorry for all you simpletons
I got no apologies; I'm an anomaly
In this shit, and I am about
To rip apart your anatomy
This is Mortal Kombat, motherfucker
And this was a Flawless victory.
Now gimme ma fucking contract.

That did it, enough had been said. The eruption of the crowd had declared Flawless the winner. At the time it had been a huge pill to swallow. It took time and death before it had been smoothed enough to slide easily down the throat. Flawless won and, in retrospect, Hannibal saw that he had deserved to win. Hannibal had always known this. Still, he despised losing to anyone. It was this competitive nature that had made these two men enemies; though he respected the man beyond par, it was also what kept them from ever being friends. At that moment Hannibal had a sorrowful thought of Micah.

Micah, damn God, he lamented to himself with eyes closed, unaware that the barrel of a gun was only two inches from his brow. Hannibal had relived his thoughts in a dreamlike state, with eyes closed, rapping along to his memory as he had that night, being senseless to an intruder's quiet creep into the room. The intruder, at first, had silently found the entire affair very interesting but after two minutes . . . he had gotten bored.

"Hello, Bull," Mook said to him calmly. Hannibal immediately recognized the voice and was awakened. He knew it was Mook, though he could not see past the gaping hole of the gun.

"Nothing like the feel of cold hard steel put to your skull to make you know if you're really a man," Mook said to him, reveling in the moment. "Who's the faggot now?"

Hannibal remained silent. He knew that he should have changed the security for the house. Business and death had been his delay.

"You don't hear me when I'm talkin' to you, nigga? I said, who's the faggot?" Mook shouted and Hannibal stayed silent. "You know what, I'ma show you a faggot. Get down on your knees." Hannibal did not move. Angered, Mook cocked his pistol and imprinted it on his temple. "On your knees, Bull," he further pressed. Hannibal could see the profound sickness in Mook's eyes and he silently acquiesced. "Good shit, nigga, good shit. Now open your mouth." Hannibal opened his mouth with a look up of abject indignation. "Good. Now suck on this." Mook propped the gun before his lips. "Naw, don't do that. That wouldn't be any fun. Better yet, suck on this." He kept the gun erect and began to fiddle with his belt in an attempt to undo his pants. It was a difficult task to accomplish working with only his left hand. In his exasperation, he abandoned the belt and went for the zipper. Hannibal could hear every ripple as it slowly went down. He could see a growing bulge behind the thick blue denim. He could already smell the foul funk of crotch as Mook put his hand inside of his pants and fingered through his crimson boxers. It was a sickening experience. At that moment, Hannibal began to accept that he might die: for he knew for certain that he would not do this.

Mook broke through the peephole and was about to bring his nature to air when both men heard the sound of footsteps coming from behind. Knowing who it was, Mook hastily readjusted himself. He turned around with the gun still pointed at Hannibal and saw Jacobin standing at the doorway with a gun in his hand and two equally armed men behind him.

"What the fuck is going on, Mook? We ain't got all day."

"Cool, I'm comin' right now," Mook replied to him. He turned his attention back to Hannibal and whispered, "Lucky bastard. I was so hard, all you woulda had to do was kiss it and I woulda came all over your face." He made a kissing motion to Hannibal and pulled him to his feet. "Let's go, the boss is waiting."

He pushed Hannibal in front of him, who silently walked over and nodded to Jacobin. As Mook proceeded out of the room, he noticed the immense television and Lecter's now-nauseating face in the corner. He pulled back and fired. The bullet lodged in the center and created a web across the screen. In a millisecond it all came crashing down in pieces.

"What the fuck you did that for?" Jacobin asked. "What kinda deranged motherfucker shoots a man's TV?"

In response, Mook merely replied, "I hate that fucking movie."

FORTY-EiGHT

No matter how big Jersey had gotten, he still held an office in the back room of Joey's Famous Cold Cuts in the Bay Ridge section of Brooklyn; yet he had bought off enough cops in the area that he felt very comfortable parking a limousine outside. The limo pulled up to the deli. Hannibal remembered it well and how he used to hate coming here to make deliveries. Unlike Harlem, Brooklyn was not a homogenous entity; it had as many facets as there were races and nationalities of people. This was an Italian neighborhood. Hannibal's lore never extended this far.

Jacobin and Mook escorted him in, past the counter where Joey junior was slicing cold cuts, past the elder occupants seated, smoking, next to the wall of framed pictures of Italian icons, on to the back, past the curtain, down the two sets of wooden stairs, into the dimly lit basement, through the door and finally into the light of Jersey's office to find him seated behind a large mahogany desk. By conditioning, Jacobin went over and stood at his post in front of Jersey's desk. Hannibal walked in and noticed the television placed on a stand in the upper lefthand corner of the office; Flawless's funeral was on the news. Mook entered last and closed the door.

"Hello, Bull," Jersey said to him.

"What's up, Jersey. If you wanted a meeting, I woulda came without the guns."

"Bull, Bull, Bull. You never call, you never write, but still I got a soft spot for you. You fucked up, Bull. You know that, right? You fucked up. You forgot your friends. You stopped doing business without even a good-bye."

"Can't sell drugs forever."

"Yes, but you can be loyal and remember those who were with you in the beginning. What did you think? That you could just write me off and that would be it? That I was just a story to be used in one of your rap songs? I almost had a fit when Jaco here made me listen to one of your records when you was detailing my whole operation. The debate first came up then about whether or not to kill you. Both Mook and I said no. Mook said that hip-hop was filled with a lot of big-mouth motherfuckers talkin' shit that wasn't true. So even if it was true, nobody would take it seriously. So I said all right. Jaco was still pissed but he got over it. Plus, we had Mook there on the inside to keep an eye on you. But now when you got rid of Mook, we said this kid is gettin' too big for his britches and needs to be brought back down to reality. So you wrote me off; now Jersey is writing himself back into the story. What did you think, that you were going to live life, fuck and be happy without me? You didn't start Cannibal by yourself. You owe us a percentage and it's time to collect."

"How much?" Hannibal asked, knowing that the conversation would sooner or later be estimated in dollars.

"Twenty million," Jersey flatly replied, as if he were asking for twenty dollars.

"Twenty million, shit!" Hannibal reacted, showing his first sign of emotion during the entire affair. "You knocking me all the way back to zero! That's fucked-up, Jersey." As he said this Hannibal wondered for a moment how it was that Jersey knew almost exactly his entire bank account but he didn't have to think long; he only had to glance over at Mook for his answer.

"No, it's not. There was a vote as to whether you should be breathing right now. I was outvoted and you're still alive. So this is not fucked-up. You have your legs, your teeth, all of your eyes; no, this ain't fucked-up. I expect the funds by the end of the week."

"Okay, dance with the devil, huh? I dig," Hannibal replied. He knew that there would be no use in debating. "So twenty mil' and that's it? We say good-bye."

"I get ma money and that's it. This is for past debts and future earnings."

"How do I know that you won't come back later down the road asking for more?"

"That's an interesting thought. But don't worry about it. I'm a man of my word, Bull. And despite it all, I loved you, man. You were one of the best. You ran the streets like a true professional. Don't know how Mook is gonna do in your place but . . . we'll see."

So that's what happened. Mook had sold him out in order to take his old seat. It was okay; he had long outgrown Cypress. At least he would leave the game in better shape than his predecessor. Hannibal turned and was to walk out when the television caught his eye and halted him for one more question. "Cool, Jersey, but one thing I don't understand. You hit me, I get it, but why did you kill Flawless and the kid?"

The question rang weird in Jersey's ear. "Flawless, who the fuck is Flawless?" he reflexively asked. Jacobin leaned over and said to him quietly, "The nigga that got shot up outside a Bergen, that's on all the news." He then pointed to the television.

"Oh, that nigga!" Jersey raised his voice in recognition. "What the fuck do I care about him? Just make sure I have my money. Mook and Jaco will take you home."

That was all the answer Hannibal needed. He would have to look somewhere else. If Jersey had done it, he would have gloated in it. Mook opened the door and the three men were about to leave when Hannibal turned around one more time.

"Oh yeah, by the way, Jersey, the package is going to be six thousand short."

"Six thousand short? What the fuck for?"

"It's for the cost of the TV Mook shot."

"What?"

"It's true. I saw it; he shot it. Blew the whole fucking thing up. It was a nice TV too. Big, big, real big," Jacobin added.

"Mook, you shot the man's TV?" Jersey barked at Mook. Mook did nothing but look stupefied. "What kinda stupid shit is that?"

"I don't know. Nigga kept on watching the same fucking movie all the time. It was gettin' on ma nerves."

"So you shoot the man's TV, like the TV did you something? You know what, you're gonna pay me back for that fucking TV," he scolded. "All right, Bull, you can deduct the six, now get the fuck outta here and get me my money."

The limo drove through Brooklyn and after a mile or two they were out of Bay Ridge and the climate became more colorful. It was a pleasant day outside but everything was always dark in a tinted limo. Hannibal was seated toward the right window, silently looking out. Mook sat beside him, closer than need be, given the great space in the vehicle. Jacobin sat on the opposing side. The shield that separated the driver from the back was down. Jacobin laughed amiably with the driver. "So I tell you; I ain't never seen nothing like it. Craziest thing. We're walkin' out, everything is cool and then Mook here just gets up and pops the TV. One shot shatters the screen, blows the whole fuckin' thing up." Jacobin and the driver began to laugh. Jacobin had been retelling the tale for over an hour now; the joke at his expense, for Mook, was already growing stale and costly. If he could have shot Jacobin, he would have. But he knew that that was an impossibility. So he grinned and bore it, though it bore into him knowing that they had never ragged on Hannibal in such a manner. Not even in the slightest. Even now, as he was leaving, there was still that air of respect.

"So Mook, why did ya shoot the TV?" the driver shouted.

Mook was annoyed at the question and annoyed even more that the driver was questioning him. Jacobin looked at him waiting for him to answer so that he could pounce on the response. After a moment he reckoned that Mook would not and so took the liberty and answered for him, "He says dat he hated the movie."

"Hated the movie? So you shoot the man's TV. What movie was it?"

"It was *Hannibal*," Hannibal said with his eyes to the tinted glass.

"Oh yeah, *Hannibal*," Jacobin added in recognition.

"*Hannibal*! You didn't like that movie, Mook? That's a good fuckin' movie," the driver added to Mook's annoyance. Then he thought maybe he could kill the driver. No, he couldn't. The driver was family; they would take his death personally.

"Yo, tell me about it," Jacobin agreed with the driver. "That shit with the pigs, that shit is true, y'know. I know a guy who got a farm just like it, does the same fuckin' thing."

Jacobin then turned his attention to Hannibal and looked at the fine beige leather interior and thought that it would be a shame. He began to think of a plan that would allow him to do what he was going to do and keep the mess as low as possible. Those stains didn't easily wash out. He would have to do it quickly and with stealth. He gave a nod over to Mook, who returned the favor, happy to see the issue reverted back to business and away from his mockery.

Mook inched himself closer to Hannibal, placed his hand upon Hannibal's thigh and gave an intimate grope of his knee. Hannibal turned and threw Mook a look, which was a ménage à trois between anger, disgust, and "I am going to blow your brains out if you don't move your hand." Mook merely smiled back and pursed his lips in a mock kiss.

"How's the cops treating you lately?" he said to him. As Hannibal pondered on the meaning of this he realized that the car was coming to a stop. He looked out of the tinted window and saw the blue-black image of Brookdale Hospital. He knew well enough not to question. He knew why he was brought here and he knew that whatever it was that was going to happen next it was going to hurt.

"You like movies, don't you, Bull?" Jacobin said to him. "You should find . . . this . . . very . . . ironic." He called to the driver, who passed back a very sharp, very large, very clean butcher's knife. Mook smiled; Hannibal remained quiet. "Mook, pull out the newspaper and place it on the floor, we tryin' to make as little of a mess as possible." Mook did as Jacobin said and Hannibal looked at his old friend with disgust. In his tenure, Hannibal had never taken orders from Jacobin and when Mook was with him, neither had he; Jersey would not allow it. How things change, he had been promoted in rank and yet demoted in stature.

When Mook was finished he returned to his prior position. "Good shit." Jacobin remarked and then turned back to Hannibal. "Never liked your ass. You was always Jersey's pet boy, huh? Not anymore. Gimme your hand, Bull." Hannibal cringed inside but outwardly showed no emotion. He complied and stretched out his hand, looking Jacobin directly in the eye. Jacobin rolled Hannibal's sleeve slowly up to his forearm and then made a mark on the wrist with the tip of the blade. It was sharp enough to cut with only just a graze. The bit of resulting blood trickled out around his wrist and made a deep crimson splash onto the newspaper. Jacobin held Hannibal's hand firmly with his left hand and fully extended his right with the anticipated motion to strike. "Now, don't flinch. It's best for you that this is as clean a cut as possible. And don't get no fucking bright ideas about pulling my hand into the blow either." Hannibal remained silent, as Jacobin gripped the helm of the blade and was about to swing.

"Wait!" Mook shouted. "Not the hand. That won't really hurt him. Cut the tongue instead." To this grotesque proposition, Jacobin replied, "Good thought. Gimme your tongue, Bull."

Hannibal looked back over to Mook, at the man he once called brother who he had allowed to sleep in his bed; he looked at him now and for the first time in his life he knew real hatred. He hated him far more than the white man who was about to do this foul deed.

Hannibal's hard veneer softened and his heart raced. Still, he outwardly fought back his emotions and the tear that was forming in his eye. There would be no pleading or bargains made. Hannibal knew very well what losing his tongue meant; nevertheless . . . he stuck it out. Jacobin grabbed a firm hold of the tip and yanked it to its extreme. He wanted to get as much flesh as he could with one blow. Jacobin knew that this was not the right knife for such an operation. A smaller one in successive cuts would have been more appropriate. But it didn't matter. The job was not meant to be pretty. Aiming at the pink flesh in his eye, Jacobin again pulled back his right hand and arched his back for one quick blow. Then he looked at Bull and smiled, "Now this is really going to hurt." And with that his hand fell.

The door of the limousine opened, Hannibal was tossed out on his back onto the concrete with the sun shining in his eyes and glistening off of a bloody mouth with the dismembered tongue lying on his chest. The door quickly slammed shut. And as it pulled off, a shivering Hannibal could hear Mook's voice calling out, "Let's see your ass do that hip-hop shit now."

FORTY-NiNE

Erika awoke in the intensive care unit at St. Joseph's Hospital. Through drowsy eyes she had no idea of her environs. She knew nothing other than the ringing in her ear, the beating of her heart, the background's brew of meaningless chatter and the oppressive brilliance that shined directly in her eye. It was a nauseating experience, thick with the fetid hospital smell. She began to intuit her whereabouts by the bed she was in and the light smock that she wore. Realizing where she was, it all came crashing back to her, why she was where she was. She had risen with a dense feeling seated on her heart. Her purple haze had gone from shades of lavender to fuchsia to crimson, in a profound sadness. For moments she thought maybe it had all been a dream. The hospital smell and garb stole this wish from her. When she tried to move, she felt a stiffness and a pain in her side. She reached for her stomach and discovered that she had been well bandaged. At the thought of all that had occurred, she wept and continued to weep there in solitude until a fidgeting finger found the call switch for the nurse. Within a minute, a doctor and a nurse were there to attend.

"Good evening, Ms. Williams, I see that you're finally up. How are you feeling?"

She had no concern for herself and merely replied through parched lips and a strained voice, "Michael, Michael?"

"*I am sorry, Ms. Williams, but your brother has passed. He died before the ambulance had arrived.*"

These were stinging words, though not surprising. She had seen the bullet blow back her brother's brow. She had hoped for a miracle; still, sensibility spoke more reasonably. Her brother unfortunately was only half of her grieving. "*Micah, Micah,*" *she called.* "*How is he?*" *She had heard the shots fired but had not seen her heart die. In her ignorance there was hope.*

The doctor and nurse looked at each other oddly in regard to the question. The doctor responded sensitively, "*I am sorry, Ms. Williams. But as I have said, your brother has passed.*"

"*No, no,*" *she repeated.* "*Not Michael. Micah!*" *The emphasis she placed on distinguishing the names strained her voice even more.*

"*Yes, Micah. Micah, your brother Michael, right?*" *the physician attempted to clarify.*

"*No, not Michael, Micah, Micah!*"

She was exhausting all of her energy in pronunciation. The strain of it reminded Erika of how she used to strain to pronounce her brother's name when she was much younger. It was a thought that had escaped her for years until just now.

"*Um, let me understand this,*" *the confused physician said and sighed.* "*Is Micah another name, or a nickname for your brother?*"

She thought for a moment and then answered, "*No.*"

"*So then Micah and Michael are two different people?*"

"*Of course they are.*"

"*So then Micah would be perhaps the other body that was found in the car?*"

"*Body? So then he died as well.*"

"*Oh, I am sorry.*" *The doctor apologized for his insensitivity.* "*But yes, he did pass as well.*"

"*Don't be sorry,*" *Erika replied.* "*You asked.*"

"*I understand. Um, there are other questions to be asked*

but perhaps we should save them for a better time. Perhaps you should go back to sleep."

"I don't believe that I'll ever sleep again and I can't think of any time being better. Ask your questions."

"Are you sure, Ms. Williams?" the nurse interjected.

"Yes."

"Well, then we have some questions about . . . Micah."

"What about Micah?"

"Well, Ms. Williams, before you gave us his name we had him listed as John Doe."

"Why?" she asked confusingly.

"Well, we weren't able to find any tenable identification on his person."

That was an odd thing, Erika thought. But then she dismissed it as being a simple misplacement of a wallet.

"As such, Ms. Williams, we were hoping that you could fill in some of the gaps for us. Tell us about his family so that we may inform them of what has occurred."

"Okay."

"Well, okay, let's start with his last name," the physician said. And all at once Erika came to a blank. And she remained so for some time.

"Ms. Williams, you seem confused. Perhaps we should continue this later?"

"No, I am fine, go ahead," she said, breaking her silence.

"Okay, then, as we were. What was Micah's last name?" he again asked. And again, she was without an answer. It troubled her deeply that she was not able to answer such a seemingly simple question. Of course she knew it, he must have told it to her. Then why wasn't she able to recall?

"I don't know," she was forced to reply.

"You didn't know him very well?" the nurse asked.

"No, I knew him for exactly a year," Erika answered. Then why didn't she know the answer when it was such a basic thing? Perhaps it was the sedatives that she had been given

that dulled her senses? Perhaps it had also blunted her memory? They had spoken to each other almost every day ever since their meeting. It befuddled her as to how they could have gone through a year without any mention of his family. Had she been in such a state of purple bliss that she took the man for the name alone and never thought to question him about his past? "I don't know, I can't remember," was all she could say to them.

"Well then, I am afraid that we find ourselves in a quandary," the doctor stated.

"Is there anything that you can tell us about him? Where he lived, where he was from, anything . . .?" the nurse pressed.

Once again, Erika found it odd that she had difficulty answering even these questions. Of his life before they met, she only had patches of memories. He fell off of a bike when he was younger. He would sit in the corner to himself in the Spit Café. He was in search of love and . . . "Oh yeah he had a younger brother and two older sisters. But I never met or spoke to them. I wouldn't know where they are. He said that they didn't really get along." Speaking of Micah's siblings reminded her of Tommy's family and his estrangement with them. "Also, he was from Brooklyn, I think. And I know that he was planning to move to Harlem but he hadn't moved in as yet."

"So then, where did he sleep?" the nurse asked.

"Many times he would sleep over at Hannibal's house or we would stay together in a hotel," she replied. The stray thought of Hannibal brought him to her attention. "Oh, and he was good friends with Terrence."

"And who is Terrence? Is there a way we can get in touch with him?"

"Terrence is dead," she answered. "Terrence is dead."

The doctor and nurse looked at each other in exasperation.

"Is there anyone you could think of who could tell us anything about him or about Terrence or about his family?"

"Hannibal. Hannibal may be able to tell you." As she said

this, passing the baton over, the strain of the conversation began to overtake her. The questions were perplexing. She searched for answers but found her memories lost in a sea of blissful purple. As she probed her mind further, sleep began to call. Perhaps answers would come in her reawakening.

"One thing though, Ms. Williams. Is there anything at all that you yourself can tell us about Micah?" the nurse asked; finally there was a question that she could answer.

"Yes. I know that I loved him and that he loved me."

It was late evening and Erika sat on the steps at the front door of Hannibal's great white house, still suited in her funeral dress. She had been waiting for hours, patiently counting all of the innumerable pebbles that were inlaid in his driveway; a great driveway much like Flawless's that extended a long length down to a large iron gate, and, like the formation of an oxbow lake, around a sward of trees and grass. The gate had been left open when she entered, as was the front door, though she would not go beyond the step. She rang the bell but no one answered. The large house appeared to be empty and abandoned. It remained so for hours but Erika waited at the doorstep, knowing that sooner or later the man would return and there were questions to be answered.

She watched as a yellow cab began to make its way up the long driveway. The cab moved at a moderate speed yet it seemed to take forever to arrive. When it had, it stayed motionless, the engine quietly purring. For almost a minute no moves were made, until finally the door opened. A figure with one hand outstretched supported his rise out of the vehicle, to stand erect by its side, closing the door behind him.

The cab pulled off and around the green lake of the driveway, making its way out of the property, leaving Hannibal by himself with a jar in his hand, looking across at Erika. They both silently stared at each other, not moving nor knowing what to say. There were a number of things that Erika wanted to say to him; unfortunately none came to tongue. Hannibal had words to say but his tongue was in the jar he carried in his hand. So they stared in silence.

Was this the man responsible for all of her sorrows? She did not know but she sought answers for this and much more, though standing here alone in his presence she found it hard to speak, hard to think. And what was he carrying in that jar?

All of those questions would soon have to be asked because Hannibal began his approach. He walked slowly across the pebbled driveway. He ascended the steps and came onto the plateau with his embers fixed on Erika. The intensity burned into her. She could do nothing but stare in return as he walked toward her, by her and went into his house.

She hated herself for her lack of courage. She had waited for hours and now she had allowed him by without a word. The anger began to seethe. It would not end like this. She was about to call him back when Hannibal did a slow about-face. He placed the jar on the floor and pulled out his pager and began typing. When he had apparently finished, he recaptured the jar and made his way back to her position. As he came to her, one of the questions could now be partially answered. The jar he carried held what appeared to be a saline solution in which floated some sort of flesh. And when her eyes left the contents of the jar, they rose to meet the embers. Only now the eyes were not as intimidating. He called for her palm. When she gave it to him, he left her the pager and walked away.

Again, he had been in her proximity and again, she had let him go without a word. But now, what was the reason for the pager? She opened it and found that he had left a message.

> *I loved him too.*
> *I loved them both,*
> *I am sorry.*
> *Bull*

With those words there came a calm about her and her questions subsided somewhat. There was some measure of lavender to be taken in this. She knew that she loved Micah and that he had loved her. For now that was enough. She reached for her mobile and called for a cab. Within five minutes the same cab that had dropped Hannibal off returned and drove her away. This had been their first and their last meeting.

Hannibal made his way up the stairs to the second level with his tongue in a jar. He made the long trek down the hall to the final room, though it mattered little which room he stayed in now. They were all empty and he was alone: no Mook, no Terrence, no Reaper, no boys, no Micah and no Flawless. What purpose was there left in life?

He came into his room, into the darkness, thought to utter the word *lights*, and then remembered that he had no tongue and looked across at the immense television and recalled how his big picture had been shattered. He would have screamed but it would have sounded like a retarded, ugly wail. So he did all that he could; he remained silent and allowed the emotions to fester inside. He thought that he could contain it but it tore at him too much. He fell to his knees and there before the shattered immense television, for the first time in a long time in darkness, Hannibal wept and he wept and he wept. He did not know that he had that many tears in him. At one point, he felt that if he continued he would surely drown in the depths of his bewailing, though it could not be helped; the tears, liberated from long years of bondage, flowed freely.

Then, while in the midst of his weeping, he noticed a figure standing to the distant left in the doorway of his bathroom. At the recognition that he was not alone, Hannibal attempted to recompose himself and make out his voyeur. It was a woman; beyond that, through the shadows, he could not discern, though he would not have to question for long as Rosa stepped forward. He wanted to ask her why she was there but the tongue in the jar would not permit. He felt frustrated at his inability to communicate.

Rosa said no words to him in her approach. She merely came and knelt silently. He cursed her viciously in his mind. He wanted her to leave and could think to do nothing else to scare her off but to open his mouth wide and reveal to her the scarred stub that was left of his tongue. His actions did not scare her as he had hoped but rather drew her closer. She crept on her knees toward him. He fought her, trying to push her off, though she would not be daunted. She kept coming and he kept fighting and fighting, until the gravity of his dole ebbed his energies and he could fight her no more. She came into him and threw her arms around him, his head fell to her bosom and she held him tightly in her tender brown warmth. And there in the arms of this woman, Hannibal felt a peace that he had never before experienced in his life. His mind gave way to his heart, he threw his arms about her tightly and he let go; losing himself completely, along with the jar with his tongue, which rolled about abandoned on the floor. And there in her arms, kneeling on the floor before his shattered, immense television, Hannibal wept and he wept and he wept.

BOOK SEVEN

FiFTY

Erika sat on the platform at what would be the side arm of the moderator. While the makeup artist dabbed her cheeks with blush, she looked out from the set at the nonexistent audience. This would be a live program, privy to millions and inclusive only of the panel and crew. She looked now at the crew as they hurried about getting everything ready. The cameramen checked and double-checked their positioning; the sound engineers were doing mic checks; a bright light wavered above as the lighting crew tried to coordinate the perfect setting. And as was being done to Erika, the makeup artists applied the final touches on the three other panelist of the show.

The show was *Carthage Tonight,* owned by the Carthaginian and moderated by Roosevelt Muhammad. Muhammad, a man with a body builder's physique and an orator's diction, was well adept at the role he played. *Tonight* was the premier news commentary for the newly founded Carthage Television Network. CTN was a cable network, much as BET was before it, and now, only in its three-year history, had a subscriber base in the millions; not yet comparable to its predecessor's but it was growing.

Erika spoke to the media rarely in the years since her brother's passing. In many ways she held them accountable. Muhammad's was in fact the only one that she inclined herself to watch from time to time. When he called her personally and invited her to be on a program in which they would be discussing the life and legacy of her brother, she agreed, understanding the importance of the topic. She also understood the necessity for the program to be done right. In the years since, there had been countless shows dealing with the topic of Flawless. Most had been to her displeasure; all featured this person or another speaking with seeming authority on a subject on which they had no intimacy.

So she sat getting ready to speak about something she had spent the last nine years trying to forget. It was therapy of sorts, she supposed. The bullet wound had long healed and laser surgery had abolished the physical scar. The mental scars of that beautiful January day still, at least once daily, stung her thoughts. It didn't happen that often in latter years. Still, at times, in quiet remote moments, she would fall to her knees and bewail in private. At times involuntarily, she teared in public whenever she thought of the life of that tear that trickled askew from his cheekbone and fell to a pool of blood, hearing her name screamed in silence. There in silence, she thought of Micah.

"Silence on the set," a voice called from beyond a light. "We are live in two minutes." At this time Muhammad came, well suited, onto the set. Bald headed and brown skinned, he sat with ease and confidence in the center of the mix. He turned to her, smiled magnanimously and offered his hand.

"Greetings, sister. Thank you so much for coming. How are you doing?"

Erika took his hand and fell into the firm support of his grip. "I am quite all right. Thanks for having me," she replied. As she greeted Muhammad, she also noticed the rotund Stalin sitting across the stage, stripping her with his eyes as he always did. He had good reason to. In the years since, Erika had grown more mature and even more beautiful. At the age of thirty, the attorney had less vim than she had at twenty-one but had still maintained her youthful frame; her skin glowed but her smile was solemn.

She then looked across at Guevara seated to the left of Muhammad. At seeing her, the Latino-locked rapper nodded respectfully.

"Hey, girl, how you doin'?" a comfortable voice called from the side. Erika turned to see Ebony and returned her greeting with kisses on the cheek. Ebony was here because she had written a book entitled *A Hip-Hop Story*. In it she created an alternate hip-hop world of sorts in which she detailed the lives and battles of Flawless and Hannibal.

"All right, everyone . . ." the voice called from beyond the light ". . . we are live in five, four, three, two, one."

"Greetings and welcome, everyone. As always I am your host, Roosevelt Muhammad, and this is *Carthage Tonight*. Thank you all for tuning in. We have a great show for you tonight. Tonight we are speaking on the life and legacy of one of our fallen greats; taken from us much too soon but one who has left a lifetime's worth of work for us to study and to be inspired by. We are talking about none other than hip-hop legend Flawless. Now, we have assembled a great panel of guests to speak about this young man and his impact on yesterday, today and the future. To my right, I am honored to have with me his sister and entertainment lawyer, Erika Williams. To her right, we have rapper and author of the best-selling book and soon-to-be motion picture, *A Hip-Hop Story*, Ebony. Across the panel to my left, we have rapper and independent movie producer Guevara; and to his left, we have the ever-ebullient, the Boss himself, hip-hop legend, Stalin. Now, before I get to anyone else, Erika, I am going to start with you. And Ms. Williams, I hope you don't mind but I will be coming back to you often throughout the night, given that the rest of us were only peripherals to the man. You knew him directly."

"That's quite all right," Erika replied.

"Now, there is still a lot of controversy as to how Flawless died."

"Murdered," Erika said, cutting into his speech "Murdered.

To say 'died' suggests that there was something natural about his death."

"You are right. You are absolutely right and I stand corrected. And rather than murdered, there are those who would prefer to say that he was assassinated." In that last statement he looked at Erika for approval and she nodded her acceptance. Having received this, he went on. "Okay, as we know, his case has never been solved, his murderers go unfound. The conspiracy theories surrounding his death run the gamut. Some say it was the Mob. Some say, as I know my brother Guevara confirms and which I am inclined to believe myself, that it was the government. Though it is not conclusive, the authorities agree with the opinion of the President of Crown Records, Steven Jennessy, that slain rapper Bin Laden and other members of his Al Qaeda Network are to blame. Some even say that the blame is on Jennessy himself. Then there are the many that still believe that the head of the Carthage Conglomerate Empire, and the owner of our Carthage Television Network, Hannibal, is to blame. We all know of the infamous battles and seeming hatred that these two men had for each other at the time. Now, all of that considered, you were there when it happened. What do you think?"

"Well, I was there but as I will say now as I have said many times, I was not able to get a look at any of the shooters. I try not to worry about the theories, although they all seem very viable. But the truth is, I don't know. I do, however, know that the blame extends further than the two or more people who pulled the trigger. As for Hannibal, I don't believe that he was directly involved. I do, however, credit him and the media, along with Crown Records, for creating the environment that lead to Michael's passing."

"Roosevelt, if I might just cut in," Guevara pardoned.

"Go ahead, ma brother," Muhammad obliged.

"I am in agreement with the sister when she says that the blame extends further than the parameters of the gun and that the media had much to play in this. The radio stations and the print magazines profited heavily from the hype of the battle between Flawless and Hannibal and, to a lesser degree, even Stalin here, which is why I believe that the government had much to gain in this entire assassination. To understand this killing clearly, we need to look at Flawless at the time of his death. He was a drastically changed man than he was when he first came on the scene. His first album, *Flawless Victory,* was an excellent work. But for the most part as content goes, it was the typical hip-hop fluff. What made it special was the extreme talent and artistry of the man. Flawless was indeed a wordsmith and probably was the best lyricist and might still be one of the best lyricists that we have seen. Now, we come to his second album, *Poorman's Philosophe*, which in my opinion was one of the most deeply spiritual, philosophical, political and substantial hip-hop records ever made. Flawless took his talent for words and he turned it toward real issues. He was talking about AIDS, police brutality, political prisoners, religion and the war against terrorism. He was talking about all of the things they don't want us to talk about. And he was talking it to the people, to the youth . . ."

Guevara wished to continue but Ebony took the break in his speech as an opportunity to cut in. "I do agree with Guevara on all of those things. And I outline the vast changes in Flawless coming up to the time of his death in my book. When he said, 'I used to be about booties and Bentleys/ Now I am about bending realities/ Debunking fallacies/ Changin' philosophies,' you know what I'm sayin'? Flawless was changing and he wanted to take us with him. But I also do think that we should be careful about always throwing the blame to the government. I think that when we are always quick to fall into the typical conspiracy theorist jargon, it makes our cause seem clichéd, contrived and ultimately insubstantial."

"What's wrong with booties and Bentleys?" Stalin remarked. "Now, listen, I had my little tiff with Flawless back in the day but overall I respected the man. I loved his work, the first album and his second, and all of the albums that have come since. I like the balance in it. I like the conscious stuff and the stuff you can dance to, which is what I make. We all can't do the same thing. You make music to make people think and that's cool. I make it to make them dance, to give them a relief from their troubles. A lot of people say the music is materialistic. I say okay, the whole world is materialistic, we just being real about it. We all just little kids from the ghetto that have been denied not just the finer but actually the basics of life. So we dream about it until we get it and when we do, we glorify it. And they say that we are offensive to the women in our videos and our songs. I'm like, that may be true but if there weren't any women to put in the videos, we couldn't be offensive to them. That's something that we have to think about."

"I hear you, brother," Ebony remarked. "But don't you believe that if we are to move on as a people we need to relinquish the whole adversarial relationship between sisters and brothers and look at each other in mutual respect? We need to build each other up and not make excuses about putting each other down. I mean, I myself am a bit taken aback that given all of the consciousness that came about in hip-hop in the new era, it still has not addressed and apologized to an acceptable extent for its disrespect of women."

"Yeah, you're right. That may be true. But I see the songs get made and the women dancing to them," Stalin returned.

"Okay, this is very interesting and very relevant. It is an issue that needs to be further addressed. But let's keep the talk to the topic at hand," Muhammad intervened.

"Exactly," Stalin continued. "Now, going back to Flawless. He understood this and he did both types of music, which is what made him great. It's what made Hannibal one of the richest men in the country right now. And now a lot of people like to say that it is because of hip-hop and the battles that were taking place why Flawless died. I think that's bull and I am not talking about the man. Hip-hop by its nature is competitive, always has been, always will be. People was battling before Flawless, Hannibal and me and they will be battling afterward. Now, if we get too scared and take that out of the game, we gon' ruin it. Hell, if you think that way, some people would be lookin' to me and my people as if we had something to do with it. Same way they still lookin' at Lil' Hitler and down south."

"I am hearing everything that everyone is saying," Guevara interjected. "And you are right, brother, we all need to dance, but I think that in this day and age we need to think more. We have made a lot of great strides but the war isn't over yet, so I think that partying would be premature. And I say this because I am beginning to see a trend swinging back to just club music and away from conscious thought in hip-hop, as I believe Ebony was alluding to. I think that we need to be vigilant in keeping the mind of the youth on track. I think that we can dance without losing our perspective, or being disrespectful.

"Going back to Flawless, I think that the battles with Hannibal are very much a key part of what happened but that they are not the sole reason behind the slaying. I believe that if we look at the facts and we understand the predatory nature of this country and its government as it regards darker people, everything makes sense." Muhammad nodded affirmatively to Guevara's last statement. "All right, and we have to understand that at the time Flawless and Hannibal were two of the biggest names in hip-hop. Millions of people were listening to them and they both put out two of the most radical and revolutionary albums of that era or any and it spawned a movement. Like Bob Marley before them and Che Guevara, Malcolm and Martin before him, they were a threat to the status quo. Remember Flawless's album was called *Poorman's Philosophe* and not just *Philosophe*. His message was specific, as was the message in *Elephant Warfare*; and it is for this reason that these two men were, in a word, silenced."

"Well, it seems that everyone here has a lot to say about the matter," Muhammad reinserted himself. "I think that a lot of interesting points have been raised. I do think that the role of Hannibal is very relevant; when we look at what happened to him, and also that he has chosen not to communicate in the least as to how and why what happened to him occurred. And this is not said to bite the hand that feeds us. None of us can deny the great work that Hannibal has done in the community in these years, in leading hip-hop into a new and profitable sense of consciousness. Nevertheless, there are questions that must be answered. But I am interested that none of you have spoken of Bin Laden and his role. Now, much like Lee Harvey Oswald or James Earl Ray, it is the established belief that he was the shooter. But to this point let me turn back to Erika for your word on the matter. Tell us, do you believe that there was someone in the grassy knoll, so to speak?"

"Well, I have listened to all of the theories and I must say that much of what Guevara says makes a lot of sense. Now, we all know about the COINTELPRO program of the sixties and also the great abuses to our liberties and rights that the CIA, FBI and HLD have brought about during their supposed war on terrorism in this new millennium. We live in a world where we are constantly watched, cash is gone, we need a biometric card to buy the food we eat, we are about to be implanted with microchips, and we have to go through a retinal scan before we can get on a plane; the era of privacy is gone. True, the movement has done a lot. I mean, yes, after many years people like Mumia and Leonard were finally freed but there is still much to be done. Then when we look at the AIDS epidemic in Africa, thank God a cure was finally found but look at all the millions of people who died in that time. And people are still dying right now while all of these pharmaceutical giants are fighting over the patent to the cure. We won the fight to say that we are due reparations but we are still debating now on just how much and how it should be allocated. Now, I am spewing all of this out but I myself wasn't aware of all of these things until I actually really started reading my brother's lyrics. So I do see how the government could have played a role. But regardless of that, like I said before, from Bin Laden to the government, I believe that they are all relevant but I try not to get into all of the theories. I did in the beginning but I realized that, on a personal level, it didn't make me feel any better. I have spent years trying to get past that one day and if I penetrated on it too much, I would go insane. Which is not to say that I have in any way given up the search to find my brother's killers. Though my focus is entertainment, it was one of the reasons, along with the fact that I wanna protect other young artists from getting into bad deals with these record labels like my brother, that I decided to become a lawyer. And also a point that I would like to make is that there were three people who died that day. Beyond my brother, the other person that I loved most in the world died as well. Now, people try to overlook it because of who Flawless was, but just because we are ignorant of someone doesn't make their life or death meaningless. . . . But let's stop talking about death. Let's talk about the lives of these two beautiful men who left us a world of literature to study, which is why I am glad that Flawless's work is now being studied in the colleges."

"Very true. That is a point I wanted us to get into later," Muhammad added.

"Yes, it was what he wanted. It was his vision for hip-hop. Being his sister and the curator of his catalogue, that was a battle I felt I had to win after I won back the rights to all of Flawless's music from Crown Records. And now that the work is being studied, it is receiving the academic acclaim that it deserves."

"You have said and done a lot for your brother. But I wonder, where do you go on from here sister?" Muhammad asked.

"I don't know. That's a hard question. I am thirty and I feel as if I have already lived a lifetime; I have been through so much." There was a break in her speech. "I guess, well, I'll just live, love and remember." *Micah*.

"I thank you, Ms. Williams, and I am sure your brother thanks you as well. But right now, we are going to take a break and we will be right back. This is *Carthage Tonight*, on CTN. Flawless: the man and the word, the power of truth is final. We will be back in three."

FiFTY-ONE

Jennessy stood with his briefcase at his side, listening to the benign tune being played overhead. The diluted saxophone was soothing but nothing in fact would fully soothe the sting of the day. With a ding, the elevator doors opened and the Armani-suited executive stepped out and into something new. He watched the workmen by the window taking down the name-plate of Crown Records. It was a disheartening sight for the late-forties executive.

Much had changed in nine years. Gray lines were beginning to distinguish the sides of his coif and wrinkles more defined the shape of his eyes. He had remained slim in frame, though gone were his denim days that gave him that youthful veneer. He had given up the denim along with his penchant for hip-hop. After his encounter with Bin Laden he had been pushed to his limit. The security force had finally arrived. The six shots fired off were theirs. The blood spilled was Bin Laden's, as the mad rapper laid shivering, cursing Jennessy to his dying breath.

After admonishing the security force, Jennessy quickly washed off the vestiges of the man. His face was cleaned but the blood had stained the denim and his consciousness. He threw out the jeans but could not so easily jettison the memory. He had been forever shaken. In the nine years he may have had nine nights of good sleep. Then when the newborn insomniac had lost the rights to Flawless's catalogue, to Flawless's sister, he had had his fill. He said good-bye to hip-hop and jeans forever. He put on an Armani suit and signed a couple of pop acts.

Jennessy's string of hit records began to flounder. Crown was no longer the belle of *Billboard*. And with its new misdirection away from hip-hop, it lost its standing with WHRU and other likeminded hip-hop radio stations in the country. The kids in the cities stopped listening and those in the suburbs stopped buying in numbers. The label was now going through recessionary times.

All of this plagued Jennessy, though far more abhorrent to his sensibility was his lack of sleep. Four or five hours a night in patched intervals did not suffice. He walked about many times in a constant daze, wondering truly if he were asleep or awake. He began to see visions of weird matter floating about him and of an opened-skull Bin Laden. He would see this and others during his daytime dozes. The urge to sleep always came to him during the most inappropriate times: never when he was home in bed but rather when he was in a board meeting, he would begin to blink in and out of reality.

Sullen-faced and fatigued, he stepped into the office and cut the familiar corner. All he thought of was sleep and not looking down because on the floor was the sign that would replace the Crown Records banner. The label had a new name. He couldn't bear to read it. He tried desperately to be as ignorant of the inevitable as possible. He turned quickly and out of habit went to the large office down the hall.

"Hello, Jane," he greeted the secretary upon arrival.

"Um, good morning, Mr. Jennessy," she replied with a puzzled expression. "Um, sir, where are you going, might I ask?"

"Why, I am going to my office, of course."

"But sir, this is no longer your office. Your office is downstairs now . . . remember?" There was a pause as what she said seeped back into Jennessy's consciousness.

"Yes, yes, you are right, Jane. This is not my office anymore, as you are not my secretary anymore, as I am no longer the president of that which is no longer Crown Records. I now am the East Coast regional director of . . . whatever," he spoke in sarcasm.

"Yes, sir. And as the East Coast regional director you are expected to be in the conference room to greet the arrival of the new CEO of the corporation."

"Thank you, Jane. Don't believe that I would have cared to remember that fact if you hadn't told me."

He gave a half curtsy-nod of the head to his former secretary and headed toward the conference room. It was at the other end of the hall. He cursed in his mind as he hurried past the workmen and went the remainder of the journey feeling a bit of shame.

Jennessy stepped into the large exquisite room that held a majestic, hardwood rectangular table in the center. Much like his old office, the room had a long encompassing window that gave view to the great expanse. The table seated thirteen; of the thirteen, ten of the fellow executives and senior shareholders were present, seated and suited, with mostly old and long, drawn faces. Jennessy was ushered to a seat at the end. This was far from the days when he often sat at the helm of Crown. Now he punctuated himself into the fine leather chair and no one paid him the least bit of mind.

With Jennessy present, the meeting began. The speaker, who called the meeting, rose from his seat and began his speech:

"Good morning, everyone. I am pleased that we are all here. Our company has accomplished much in its tenure. We have truly stapled ourselves in the annals of music history. We have always been at the forefront of vision and as such we shall continue to be. But like all things, we will adapt, we will evolve or we will perish. Now, we are far from perishing, for we have with us vision. Whenever there is vision, there is life and progress. We are upon a new threshold, a new era, and for that we have a new leader. And it is my pleasure to introduce you all to the man who will lead us into our evolution, the new

CEO of the newly merged Carthage/Crown Records, Mr. Hannibal."

The name of the Carthaginian evoked in the hearts of the committee either a twinge of fear, reverence, or in Jennessy's case, the feeling of "I can't believe this shit is happening." They all remained breathless, rising to their feet in applause as the man of silence entered the room with Rosa at his side.

In these years the thirty-five-year-old had grown much in thought but little in demeanor. Other than crow's feet in the corner of his eye there was no real mark of aging. He had maintained the vigor of old, and likewise attired himself as he always did. The difference now was that the baggy jeans and work boots were of his own Elephant brand. Of the many ventures that Hannibal explored, fashion had been one of his most successful. Rosa took the vacant seat to his right and Hannibal rightfully took his seat at the head of Crown. How far I have come, he thought to himself.

It was never Jersey's wish that anything should happen to Hannibal as he left. When Jacobin reported what had been done, Jersey beat him viciously and then he forgave him. They were family, after all; what was a tongue between cousins? Hannibal had been left in a predicament; he could no longer speak; more importantly, he could no longer rap and had been stripped all but naked. All he truly possessed was his name and a now-weakened independent record label, of which he was the only artist. He, however, did have the rights to his new album. When the news about what happened got out, the people recognized the significance of an album which would be Hannibal's last. For months the stores couldn't keep any copies of *Elephant Warfare* on the shelves. When the year's total had been calculated, *Warfare* had sold close to twelve million copies. The only other album that had a better year was Flawless's *Poorman's Philosophe*. After his death the sales of the album moved drastically. That was their final battle. Again, Flawless had won and again, it had been close.

Though the successes of *Warfare* and *Philosophe* were far more significant than the battle between the two. They spawned a new seed of thought in hip-hop. Substance, for a time again, had proved to be profitable. What was once considered divergent, radical and ignored for a moment became mainstream; likewise, many of the youth in that moment streamed to the cause. It was this newfound consciousness, with rappers such as Guevara and Ebony at the helm, and through their mass outcry that forced the freeing of men such as Abdullah Al-Amin, Leonard Peltier and many of the other unjustly imprisoned. And in the sync of the beat, they rhymed against the war on terrorism and the war for man's civil liberties, staying off some of the state's planned progression toward marshal law. The music and the movement meshed for a time and for years it was the grove of dissidence, until recently, when there came a resurgence of the club banger. As before, the beat preceded the lyrics, the production preceded the word; as all things are cyclical, the people again wanted to dance their cares away. Again, there came about the battle in hip-hop over the issue of matter and materialism.

As for Hannibal, the revenues of *Warfare* gave him a new life, with Rosa by his side. Like Aaron to Moses, she became his voice and so much more. With her aid he signed more artists and when his contract with Crown had expired, he merged with a fledgling distribution network. At first they only catered to the small chain record stores; given the nature of the music, all done in the vein of *Warfare,* this was best, though soon, because of the caliber of artists and the great demand for the product in the new climate in hip-hop, major chains came calling. Hannibal absorbed Rebel Distributions into Carthage and now had a lock on all aspects of music.

His vision would not be halted there. He partnered with a young designer and created his own clothing line. Within three years, Elephant wear had become one of the biggest manufacturers of urban clothing. Hannibal also partnered with others and created Elephant Pictures, as well as the cable network Carthage Television. He was now in the planning stages of making *A Hip-Hop Story*. It would be the film adaptation of the book written by Ebony.

With Rosa, seemingly, everything was set. Why she loved him he did not know, nor did he know whether if in the years he had grown to love her. To love a woman, it was something he once thought himself incapable of. Now he wasn't sure. He knew very well that she had saved him and that he could not live without the mother to his three children. Always the only child, Hannibal hungered for a large family. So he loved this woman, perhaps, he thought. He knew he cared, though overall he tried not to question these matters. Whatever it was between them worked for him and he would exploit this circumstance for as long as his vision permitted. At least. so he told himself.

His vision and Rosa had brought him home to Jamaica; this they did after visiting her family in Cuba. Being back to the island for the first time since he was three was an incredible experience. He remembered nothing of the land, which to him was both foreign and natural. When it became known that he was also Jamaican, the people cheered him in the streets of Kingston as a hero. "BULL, BULL!" People numbering in the thousands shouted his name as he walked with them, spoke with them through Rosa, and saw how they dreamed, how they suffered and how they hungered. Being home again, he knew then that the big picture was not his alone. Far greater things he was still to accomplish, for far greater reasons. His story would not end here.

Throughout these nine years he had bought an even bigger television but he never watched Lecter again, nor had he spoken a word. His fanaticism went with his voice. He could only utter semblances of syllables. The nerve endings had been forever severed. The remnant existed as senseless dead weight in his mouth. With the nerve endings gone, so too was his sense of taste, though not completely. He could still acknowledge the bitter but all things sweet and sour were forever lost to him.

He had not spoken for so long that he at times forgot how his own voice sounded. The sound of his thoughts became confused and mumbled. He had to listen to his old records to get some memory of it. When he heard just how rich and powerful it was, he recalled what his father had said to him long ago about the power and gift that was in his tongue. Listening to the old CDs soon began to upset him. He was envious of his former self. He was envious of the youth who went about and battled on the street corners as he once did. He missed those sweet, simpler times.

He missed Terrence. There would never be another comparable to the man in spirit and loyalty. He had no love lost for Mook, who just two years later was shot and killed. He could never garner the full respect of the boys and one of them, on Jersey's prompting, put a bullet to his head and took Mook's position. This was how Rome had repaid him for his betrayal.

He missed that beautiful spirit that had come to him and taught him who he truly was. It was his words that had saved him when all else was lost. For that he would always be thankful and regretful. An only child bred into a strict Christian home, he had always wished for a little brother. He prayed for him and when his wish came true, he treated him badly. I am sorry, brother. You lived to bring me a love that I was not yet ready to understand.

Hannibal thought about a lot of things as he stood before the board of Crown. When he was seated he looked over to the speaker to continue his speech.

"As for reasons we all know, Mr. Hannibal has crafted a statement that he would like me to read." He began to read aloud: "Thank you everyone, I must tell you that I am very pleased to be here. Of the many companies that I have acquired, I must say that this one is extra sweet. I began here at Crown, just some ten years ago now. I was able to grow here and eventually leave the womb. I took the knowledge and lessons learned here and I built an empire. For that, I am thankful and grateful. I have been through a lot in my life. I went from nothing to a lot, to nothing, to being here. And I am happy to be here, with an ever-expanding vision to the future, as we shall trumpet our voice and our stories into the annals of history. Carthage is born anew, born again. I will say no more other than there is a world out there to be conquered. And, in the spirit of a very wise man, let's take it over." The speaker hesitated a bit as he came to the end, "All right . . . ma niggas, let's get to work."

All in attendance rose and applauded. Hannibal likewise rose and gave an eye to Jennessy, who was busy nodding off. Hannibal smiled to himself, knowing that a purge was coming. And as he did, he noticed another man, a man who appeared to Hannibal to be his peer in many ways standing by Jennessy's side. He wore a black suit with a crimson tie and an omnipresent grin. Of all the others, he applauded the loudest. Hannibal thought it was strange but, for his emphatic affections, he gave his peer a complimentary nod of the brow as he walked over to the window. With the applause behind him he looked out at the gates of Rome, at the great expanse, at New York City.

The big picture, he thought to himself, while still being hungry for more. And there in the sky the clouds took on an organic likeness. It seemed to him that they resembled Flawless. It seemed to Hannibal that even in the heavens the man still baited him for a battle and Hannibal welcomed it with a smile. "Don't worry, god. I'm coming."

FiFTY-TWO

It was spring again and Erika sat on a park bench in Queens, looking across a sea of young faces, upon a wall, into the eyes of her brother. It was a mural, large and well imagined, in his likeness. They had done a good job; it looked just like him, as did the opposing picture of Hannibal. It seemed that with this composition of the two set against each other, a reproduction of the famous picture published years ago, they would battle each other unto infinitum. It would carry on for generations, as a younger generation moved in their footsteps, and of the many others who came before and after in the eternal battle of hip-hop. It seemed as long as there was a tongue and a heartbeat, the word would be heard and there would be a battle to see whose word would take precedence.

Under the big picture of Flawless and Hannibal, a young man in his teens flowed with his opponent at his brow before a goading crowd. It was obvious that he had studied Flawless, word for word and inflection for inflection. To Erika, it was very complimentary. She knew that Michael would feel the same as well. And as was the case from the beginning, she could not think of Michael without thinking of Micah. "My handsome Micah." She many times recalled what he had said to her on the train: that he would never acknowledge death and stay with her in that moment forever. As she did now, she many times still felt as if he were with her, in a purple haze: holding her, touching her, kissing her, looking at her and in those moments in his spirit, she felt whole.

In her remembrance of this man, who was more spirit than man, her handsome Micah; she remembered when she went to identify the body. There he lay on the cold slab of steel, exposed to the drear of the morgue under a glaring crimson light. The matter before her held no resemblance to the mind of the man she knew and loved. What existed now was merely raw flesh. It took much prompting on the part of the attending officers to convince her that that was the body pulled from the car, the body that had died on top of her. "But that was not Micah," she told them. To that they offered no rebuttal. But if he was not, then who had Micah been? Where did he come from: this man who was Flawless's reflection, Erika's love and Hannibal's little brother? The desire of man manifested, who it seemed had come into view from out of the periphery of meaninglessness, born big, without a history. Just a name, a word made flesh from a trinity of wants, immaculately conceived. A thinking thing, a thought brought into being, unbeknownst to itself and to its creator, or perhaps creators, as the light had been to the darkness. Erika thought of all this but she did not know for sure. Could a wish come to life?

Without the answer to these questions, Erika saw to the burial of the unclaimed body. With her mother alone, she laid her heart to the earth seven feet deep for a second time and was unaware of the dark, silent figure looming in the distance of the cemetery, looking on.

From that moment throughout the years, Erika had never truly been able to resurrect her heart. She remained sane by believing that what she buried was merely matter and not spirit. And Micah, to the best of her understanding, had been a spirit, a beautiful spirit, a living dream gone too soon, written into being with no other purpose but to love her as she had been written to love him. That was the narrative. It was not until she came to some understanding of this that she came to some understanding of Trish. A dream can only exist under the pretense of being real. It must be accepted and never questioned. If not, it will fade away to nothingness, as if it never existed. And so she did, gone without a trace, as one awakes going from a haze of purple to fuchsia to crimson. However, what is real and who was writing reality? The heartbeat was hers, but who rhymed over it?

Was she just a "pretty brown thing," a character in a narrative, rhymed for amusement? Were her joys, and now her pain and sufferings, all felt solely for the purpose of being thought provoking to someone turning a page or bopping their heads to a beat in a club? She did not know the answer and at times she hated and cursed the Creator for bringing her into being with such happiness and then snatching it away, expecting her to live on without. Give her to me. Give hurt to me. Maybe the wish had come true. Now how was she supposed to truly live again? How was she supposed to love? She did not know the answers to any of these questions, as she sat there on the park bench in the fickle of spring, watching the young brothers rhyme before her.

Perhaps it was not written nor rhymed for me to love again? Perhaps the plan of my life had long been laid out? I had signed a contract without my knowing and I am now merely a slave to play out the part until my contract expires. Or maybe I was created without forethought and, like a freestyle rap my life is left to happenstance and the fickle nature of the spirit or the weather? Or perhaps there is a set pattern to it all, but every once in a while an unexpected ad-lib is thrown into the mix, merely to make the rhyme more interesting or perhaps more insulting? Am I just an insult? Is Erika just a name? Is Erika only a word; was Micah?

No answers came, and in time Erika came to accept her ignorance as she did before. She accepted that there were questions out there that perhaps would never be answered, and with that she was able to find some measure of bliss. She would love again but never as she did for the first time. The color purple was gone. Micah had been her first on every level and for that she would love him unequaled forever. But for now, she sat there with the thought of her head to his chest, happy and in peace, in the midst of the eternal battle between Flawless and Hannibal and the cheering crowd around them.

The lights came on, the curtain opened, the audience anticipated; Flawless came to the stage, a mic in his hand, his DJ behind him, his heart racing, his mind ablaze. It was the Source *Awards, the final performance, two hours after Hannibal's performance, two hours after his embarrassment. Now he debated what to say, what to be, who to be; the crowd knew what they wanted: "Bullshit," they chanted. "Bullshit," he taunted, while Hannibal's words haunted him, he still felt the sting—it had not been the plan, but he could give it to them, or something new, a freestyle, something harsh, hard, the hardest ever. But then this would go on forever, when would it end, it would never end, never end; but it had to end, now; it had to mean more than this, he would mean more than this, he had to . . . he had to . . . He made his decision, he looked back to his DJ, alone without Tommy beside him. "Aftermath," he told him; "Aftermath," the DJ affirmed; and so the rhythm played. They debated him at first but then after the first verse, the crowd tamed and listened, attentively.*

> *One man's madman is another man's martyr*
> *But murder is murder; slaughter is slaughter*
> *Too many mothers and sons*
> *Lost to politics and perspective*
> *Back to politics as usual*
> *As usual, more funerals*
> *The innocent die so that*
> *The innocent have to suffer*
> *Rich men fund wars*

To have them fought by the poor
The military marches on
The earth is a playground
For Martians, but first martial law
Comes as a Marshall plan
'Cause the Monroe Doctrine been mocked
Now everyman wanna wiretap
It's like living in The Wire
Your phone's already been tapped
They'll put taps in yo' toilets
To make sure yo' shit's in check
Soon I won't be able to cash ma check
Unless ma biometrics mesh
Used to have a chip on ma shoulder
Now I got a chip in ma wrist
Still got the freedom of speech
But only when I'm pleading the fifth
Still, I'ma teach the children
That the Kremlin had fallen
The CIA needs justification
Now terrorism is our communism
And Ashcroft is our McCarthy
A motherfucker mocking me
Got agents watching me
They already questioning me
Are you now or have you ever been a terrorist?
Have you ever given a terrorist patronage?
Do you love your president?
Do you support your Congress?
Well, now I'm terrified because
I don't know what's a terrorist
An' pres' sez if you not with us
Then you must be with the terrorist
But I'm not with bombing clinics and killing kids
With crashing planes into buildings

In order to pass some bills
You see, I see past yo' bullshit
The true shit is, you blew it up
In order to build it up
Now president's polls are up
CIA budget is up, FBI powers is up
Homeland Defense is up. An what's up is that
There is a warranty on yo' freedom
Because we're in a new season
An' fascism is fashion; and I guess that means
Standing here in my black Guess jeans
That a part of me still leans
To be part of the American dream, it seems
Like a hypocrisy, but you see I'ma supporter of
America "ideally," but I'm the victim of its reality
So really, I'ma rally to the cause
Until it's the cause of my death
To my dying breath I'ma spit it
Until I spit it on yo' grave.

And so it ended, the beat faded and the light gave way to the dark . . . and in the dark, Hannibal watched Flawless exit the stage for the last time. And in his heart he admired him and in his mind he couldn't wait to surpass him; he knew he would one day, perhaps the battle would end one day: one day, he smiled to himself . . . but not today.

ACKNOWLEDGMENTS

I would like to thank my mother, for my heart, my father for my mind, and the creator for the semblance of the two. But again I am without words to express my extreme gratitude for my mother, Venice, and the sacrifices she has made for me. To the hardest workingwoman I know, we will soon have that kitchen with the island in the center. Special acknowledgments to my inner family: Michelle; Shanice; Jay, big ups to becoming the first doctor in the family. Big shout out to Uncle Mickey and to Lomalee and her crew: especially Kimmy, thanks for giving the book a good read when it was in its earlier stages.

Next I would like to give special thanks to the Queen of the world, my beautiful Monifa Powell; thank you for teaching me the meaning of love and for being Erika's inspiration. I love you, girl; I love you for life.

Big shout out to my friend, my inspiration, my brother, my fellow kemite: Tehut-nine. Thanks for always being there for everything. I love you brother. Special shouts to the family: Marcia "Slim" Morris, and the already-crawling, Masai "Tehutten" McAplin.

Big shouts to my cousin Troy; Moses; M-one, thanks for giving the book a good read, giving me the blurb and putting me up on how the industry works; Abu; Big Tahir, for the love and support and helping me produce my album; Herb Boyd, for the edits and the blurb; Omar Tyree, I can't thank you enough for the blurb; Jehvon and Yaw, for your love and energy; Dacia Morris, for your meticulous edits, they helped me so much; Tania Cuevas, for your spirit; Tania Small, thank you for being a great friend, can't thank you enough for the copies; Frances

Goldin, thank you for all of the love and energy that you put into the project; Mumia Abu Jamal, brother I cannot thank you for all the love you have shown me, I have already written it into being and soon very soon you will be free; Mshindo I. Kuumba (the greatest artist in the world), thank you for your love and support and for doing my cover for me for practically nothing. To Jacob and Damian and everyone else in the MTV/Pocket Books crew. Thank you for seeing the big picture.

To my father Anthony Richards, thank you for giving me my life and my name. Our renewed relationship in recent years has taught me a lot about you and myself. Here's still looking at thirty-five. Finally I would like to thank the Creator for life, love and creativity. And to any and everyone who has taken the time and the love to read this book. I thank you all. Much love—Heru.

ALSO PUBLISHED BY SUNRASON

Love, God and Revolution (poetry) by Heru Ptah
ISBN: 0-9677644-1-6 $20.00

The Fire in Me (poetry) by Tehut-nine
ISBN: 0-9677644-0-8 $20.00

Mental Eye-roglyphics (poetry) by Tehut-nine
ISBN: 0-9677644-3-2 $14.95

Mind Magician (CD) by Tehut-nine $10.00

COMING SOON

A Hip-Hop Story: The Soundtrack (CD)

The Reluctant Revolutionary (CD) Heru Ptah

All items above available online at
www.sunrason.com

You can also mail order:
Send check or money order to:
SunRASon Prod, Co. P.O. Box 2020
Canal Street Station NY, NY 10013
Include $3.00 for shipping and handling.

Like this is the only one...

Floating
Robin Troy

The Fuck-up
Arthur Nersesian

Dreamworld
Jane Goldman

Fake Liar Cheat
Tod Goldberg

Dogrun
Arthur Nersesian

Brave New Girl
Louisa Luna

The Foreigner
Meg Castaldo

Tunnel Vision
Keith Lowe

Number Six Fumbles
Rachel Solar-Tuttle

Crooked
Louisa Luna

Don't Sleep with Your Drummer
Jen Sincero

Thin Skin
Emma Forrest

Last Wave
Paul Hayden

More from the young, the hip,
and the up-and-coming.
Brought to you by MTV Books.

© 2003 MTVN

books

POCKET
BOOKS

The Alphabetical Hookup List

A new series

A–J
K–Q
R–Z

Three sizzling titles
Available from
PHOEBE McPHEE
and MTV Books

www.mtv.com

www.alloy.com

As many as one in three
Americans with HIV...
DO NOT KNOW IT.

More than half of those
who will get HIV this year...
ARE UNDER 25.

HIV is preventable.
You can help fight AIDS.
Get informed. Get the facts.

www.knowhivaids.org
1-866-344-KNOW